DE'LURE PUBLICATIONS PRESENTS

PASSION ABSOLUTE

Radicon's Princess

DE'LURE

Passion Absolute

(Radicon's Princess)

De'Lure

Published June 2016

Author Quotes

*"Always remember that the **trouble** in your past is already done and it never changes... so in turn never be discouraged when fighting a battle that you've already fought so many times before, look instead to your inevitable future."*

Delure

"I will die a dreamer... A dreamer with the heart and the talent to realize their dream is more powerful and blessed than the richest man on the planet..."

Delure

*"Once you recognize the fact that **NOTHING** in your past be it lies or truth, can discount your present accomplishments, or the things you will achieve in the future, life becomes much simpler."*

Delure

*"We are taught to believe that our **names** and our **images are** everything... If so that's a good thing because **we** are **in control** of **all of the above**..."*

Delure

"To read my work... is to peek inside of my very heart and experience my vivid rainbow of imagination"

Delure

"When people can't compete with your **present,** and they fear your **future,** they have no choice but to bring up and attempt to distort your past"

Delure

"We are not who **THEY** say we are... but exactly who we choose to be"

Delure

"If we let the ghosts of our past affect our present and our future... well then we were much better off dying, along with those nagging ghost of long ago..."

Delure

"Foreword"

Being talented with an amazing gift of writing is a blessing in itself from God and that's exactly what Michael possesses. I've known Michael De'Lure as a close friend for three years now and if I can describe how he is as a person, I would say he's very dedicated. As an author, he's passionate about his novels; he gives his all, and spends the majority of his time making sure that he is creating amazing masterpieces. As a witness, he has taken me on some unimaginable journeys with his novels; I fall more and more in love with his books because he has that special gift to capture your attention with his unmatched imagination and his amazing descriptive writing ability. This novel, Passion Absolute is different from other novels in this genre because, the storyline is so good that it will keep your attention within just the first chapter. I can firmly and honestly say that you won't be disappointed with any of his creations you so decide to purchase and experience firsthand. De'Lure is truly one in a million, much different from any other authors that I have ever read. I'm honored, grateful, and proud to be a part of his journey as a writer, an author, and as a close friend. Being able to meet him and see how much he has grown as a writer has been a great fortune in my eyes. He has proven that he's a force to be reckoned with

V. Olivier

"Dedication"

T his novel is simply and in the same respect greatly dedicated to all of my readers worldwide. I feel as if each one of my readers becomes a special friend of mine after we have at least one interaction with one another. To read me, as many of my readers know and feel now, is to understand and know my heart and my passion. I will never stop writing, creating, and loving the things I'm creating, until I'm hailed one of the greatest storytellers of all time. That is my sincererest dreams. So to you, all of my gorgeous, intelligent, mindfully supportive readers/ friends I dedicate this, my 5th published novel, "Passion Absolute" (Radicon's Princess).

"If you're scared of becoming *great* just attach yourself to somebody who already knows how to fly. You'll never learn how to *soar* until somebody shows you how to grow your own *wings...*"

M.L. De'Lure

Acknowledgements

Carole Burton, Valerie Olivier, and Katrice Brown all three of you wonderful ladies again spent countless hours reading and editing this book just like you did many of my other projects, I can't thank you ladies enough and no words could ever express my true appreciation for all that you have done for my blossoming writing career.

My Personal Investors

These events and the characters you are about to read about are all fictional. The things I write about are always born through pure imagination.

To my personal Investors, I love you all very, very much. Your love and belief in my talent will live inside of my books and my heart for eternity and for that I am so grateful. Thank you all for going out of your way to invest in my dream in many different ways.

Edna Rowell AL
Valerie Olivier NY
Carol Burton AL
Brandilyn Hayes AL
Britney Latrice AL
James Bryant OK
Lamar Jones AL
Alexus Calvin AL
Pashale Calhoun AL
Rita Lowry AL
Quana Lane AL
Paige Marie NY
Terrilynn Dunning AL
Ravon McDade AL
Chantay Calhoun AL
Martenia Shyne IL
Cheryl Cece Curry AZ

Charita Calhoun AL
Kela King AL

Samantha Blackmon
FL Regina Kennedy AL
Brittany Williams AL
Jordan Lee Aune MN

(Prologue)

M iami, Florida is located on the Atlantic coast
in southeastern Florida and the county seat of
Miami-Dade County. It's no secret how exciting the city
of Miami is from sun up, to sun down, and beyond. Sex,
drugs, and money bursts from every single street corner
and establishment. You can get married, laid, high, or
killed all on the same block. You can become a millionaire
or you can die broke and alone in a cold dark gutter.

Love exists everywhere, and every being at some point
is capable of loving another being. In Miami though it's
a lot harder to know and distinguish real love from
carefully calculated deceit-filled pseudo affection. This is
true especially among the elite. There are so many
seemingly beautiful, successful people of all kinds of
backgrounds, its damn near impossible to tell if someone
is actually who and what they say they are.

3185 Dunbarton Lane has been the home address of the
extremely wealthy Radicon clan for forty plus years. Old
man Raymond Radicon had the estate built from the
ground up in 1971 when he was just twenty-one years old.
His father Dorian Radicon was a simple man, very
affluent as well but he was complacently satisfied with
the uncomplicated things in life. Dorian could have built
a home equally as grand as the palace Ray had built on
Dunbarton Lane, but he wanted his money to last
generations and not to be squandered off on expensive
meaningless things.

(Carolyn)

Ch. 1

"Night Rider"

T he night air is wafting in through the car window
gently bathing both of their warm bodies with a
calming breeze. The air in Miami is so sweet, it opens
you up to so many amazing possibilities that you would
have never even considered before.

The unlikely couple is riding along the strip quietly
without a care in the world. Well, at least he is. She's lost
deep in her heart's desires as she ponders her inner most
thoughts. There is real beauty to be found in that anxious
moment when you hope, and ultimately think the person
sitting right next to you feels exactly the same way you
feel.

Not that you actually want to know the answer, because
there's always that chance that you're all alone in your
fantasy love connection. But that's the beauty of love,
isn't it? It's you stepping out on faith and taking chances;
showing someone pieces of you that the rest of the world
isn't usually privy to see. You can't delve into a potential
love with training wheels on, that's the fastest and surest
way to crash.

You have to be open and insane when it comes to love.
If he or she is really worth your time, don't be afraid to let
that person know you're open to them and their way of
thinking. Be very careful about that. Carolyn is sure she
has everything under control with Mr. Radicon.

On the radio Mariah Carey is singing her 90's hit, "My
All". This is one of Carolyn's favorite songs of all time. As

a young teen she used to believe in everlasting love that could never grow dull and useless.

Then she got married to *him*, and realized a love like that only truly exists in fairytales. Or maybe not... Real love she thinks, with the right person, and in the right circumstance can be sustained far longer than her personal situation.

Her personal situation could end right now, this very second and she'd probably be happier. Being alone would be a major upgrade as opposed to being with her husband.

Carolyn Olivier is only twenty-three years young and she's been married every day since her 19th birthday. The wedding was small but cozy. Her parents came ahead of time, but his parents were late.

They're always late for everything, but somehow they always have the most to say. Carolyn's just glad her in-laws finally moved away. Her father-in-law Greg Olivier got a management job at a car dealership in Orlando which caused him and his wife to move away two years ago.

His wife Marilyn, her husband's mother is a professional church member. She's one of those women who are at church *every single time* the door's open. She's in every choir, every program, and has to speak at every function. It makes you wonder, how fucked up she must have been in the past, that she's working overtime just to make herself believe she's saved and forgiven. However; in the event of raising their son, they did a terrible job.

He definitely tricked Carolyn, and ultimately guilted her into saying yes to his lofty marriage proposal four years ago. He told her she was never going to find any man that was going to be faithful to her, love her unconditionally, and be man enough to marry her.

She believed him; maybe he was right. After all she was only eighteen, who the hell finds true lasting love at eighteen anymore?

Ultimately she married him on her nineteenth birthday, and became a slave to a dry, monotonous, robotic, lifestyle. The type of lifestyle that plagues so many marriages across the globe today.

At first she just endured it believing that her life was just the way marriage were supposed to be. Then she started smoking, and smoking turned into drinking. Neither habit lasted long because she had never been the type to stick with anything too long good or bad, including substance abuse.

Next she started buying overtly erotic novels by the bundle, mommy porn as they call it.

She also owns an impressive arsenal of sex toys that she hides in the drawers of her nightstand on her husband's side of the bed. Of course he has never found them or noticed; just like he doesn't notice anything else she does for that matter.

Honestly she was hoping he'd find her dirty little toys, and that maybe finding them would spark his interest and imagination and make him want to start exploring with her sexually. They could begin a new erotic journey together and send their humdrum marriage down a new blossoming golden path of eternal orgasmic explosions. But of course he never noticed her toys, and if he did he never bothered to mention to her that he had. Oh God, the man is so boring and predictable it's almost comical.

Carolyn once had a ridiculous pink streak dyed down the back of her hair just to see if he would notice it. He did, a month later while he was giving her some routine mediocre sex from behind.

It's always from behind with him, she wonders if he's maybe no longer attracted to her, and in turn prefers to have sex with her from the back so that he can imagine she's someone else. This wouldn't bother her at all. In fact, for the past two and a half years the only way Carolyn has felt any pleasure with her husband, is to imagine during sex that he's some stranger she met on the street, fucking her in a random alley for cash.

She relies on her extremely vivid imagination, because that's the only way the poor woman can feel even an ounce of pleasure for the five minutes he humps her quickly from behind once or twice a week.

Four years and two kids later her body is screaming for some much needed excitement. Carolyn has grown even more beautiful with each passing year. Along with her beauty, her painful unhappiness has grown as well.

Carolyn is 5'4, sinfully curvaceous, with hazel eyes, and toasted caramel skin. Her long brown hair is pulled back into a tight ponytail tonight. She can't see a thing as he blindfolded her tightly the second she got inside his expensive vehicle. She's wearing a gorgeous yellow fitted body dress that he made her change into moments ago.

To change into the dress, she got completely naked as he drove down a crowded Miami street never knowing if anybody driving near them saw her nude body or not. But she knows he doesn't care. If anyone did see her perfect naked body, that probably turned him on even more.

James Radicon, the son of Raymond Radicon is the richest man in Miami, Florida. His late father left him everything he had in the world in his last will and testament. And by everything I do mean an eternal fortune.

The origin of the Radicon's wealth was unknown even to old man Ray Radicon his entire life. All he knew is he was born rich because of his father before him and he was going to die rich, just like his grandfather did. James on the other hand is close to unveiling the true secret behind his family's age old fortune.

"Where are we going James?" Carolyn asks finally breaking the silence.

"Shut up." he replies blankly. Carolyn tries to sneakily readjust her blindfold so she can sneak a glimpse of their current location. James quickly looks over at her.

"Bitch if I so much as see either one of your eyes you're gonna get it. Her hands fall helplessly back down to her lap. "Well where are we going James?" she asks again. He doesn't respond.

She exhales abruptly trying to pretend she's angry. She can barely sit still riding next to this man. She's wanted him for as long as she can remember. She had never been noticeably attracted to white men before him, and she knows after him the attraction will most likely cease to exist.

James Radicon stands six feet two inches tall, with an impressive athletic body shape. His blond hair is exquisite and always trimmed to perfection. His nose is small and narrow but distinct. His ears are not too big and not too small they're adorable just as cute as he is. His blue eyes are absolutely hypnotic and they fit his face to classical perfection. The man has never known rejection in his adult life. His sinfully sensual eyes have never failed him they always close the deal.

"Damn it James, just tell me where we're going!" Carolyn yells, forgetting momentarily just how dangerous James Radicon really is. He looks towards her smiling sadistically at her blind face, and her weak attempt at bravado.

"Tonight all your fantasies become instant reality once again my dear." he promises in a grandiose tone.

"My fantasies," Carolyn scoffs, "I'm allowed to have those? I thought only your fantasies mattered."

"Shut the fuck up Carolyn," Mr. Radicon fumes, "what deeper fantasy could any bitch ever possess other than satisfying me? I am *your* God, never forget that!"

"Some God." she turns her head. James quickly reaches over and slaps her hard across the mouth. She doesn't speak. Instead she just wisely holds her throbbing mouth in complete fear and silence.

"Now we're almost here," he looks at her, "do not embarrass me."

"Yes sir." she mumbles meekly.

"You will speak only when spoken to and do exactly as you are told," he grabs her right knee gently; "if I do not object to something you are told to do... you will not object either." "Yes sir Mr. Radicon." she mumbles again.

James parks his expensive SUV on the street near the deserted looking mansion. "Hell, I might as well go first." he smiles to himself.

He unzips his tight jean pants. She knows exactly what that sounds means for her. Carolyn seductively wets her voluptuous lips with an anxious smile plastered on her beautiful light brown face. James loves her lips almost as much as he loves her behind.

As he grabs her ponytail, she readies herself mentally for the oncoming oral intrusion. He holds her head just close enough to it so she can lick the tip thoroughly just the way he likes it. Then she begins to take him deep in her mouth and throat. His eyes are closed and his mouth is wide open. Suddenly there's a knock on his SUV window.

"What the hell..." James jumps.

"The Master said bring her inside immediately." the masked man tells Radicon. Radicon nods. Then the masked man turns and makes his way back up the hill to the dark mansion.

Carolyn continues to service him with no hands. James has trained her perfectly. Looking down at her he can't quite figure out how to make her stop. He realizes she's enjoying this even more so than he is.

"Let's go." Radicon tells her finally. She doesn't stop. Her wet hungry mouth just can't tear itself away from him.

James pulls her ponytail as hard as he possibly can, ultimately ripping himself, out of her lustful oral grasp.

Carolyn is in sudden pain from her head down to her neck. As she caresses her own shoulders and neck silently she is relieved that the hair in her ponytail was her real hair, because had it been a weave Radicon would have surely snatched it right out of her head.

James opens his door and steps out calmly, and then begins brushing his clothes off as he notices a few pieces of lint on his tight black V-neck shirt. After peeling each piece off, he makes his way around to her side of the truck. He opens her door and takes her by the hand. She hesitates now.

"Wait James," she whispers, "I can't see." she complains.

"Of course you can't see you *idiot*, that's the whole point of the damn blindfold." he tells her.

"Geez Carolyn," he continues, "you're already black, please don't continue to say stupid things like that... It's so expected." She doesn't respond.

Using his hand to find her balance she carefully steps down out of the SUV. "Lead the way." she tells him.

As they make their way up the hill Radicon finds his adrenaline pumping through him fiercely. He so loves these random late night rendezvous. He has been a student of the Master for quite some time now, and he lives in his large shadow. Radicon only breathes to learn more and more about the art of sexual pain and pleasure.

As they approach the large stained glass door Radicon smiles at the genius of its design. He has seen and walked through the exquisite door many times before but tonight its detail is screaming for his undivided attention.

In the center most part of the door is the Virgin Mary holding the precious baby Jesus, standing in front of an upside down five-point star, with red rose petals all around their feet. In the air flying all around and above their heads are beautiful winged angels and demons battling for their souls, or at least this is Radicon's interpretation of the art piece.

He does know that the Master is absolutely obsessed with the book and movie "The Da Vinci Code" so the occult symbolism James suspects in the door's art is very real.

As he and the still silent Carolyn enter the Master's mansion he feels a very real chill come over his body. He should be used to it all by now, but whenever he's in the presence of his mentor his body always goes through real changes that he can't help but to feel.

Radicon kneels down close to Carolyn and removes both of her shoes from her tiny feet. Then he stands back up and begins leading the gorgeous young woman towards her unchosen fate for the evening.

"James..." Carolyn whispers. He spins around and slaps her hard across her mouth again. "Bitch you only speak when you are spoken to." he reminds her.

As they near the entrance to the large living room Carolyn's entire body has caught a chill because of the ice cold marble floor beneath her unsure feet. Music begins to play. It seems to be an old "112" song from an album that Carolyn can't quite remember the name of.

(Carolyn)

I want nothing more than to be this man's deepest fantasy. I owe him that much, because he is already my deepest fantasy. His voice, his lips, his regal eyes... damn it the way he walks carrying with him the absolute perfection that he calls his body. His confidence bleeds through honestly via his impeccable style and swagger.

I will do anything he asks of me. I could... No I should be his one and only wife, and not just his, his submissive whore. But I would be this creation he has fashioned me into, and do the freaky sometimes near unbearable things he makes me do until I stop breathing... Just to be near him.

I don't deserve his time; he shouldn't even know my name or that I even exist. Because he made me, I was not really alive until he awakened me mind body and spirit. Of all the wonderful and at time subpar lovers he has afforded and or force upon me in the past six months he is still by far the best lover I have ever had the pleasure of being used by.

The only man who may top James is the man he calls the Master. James seems to worship this man whom I've never actually seen, but I feel like the Master is always near me when I'm with James because everything we do together seems to at some point have been planned or mandated by the Master himself. The Master is supposed to be some kind of sex genius...

"And who is this delicious dark dish?" a deep raspy voice inquires as they reach the room that connects to the huge living room.

"How are you, this evening Master," Radicon asks, "and this my friend is Carolyn Olivier one of my... more special pieces."

James studies the Master's face carefully like he always does. The old man's face isn't pretty to say the least. The Master isn't an ugly man, but he does look like he was in a terrible accident and had to have his face surgically reconstructed.

"And special she is my son," the Master replies, "tell me James, why is it exactly that you are subjecting such a gorgeous specimen to my unorthodox brand of entertainment?"

James looks at Carolyn for a moment, and then squints, his eyes as he looks at her from head to toe.

"She's beautiful," Radicon agrees, "but I have no room in my life to realistically fall for any woman. It's all just a game... Right Master it's all just a game we play, and in turn bless a select few to join and enjoy our brand of entertainment?"

"So," the Master says, "you're telling me that you have no value for, or recollection of what true love is?"

"Absolutely none at all," Radicon claims, "sex and love have no true value in this world. Once people realize that, they open themselves up to the opportunity of being a lot more successful in life as a whole."

The Master smiles a knowing smile.

"How so son?" the Master asks. Radicon doesn't reply.

"No, please explain James." the Master insists.

"Sir we are getting way off track here, we should all be jumping Ms. Olivier like hungry horny dogs by now." Radicon laugh nervously.

"In due time," the Master points towards the girl giving two of his masked men some sort of signal, "how is it that you a married man put no value in love?" the Master asks. "I learned from my father." Radicon replies coldly.

The two masked men escort the blindfolded Carolyn towards the Master. Now that she is standing right in front of him, he explores her face thoroughly and the curves of her explosive young body. With his left hand he begins to lift her skirt slowly.

She doesn't resist. With a hand on each thigh he prompts her to spread her legs more. She obeys the obvious instruction. The bottom of her new tight yellow body dress is now resting atop her soft round caramel behind.

The Master grabs hold of her soft wet center as if to check her pulse. With his right hand on her stomach and his left hand groping her vagina he begins to wildly massage her throbbing wetness. Her moans are delightful.

James closes his eyes in the distance as the sounds of her pleasure wash over his joyous ears like the soft tones of an angel's voice.

"Master..." she moans.

"Yes Carolyn." he replies. "Do what you will, to me..." she cries impatiently. "Oh I am," he smiles, "trust me my dear your ass belongs to me... at least for tonight."

The Master glances over at James to check his facial expression. Just as he thought the look on James' at this point face isn't quite one of jealousy but it's not exactly one of pleasure either.

"Come close son." the Master says with his smile still completely intact. Radicon obeys. Standing by the Master's side he can't take his eyes off of the beautiful entranced black woman before him.

The mystery of the Master's touch is all James can think about. Carolyn seems to thoroughly enjoy the sex they have together, but the noises she's making now have never graced his corner office, the utility closet during his daily lunch break, of the back seat of any of his luxury vehicles.

What is this? I'm not jealous, I can't be jealous. I am the son of Raymond Radicon. I can literally screw any woman I want. There has never been one woman, in my adult life that I've wanted to fuck that I haven't. I'm perfect. So why now would I be... How could I possibly be jealous over this little black employee of mine? I mean sure she has a great ass and she's not bad to look at, okay she's perfect. But, she's just a part of my fantasy she doesn't really exist to me.

The room is very well lit. The Master insist on the lighting to be as such because his eyes aren't what they used to be and he always says more than anything he enjoys watching. The two masked men are shirtless and covered in oil, wearing black leather pants, and black combat boots.

The Master motions for one of the masked men to come near to him. The man begins carefully stripping her clothes from her throbbing wet body. She's soaked with sweat, and passion. She could have never imagined being this fully aroused in a room full of strange men.

(Hours later)

As they pull up to the small brick house on the corner of Jefferson Street, it appears to look just the way it did when James picked Carolyn up hours ago. Not one light on inside the home. James parks his SUV just across the street from the house. Carolyn staring out of the passenger window towards her house hesitates to exit the vehicle.

"Is something wrong baby girl?" Radicon asks in genuine concern. She looks at him, but she remains silent.

"Hey," he starts, "if what happened back there was too much..."

"I loved it." she interjects.

"I love pleasing you James," she continues, "the passion and intrigue on your perfect face and the look in your enchanting eyes was enough to will me to do almost anything."

James isn't sure how to respond. He wrinkles his left brow, and then gently clears his dry throat so that he can attempt to speak. "But Carolyn," he starts, "you have a husband I'm just you're..."

"A husband," she starts, "in my mind at least... is a man who possesses a woman's mind first, then her body, and then finally her spirit. A woman's true husband is the man she pheens for constantly, the one she dreams about. You, James Radicon embody all of my sweetest dreams and I wake up every single morning wishing it was you lying next to me."

James turns around to look out of the driver's side window. He wipes some warm sweat from his forehead, clears his throat again and begins scratching the top of his well-kept blond head.

"It's um... Very late Carolyn," he mumbles, "you should get inside before he..."

She opens her door and steps out of his truck. She immediately looks down and tries to straighten her soiled yellow gown. Before walking away, she turns back to look at him with an awkward grin on her face.

"I may be just a fool to you Mr. Radicon," she says, "but what wife doesn't play the fool sometimes? Goodnight James."

She closes the door and makes her way towards her house where she lives with Ralph, her actual legal husband of four years now. James drives off into the distance, all the while secretly watching her in his rear view mirror to ensure she makes it inside the house safely.

Once she's inside he readjusts his mirror and sets his mind on what may be possibly waiting on him when he gets home himself.

Before retiring to her room she takes a left in the front room towards her children's room. She opens their door quietly and tip toes in completely undetected. She finds her three-year-old Ralph Jr. sleeping quietly in his Spider-Man bed. She smiles down at him as she makes her way to her 11 month old Karan's crib. Looking down at his tiny angelic face she's in awe. She feels as if she's being showered with love as her eyes find themselves lost in the perfect design of his adorable face. Her son's beauty has washed away the memory and the sins of the lustful evening she just encountered.

She bends down to pick him up, and then she kisses him gently. After laying him back down safely in his little crib she turns around to find Ralph Jr. smiling up at her.

"Hey mommy..." he whispers.

"Hey Mama's baby." she whispers back returning his infectious smile. The three year olds smile quickly fades into a sad frown.

"I miss you mommy," he tells her, "you don't love me and Karan anymore." the toddler begins to cry. Carolyn quickly picks him up in her soft arms.

"No, no baby, don't cry," she tells him, "you're my big boy."

"You don't love me Mama." he cries.

"Don't say that Junior." she tells him.

"You never come home and play with me no more mommy." he tells her crying harder with each painful syllable.

Carolyn picks her older son up high in the air so that he is face to face with her. "Baby," she says, "I do love you. Mommy just has a lot going on at work. But you know what..."

"What..." he whines?

"Mommy is going to leave work early tomorrow," Carolyn tells her son, "and come straight home and play with you *all* the way until it's time for your bath."

"What about my baby brother?" the three-year-old asks.

"Of course baby," she smiles at his adorable serious demeanor, "I'm going to play with you and your baby brother. Now little boy it's time for you to go to sleep... Okay?"

"Okay mommy." Ralph Jr. grins.

She kisses him on the lips three times and then tucks him safely back in his Spider-Man bed. Then Carolyn leaves their room and heads towards her own.

Back inside her bathroom Carolyn walks solemnly to her large window that looks out across her nice sized back yard.

"Is this my choice," she whispers, "is anything in my control? Or am I just trapped in this man's fantasy until he decides he's finally finished with me? I'm far from stupid, I've seen "The Family that Preys" I know James Radicon will never be my husband... But even still the rush I get just from being in his presence feels much better than anything I've ever felt with Ralph. Lord I guess these rambling words of mine are some kind of sick prayer. When you pray you have to ask for something right? But I don't know exactly what it is I want or need. Yes, I do... make me white Lord. Please God just make me white so I can be good enough to be James' wife, I don't want to struggle with Ralph anymore in this tiny house. Damn it. Poor Ralph and I know how much he loves me. If he ever found out about this, he would..."

Carolyn shakes her head nervously as she makes her way to her bathroom mirror. Looking at her reflection, she has no clue who this woman is staring back at her. She sees a black whore who would do anything and everything to satisfy a man who could never righteously marry her. The bags under her weary eyes are bold or at least they seem that way to her.

The makeup that's left on her face looks absolutely atrocious. She looks to herself like an ugly old dark clown waiting to pop out from behind a tattered old curtain to perform in front of some cheap circus crowd.

And oh God her breath, she can still taste and smell all four men on her own breath and her entire body is still throbbing in both pain and pleasure.

She grabs her tooth brush and an old tube of Colgate toothpaste. She covers the brush with a generous amount of tooth paste and then begins brushing her teeth vigorously.

After she rinses her mouth out after brushing her teeth she stares back in the mirror again. Her hair is a mess. Her tight ponytail didn't last ten minutes after the evening's festivities began. Her brown curls are all over her head stretched out from being tugged and snatched back and forth for hours.

Carolyn turns around and approaches her lonely shower. She leans on the glass door of it as she turns it on. In her mind she can't help but ponder all the secrets only her bathroom walls know about her inner most thoughts and sentiments.

She smiles, but not for long as she turns back towards her mirror the warm tears begin to storm her pain-filled face like never before. "God I don't want to be a fool forever. Lord, please save me from my own mind." she cries silently.

After a long steaming hot shower Carolyn finally steps out of her almost clean tub onto the bathroom floor. The tile floor is uncomfortable to her touch. All of the bathroom rugs are in the laundry room on the floor where they've been for about eight days now.

The rugs are stuck there because neither she nor Ralph, have been considerate enough to take a moment to go in there and actually wash them. This would be the first time their dingy orangish bath rugs have ever been washed in over three years. The only reason they were going to wash them now is because one of their children threw up all over their bathroom over a week ago.

With a towel she found hanging on the back of her bathroom door Carolyn begins to dry the excess water off of her beautiful, drained, naked body. After sliding into her old purple bath robe she uses a towel from the bathroom closet to dry her wild hair.

With her robe on and a towel wrapped carefully around her head she opens the bathroom door. Standing there staring into her bedroom Carolyn is forced to think about how different her life would be if she was Mrs. James Radicon and not just Mrs. Ralph Olivier.

Looking at her queen sized bed she sees him lying there sound asleep. He doesn't seem to have a care in the world. And he doesn't, he has his pretty little trophy wife, a dead end factory job, a car and a home. He's content.

At twenty-four years old Ralph Olivier has the body of a forty-year-old man. He was never a very physically fit man, but the past four years he really let himself go. He's dark skinned and he wears his hair in a low buzz cut with a silly childish part cut in the side of his plain head.

Everything about him is plain, his face, his walk, even the things he says. He's just a dull guy. Ralph stands about 5'7 and he wears the same three or four outfits year round.

Carolyn is well aware that he prides himself on the fact that she, his wife is prettier than all of his friend's wives and girlfriends. If only he knew his wife was in love with and sleeping with another man. What's more, Ralph actually had the audacity to cheat on her first. He's cheated on Carolyn and gotten caught multiple times over the span of their four-year marriage.

That's part of the reason Carolyn didn't even pretend to be resisting her bosses' sexual advances once they became more obvious.

As Carolyn walks towards the bed her heart is pounding in her chest. Not because she fears or cares what Ralph might think anymore, but because she's can't get the Master and his men out of her mind. The things they did to her, the things James let them do to her were extraordinary.

She would have stayed there in that creepy old house forever if James would have allowed it. She would have lived there forever chained to a bed in one of the Master's many bedrooms completely nude waiting to satisfy any takers. James has awakened in her an inner sexual goddess that she never even knew could exist.

As she lies down next to her husband she continues to mentally relive the evenings many pleasures. Ralph instinctively rolls over close to her in his sleep and wraps his hairy dark arms around her. She cringes at the smell of his natural body odor. It's nothing new; he's always had that smell, even fresh out of the shower his smell remains. She closes her eyes to endure yet another night trapped in his unsuspecting arms.

Ch. 2

"Doughnuts and Tea"

The sun is shining in brightly through the large window in the master bedroom. The trees outside the window are filled with happy birds singing praises to the clouds. James wishes they would all just shut up. He's never been anything close to a morning person. But for some reason this morning as he rolls over and detaches his cell phone from its charger he has a real smile on his face.

The text message on his screen reads, "good morning sir can I do anything to make your morning better?" He covers his head with one of his large fluffy white pillows to hide his obvious happiness.

"She actually does wake up thinking about me." he mumbles through the pillow.

"Who does darling?" a soft voice startles him from across the room. James quickly looks from under his pillow at his wife's pale curious face.

"No one darling," he lies, "how are you feeling this morning?"

"Like you're hiding something from me," she replies, "now please answer my question."

"I'm thinking of penning an autobiography," he lies to her, "you know a chance to reflect back on all my memoirs and achievements, most notably marrying you Jessica."

Mrs. Jessica Radicon is thirty-six years old and has loved James Radicon since the moment she laid eyes on him.

She knew he was richer than God when they first started dating, but that didn't matter she never wanted his money. He was worth much more to her than material possessions, cash, and an eternally glamorous lifestyle. To her, he was her soul mate. Jessica's gray eyes are clear and wise. Her strawberry blonde hair is much more strawberry than it ever was blonde. She's a natural red head, but she started tinting her hair with blond highlights a few years back to liven up her appearance. Now that Jessica is getting older, although she is still quite stunning herself, she's sure her husband's handsome eyes are going to begin to wonder soon.

She always suspected he might be cheating, but she's well aware that the life he has afforded her would never have been possible without him. Before they were married she insisted they sign a prenuptial agreement just to prove that she wasn't there for his money. She really wasn't, and she would love him just the same if he was homeless.

"Your memoirs huh..." she says.

"Yes baby," he lies again jumping out of bed to approach her, "Jess you know there's only one woman for me." He kisses her softly on the forehead and then makes his way to the bathroom.

After closing and locking the bathroom door behind him. James pulls his cell phone out of his pocket. He quickly texts her back and then places his phone back safely in the pocket of his Polo sweat pants.

Next he grabs his tooth brush and begins looking for his favorite Crest toothpaste. He looks around all three sinks on the top of his beautiful marble bathroom counter top. He can't find a tube of toothpaste anywhere.

He opens the medicine cabinet to his right. He sees every possible pill and ointment for any ailment or disease imaginable, but absolutely no Crest toothpaste. One by one he opens each of the five drawers going down the front of the sink. No Crest toothpaste.

"Oh damn it, that's right. She threw it all away." he whispers to himself.

In the very back corner on the right side of the black marble sink top, he sees a transparent blue bottle baring the words, "Blue Tooth Technology" and the name Dr. Gregory Blue. Jessica was watching some late night infomercial about some crazy dentist out in Waco Texas who invented some kind of miracle salve that is supposed to replace your regular tooth paste and mouth wash, strengthen your teeth and gums, and restore your teeth to their most healthy form.

James shakes his head silently. Holding his yellow Crest tooth brush beneath the dispenser he pushes its top down to release the miracle goo. The weird watery concoction immediately begins to spill out on and around his toothbrush and on the sink-top.

After each bristle is covered James prepares himself for how bad this stuff just might taste. He would turn on the sink and wet his toothbrush first, but Dr. Blue's goo has wet the brush quite enough already.

As he puts the brush in his mouth and begins to brush, amazingly the taste of the salve isn't bad at all. In fact, it tastes like fresh fruit, and it's foaming up nicely prompting James to brush more thoroughly than he normally would. He can definitely feel the salve working fiercely through his mouth. Jessica may not have made a mistake with this particular purchase, he thinks to himself.

After rinsing his fresh mouth out, James strips down completely naked and jumps in the shower turning it on full blast. As he lathers his towel with some ridiculously expensive West African soap Jessica bought and insists he uses, James is mentally preparing himself for the day he has ahead of him at the office.

After placing the black bar of soap back in its crystal dish on the side of the shower he begins to rub his body thoroughly with the soapy towel. As his hands glide across his chiseled white body, he's imagining his hands are Carolyn's hands. She's taking immense pleasure in exploring every inch of his body.

From his strong neck, to his tense broad shoulders, a l l the way down to his ripped abdomen. As her hands caress his back with the soft towel she notices his sudden arousal. She takes hold of him as he throbs fiercely in the palm of her hand.

James smiles to himself as he realizes his imagination was never this vivid before he met Carolyn Olivier. Her hands feel so soft on his strong pulsating penis.

As she begins to stroke him masterfully he leans back against the side wall of the shower. Her strokes are becoming more intense as he rises up on the tips of his toes balancing himself with one stable hand on the glass shower door in front of him.

His throbbing member feels huge and powerful in her hands; it's almost too much for her to stroke. She begins to use both hands. He can't take much more of this; the speed at which she can force him to climax is unreal. Just the thought of her is an insanely powerful aphrodisiac for him. Up even higher on the tips of his toes now stroking himself full force James' entire body grows extremely tense.

"Oh Carolyn..." he moans as he spills his seed forth all over the glass shower doors. As he watches his semen squirt out all over the glass he can barely contain himself. He wants to scream her name out, but he thinks better of it realizing his wife Jessica is right outside the bathroom reading a book.

After lazily toweling himself off sitting on his gorgeous immaculate marble toilet, James slides into a pair of cocaine white Polo boxer briefs. With his yellow towel secured around his neck he opens the bathroom door and makes his way back to his enormous bed.

Sitting on the edge of the side of his bed just across from Jessica's reading chair James stares over at her. She feels his eyes on her but she doesn't look up at him. Lost in a trance Radicon begins to think to himself...

Where did I go wrong? I'm a good, strong, white, Christian man. I'm handsome, intelligent, more than affluent... hell I live in my very own mansion. I have a wife who loves me there is no doubt about that. But is she still enough... obviously not. As a man, as a good

white Christian man the last thing I want to do is embarrass and rip apart my family by getting caught being unfaithful to my wife Jessica. Damn it we said real vows... and bound our hearts and lives together sixteen years ago. We have two gorgeous children, a son Lucas 16, and a daughter Katherine she's 15. If their friends, my friends, or my wife's friends ever found out what I was doing with Carolyn they would never understand or forgive me. So in turn I must stop the madness now. I'm going to fire her today and rid my life of her disruptive black ass forever.

James' clothes are laid out on the bed perfectly. For some reason today he's noticing all the things he usually doesn't. This woman, his wife works very hard to make, and keep his life as simple as humanly possible.

For years he's felt as if after finishing his morning shower his outfit for the day has just always magically appeared towards the foot of the bed, always in the very same spot. But it was never magic. It was the carefully thought out love and dedication of his wife Jessica.

As he puts his clothes on he glances at his rose gold MK watch. He's late. James throws on his suit as quickly as he can, kisses Jessica softly on the lips, and then storms out of their room and all the way down stairs.

The tasty aroma of pancakes, scrambled eggs, and

bacon could be smelled all the way upstairs in the master bedroom. Without much time to eat James grabs a plate and a fork on his way out of the door.

"Hey Dad..." his son Lucas Radicon calls out to him wearing white Ray Ban sunglasses with clear lenses, a baby blue neatly tucked in Polo shirt with a pink logo, white Polo shorts with a baby blue logo, and pink and white Polo shoes. James looks at his teenage son for a moment, and then heads out of the door as if he hadn't said a word to him.

As James drives off in his black on black 2015 Mercedes Benz coupe he ponders why he never deals with any of his family issues head on. He wonders if he's afraid or if maybe he's just not capable of dealing with these sensitive issues appropriately. If there's a problem at one of his many businesses he's right on it.

He listens to the problem, weighs out his options carefully, and then executes the best possible course of action to resolve said problem. But when it comes to his family he always closes the door and blocks their problems out until he can make himself believe he's forgotten all about whatever the issue was.

Thirty minutes later Mr. Radicon pulls up to the large building that houses his main company, the gorgeous Radicon Winery. James has his hands in hundreds of successful business ventures, but his winery is the one he is the most passionate about.

The great Radicon Winery sits on 7.5 acres of land. The majority of the land is covered in grapevines. Grape growing is both simple and confounding. While it is easy to keep a grapevine alive it is one of agriculture's great difficulties to continue to produce grapes of good enough quality to produce a fine wine. Radicon Winery boasts some of the tastiest wines in not only the U.S. but the entire world.

The building that sits at the very center of the largish vineyard is where the business side of the winery is handled. James has hundreds of offices from corner to corner of the five story structure. These offices are inhabited by his many sales reps, marketing execs, and other various employees that help his company run smoothly from day to day.

Carolyn Olivier started working at the winery two years ago as a field laborer in the vineyard. Five days a week she and her 200 plus coworkers would all go out into the vineyard and tend to the grounds.

Some were equipped with backpack sprayers that they used to spray the vines to keep them pest and disease free. Others trimmed the vines, took care of pesky weeds, and even mowed the lawn around and in between the vines.

Carolyn though was a grape picker. James knows countless other top notch Vineyard owners use mechanical harvesters to pick their grapes, but he likes the old fashion way much better. When he tastes a glass of his wine he wants to know that some hardworking soul took time to carefully pick each one of the delicious grapes he's drinking with love and purpose.

Carolyn wasn't too fond of her job in the vineyard, but she never once complained. She needed the money for her family and the pay wasn't bad at all.

James still remembers the day he met Carolyn Olivier like it was just yesterday. It was about 14 months ago. He was riding through the vineyard in one of his personal golf carts when out of the corner of his eye he saw a woman bending over displaying her round, perfect, voluptuous behind. He stopped his cart immediately, got off and began walking calmly in her direction.

On his way to her he divisively engaged in a couple meaningless conversations with some of his other vineyard employees as not to make his current mission to obvious. By the time he reached her she was standing up right again carefully picking each grape in her section one by one.

Standing not far behind her James cleared his throat and said, "I think you missed one." Carolyn immediately threw her bucket down to the ground and spun around to him with a venomous scowl on her face.

"Listen wise ass," she said, "I don't know who you think you are, but I work very hard in this damn vineyard. I don't bother anybody; I don't gripe or complain I just work damn hard. So if you think your little comment was funny... Then you can just kiss my black ass." James smiled at her sassiness as she bent down to recapture her large grape bucket.

"I'd love too." he replied. She spun around to him again refusing to acknowledge his unmistakably white teeth, his bright light blue eyes, and his radiant smile. "Excuse me," she said, "you would love to what... Kiss my black ass?"

"Why yes ma'am." he said through that perfect smile. "I am a married woman," the 22-year-old Carolyn told him, "and this is sexual harassment. If you don't turn around and leave now I'm going to be forced to march right up to the main building and tell Mr. Radicon about your behavior." "Well is that so?" James asked Carolyn in animated amusement.

Just then a white gentleman approached the two of them. "Mr. Radicon," he said, "your wife left a message for you to call home... It's about your son Lucas."

"Okay Brad I'll call her." Radicon said shaking the man's hand just before he turned to leave.

Carolyn at that point had dropped her grape bucket again and was covering her mouth with both hands in total embarrassment. James smiled at her and extended his hand in her direction. "It's nice to meet you... my name is James Radicon, and what's your name?" he asked in a charming tone.

"I am so sorry Mr. Radicon, I had no idea it was you... Well that you were him or you... Oh damn it I'm sorry." she said laughing at herself as she shook his large hand. They exchanged phone numbers and a week later Carolyn had a job inside the main building. James couldn't help but feel like their situation was reminiscent of a slave and her master 300 to 400 years ago, but this fact for some reason enticed his unorthodox mind even more.

"Good morning Mr. Radicon." a familiar voice says from the door of his office snatching him away from his daydream. He looks up to see her. She's wearing a gorgeous yellow pant suit and black heels. She knows yellow is his favorite color.

Her naturally curly hair is pulled up into a tight neat bun on top of her head. Her yellow blazer is open just enough to playfully expose the top of her perky bosom. James is trying to ignore how pretty she is because his plan is to fire her this morning.

"I brought your doughnuts and tea sir that you asked me for..." she tells him.

"Doughnuts and tea..." he says.

"Yes sir," she replies, "You know the ones you asked for in your text this morning." she smiles.

He doesn't respond. "Is there anything else you need me to do before I head to my office and begin work on the Brown & Nielsen project?" she asks trying to accurately read his mood.

He remains silent. "Are you okay... James?" she asks closing his door behind her and stepping towards him.

Standing over him now, as he holds his head down in his large hands she puts a soft hand on his left shoulder.

James looks up into her caring hazel eyes.

"Carolyn," he says, "I have to... Tell you something."

"Anything," she kneels down in front of him, "baby you can tell me anything."

Holding her angelic caramel face in between his milky white hands he says, "I have to tell you... You are... an absolutely gorgeous woman." Pulling her into his chest he kisses her long and passionately on her full lips.

(Later that afternoon)

"Come on Ralph Jr., it's time to go baby..." Carolyn calls out from near the front door holding her younger son Karan in her arms tightly.

"Coooooming mommy." He says running into the front room with one shoe on and the other in his left hand.

Carolyn smiles down at his wide eyes.

"Now I just knew you would beat me to the door little boy," she says, "You told me you wanted mommy to play with you and your baby brother and spend more time with you. Now I cleared my entire schedule for the rest of the day just to take you two to..."

"Chuck E. Cheese!!" Ralph Jr. screams vibrantly.

"Chuckuh Cheese!!" his lovable baby brother tries to mimic him.

"That's right," she smiles opening the front door, "now let's get you both strapped in so we can head over there before it gets too crowded."

Karan nods his adorable little head up and down as his mother walks him to the car in her arms.

"Mommy," Ralph Jr. says walking a step behind her, "Is daddy coming too?"

"Daada, Daada." Karan whines.

"Of course your father is coming." she replies placing Karan down on his feet so she can open the door.

After securing both of her sons in the backseat Carolyn hops in the front seat and straps her seatbelt on just before cranking up her car. "Conquerors mommy, play conquerors..." Ralph Jr. says from the back seat.

Carolyn smiles as she shakes her head and turns her radio on.

"Please mama..." Her older son begs.

"Please... please." Karan joins in with the begging onslaught.

"I'm trying to find it children," she placates them as she searches her phone, "mama is happy ya'll's favorite song is a gospel song, and I'll play it as many times as your tiny ears wanna hear it."

She finds the song and presses play as she backs out of her long driveway.

"It was your favorite song first mommy." Ralph Jr. says.

"That's right," she confirms, "when mommy was a little girl she used to always lead this song in the youth choir."

"What's a lead mommy?" Ralph Jr. asks playing with his baby brother's toes.

"A lead," Carolyn says, "or a leader is the person everyone else looks up to or follows."

"I wanna be a leader mommy." Ralph Jr. proclaims.

"Well," she smiles at him in her rearview mirror, "If you're anything like your mommy, you will be a leader one-day baby boy."

"Is daddy a leader mommy?" Ralph Jr. asks.

"Daada..." his baby brother smiles.

"Your father," Carolyn hesitates, "is... the leader of our household. Every man should be the leader of his house baby."

"But mommy," Ralph Jr. whines, "you said a leader was the person everyone is posed to look up to and follow. Daddy looks up to you mommy."

"Where on earth did you come from child?" Carolyn smiles at her remarkably attentive son.

As they pull into the parking lot of Chuck E. Cheese Carolyn pulls out her cell phone to call her husband. As she pulls into an open space near the front the phone is still ringing. She steps out of the car, hangs up, and tries to call again. No answer. With the phone to her ear calling a third time Carolyn opens the backdoor to get her children out of the car.

Once inside Karan follows his big brother towards a racing game. Carolyn watches them both carefully with a distant smile painted on her tired face.

"Come on Ralph answer the phone," she mumbles, "we agreed to meet here and spend time with the kids together for once."

Carolyn hangs up again and slips her phone in her purse as her sons' rush towards her carrying the two powerful smiles that always seem to wash all her pain away.

"Boys," she says looking down at the two of them huddled between her legs, "mommy knows she doesn't spend a lot of time with ya'll right now but I will always be your mama and I'll never let anything bad happen to you. I love you both very much."

"Okay," Ralph Jr. smiles, "can we have pizza now mommy?"

"Pissa, pissa!!" Karan squeals.

"I'll take that as a *we love you too* mommy," Carolyn smiles as a lone tear streams down the left side of her beautiful face, "and yes ya'll go play mama will go get you a pizza."

Ch. 3

"The Brown & Nielsen Project"

Justin

P atrick Brown and Renaldo Nielsen are the joint owners of the Los Angeles based "Brown & Nielsen" Winery. The last few years have not been very good to them.

After researching their company and their decline in sales over the past three years, Carolyn reached out to Mr. Brown himself via email to discuss the possibility of merging his company with Radicon's Winery or just selling his winery to Mr. Radicon outright. For about six months he played hard ball, but just last week Carolyn got a call from Mr. Brown's partner Renaldo Nielsen saying he was interested in selling his half of the company to Radicon. His only stipulation was that he wanted to meet James in person in California.

James looks up from his desk to see Carolyn standing just outside of his office door speaking to a handsome, young, biracial kid named Justin Tolls. James knows the young man's name well. He actually hired Justin on at the winery full time himself recently.

Justin is a standout student in the School of Business Administration at the local University of Miami. He interned at the Radicon Winery for three months, and just last week James called him into his office to hire him on full time. But if he's sweet on Ms. Carolyn Olivier, his tenure at this particular Winery may be cut a little short.

Carolyn finishes her obviously delightful conversation with Justin, shakes his hand a little longer than James thinks she should have, and then she looks through his door at James. Her heart quickly sinks to her stomach. His gaze and its meaning are definite.

He's not happy with her.

She looks down at her shoes knowing her face must be red with fear, and confusion. She straightens her long pink dress and knocks politely on his thick office door.

He spins his expensive office chair around to face in the opposite direction from where she's standing. She walks in his office anyway. "James..." she speaks. He doesn't respond. "I uh... Spoke to Mr. Renaldo Nielsen in California." she tells him.

Radicon spins back around to face her.

"Well come on with it," he says, "what did the old fool say?"

"He wants to sell." she says.

"Finally," James flashes a greedy smile, "Cheer up girl this is great news!"

"Not quite." she replies.

"What do you mean not quite," he asks, "of course this is good news... all of it. If I can get the controlling share of the "Brown & Nielsen Winery" I can expand my brand and my genius methods all across the West Coast."

Carolyn looks down again. James stands up from his chair, his face and neck turning bright red now.

"Damn it bitch, speak," he fumes, "what is this? What the hell is all of that looking down at your feet crap? Women are such weak pitiful creatures, especially you black ones. What in God's name is wrong with you now?"

She looks up at him. "You hate to travel sir." she mumbles.

"Damn it, speak up," he growls, "I can't understand you people... You, you... All of you speak too fast and you don't form your damn words."

"You hate to travel." she repeats a little louder this time.

"I don't speak Ebonics," he tells her, "you people just make up your own damned words and just form sentences however you damn well please. Ignorant it's just stupid..."

"Damn it James," she interjects throwing her paperwork down on his floor, "I said you hate to travel. I said each word very clearly. I pronounced and enunciated each word perfectly. Your speech on the other hand leaves much to be desired."

"And what the hell is wrong with the way I talk?" he asks.

"Nothing James." She replies realizing how angry she allows him to make her.

"You're even more beautiful when you're mad... you know that?" he tells her.

34

She blushes.

"Well thank you, I guess," she replies bending down to retrieve the papers she threw on his floor, "but as I was saying; I know you hate to travel, but the only way Nielsen will agree to sell his share of the company to you is if you fly out to Los Angeles and meet him in person... *Next week.*"

James' pleasant smile fades instantly.

"Out of the question." he sits back down in his chair.

"But sir..." she starts.

"There are no buts, girl," he growls, "You know I hate to travel."

"Well yes sir I know, but..." she tries to finish her statement again.

"I am not getting on an airplane Carolyn not now, not ever." he interjects. "But why not James," she asks, "you have all this damn money and now you're faced with the opportunity to at least triple your fortune, but you are scared to fly. Why?"

Radicon spins his chair away from her to face the back wall of his office. "My father," he starts, "Raymond Radicon got on a plane one day 26 years ago and I never saw him again."

"Oh my God," Carolyn gasps covering her full lips with her left hand, "the plane James, whatever happened to the plane?" "It was never found, and neither was my father." he tells her.

Carolyn walks over to close and lock his office door. Then she carefully closes all of his blinds so no one can possibly see inside of his office.

With both hands she pulls the straps of her long dress over her shoulders and lets it fall to the floor. Standing there in a matching white lace bra and panty set, she reaches up to undo her bun. After shaking her heads to release all of her glorious curls she speaks.

"I'm sorry about your father James," she says, "but I will not let you miss out on this deal that I worked so hard to land for you. You are going to California next week..." He stands up quickly from his chair and then turns around to face her.

"Damn it I said..." his words get caught in his red throat as he stares at her perfect seminude body.

"You're going James," she tells him, "and I'm going with you."

"Hell yes you are." he rushes towards her.

As he reaches her she jumps into his massive arms wrapping her anxious legs around him. Her sexy caramel skin looks gorgeous next to his almost tan white skin.

He begins to kiss her ever so passionately gripping her round soft behind never closing his eyes. As they stare into each other's knowing eyes they continue to hungrily devour each other's mouths.

"Damn it Carolyn," he moans carrying her en route to his huge mahogany desk, "I was going to fire you today."

"For what?" she asks, as she sucks and bites the left side of his thick neck.

"Are you not satisfied with my efforts?" she continues.

"Oh shut up." he smiles down at her.

Then James begins to push everything on his huge desk towards the back of it. Carolyn drops down to her well trained knees and unbuttons his pants, and then rips his zipper open.

He's already more than ready for her. She masterfully grabs hold of his enormous member. Licking the sides of it she strokes him softly with both hands.

"Not today..." he moans. He grabs her by her hair forcing her to stand up straight. Then he picks her up and sits her on top of his desk. Radicon takes a few steps back to admire his Nubian queen. With her heels down flat on his desktop she has her legs spread wide for him. James throws his luxurious blazer on the floor and then button by button he opens his Polo dress shirt exposing his rock hard six pack. Pulling his undershirt up, he unveils the perfect V-cut above his private area. She loves his V-cut; it gets her wetter than anything else.

She can feel her breathing pattern changing rapidly. She can no longer contain herself; she needs James Radicon inside her right this instant.

As he approaches her she quickly takes off her passion soaked underwear. He stopped using condoms with her months ago. He puts the head in, struggling to get all of him inside of her small frame.

It always feels like the first time when they're together. If only either one of their marriages could feel the same way, they wouldn't be locked in this office screwing each other's brains out right now.

Yes. He finally breaks through again. He runs his long, strong, penis as deep inside her as she will let it go. She closes her eyes as she bites her quivering bottom lip. "James..." she cries.

"Open your eyes Carolyn," he whispers, "I want to stare at your soul while I fuck you. Look at me... ***Every fiber of your being belongs to me... forever.***"

She stares back at him obediently. Carolyn's passion filled screams and moans are growing louder with each powerful stroke. James reaches over and grabs her panties. "Open your mouth." he demands. She obeys. Then he stuffs her wet panties in her unsuspecting mouth. "Don't take your eyes off of me..." he moans. She obeys between her muffled screams.

His blue eyes are hypnotizing her as he strokes harder and deeper inside of her cum drenched center. "You are one of my most prized possessions..." he moans.

"I'm all yours James..." she mumbles through her tasty wet panties.

Ch. 4

"Kate Radicon"

Kate

It's never easy being the product of an affluent family. I mean sure you get a lot of stuff. But all the stuff in the world can't make you whole or happy.

To be rich is one thing, but to be a Radicon is something completely different. My big brother Lucas and I don't even know how rich we really are. I mean sure we have googled our dad's net-worth; it says he's worth   like $870,000,000.

We also know about his private offshore bank accounts and business ventures. How rich my dad is doesn't really matter though, I know full well I'll never have to work, I do know he's that rich. He has transformed my Great-grandfather's fortune into an eternal gold mind. I'm very proud of my father and the shark of a businessman he is; I just wish he knew I existed.

I love all of my material possessions, my clothes and shoes, this house, hell I had a pink Lamborghini when I was fourteen. I would never change who my dad is... I just wish he was a father too. Life is so easy that it gets extremely hard sometimes.

Katherine talks to herself often alone in her private bathroom that connects to her bedroom. She is her own best friend, because her actual best friend Scooter isn't in her life consistently enough to hold that title. Katherine is 5'3 and she weighs 93 pounds on a good day. Her strong flowing hair is sinfully red, with streaks of blond in it that her mother suggested she get a few months back. She has her father's blue eyes.

Her skin is more than pale and her tiny face is covered in pimples that look like they're all ready to burst at any given moment. She does hide them well enough though, with the expensive makeup her mother prompted her to order online.

Her teeth are a goner. She's had braces since she was 12, yeah she's had them for three years already. Katherine's orthodontist Dr. Dorothy Blanchard Rose said she'll have to wear them well into her seventeenth year on this earth.

The structure of her teeth was *that* bad, and they're still placed and shaped horribly wrong now. Katherine isn't all that ugly, but she just has so much going on with her face and the way she speaks it makes her even harder to look at. Her lisp is terrible and she spits when she   talks because of her braces.

Needless to say her peers and classmates are not usually kind to her. Sitting here in her bathroom now she's trying to think of reasons not to take her own life. People can be so cruel. She's far too young to understand that those mean people are the way they are because they are weak and not happy themselves, so in turn they lash out and torment people who are even weaker and less happy than they are.

"Katherine you're *so ugly*," she whispers to herself mocking some of her bullies,

"God, do you ever eat? You look like *a little poor white African kid*. Come here bitch let me play connect the dots with your bumpy ass face. All that makeup ain't hiding shit! I'm gonna beat your ass *like a red headed step child*! You can't be Radicon's daughter... he looks too good to have produced an *ugly duckling like you*!!"

Their evil, obnoxious, and incessant laughter after each joke is always the worst part. The laughs make the jokes and name calling hurt so much more.

Damn it the tears begin to fall again. Her pain seems eternal to her. She can't even begin to imagine her life being any other way. Being completely invisible until her classmates get bored enough to pick on her; that's just what her life is, and will always be. Her red face hurts and she's so tired of crying.

Katherine stands up from her toilet and makes her way to her mirror. She grabs a towel from a nearby towel rack and turns on the water full blast. She drenches the towel with Clearasil Ultra and some new Proactive cream her mother bought for her online.

Then she begins scrubbing her face with the towel as hard as she possibly can. In her mind maybe, just maybe if she scrubs hard enough she can wash all the ugly off of her face. Or even better maybe she will bleed to death from the pimples on her face all rupturing at the same time.

Her screams and cries can't be heard because she's locked inside her room and inside her bathroom with its door also locked and closed tightly.

As the pain of the scrubbing finally becomes unbearable she throws the bloody towel on the floor behind her and falls to the floor covered in tears and blood still crying fiercely. Her entire body is shaking and her vision is no longer clear.

From the left pocket of her cargo shorts she pulls a small sharp razor. She holds the dangerous weapon up towards the ceiling of her bathroom as if she's offering it up to God as a solution to rid his beautiful earth of such an ugly creature he couldn't have possibly created himself.

She slices her left wrist hard and deep.

"My own damn father won't look at me," she cries, "He doesn't love me. Hell, how can I blame him? I don't even love me. How could I ever hope to get a boyfriend when my own dad can't stand to look at me? Oh God... die, I just wanna... God please just let me die right here right now. You owe me that much!"

She cuts herself again in the exact same spot. Bright red blood squirts out everywhere all over her floor and clothes. "God damn it," she screams, "my mother, she wants so badly to love me and be proud of me... But I'm so ugly even my own mother hates me."

Hurting herself feels wonderful; she has never felt so alive in her life. She begins slicing her arm even higher now. She wants this rush to last forever.

"Kate..." her mom calls out from inside her bedroom.

"Kate where are you?" Her mother tries to open her bathroom door.

"Kate your school just called, they said you haven't been to any of your classes all week." Katherine remains silent rocking back and forth still crying her blue eyes out on her cold, dark, lonely bathroom floor.

"Damn it Katie answer me," her mother demands, "Your father is paying college tuition prices for you to attend this very prestigious high school and you don't even show up..."

Katherine still doesn't respond, she feels shitty now looking down at all the blood and gashes in her arm. She feels so weak and stupid for hurting herself like this. These scars in her mind have only amplified her hideousness.

She can hear her mother attempting to unlock her bathroom door from the outside. Katherine would get up and run to her large bathroom window and open it, so she can dive out of it killing herself in the process but she doesn't even have enough strength to lift an arm.

"Damn it Katie you open this door right now!" her mother cries.

"Katie, please... Are you okay?" her mother continues, completely drowning in panic now.

The door swings open violently. Her mother screams out at the top of her lungs.

"Kate! Baby no," Jessica cries out rushing to her confused daughter's limp body, "baby I'm sorry for yelling... what are you doing to yourself Katherine?"

Jessica grabs the bloody razor from Kate's limp hand and puts it in the pocket of her garden apron. With her arms wrapped tightly around her tiny daughter she begins to rock back and forth. Kate can feel her mother's tears dripping down on her almost numb face.

Jessica picks Kate up in her arms and carries her all the way downstairs and into the garage. Then she carefully lays her down in the back seat of her black Mercedes van. Seconds later Jessica speeds out of the huge garage towards the emergency room

Ch. 5

"Emergency Dad"

The University of Miami Hospital is located at 1400 NW 12th Ave, in Miami, FL. The hospital boasts some of the best service in Florida; they're always fully staffed with thoughtful intelligent nurses and doctors.

Room 820 at the University of Miami Hospital is cold and dark this morning. A little red headed girl is lying in a hospital bed with her left arm all taped and bandaged up. Her mother is sitting close to her bed in an almost comfortable chair holding and caressing her right hand attempting to soothe her.

The teenager can't feel her mother's touch at the moment. The meds the doctor has pumping into her body put her to sleep almost three hours ago.

The door opens. Jessica jumps up and rushes into his protective arms.

"Oh James..." she cries.

Radicon who is out of breath obviously from running as fast as he could to reach his daughter, kisses Jessica softly to calm her nerves as much as any kiss could. Then he quickly makes his way to his baby girl.

Taking his wife's seat next to their sleeping child, he takes hold of her cold, pale, limp hand. He kisses her hand several times trying to warm it up. Then he leans forward to kiss her on the forehead and cheek.

James turns to look up at his wife for answers.

"Why... Why would she do this to herself?" he asks. Jessica turns to look at the lone nurse in the room.

"Betty, can you give us a few minutes please?" Jessica asks her. "Sure Mrs. Radicon," the nurse replies, "if you need me just press the red button okay love?" Jessica nods in acknowledgement.

After the nurse walks out allowing the heavy door to close behind her Jessica makes her way to her beautiful blue Hermes Berkin handbag. She opens the purse and immediately grabs a bloody piece of purple notebook paper. She looks at it, and then walks it over to her husband.

"Here..." she hands the piece of paper to him.

"What is this," he asks gently letting go of Katherine's tiny right hand. He opens the paper and instantly covers his quivering mouth.

"Was this a... suicide note?" he asks looking up into Jessica's red teary eyes.

"Not *was* James," she says, "It *is* a very real suicide note that our 15-year-old daughter was leaving to you."

James clears his throat twice. "Dear Daddy," he reads aloud, "I love you and Mommy very much. I am so proud of all of your accomplishments, I apologize for being an ugly blotch on the canvas of the perfect picture our family could be, or should be without me. I know how hard it must be to have to explain to all your friends why your daughter is so ugly. I'm so, so sorry Daddy..." James breaks down in tears.

"I am ridding your picture perfect world of me," he continues to read; "I am only holding you all back. I know I'm the reason we never win the family of the year award; I wouldn't want to put my face on the cover of the Miami Beat either, next to all of your perfect faces I would look more than out of place. You, mommy, and Lucas belong together I will never fit in your beautiful mold. My own best friend is embarrassed to be seen with me in public. I was the only virgin in our class. Scooter Robison, my best friend tried to force me to have sex with several different really mean boys. She said that if I just did it and got it over with I would change... She said having sex would make me cool and popular. I was so close but I just wasn't ready for that Daddy. Well I wasted enough of your time; I guess this is goodbye Daddy. I only have one request in death... Please when you approach my casket at my funeral, when you look at me Daddy please really look at me. Try to find my beauty in my tragic imperfect face. Kiss me Daddy... and tell me you love me. Tell my mamma I love her."

James; crying in full force, now falls to his knees next to her hospital bed as he recaptures her limp right hand. Jessica takes a seat in the chair behind him leaning forward to wrap her arms around him.

In his left pocket James can feel his second cell phone vibrating violently. He reaches down to grab it. It's a text message. As he reads it quickly, Jessica catches a glimpse of the message and the name of the person it was sent from.

James stands up. He kisses his daughter on the lips twice and then he places her right hand gently on top of her stomach. He turns to Jessica and kisses her on the forehead. "I have to go baby." he tells her. She doesn't speak.

"Take care of my baby for me." he leans down to kiss her. Jessica dodges his lips.

"Why don't you stay and take care of your own damn daughter," Jessica contends, "damn it James... She was killing herself for you. She thought she was doing you a favor... Hell maybe she was."

Jessica walks away from James. He turns back to Kate and kneels down to kiss her once more. He pulls out his phone and sends a quick text. Then he looks at his crying wife. "I love you Jessica." he walks towards the door.

"Hey," she says just before he walks out, "that's a very nice outfit you have on, but it's not you. Who picked it out for you?"

James looks down at his blue and yellow striped V-neck Polo shirt, his dark blue Louis Vuitton jeans, and his dark brown Sperry shoes.

"I um," he pauses, "I picked it out myself, and I like it. It's comfortable." Jessica smiles a dangerous smile as she shakes her strawberry blond head.

"Yeah okay," she replies, "have a safe trip James. And tell Carolyn I said hello." The look in his eyes would tell any woman everything she needed to know.

Ch. 6

"The Flight"

As James arrives at 2100 NW 42nd Avenue the Miami International Airport in the backseat of a taxi cab; his face is still red from crying.

After paying the cabbie he grabs both of his brown matching Louis Vuitton duffel bags, closes the cab door and heads towards the airport entrance.

As he approaches the main entrance of the airport he passes several foreign families who have obviously just arrived here in Miami on vacation, as they're all happily snapping pictures of everything. Now a group of older women are smiling and waving at him as he passes by.

"My brother," a raspy voice says from down below, "can you spare a little change I ain't ate in four days."

James looks down to find an old balding black man who's clearly fallen on hard times. Just before James can curse the man out, he looks up in the doorway and sees Carolyn watching him. He looks back down at the man and sits one of his expensive LV bags down on the ground.

"Sure man." James reaches in his pocket to retrieve some cash. He counts out five twenty dollar bills and hands them to the man.

"Thanks my brother." the man says.

"You're very welcome sir." James replies.

James turns to walk away. Before he can the homeless man grabs his right leg. James looks down at him filled with confusion.

"Can I pray for you James Radicon?" the man asks.

"Wait how do you know my name?" James asks.

"Everybody knows who you are James." the man tells him.

James looks towards the door where he sees Carolyn still watching them closely.

"Um..." James says.

"Please sir," the man stands to his old tired feet, "I won't keep you long."

"Fine," James replies, "my mom used to always say, prayer is something you can never have too much of."

The man puts a hand on each side of James' head and closes his eyes.

"You will travel safely to Atlanta, Georgia," the man says in a deep thoughtful voice, "you'll leave behind a lot of pain, and dark secrets filled with lustful blood... no matter what you do or where you go James Radicon, your secrets are always with you. You are a good man; your sins will be forgiven in time. When the smoke is long cleared, eventually confess what you've done to the woman you love. Protect her always, the devil is very busy. If you're not careful one of you may fall still forever in Atlanta. Lord I pray right now that you keep a hedge of protection around my brother in Christ James Justin Radicon, that bullet is not meant for him Lord. Amen."

The old man opens his eyes, to find James' eyes filled with tears.

"What is this?" James asks.

"God loves you my brother," the man says, "now go... your lady friend is waiting for you."

"I'll be honest," James wipes his face roughly, "I do feel real power in your words, but why are you talking about Atlanta? I'm not going to Atlanta; I'm going to…"

"California." The older man interjects.

"How did you…" James wrinkles his brow.

"Protect her always," he tells James, "she is the vital piece to maintaining your sanity. Atlanta will come to you after the smoke clears and the clouds crowd your mind with confusion."

"I have no clue what that means, but please take this card." James hands the man a business card and then shakes his hand firmly. The man pulls James close and hugs him tightly.

"I want you to get yourself cleaned up sir," James tells him with a subtle genuine smile, "and come see me at the address on that card at 8am Monday morning if you're interested in a job."

The old man smiles harder than he has in years.

"Yes sir my brother I'll be there. Thank you and God bless you." the man says as James heads inside the airport.

As he steps inside Carolyn wraps her arms around him tightly. James chuckles happily to himself.

"Now what is all of this?" he asks.

"What you just did was amazing James Radicon," she says, "and I am very proud of you. There may be some good in you after all *Scrooge*." she laughs at her own joke.

"Ha ha ha," he playfully mocks her laughter, "real funny. Where do I go? What do I do, these bags are heavy and I'm nervous as hell?"

"James," she searches his red eyes, "have you been crying?"

"Yeah," he shrugs, "I'm fine. My daughter's in the hospital, but she'll be fine. Really I'm okay, where do I get my bags checked?"

"No worries," she tells the gorgeous millionaire, "just follow me."

He follows her to the front desk. Carolyn looks absolutely breath taking in her short cut white and pink summer dress. Her light brown hair has been straightened and a small bang is hanging down subtly over her left eye. Her hazel eyes are glowing with life, and her Melody Good worthy lips look like ripe fruits that Radicon can't wait to taste again.

"Give this nice lady your ticket James." Carolyn says as they reach the front desk.

He obeys.

The young Mexican woman thanks him and takes the ticket.

"May I see your I.D. please?" she asks. James hands it to her. Then she begins clicking away on the keyboard in front of her. Finally, she hands the ticket and his I.D. back to him.

Then the young woman looks up at James and pauses. "Are you the James Radicon," she asks, "the millionaire wine tycoon?"

"One and the same…" James flashes her that infectious Radicon smile.

"Well it is very nice to meet you sir," she says, "now if you will Mr. Radicon please sit both of your gorgeous bags up here, we'll take care of them for you. And just follow your wife she has your entire travel itinerary.

James chokes. "My wife," he laughs, "no this woman obviously isn't my wife... She's..."

"I'm what James?" Carolyn interjects. "You're just not," he pauses to clear his throat, "can we talk about this later..."

She walks off. He follows closely behind her. "Carolyn," he calls out, "Carolyn baby please..." She turns on a dime to face him.

"Oh so now I'm baby again right," she says, "as long as no one can hear you... I can be *baby,* right?"

"Yes," he replies, "that's exactly what I'm saying."

She steps closer to him. "And why the hell is that James?" she asks. He hesitates to look around to see if anyone is watching them.

"Listen baby..." he starts.

"Do not call me baby," she interjects, "I'm no one's secret baby."

"Carolyn," he says, "listen..."

"I am listening." she interjects again.

The look on Radicon's face changes instantly.

"Bitch, do not interrupt me again," he growls, "I think you are getting beside yourself and forgetting who I am. You belong to me... I am your god. You obey me! Now as I was saying I like you, I like you a lot. What we have is amazing, and we do have a lot of fun together... In private, but outside of the shadows, what we do in the dark... *This* does not look right, and we're both married."

"What doesn't look right Radicon?" she asks   trying hard not to raise her voice.

"Me and you," he tells her, "us, and *this*... We don't fit outside of our own private fantasy. And I do not do love period. My wife is the only woman I will ever love."

Carolyn shakes her pretty head.

"I see," she replies, "she's the one you love right?" "Of course she is," he laughs, "that's why she's my wife."

Carolyn crosses her arms and searches Radicon's eyes intently.

"Tell me James," she hesitates, "your wife, does her laugh... Give you life? Can she effortlessly make you cum three times in a day? Oh and you've been married for over sixteen years right... if you love her so much how come she never had the power to get you on a damn airplane?"

James clears his throat several times, and then licks his lips twice as he searches his brain for something; anything he can say to pretend like his way of thinking is okay.

"Yeah that's what I thought." she turns to walk away from him again.

James looks around, shakes his blond head, and then hesitantly follows behind Carolyn. She quickly passes through the metal detector, and leaves him there to fend for himself.

In the waiting area near the gate through which they will board their plane James finds Carolyn sitting next to a moderately attractive older white man. She has her legs crossed and one arm folded across her stomach as she's scrolling through her expensive new smart phone that he bought for her a couple of weeks ago. Not because she's special, just because he was bored one day, or at least that's what he told her.

With Carolyn sitting in an end seat and the older gentleman sitting next to her James has no choice but to sit somewhere else. He looks around and finally spies an empty seat a few rows away facing in Carolyn's direction.

Sitting there he never takes his eyes off of Carolyn, and the gentleman. The man leans over to whisper something private to Carolyn. She smiles. James' heart begins to pound loudly in his ears and his brows furrow tightly as he starts to stand up, but he pauses when he sees Carolyn reach in her purse and simply hand the man a piece of chewing gum.

(James)

What is this feeling? Why is my heart pounding so hard? This woman or this girl that is, is only my employee... that I occasionally have wonderful sex with, and kiss, and text frequently. But kissing though? I never kiss anybody on the lips except my daughter and my wife Jessica. What makes her so damn special? I hate her so much, and the things she naturally makes me feel. Who's this old fart she's sitting next to? And why is he touching her damn arm? She's handing him her phone. They're obviously exchanging numbers, damn it. What am I doing? Carolyn is a grown woman, who can do what she wants outside of me, she is not my wife. She's just a girl that works for me, one that helps run my company, one that brings me warm doughnuts and tea in the morning, a girl that I never stop fucking thinking about. I have to end this now. When we return from California I'm going to fire Carolyn once and for all.

"Flight number 082453 you can begin boarding now." a loud voice says through the overhead speakers. James sees Carolyn standing up, she shakes the man's hand after he hands her, her cell phone back. Carolyn looks at James and smiles. His heart starts to race again; he wonders if this is a good smile or if maybe she's just playing with his mind. She's heading to the gate; he quickly makes his way to her.

As he reaches her Carolyn is handing the gate worker her ticket. James does the same. She politely scans each of their tickets and then hands them back to them.

"Enjoy your flight." she tells them.

As they enter the long hallway that leads to their plane James is trying hard to figure out what he can say to her to fix what happened before. Up ahead, James sees a man standing to the right of where he and Carolyn will obviously board their plane. As they near the man and the plane James calmly reaches over and grabs Carolyn's bag from her and puts it over his own shoulder. Carolyn looks up at him in confusion.

"I'll take that sir." the man standing near the plane says as he reaches for the bag. James pulls back. "I can handle it." James tells him.

"No sir you don't understand." the man says.

"No I don't think you understand," James says, "you are not touching this bag, she's with me and I..."

Carolyn gently grabs her bag from James and hands it to the man.

"It's okay James he's just doing his job," Carolyn says, "now come on let's go find our seats."

James looks at the man.

"I uh, um..." he stutters.

"Its fine sir," the man assures him, "it happens all the... No actually I can honestly say this has *never* happened before. But its fine you can go take your seat now sir, enjoy your flight."

James smiles nervously and then follows Carolyn inside the plane.

Once she's seated Carolyn begins searching her bag vigorously.

"Damn it," she whispers, "now I know I had more. It's gotta be here somewhere."

"What are you looking for?" James asks.

"Got it." she pulls out a lone stick of gum. She breaks the stick in half and hands one half to James.

"I'm fine," he tells her, "you go ahead."

"You're going to need it... now take it." she demands.

"I will not need it," he replies sternly, "chew it yourself. Or give it to the elderly white man you were engaging with so freely in the airport. What a slut."

Carolyn quickly sits forward in her seat with her hands positioned firmly on her seat's arm rests.

"First of all Mr. Radicon," she starts, "Mr. Thomason is not elderly by a long shot. In fact, he's only three years, your senior. Second why the hell were you watching me?"

"Why not..." he asks.

"Really James," she says, "why not? Because I'm not your precious wife, that's why. And you don't love me. I'm just your employee remember."

"Don't be so dramatic Carolyn." he leans back to close his arrogant eyes.

Carolyn instinctively grabs his penis as hard as she can. James opens his eyes, covers his mouth to muffle his outrage, and hastily sits forward in his seat.

"What the hell was that for?" he cries.

"You are impossible," she fumes, "one minute you don't even want people to know you know me, the next you're a raging jealous madman. Now either you care or you don't James, make up your damn mind!"

"What the hell are you talking about baby?" he asks with his brows wrinkled tightly in pure frustration.

"That," she points at his wide open mouth, "one minute I'm your baby, one minute I'm your bitch, then the next minute you don't have a clue who I am. Now this is not "Fifty Shades of Grey" you are not Christian Grey, and I am definitely not Anastasia. I'm much prettier and I have way more ass than her. Damn it James, I am not some animal you can just keep locked in a cage until you decide you're horny enough to play with me!"

"Tell him again girl." a young white lady sitting behind Carolyn leans forward and says.

"Fine." James pouts.

"Fine what James?" Carolyn ignores the woman behind her.

"I won't call you a bitch anymore." he claims.

"James that is not what this is about," she tells him firmly, "I don't mind you calling me your bitch; in fact, I actually like it. I wouldn't allow another man to say it, but I don't mind being your bitch because I..."

Carolyn catches herself before she makes a grave mistake.

"Because you what Carolyn?" James asks.

"Nothing," she replies, "sit back, and fasten your seatbelt the plane is going to take off soon."

He obeys.

"What, were you going to say Carolyn," he asks again, "you don't mind being my bitch because you..."

Carolyn does not respond to him. She opens her half of the gum, places it on her tongue, and then tosses the other half in James' lap.

"Put the gum in your mouth and chew it James," she says with finality, "if you don't your ears are going to pop terribly as the altitude changes during our ascent."

Again he obeys.

Carolyn places earplugs in each of her ears and turns towards the window closing her gorgeous hazel eyes. She absolutely refuses to have this dead end conversation with this obviously confused married man. Her plan is to sleep all the way to the airport in Dallas Texas, where they will switch planes before continuing on to California.

James knows exactly what Carolyn was going to say, and he wanted very badly to hear her say it. He knows it's probably best she didn't though, because he would never say it back, or would he?

(Back in the hospital)

"Mama..." a weak voice cries, rudely snatching Jessica Radicon away from her long awaited sleep. She looks up to see her daughter's eyes finally open and fixed on her. Jessica immediately leans forward in her chair, taking her daughter's cold, pale hand in hers. "Yes, Mama is here baby." she whispers. "Baby, you scared mama," Jessica continues, "I thought I was going to lose you."

"What happened mama," Kate asks, "how did I end up in the hospital?" Jessica starts to cry again.

"It's okay Katie," her mother assures her, "the doctor said you might wake up with mild amnesia after you fainted and hit your head a couple nights ago."

"A couple nights ago," Kate repeats, "how long have I been here? What happened to me?"

Jessica stands up and bends down to kiss her confused daughter on her red forehead. "Are you hungry baby?" Jessica asks her.

"What the hell Mama," Kate panics, "I can't feel my left arm at all."

"Watch your mouth Katherine," Her mother tells her, "you just have some nerve damage in that arm. The cuts were very deep but the doctor said some of the feeling may return in a few days."

"The cuts," Katie cries sounding barely coherent, "what cuts? Who cut me Mama? You let somebody cut on me; you said you would always protect me Mama."

"Oh baby," Jessica leans down to hug her teenage

daughter, "I will always protect you. I have never been a fighter or a killer, but I would fight, kill, and die for you Katherine Marie Radicon."

"Mama who cut me," Kate cries, "I don't understand. I know I'm ugly, but why would anybody..."

"No Katie," Jessica looks deep into her daughter's eyes, "stop it right now. You are not ugly, and you never have been. When I was your age I went through the same struggles you are experiencing now."

"You don't have to lie to me mama," Kate insists, "I've seen pictures of you when you were 15, you were gorgeous."

Jessica smiles at Kate. Then she takes her seat back in the chair next to her hospital bed, never letting go of her small, pale hand.

"Thank you," Jessica wipes a few tears away, "but, tell me Katherine have you ever seen a picture of me when I was 12 years old?"

Kate hesitates to respond. "No mama I haven't." she finally replies.

"What about when I was thirteen?" Jessica asks. "No ma'am." Kate replies.

"14..." Jessica asks.

"No mama I haven't." Kate says.

"Neither have I." Jessica admits.

"Why mama," Katie asks, "what happened to all those pictures?"

"They don't exist." Jessica tells her.

"How can they not exist Mama," Kate asks, "what happened to them?"

"From age 12 to 14," Jessica starts, "I had very, very low self-esteem. I had braces, and acne... and absolutely no friends. I skipped school on picture day for three years in a row. And you know what hurt the most?"

"What Mama?" Katie asks.

"My parents never even noticed," Jessica laughs solemnly, "I was so ugly my mother and father never even noticed for three whole years that I didn't have a school day picture. I was missing completely from my school's yearbook for three years and nobody noticed. Of course my parents didn't have much money back then so we couldn't afford the actual yearbook anyway... but they never even noticed, I was that invisible."

Jessica begins to cry much harder than before.

"Mama," Kate cries, "Mama... Please don't cry. Don't cry Mama I didn't know, but it doesn't matter anymore because you lived, and you are beautiful now."

Jessica looks up at her daughters scarred and bruised face.

"So are you Katie," she says, "you are beautiful, and you will live, and grow, and blossom into a gorgeous young woman."

Kate looks down.

"Mama..." she says.

"Yes baby?" Jess replies.

"I cut myself... Didn't I?" Kate asks.

"You made a mistake baby that's all..." Jessica cuts her words off as Katherine's eyes roll back into her head and she begins to shake violently.

"Nurse!" Jessica screams as she pushes the panic button over and over again.

"Nurse... Somebody, anybody please help me!!!"

Seconds later the hospital door flies open as ten or more members of the hospital staff rush into the room.

"What's wrong," she cries out hysterically, "what is wrong with her? Doctor... Doctor please you said she was going to be fine. You said there might be some   amnesia or nerve damage but..." Jessica falls down hard on her knees, screaming out in pain, right there in the center of her young daughter hospital room.

(Flight 082453)

The flight has been very peaceful for almost every passenger on flight 082453 from Miami to Dallas, all except for first time flyer James Radicon. Everyone around him is asleep. To conquer his nerves, he realizes he will have to do something to take his mind off of the flight itself.

He looks over at Carolyn. She's sound asleep like everyone else. She's lying towards the window but her legs are straight forward. James puts his right hand on her left knee. She doesn't move. Inch by inch he begins to pull her skirt up towards her supple upper thighs. Finally, her bright pink panties are exposed to him. He softly uses his right hand to spread her gorgeous caramel legs.

He looks around again to ensure everyone near him is still asleep. Carolyn's vagina is all but bulging through her tight fit see through lace panties.

James begins to rub her softly. She stirs but never quite wakes up. He begins to caress her magnificent vagina a little harder now. Her underwear is beginning to moisten now. His adrenaline is pumping from his brain, to his penis, down to his toes.

Skillfully using his fingers, he pulls her panties to the side and enters her with one large finger. Carolyn begins to slowly grind on it, never once opening her eyes. She must be dreaming he thinks. She spreads her legs wider now inviting him to go a little deeper.

His arousal is uncontrollable at this point. He removes his large finger and makes his way down to the floor of the plane. From there he reaches up and begins to hastily pull her panties down. After removing them he   pushes them down deep in his left pocket. One at a time Radicon places each one of Carolyn's sweet caramel legs over his shoulders as he slides his well-groomed blond head towards her center.

She tastes magnificent to him. He continues to kiss and lick her from the inside out. He takes a break to bite her tender inner thighs. Back to work now he begins to suck hard on her wet center that does it.

"James..." she gasps looking down at the handsome madman who's openly feasting on her vagina in the middle of the crowded airplane.

"Baby," she moans quietly, "What are you doing?"

He doesn't respond, his mother taught him long ago to never talk while his mouth was full. Carolyn's plump vagina would be quite a mouthful for anybody.

The ecstasy trapped black goddess grabs hold of James' hair and pulls his face deeper in between her supple thighs. With one hand James reaches up to feel her perky breasts. They feel so firm and warm to his touch as both of her nipples are protruding through her shear dress. With one tug he pulls the top of her dress down beneath her breast exposing both of them for the world to see.

Carolyn gasps as she let's go of James' hair and immediately covers both of her breasts with her shocked hands. "Damn it James," she whispers pulling her dress top back up, "what if somebody sees me naked?"

He reaches up again as if she hasn't said a word. For the second time he snatches her dress top down below her shy bosom. "Let em look." he moans taking a break from swallowing all of her sweet juices.

The look in his eyes quickly melts all her doubts and insecurities away. She takes hold of his hair again in both hands pulling him into her as he kisses, licks, and s u c k s her vagina relentlessly. The man's mouth is like a diesel fueled motor. "Yassss..." she moans quietly.

"Yes baby." Carolyn has never felt so free in her 23 years of life until this very moment. The entire plane could be watching them and she wouldn't give a damn. She is secure, she is sexy, she is confident beyond measure because he made her this way. "Oh James I love when you look me in my eyes while you're eating me." she growls passionately.

If the plane crashes, Carolyn could die happy right now, or at any moment amidst one of the multiple explosive orgasms he's continuing to bless her curvaceous body with. Gripping her round light brown ass, he pulls her forward so that she is now squatting on his strong face, supported only by his neck and wrists.

She's shaking now in triumphant orgasmic pleasure, and she's lost deep in his trance and the perfection of this man and this moment. "James..." she moans.

"Yes my queen..." he moans back.

"Tell me I'm pretty." she demands.

"Are you kidding me," he whispers between powerful flicks of his freakishly long tongue, "you are not pretty at all Carolyn. No, you are the archetype of complete loveliness. I wouldn't change a single hair on your gorgeous head. I lo..." He dives in again.

He pushes her shoulders back on her seat. She lies there open, waiting for his next move. Up higher on his knees now, he unbuckles his belt, unbuttons his Louis Vuitton jeans, and then unzips them completely. With a couple of strong tugs he finally unleashes all of himself.

Her eyes bulge in fear as if it's her first time seeing the impressive girth and length of him all over again.

James anxiously pushes her legs even further apart now. He tries to enter her body, but she's way too tight for him. Carolyn's vagina always snaps back to the tightness of a virgin after each of their sexual sessions.

After fingering her fiercely for the better part of five minutes Radicon tries yet again. This time his head just barely breaks through the barrier as she closes her eyes, bites her bottom lip, and covers her mouth for security. As he begins to slowly stroke his head inside and out of her, he reaches in his pocket to retrieve her wet pink panties.

He hands them to her, and she knows exactly why. James pauses as she quickly stuffs her underwear in her own mouth and bites down hard. Once her panties are in place he slides in again, much deeper than before. Stroke after perfect powerful stroke James single handedly forces the release of so many wonderful, blissful chemicals in Carolyn's brain. Her head falls to the side involuntarily, she believes she's no longer conscious, but it's clear that she is because she can still see, hear, and feel James' huge penis invading her body as if he's trying to destroy it, or at least alter it in a major way.

James can feel his phone vibrating in repeatedly in his pocket. He realizes several old texts must be coming in at once due to the poor cell connection on the plane. He pulls the phone out of his pocket, as he continues to stroke. After reads the first text he pauses. After reading the second one he feels his erection becoming weak. He reads the third text... his heart stops. He reads half of the last text, and then deletes all four of them.

He sheds a few tears as he leans forward on Carolyn, to hide his face from her. James runs the length of himself as deep inside of her as he ever has before.

He kisses her twice and then bites her bottom lip softly. "I live to make moments like this with you..." he whispers just before unleashing one final power driven stroke that she can feel deep within her stomach. She inhales deeply as James spills his precious white seed all inside of her wet throbbing body.

"Lucas Radicon"

Lucas

In one of the upstairs bedrooms in the Radicon mansion a blond haired, tanned, teenage boy is alone in his room sitting on his bed. His bedroom walls are covered with posters of various musical artists both male and female. His large radio is playing a new August Alsina song. He's never heard it before, but he feels absolutely drawn to the flow of it.

He's wearing coral colored cargo shorts, a white tank top with coral letters on the front of it that say "Born to Ride", and bright white ankle socks. His blonde hair has been cut low on the sides, and he has allowed the curly hair on the top of his head to grow out considerably.

Sitting here alone he can't help but ponder his greatest obstacle in life. One day he will be expected to become his father. He realizes filling James Radicon's size 13 dress shoes is going to be damn impossible. Up off his bed he makes his way to the large vanity mirror attached to the top of one of his dressers. Staring into the mirror he can clearly see his mother's eyes embedded in his father's young handsome face. Lucas Radicon squints his regal gray eyes at himself as he considers his future.

My father James Radicon is the walking American dream. I mean sure he was born rich, but he still dug down deep and came up with his own company to multiply our family's fortune instead of just blowing what his father and grandfather built.

Wine... Who woulda thought a little spoiled rich kid could evolve himself into a tycoon and a wine savant? My father's fortune easily trumps that of his father's and his grandfather's. And so now that leaves me... Lucas Radicon the sole heir to the Radicon throne. I'm not just the heir to my father's wine empire, but also the hundreds of other thriving companies that we hold ownership and or massive stock in.

The thing is I don't want it. I mean sure most people want to live and die rich. And even more people want to do so without having to build their fortune themselves. Not me. I want to earn my keep and make my own way. I want to build my own new leg of my family's legacy and fortune. I just don't have a clue how I'm going to do that.

I'm not noticeably good at anything, which I guess is normal and okay for normal people, but I am definitely not normal. I'm a Radicon for God's sake. In two years

I'll turn 18 and I'll get the family crest tattooed on my left wrist and everything. I'll be branded for life just like every other adult man in my bloodline. Then everything will truly be official.

The only thing I wish is that I was more like my father. The man is the true alpha dog; he bleeds the much needed natural confidence that is key to run super successful companies. And I'd like to think that gene is hidden somewhere deep... deep inside of me because James Radicon is my father.

God bless his soul, he tried. Lord knows he tried. He did everything in his power to mold me as a boy into his own image. As I got older he finally saw me for who I am. So eventually he quit trying to change me, and ultimately make me into a younger version of h i m.

I honestly don't think I was quite finished cooking when God sent me into the world. My chemical balance isn't quite right to be a successful, notable Radicon man.

There are so many things I want to tell my father. He used to talk to me, and spend time with me, and actually notice me. I'm his only son, so I understand how huge the disappointment must be. I'm his only chance at his name being carried on into a new generation. That burden is all mine. Lucky me right?

It probably won't turn out the way I would prefer but soon the old man and I are going to have to talk about our differences. Hopefully we can agree to disagree, and meet somewhere in the middle.

I am every bit as handsome as my father and probably even more intelligent than him, but that's where our likeness ends. We are two completely different creatures. I love my father James Radicon... Maybe one day I will be able to make him respect me enough to love me back.

Ch. 8

"Lost Angels"

As their plane from Dallas to Los Angeles nears their final destination James and Carolyn both begin to mentally prepare themselves for what they have come all this way to accomplish.

James looks at Carolyn and smiles.

"Well somebody's in a good mood huh?" she returns his infectious grin.

"I'm just not worried." he tells her.

"Worried," she repeats still smiling, "why should James Radicon ever worry about a thing? You live in the clouds, eating and drinking the fruit and wine of the gods."

He looks past her now out of the window to the world below.

"I will never worry again." he assures her.

Carolyn pats him on his left knee.

"Well good James, I should hope not." she says.

"I know that the way I think is not a good path for most people," he says, "the normalcy of tradition, subtlety, and relationships do not hold much purpose in my world. People should all matter, but to me they just don't. People come into your life, if they remain wonderful... if not, so what there are billions of other people to meet and experience."

He looks at her. Carolyn can't help but to stare back at him in awe.

"You're gawking Carolyn," he tells her, "Never gawk it's not polite."

"I'm sorry," she whispers, "but where did this revelation come from? If... You don't mind me asking that is."

"I have always thought and been this way," he tells her, "but I just recently saw two movies that had absolutely nothing to do with each other to the naked eye... But to me their connection was clear and explosively relevant to me."

"What two movies James?" she inquires.

He smiles again returning his gaze out of the window.

"The two movies I saw were "Lucy," and "Get on Up," the James Brown biography." he tells her.

"Seriously," she laughs, "Lucy" ... And "Get on Up? I saw both films as well and I must admit I didn't draw even one parallel between the two."

"To each his own," James says, "In my mind the message in the two films went hand in hand. For instance, the late great Godfather of Soul, James Brown basically said that being fathers and or husbands gives men a purpose. He said people need purpose, but a man is going to do what a man is going to do, and he is going to be what he is supposed to be. Ultimately nothing is going to stop that. And Lucy, as she gained more and more access to her brain began to discount her regard for people, and or relationships. To me the things we are taught... and built to value as children don't really make a damn. None of it means anything, or defines who we are. Sure; love exists, but only when and where we as weak human beings acknowledge it. Therefore, giving into the vulnerability of giving another mortal human being instant gratification, and or control of our own personal emotions. No, not me I am the most efficient American I know, even more so than my father was. I will be a multi billionaire by the end of this trip, and not because I was born a millionaire... But because I understand people, money, business, success, God, and ultimately my loyalty to Him and myself alone."

"Damn," Carolyn searches the recesses of her mind trying to find more meaningful words to respond with, "Damn." she fails.

"It's 7pm we should be getting close." he breaks the awkward silence.

"You really got all that from those two films?" she asks.

"No Carolyn," he smiles, "I got that from me. I built that basic philosophy within myself when I was about my son Lucas' age. But I'm starting to hear, feel, and see confirmation of the truth in my philosophy in all things."

"Well that is... That's very beautiful," Carolyn admits, "Dr. Radicon... Yeah, I'm going to have to start calling you Dr. Radicon. You never cease to amaze me sir."

James leans back in his almost comfortable seat and studies Carolyn for a moment.

"Tell me Mrs. Olivier," he begins, "what do you think about my newest full time recruit at the winery, Justin Tolls?"

Carolyn's heart drops. She tries not to panic as she clears her dry throat twice, and attempts to lick her sandpaper-like lips.

"Just... Justin Tolls?" she asks.

"Yeah," he replies, "you know the mixed kid that I hired on from the University of Miami? The one you were flirting with in front of my office a few days ago?"

"I was not flirting," Carolyn assures him, "we were just talking..." "I'm sure," James interjects, "talking, talking, everybody's always talking right? But what does it all mean or amount to?" Carolyn remains silent sensing something frightening in his voice.

"That question was not rhetorical." he tells her. "Oh I," she stutters," I don't really remember what..."

"I, I don't really remember," he mocks her with an unattractive sneer on his contorted face, "bitch don't ever play with me. I see all, I hear all, and I know all. I may let things go for a time... But I never forget a thing."

"Where the hell did this conversation even come from," she asks, "I swear you're bipolar."

"Maybe I am." he admits.

"Oh there's no maybe about it," she tells him, "you change like the wind." Looking past her James focuses his attention outside of the window yet again.

"You know Carolyn," James says, "over the course of our lifetime's boys and men ruin so many girls and women. Not on purpose in most cases, no we're all just trying to figure out who we are as men. We exercise certain tactics to see how much power we possess over women. That power if not abused can be a very good thing. But in turn the men who understand this idea, and ultimately fear the women they have destroyed and or molded... These men are smart enough to find a young woman in her twenties, who has not been tainted yet, and sweep her off her feet and show her the world as they want her to see it. They give the woman they select the opportunity to experience life, love, submission, and control without many of the bumps and bruises that years of sporadic dating can brand on a person. These women have an actual chance at happiness, because the man that has chosen them has been tried and tested, and is more than likely ready to give her all of him."

"And you James... Are you one of those men?" she asks.

"I um," he smiles, "I'm married."

(An hour later)

James and Carolyn have been riding along in a smelly old cab for 15 minute completely silent.

"I still can't believe you've never flown before," Carolyn breaks the silence, "what did you think?"

"I think... I want this cab to get us to our hotel so I can shower, change, and then find something to eat." he tells her.

"Did you not hear my que..." she starts.

"Yes of course I heard you babbling," he admits, "never small talk me. Your vocabulary is already limited as it is. When you speak make sure your words have actual purpose."

"Wow." she replies as the cab pulls up to 251 South Olive Street, the Omni Los Angeles California Plaza hotel. The front of the magnificent monstrous building is lined with gorgeous palm trees. The structure itself is more than breath taking in all of its modern unorthodox architectural glory.

After paying the cabbie James makes his way to the trunk to retrieve his bags. He calmly waves off the anxious bellhops. He and Carolyn carry their own bags inside the beautiful hotel. After checking in at the front desk the odd couple takes the elevator to the presidential suite on the 8th floor.

Once inside the room Carolyn throws her luggage on the bed and stands planted firm with a defiant hand on each hip.

James looks at her.

"What the hell is your problem?" he shrugs nonchalantly.

"You're my problem James," she tells him, "your mouth. You have no regard for people's feelings."

"Carolyn please shut the hell up," he drops down into a huge lounging chair, "we've had a long flight and I just want to rest."

"Stand up James!" she demands.

He laughs.

"For what," he inquires, "look, look I know you're angry, and I know you people enjoy assaulting each other in your trivial little domestic violence spats, but I'll pass. Thank you though. Just go take a shower and get over it." He continues to laugh to himself.

Carolyn removes both of her earrings and her shoes. Then she stalks towards him with specific intent.

Wham! She slaps James hard across the face, and then begins to slap, punch, and kick him repeatedly.

James stands up and with one hand James lifts Carolyn high above his head. Even suspended in air the angry beauty continues to swing at her boss.

"Calm down!" he demands. Without much effort at all he tosses her on the huge bed a few feet away from him. Then James turns away from her because she obviously isn't a threat to him.

As soon as Carolyn lands on the soft bed she scrambles back to the foot of the bed on her hands and knees. Then she dives off the edge of the bed wrapping her arms around his neck, bringing him down to the floor with the help of her swinging body weight.

Down on the floor Carolyn never loosens her grip, she believes she can and will choke the life out of this rude, angry, impossible man.

With all the strength left in him James puts a hand on the bed and pulls himself upright. Now back on his feet with Carolyn hanging onto his neck with a deadly grip, James forces her around to the front of his body. With her hands around his neck now Carolyn continues to choke him as she digs her French tipped nails in his reddened skin.

His eyes. She looks into the pure blue serenity of his perfect eyes and instantly loosens her grip.

James knows he's back in control now. He puts his massive hands around her neck and lifts her high in the air above his head once more, shaking her with certainty.

Carolyn cannot breathe at all. She doesn't care if he kills her right now she will forever be connected to him even in death.

James looks up into the innocent pools of her caramel eyes and calmly pulls her back down to his body. He kisses her once. Then with one strong toss he throws her on the bed once again. She doesn't move.

James slowly pulls his striped Polo shirt off over his blonde head and drops it on the floor. Then he kicks both of his comfortable shoes off. From the foot of the bed he begins to crawl towards her small caramel frame; stalking her like a hulking beast in the wild, ready to pounce on his weak submissive prey.

Carolyn inches back towards the headboard unsure of James' intentions.

"Bring your ass here..." he demands. She doesn't move.

"For what..." she cries.

"Get off the bed." he tells her.

After getting up off the bed himself, James walks towards the head of the bed. Standing near the headboard he grabs the phone beside the bed snatching it out of the wall. Then he disconnects the wire from the back of the phone. James grabs Carolyn's left arm and forcefully ties it to the middle of the left bed post with the phone cord. Then he jumps up and stalks around to the opposite side of the bed. In one of his LV duffel bags he finds the cord to his cell phone charger and a black and gray checkerboard LV belt. After zipping his bag back up he makes his way back to the stranded Carolyn.

Next to the bed is a full bar. At the edge of the bar is a gold plated knob. James has no clue what the knob is for but he ties Carolyn's right arm to it nonetheless.

"James, what the hell..." she protests.

"Shut up." he snatches one of the pillowcases off one of the large fluffy white pillows. He puts the pillowcase all the way over her head instantly blinding her.

Bending forward slightly due to the awkward position her arms are tied in Carolyn waits quietly on Radicon's next move.

She can hear him unzipping a bag, and now searching the contents of the bag for something seemingly specific. Next she hears him cut the shower on. For the better part of thirty minutes Carolyn stands there blindfolded, tied to the bed and the bar with no clue how long she's actually been standing there. She's not sure if she should be aroused, or frightened, or both.

He turns the shower off. She can hear him doing something close behind her. She figures he's probably just drying off and putting on some clothes.

The music comes on loud and clear. It's R. Kelly's "Black Panties" album.

"You like that?" he whispers in her left ear. She doesn't respond. "Don't you people love getting fucked to R. Kelly," he asks, "I googled it. What artist do black women

have sex to the most? This was the answer it gave me."
Carolyn still doesn't respond.

"Speak you little dirty black wench!" he demands. She remains silent.

Her legs and arms are growing tired, and she wants nothing more than to take a hot shower right now. He's close enough now that she can feel his intense body heat. He's leaning over her, breathing harshly on her neck. She can feel his warm breath even through the thin pillowcase. Carolyn can feel every hair on the back of her neck rising one by one.

James uses his left hand to lift her dress up completely exposing her bright pink panties. He smacks her ass with his right hand twice. She flinches both times. As he rubs her soft round behind, Carolyn rolls it in an almost circular motion. James backs away from her.

She waits. Just barely over the music she can hear the hotel door open and then close. She waits.

Whap!

"Ahhh!" Carolyn screams as the left side of her ass feels like it's on fire. Whap!

"Damn it James!" she screams. "Bitch you better shut the hell up!" he growls.

Whap! He hits her again with his strong leather Louis Vuitton belt. He hastily snatches her panties down to her fatigue bent knees.

"You're gonna learn," he says, "to not disrespect me!"
He hits her again.

"Don't you ever again in your miserable black life engage in a conversation with another man in my face!" he hits again.

Her caramel buttock is red with belt marks. She smiles as the warm tears begin to fall.

"Tell me I'm your daddy!" Radicon growls.

Whap! He strikes her again.

"Harder!" she screams.

Whap! Whap!

"Tell me!" he demands.

"Ooooh hit me harder Daddy..." she moans.

He does, Radicon strikes her much harder three more times. Her ass has become more than numb, her adrenaline is pumping at full force, and her passion box is wetter than she remembers it ever being before. The pain has turned into the deepest pleasure her body has ever known.

"Daddy," she cries, "Daddy don't stop now, I've been a very naughty girl."

Whap!

"Ooooh." she moans.

Whap!

"Yes!" she screams.

Whap!

"Yes daddy!!!" she cries out.

"Enough!" he growls.

Snatching his fluffy white bath robe off and tossing it to the floor. He steps close behind her. With one rough shove he forces her to bend over completely. Her head and face are down by her ankles, as her arms are still suspended in the air tied to the bed and the bar.

James sticks two of his large fingers in his mouth wetting them thoroughly, even though Carolyn's body is nowhere near lacking in moisture. He then shoves both fingers in her hard from the back. She inhales. As he impales her with his two massive fingers she trying to take more air but she can't. She's forgotten how to breathe. He's pushing his fingers in her with a strong twisting motion. She's grinding slowly to the beat of the music, and Robert Kelly's smooth voice. She can finally breathe.

Radicon slowly pulls both of his passion covered fingers out of Carolyn and buries them both in his anxious mouth.

"Like crushed apples..." he moans.

"Do me," she begs, "Daddy please just do me."

Radicon spies two condoms on the table on the other side of the bed.

He points to them before plunging his enormous member in Carolyn from behind. She inhales again. He pumps long, hard, and strong.

"Harder daddy!" she screams.

"Shut up!" he growls.

"Okay daddy. She moans quietly."

As he strokes he points towards her bobbing head. James lifts Carolyn's upper body up slightly, so that she's still bent over but now her back and legs are completely straight.

James continues to stroke masterfully. Radicon has both of his huge hands on her hips as he continues to give her all of him. Carolyn can feel the pillowcase on her head being pulled up. Once it is high enough to expose her nose, and mouth Radicon reaches forward and ties the pillowcase in a knot around her face.

He continues to hit her from the back, pulling her back against his rock hard body.

"Open your mouth..." he tells her.

She obeys. Then she chokes as her mouth is filled with something warm and pulsating. She opens her mouth wider to accept all of it, but Carolyn is confused as to how this is even possible. How is James behind her, and in her mouth?

"You like that..." James moans.

"Mhmm..." she mumbles with a full mouth. As the R. Kelly album, begins again Carolyn realizes this is going to be a long night.

(Brown & Nielsen)

James and Carolyn arrive at the "Brown & Nielsen" Los Angeles winery at 8:30am. They're thirty minutes early for their meeting with Mr. Renaldo Nielsen, one half of the owners of the winery. The fact that they are even awake is amazing in itself since they stayed up well after 4 am screwing each other's brains out.

James reaches forward to pay the driver handsomely, and then he jumps out of the cab, and walks around to let Carolyn out.

"Thank you." she takes his hand as he helps her step out of the car.

They are both dressed to the nines. Carolyn has on an exclusive long black Alexander McQueen dress with a slightly plunging neckline, black jewelry, and black stone Lorenzi heels. James has on a black three-piece suit, black Tom Ford boots, and his large gold Michael Kors watch. His hair is perfect, almost prettier than hers. Carolyn's subtle pink lipstick, and skillfully applied makeup elegantly bring out her deep hazel eyes.

As they walk Carolyn is searching her mind trying to understand what happened the night before.

"James..." she says.

"Yeah." he replies.

"Who was that last night," she asks, "the other man in our room with us..."

"Some bellhop I paid." he admits.

Carolyn gasps with a hand across her chest, as he opens the front door for her.

As they walk in the front door together, all eyes are glued on them.

"This conversation is not over." she assures him.

There are two receptionists at the front desk as they approach it. "May I help you?" a moderately attractive young white woman says.

"Ah yes," James says, "I'm..." "I know exactly who you are Mr. Radicon," she interjects flirtatiously, "I have calendars, and posters of you at home... Not to mention countless magazines with long descriptive articles about you and your company. What I was asking is if you wanted to speak to Mr. Brown, or Mr. Nielsen."

The left side of Carolyn's lip begins to curl upward as she glares at the woman through absolutely poisonous eyes.

"We're here... together to see Mr. Nielsen thank you." Carolyn informs the blushing receptionist.

"Perfect." she never takes her eyes off of James.

She picks up her phone and dials three numbers.

"Renaldo," she says into the phone, "Mr. Radicon is here to see you. Yes, sir. Okay."

She hangs up the phone.

"He's on a call, but he will be down to get you shortly Mr. Radicon." the receptionist smiles at him.

Carolyn's heart is racing faster than the speed of light.

"So you can wait over there on one of our benches, or you can stand here and talk to me..." she tells him as if Carolyn isn't even standing there.

"I think I'll wait here with you." James flashes his million-dollar smile. "Hmm... I bet." Carolyn mumbles.

"Tell me James..." the receptionist starts.

"His name is Mr. Radicon." Carolyn informs the young lady sternly. "May I call you James." the receptionist asks him. "Sure." he replies. "Thank you," she gushes before rolling her small blue eyes at Carolyn, "So James, the rumor around the winery is that you're going to buy Renaldo and Patrick out... is that true?"

"That's the plan." he replies. "Oh my God," she says, "I would love to work for a man like you. I mean your philosophies, and wining techniques are more than genius, damn it they're inspiring."

"Why thank you," James says, "I look forward to bringing my ways out west to all of you young bright vibrant people." "Can't wait." she tells him. "Bitch, wait on it." Carolyn interjects.

"James, Carolyn," an old raspy voice says from up above, "come on up. We can talk in my office." James waves his hand at Mr. Nielsen to acknowledge that they are on their way up.

"Before you go James," the receptionist says, "please take my card, this is my personal number right here at the bottom..."

"Thank you," Carolyn snatches the card as she takes James by the hand leading him towards the elevator, "Let's go turn your millions into billions my love."

Once on the elevator James snatches his hand away from her.

"You embarrassed yourself, and more importantly you embarrassed me." he growls loudly. "How so James..." Carolyn inquires with a pleasant smile. "Never be hostile with good clean white people again." he tells her as he looks down to straighten his expensive tie. Carolyn's mouth drops, as James presses the number 3 on the elevator's button panel.

"What the hell did you just say to me...?" Carolyn steps towards him. "Calm down Carolyn," he says, "she's just a harmless fan."

"No," she replies, "she... Is a groupie and a jump off? There is a difference."

The elevator door opens to reveal a short, overweight, balding, black man. "James, Carolyn it's wonderful to meet you both." he says with a genuine smile, reaching out to shake both of their hands. His face and smile are almost as pleasant as his demeanor.

"Please, follow me." Mr. Nielsen leads them down a long clean hallway lined with mind bending abstract paintings up and down the walls.

James looks down at Carolyn as they walk. "Why didn't you tell me they were black people?" he whispers. Carolyn sticks her tongue out at him playfully. "You never asked." she replies.

"Come on in please." Nielsen opens the door to his huge corner office that overlooks downtown L.A.

Inside of his office Carolyn and James take a seat in front of him at his huge mahogany wood desk.

"Tell me James," Nielsen starts, "what exactly do you have in mind for my winery if in fact I sell my share of it to you?"

"Well Mr. Nielsen..." James says.

"Renaldo," Nielsen interjects, "just call me by my first name. Everybody does it's more personal that way you understand?"

"Sure," James clears his throat, "well Renaldo I basically want to come in and do an entire reform of your company from the inside out. My best employee here, Mrs. Olivier has done quite a bit of research on your company and she believes she has cracked the numbers that can turn this ship around."

"I see," Renaldo says, "and you believe in her do you?"

James looks over at Carolyn with a smile and then back at Renaldo.

"I do... very much so." James says.

"Good enough for me." Renaldo says reaching over his desk to shake James' hand.

James leans forward to shake Renaldo's hand and then turns around to look at Carolyn with both of his blond brows wrinkled tightly.

"So that's it?" James asks.

"That's it for me," Renaldo tells him, "now Patrick on the other hand is a whole nother ball game. My only request is that you keep me on as a top salaried manager to help run the winery. We will follow all of your methods and bylaws of course, I just don't want to sit at home and die. No, continuing to work here will add twenty years to my life at least."

"I don't know," James says, "I'll have to check..."

"That's no problem at all Renaldo," Carolyn interjects, "you will always have a job at the Radicon winery here in Los Angeles."

She shakes his hand firmly.

"I like her." Renaldo says shaking her hand and smiling at James.

"So," Carolyn says, "when can we meet Mr. Brown?"

"He's in his office now," Renaldo says, "but I must warn you my partner Patrick and I are polar opposites. He's a real handful if you catch my drift."

"He can't be that bad." James says.

Mr. Nielsen laughs aloud.

"Let's just put it like this," he says, "if Mr. Brown was to tragically die no one would miss him, or even notice he was gone."

James and Carolyn thank Mr. Nielsen again and then leave his office in pursuit of his partner.

As they march down the hallway towards the corner office at the other end of the hallway Carolyn and James are trying to figure out what they can possibly say to sway Patrick Brown's mind to make him sell his share of this company that he built for the past forty years.

As they stand there in front of his large wooden door, James looks down at Carolyn.

"You ready?" he asks.

"I always got your back, never question that. Everything's gonna be just fine." she assures him.

He clears his throat twice and then he knocks on the door.

"Who the hell is it?" a squeaky agitated voice says from the other side of the door. James hesitates as he looks back down at Carolyn again.

"James Radi..." he starts.

"Damn it I said who the hell is it." Mr. Brown says angrily opening his door.

"Oh it's you." he says looking up at the much taller Radicon.

Patrick Brown is 5 feet 2 inches tall and probably weighs 120 pounds soaking wet. His pale white skin looks as if it hasn't experienced any sunlight since the year 2000. His face is dry and pointy like a miserable little rat. His small wrinkled khaki pants, heavily scuffed brown dress shoes, and fading stained blue color shirt appear to be the outfit he has worn to work every day for the better part of the last ten years.

"Come on in if you must," he mumbles, "but I am not going to sell."

"Then I guess we'll be leaving then." James says turning around. "Wait!" Brown exclaims.

"For what?" Carolyn asks smoothly following her boss's lead.

"Don't you want to at least know why I refuse to sell?" Brown asks.

"No, not really." James responds.

"Sure you do," Mr. Brown continues, "picture it Riverside, California 1973. A young Italian kid and a skinny black kid, both 21 years old, both were trying to figure out life, both hungry for success. Renaldo and I have been best friends for 40 years. Of course we both had full heads of hair back then. But we looked at the world together and decided we were not going to settle for the status quo and just become what everybody else in our environment was becoming. We quit our job at the local factory, came out here to L.A. with my Grandpa's wine recipe, a hundred bucks each, and a dream. We never looked back. We started selling our booze on the street for 16 cents a bottle. From that we eventually opened our first corner store and grill. Neither one of us were really good at cooking so eventually we just started selling our wine. We needed a name right? Well there was no better name we could have ever come up with than ours; I mean what the hell... our names were just as good as anybody else's right? Nielsen & Brown. Our brand and our wine were selling like hot cakes. We were a household name overnight. We built this winery in 1985, and we've been here ever since."

"Now that is a beautiful story Mr. Brown," James tells him, "but the wildfire dream you once had, has all but been extinguished now. You're in the hole with taxes and rent upwards of about 23 million dollars. You need me much more than I need you."

"Patrick Brown don't need nobody!" the old grouch contends as he walks towards his desk. Carolyn approaches him first. "Mr. Brown..." she says.

He turns to look at her for the first time since they arrived at his office door.

"Who the hell are you?" he asks. "I'm Carolyn Olivier," she tells him, "we spoke on the phone several times..."

"Oh you're the lady from Miami," he asks, "I woulda never thought you were colored over the phone." "I'm not," she tries to remain professional; "I'm black."

"Black, colored, nigger same thing," Brown says, "Point is you sounded white on the phone."

Carolyn looks back at James who's shaking his blond head in disbelief.

"In any event," Carolyn steps closer to Brown's desk, "I have come up with the only financial plan that can put this winery back above water and sustain it for the next twenty to thirty years."

"Is that so?" Brown asks. "Yes sir it is," she replies, "but you will need available capital that you obviously don't have... But we do. But in order for us to keep this winery up and running you are going to have to sell your share of the company. Now you seem to be a history buff Mr. Brown... I'm sure you would rather it goes down in history that your company merged with Radicon and began to thrive again, not that you were too stubborn to sell and you single handedly causes the full collapse of your own company. Nielsen is already on board with us. We have agreed to keep him on as a salaried manager; we would do the same for you."

"Renaldo, that idiot." Brown says.

"I thought you two were best friends." Carolyn says. "That doesn't change the fact that he's an idiot. Well he's black what the hell do you expect? No offense to you lady, you act white."

"None taken asshole," Carolyn smiles, "now do we have a deal or not?"

Mr. Brown walks away from her towards a shelf on the back wall of his office. The long shelf has about fifteen tiny handmade and painted boats lined up on it.

"Do either one of you kids like boats?" Brown asks.

"Yes sir I own quite a few back in Miami." James tells him.

"Uh huh," Brown replies, "and on your boat are you the captain?"

"You're damn right." James allows his southern drawl to creep out a bit.

"A man should always be the captain of his own ship," Brown takes one of the boats down from the shelf before turning around to look at Radicon, "and do you know what you as the captain of your ship are supposed to do if your ship ever was to... Go down as they say?

"Go down with it." James replies.

"Ding, ding, ding, ding," the man with the rat face yells, "You are correct son. You just answered the million-dollar question. So I... as the only remaining captain of the "Nielsen & Brown" winery have to stand strong forevermore and proudly go down with my ship in a blaze of glory."

"But sir..." Carolyn starts.

"Girl didn't you just hear what I said," Brown says, "I and my share of the company are not now or ever for sale. Goodbye."

"Mr. Brown..." James says.

"Goodbye... both of you," Mr. Brown says, "now either leave, or I'll have security escort you."

Carolyn quickly reaches in her purse. She can feel it, and all of its deadly power. But is it worth it, is Mr. Brown worth it, is James worth it? Hell yeah, she thinks to herself.

James approaches her.

"Come on Carolyn," he says, "let's get out of here." She takes her hand off of it and follows James to the elevator.

On their way down Carolyn's head is hanging low as she sheds a few tears.

"I failed you James." she cries.

"No," he wraps his passionate arms around her small body, "are you kidding me, you were good, no you were better than good you were perfect in there. In fact, when we get home I'm promoting you to my personal assistant."

She smiles up into his strong blue eyes.

"I'm already your personal assistant James." she tells him.

"Well now you will have the actual title and the pay to go along with it." he promises her.

"Thank you." she says.

The elevator begins to open as they have reached the lobby floor. James quickly stops hugging Carolyn before anybody sees them. She looks up at him in confusion.

"We are here on business," he reminds her, "no P.D.A."

"Sure Mr. Radicon whatever you say," she mumbles,

"not here, not at the airport, never unless we're locked in a dark room together somewhere is it okay for you to show me any affection."

Carolyn storms past the receptionist desk towards the door to exit the winery.

"See you later Aunt Jemima." the receptionist laughs and waves mockingly at the already angry Carolyn.

Carolyn turns around to look at James, and then pushes the front door open with all her strength as she storms out

James approaches the receptionist's desk calmly with a strange look on his face.

"Let me tell you a secret." he whispers to the young lady.

"Anything James." she gushes leaning over the desk towards him to hear the secret better.

"If you ever... speak to Mrs. Olivier like that again I'll have you flippin' pancakes at IHOP for the rest of you miserable fucking life. And my name is Mr. Radicon to you." he tells her.

Without another word he exits the building where he finds Carolyn waiting for him on the front steps in tears.

"Carolyn..." he calls out to her.

She turns away from him continuing to cry her eyes out. James rushes to her, throwing his arms around her in public, in broad daylight for the very first time ever. He pulls her in close to his strong comforting body.

"No baby please don't cry." he begs her from the depths of his soul. Carolyn's painful tears instantly become tears of joy. She would lose her life or her freedom for this man without hesitation.

"I guess the asshole is taking an early lunch break." James looks off in the distance.

"What?" Carolyn whimpers.

"Patrick Brown," James says pointing towards him, "He's right there headed around to the back of the building."

Carolyn pulls back from James' embrace, and dries her face with her hands. She knows what she has to do now, to make sure this trip is a complete success.

"Wait here." she tells James.

"What?" he says.

"I'll be right back James, do not move." she says with finality.

"Carolyn don't waste any more time talking to that idiot please..." he yells to her as she reaches the corner of the building in pursuit of the stubborn old man.

As she walks Carolyn reaches in her purse to pull it to the top of the bag.

"Brown!" she calls out to him. He turns around, after seeing who it is he continues on to his car as if she hadn't said a word. Once Carolyn makes it to his old rusty Toyota Camry she sits her purse on the back of it. Then with both hands she reaches in her purse. Click clack! She picks her purse up off his car and walks around to the driver side door.

She snatches his front door open. He cranks his car.

"Lady what do you want?" he asks with a hideous glare on his little pointy face. Carolyn holds her purse on her right hip as she put her left foot up on the base of his car, exposing her panties to him. With her left hand she grabs his left hand and puts it on her plump passion box. He licks his old dry lips.

"Look, I only have twenty bucks on me," he tells her, "but if you wait till I get back I might be able to get about ten more. This makes more sense. I was wondering why Radicon was keeping company with someone like you... But now I see your true value clearly."

Carolyn puts her foot down.

Mr. Brown reaches around and smacks her behind as hard as he can.

"You like that?" she teases.

"Hell yeah I do." he replies.

"I bet you do," she says pulling a brand new all black handgun, out of her purse and aiming it at him, "what about this you miserable old fuck? You like this too?"

"What are you gonna do with that," he asks with a smirk on his homely face, "you wouldn't shoot me you black bitch. Have you completely lost your cotton picking mind?"

"Shut the hell up." Everything goes black as she squeezes the heavy trigger twice killing the old bastard instantly.

"Carolyn no!!!" James yells from the side of the building. He runs to her full speed.

Carolyn's tears have returned; she's completely frozen in shock. James snatches the gun away from her and throws it in the back seat of Brown's car. Then he quickly pushes his tiny limp body over onto the passenger side of the vehicle.

"Get in!" he yells as he jumps in the driver's seat. Carolyn quickly opens the back door and climbs in the backseat, as James speeds off out of the parking lot at top speed.

"James what I'm I gonna do," Carolyn cries, "I just wanted to help you." James looks at her through the rear view mirror. "I always got your back, never question that, "he tells her, "everything's gonna be just fine."

Ch. 9

"PinkSlip"

Ralph

E ven though it's storming badly tonight, it feels so good to James and Carolyn to be back in Miami. As they pull up to the small brick house on the corner of Jefferson Street, James is so happy to be driving his own car again. Waiting around for rude, smelly cab drivers all day is definitely not his style. He has always preferred to drive himself wherever he goes.

He looks over at Carolyn. She's still looking down in

her lap; she's been that way ever since the cab dropped

them both off at Radicon's mansion so he could pick up one of his cars to drive her home himself.

"Caro... Carolyn." he places a strong hand atop of hers. She doesn't respond.

"Carolyn don't worry about it," James says, "we are back home in Miami. Whatever happened in L.A. stays in L.A. I mean you heard what Renaldo said right? If something tragic ever happened to him no one would notice because no one loves him."

She looks in his eyes before she speaks.

"I know but..." she starts.

"No buts," James interjects, "what's done is done; we dealt with it, now we're back home. That's it, the end."

"Okay." she wipes her eyes again.

"Now go inside and get some rest," he says, "take a couple days off from work, and when you come back in on Friday your brand new office will be waiting for you... Ms. Personal Assistant."

Carolyn smiles lightly. James reaches in the backseat and grabs a company umbrella to give her so she won't get too wet in the rain.

"Thank you James..." she takes the yellow umbrella and still wiping her tear stained face.

"Well, I can't just let you walk through the rain uncovered Carolyn." he replies.

"No," she says, "I'm not just talking about the umbrella... or the job. Thank you... for everything you do for me."

"Don't mention it." he leans over to kiss her on her reddened forehead.

"Well back to reality for me," she unlocks her door, "boring house, boring husband, noisy kids..."

She opens the passenger door and climbs out of the car with her purse and her small suitcase in her right hand.

"Hey..." James reaches out to grab her left hand.

"Did I forget something?" she asks.

"No," he says, "just remember... What happened   in L.A. never happened okay?"

"Taking it to the grave." she promises him.

"Okay," he smiles, "see you Friday?" "Yes sir," she smiles back, "I'll see you Friday."

As she walks across the street to her house Carolyn never opens the yellow umbrella. She wants the rain to wash her nerves, pains, and fears away.

In her heels it's really hard for Carolyn to dodge the puddles in the middle of the street, caused by the huge potholes that the City refuses to take care of.

James is driving off slowly, watching her in his rear view mirror as always to make sure she makes it to her front door safely. Once she does he speeds off, down the street.

As she takes each step up her porch Carolyn is trying to flood her mind with new peace and hope. She just wants to be okay and completely at peace again.

As soon as Carolyn sticks her key in the door, she hears it unlocking from the inside. The door flings open wildly. Ralph is standing in the doorway shirtless, smelly, and breathing irrationally.

Smack! Carolyn stumbles back from the force of the blow and falls into one of her grossly untrimmed bushes, breaking both of her new heels in the process. What did he see, she thinks to herself lost in an uncontrollable panic attack?

Within seconds he's upon her. He snatches her up out of the bushes and throws her over his shoulder like a caveman. He stalks back in the house with her in tow, slamming the door behind him. Her purse, her suitcase, and James' umbrella are all still out on the front porch and lawn.

Ralph throws Carolyn on the floor like a sack of cheap potatoes. Tiny footsteps are heard entering the room.

Ralph Jr. stands there in the doorway staring down at his silent immobile mother laying there on the ground. "Daddy," he says, "Mommy hurt..."

His father ignores him. Ralph Sr. rushes toward Carolyn and kicks her hard in the stomach forcing her body to turn around in the opposite direction.

The pain is so deep she can't find the strength to scream. "You bitch," I'm gonna kill you!" he yells in a drunken slur.

Carolyn stares up at her angry husband through unclear eyes, drowning in tears and weak sentiments. Her thoughts are cloudy but very real.

No matter how strong we women think we are, anytime a man wants to overpower us what can we do? Submit, scream, and then cry about it. But this man... He will pay dearly.

Ralph kicks Carolyn again. Junior screams out at the top of his tiny voice. Startled by all the commotion his baby brother Karan who was asleep in their room immediately wakes from his sleep and starts crying loudly.

Ralph disregards them both as he harshly kicks his wife in the back twice. Junior runs to his father and pushes him in his chubby side. Ralph turns around and pushes his three-year-old son back, sending him sliding across the floor into a wall on the other side of the room. The baby cries out in pain.

Down on his knees now, with his back to his son, Ralph Sr. begins to choke Carolyn with all of his might. "I hate you Carolyn Williams." he tells her.

As he leans over her with a notion of perfect control, he suddenly feels tiny hands hitting him in his back repeatedly. "Leave my mommy alone!" Junior cries finishing his sentence masterfully. He continues to hit his father as hard as he can, his tiny high pitch voice going up another octave with every painful scream.

Ralph stands up and turns around to look at his protective young son. He looks down into his teary eyes knowing full well this little boy would die right now for his beautiful mommy without hesitation.

Junior steps around his daddy and lies down on top of his silent and still mother. He kisses her face several times. Carolyn can taste the baby's salty tears as he cries on her. "I saved you mama..." he cries.

WHOOM!!! Junior finds himself instantly suspended in the air by the back of his underwear. His father carries him just like this by the back of his tiny underwear back to his small bedroom and tosses him in his Spider-Man bed. Baby Karan is still in his crib crying his tiny hazel eyes out. As their father storms back out of the room he closes and locks their door behind him.

As he approaches his wife, he knows he has made a huge mistake. He leans over Carolyn again for a moment and then he falls forward on top of her. His uncomfortable weight on top of her snatches her back to consciousness. Carolyn bats her blurry, teary eyes, trying to focus on something, anything.

"I'm sorry baby," Ralph cries, "I don't know what to do..." "It's okay..." she mumbles through her busted lip.

"I lost my job," he says, "and I don't know how to do anything else. What the hell am I gonna do now?"

He stands up and walks towards the door.

"Ralph you got fired?" Carolyn asks trying to sit up.

"Fired," he says, "hell no, they had to lay off 175 people and I was one of the people who got cut."

Ralph opens the door and walks out in the rain to retrieve his wife's belongings.

"Damn it." Carolyn whispers to herself.

As Ralph walks back in the house he finds his bloody wife lying on the sofa.

"Carolyn," he says, "we are three months behind on rent."

She immediately sits up. "What the hell are you talking about Raphael?" she asks. "I don't know..." he mumbles.

"Yes the hell you do." she walks towards him wiping more blood from her mouth.

"I have a problem." he admits.

"I know it's called being homeless," she yells, "why the hell are we three months behind on our rent?" she asks.

"I started back... Gambling." he says.

"Damn it Ralph," she says, "what about the kids, what about me, and the house... Every penny we had is in this damn house!"

"I'm sorry..." he cries.

"Sorry doesn't work in this situation Ralph. It's not going to pay the bills and... Three months Ralph!" she exclaims.

"It wasn't supposed to be like this," he whines, "I was just trying to make some extra money for us."

"Are you fucking kidding me Ralph," she yells, "you work to get extra money, you take on a second job to get extra money, you do not gamble money you don't have in pursuit of more fucking money!"

"I'm sorry baby." he cries as he takes a seat on the newly blood stained couch. "I'm done." Carolyn says walking back towards their bedroom."

"Wait baby no..." Ralph yells out. "Goodnight Ralph," she says over her shoulder, "and get comfortable you're sleeping on the couch."

As Carolyn walks in her room she finds all the lights off. She walks to their bed and calmly takes off her broken heels. She tosses both shoes in a nearby waste basket. Then she stands up to pull her bloody dress off over her head. The ruined, once exquisite garment cost James twelve hundred dollars when he bought it yesterday at that mall in California, but she knows he wouldn't lose sleep over it. He makes more than that in an hour.

In nothing but her panties Carolyn tries to find the strength to get up off her bed and walk to her bathroom. This weekend has been more than she's built to handle alone. But she's not alone, she believes in James one hundred percent when he says that everything is going to be just fine.

Finally, up on her feet she starts towards the bathroom. She puts one foot in front of the other. God the pain is spreading and worsening. She thinks maybe she should go to the emergency room. But if she does she knows she will eventually have to file a police report against Ralph and things are going to get really messy then.

As she approaches the door to the bathroom, a strange feeling comes over her. Carolyn stares down at the door knob, to her bathroom door that is curiously just barely ajar. That smell, what is that sweet and foul smell? Sex!

Carolyn pushes the bathroom door open quickly. She finds nothing. The smell is definitely louder the further she walks inside the bathroom but there's no one in there.

She decides to leave the light off, the bright moonlight shining in through the window is sufficient enough for her tonight.

Carolyn tries to steady her sporadic heartbeat as she stares into her mirror. Her face doesn't look nearly as bad as it feels, thank God. She grabs a scrunchie off the sink top and pulls her hair up into a ponytail on top of her head.

With her phone Carolyn takes two pictures of her bloody face and sends them both to James' phone.

Seconds later he texts her phone and says, **"WHO DID THIS!"**

"My husband Ralph," Carolyn texts back. James' reply is simple, "HE'S DEAD!"

Carolyn's blood turns ice cold. She quickly presses his name on her screen and calls his phone. James doesn't answer.

Carolyn hears something strange. Her heart stops. In the mirror she can see the closet door behind her slowly opening. On the floor coming out of the closet she can see a foot.

She tries not to panic, pretending she doesn't see it. Ralph has some nerve she thinks to herself. Her heart is steady, she's ready now.

The closet door flies open as the person inside of it makes a dash for the door. Carolyn reaches out instinctively and grabs the person by their long fake hair and drags them down to the floor. Carolyn quickly straddles the person and starts punching them in the head and face.

"You come in my house," Carolyn chastises between punches, "and sleep with my husband, you trifling bitch!"

"Wait, wait Sissy stop!" the familiar young voice cries out. Carolyn jumps up and rushes to cut the bathroom light on. What she sees turns her heart and blood ice cold.

"Kayla!" she screams.

"What the hell," Carolyn continues, "how the hell did you even get here?"

"Well I don't drive so..." she replies through a snooty little smirk.

"Ralph... Get your old, fat ass in here now!" Carolyn screams.

He waltzes into the bathroom with his guilty hands pushed deep inside his pockets. "It's not what it looks like baby." he says unable to look Carolyn in her eyes.

She stalks towards him and puts her nose to his nose, staring a whole through his black skull. "It's not what it looks like..." she repeats venomously.

"No..." he says.

The strong scent of vagina and liquor are still lingering on his disgustingly putrid breath.

"My little sister though Ralph," Carolyn questions, "she just turned eighteen last week!"

"Oh trust me, he knows." Kayla says, childishly sitting Indian style on the floor.

"Little girl," Carolyn never takes her eyes off of her bastard husband, "you better shut the hell up right now!"

"You don't have to talk to her like that Carolyn." Ralph says.

"Nigga are you fucking kidding me," Carolyn asks, "You're taking up for my little sister too? How long have you two..."?

"Bout two years." Kayla boasts. Carolyn slaps Ralph hard across his fat face.

"Since she was 16 Ralph?" Carolyn asks.

"She's lying, baby," he claims, "I don't even know what she's doing in here. I never touched her."

"Ha," Kayla stands up from the floor finally, "Ralph baby don't lie, you know you were my first...everything."

Carolyn turns and slaps her baby sister knocking her back down to the floor again. Then she quickly turns back to her husband.

"Baby she is lying!" he says again.

"I am not," Kayla cries holding her cell phone up, "I have the text messages to prove it."

Carolyn grabs the phone and begins to hastily scroll through their texts.

"You're sick Ralph!" Carolyn tells him. She throws the phone back down to her baby sister.

"You lying bastard," she says, "you pick her up from school every day, and fuck her in our car... Every day, what else have you been lying about?"

"Nothing..." he replies.

"Everything," Kayla interjects standing up again, "he did lose his job but he didn't get laid off. They fired him because he was taking unscheduled breaks to pick me up from school. He couldn't get enough of my goodies. And yeah your rent here is behind, but not because he started back gambling... Hell no! I wouldn't allow that. He has a Kayla addiction. Every time your husband gets paid baby... he gives his whole check to me."

Carolyn back hands her little sister with more power than even she knew she had. This time Kayla isn't getting back up so fast. "He's still gonna take care of me you old bitch!" Kayla exclaims.

"He might," Carolyn agrees kneeling down close to her little sister, "but you and who else... Huh?"

"What do you mean?" Kayla asks.

"Oh you thought you were the only one?" Carolyn asks her.

Kayla doesn't respond.

"So he didn't tell you about all his other sluts he sleeps with on the side," Carolyn asks, "yeah this little scene isn't new... You're just the newest slut to get caught with him."

"What is she talking about Ralph?" Kayla asks.

"I can't see you anymore kid." he walks out of the bathroom.

"Kid," Kayla cries, "I wasn't a kid when you were screwing me and spending all your money on me!"

"It was about the sex Kayla," Carolyn tells her, "Ralph never loved you. His fat ass will screw anyone who will spread their legs for him."

"So he played me?" Kayla asks as she stands up. "No, you played yourself... like a PlayStation 4 little girl." Carolyn replies.

Kayla grabs one of Carolyn's hand mirrors, screams at the top of her lungs and then throws the mirror hard against the wall breaking it and covering the floor in shards of glass.

"Let's go." Carolyn says.

"Go where?" Kayla asks. "I'm taking you home to Mom and Dad's."

"No you're not." Kayla tells her.

"Do you wanna get hit again?" Carolyn asks raising her fist.

"Ugh." Kayla groans knowing this is a battle she is not going to win.

Ch. 10

"The Williams'"

(Carolyn)

*L*ife for a little black girl growing up in a middle income family is no different from the life of a black girl in the actual hood. We're all poor; I guess there are just different levels to our distinct phases of poverty. But we all go without things we want and need. Our lives are an extremely far cry from those of the Rich and Radicon. But you get used to it, live through it, and you move on.

My father Marcus Williams was the best provider he could be when I was growing up. He worked mainly as a professional in the field of MLM. That stands for Multi-Level Marketing. For anybody who doesn't know what that means, it's what most people view as a pyramid scheme. I don't know and I don't care, call it what you want. We didn't have steak on the table every night, but we did eat every single day, and every single night. Dad paid the bills and Mama kept the house. My father is a dreamer, but he has always been a simple man. He wants a lot and he shoots for the moon, but he's satisfied with what he has. He never gets down on himself for not being wealthy, or driving the best cars, or wearing the most expensive clothing. He's content and he loves his girls.

My little sister Kayla, our mother, and I are his entire world.

My mom Marilyn Williams was a part-time substitute teacher well into her fifties, until finally the students just got a little too grown for her taste. So she eventually just retreated completely into her household duties. She's always been my biggest supporter no matter what. She's the only person who knows about me and James. I told her about him the day we met. I knew she wouldn't judge me, and she always has the very best advice.

My mother and father both did a phenomenal job raising me... I just don't know where they went wrong with my little sister Kayla.

Kayla and I are in my car headed to my parents' house all the way on the other side of Miami. And even now I still can't believe she's been sleeping with my husband Ralph for two damn years. Neither one of them have any respect for me or my feelings. Now in actuality it doesn't hurt that much because my heart belongs to someone else, but it's still the whole principal of my little sister sleeping with my husband, this shit is unbelievable.

I don't know if I should kill her, or just turn his old ass in to the police. I can't tell my parents. This would destroy my family and make my marriage and all my choices as an adult look careless and downright stupid. Nope, I definitely can't tell my parents. I'll just have to handle this on my own.

"Carolyn..." Kayla whines.

"What Kayla Marie?" Carolyn replies with no obvious emotion.

"You're not gonna tell Mom and Dad are you?" Kayla asks.

"Of course I am," Carolyn lies, "Ralph will go to prison for twenty years for child porn and statutory rape, and Mom and Dad will just look at you as the little slut you are for the rest of your natural life."

"Sissy, please don't..." Kayla begs.

"Oh, Sissy please," Carolyn mocks her baby sister, "yeah, Sissy please my ass Kayla. You don't care about me, you never have. You little bitch... You slept with my freaking husband. Not once, not twice, but for two long ass years. What the hell do you have to say for yourself?"

"I'm sorry..." Kayla cries.

"I'm so sorry," she continues, "I won't do it again Sissy. I swear to God I won't sleep with Ralph anymore."

"Who the hell are you over there texting?" Carolyn asks.

"I'm not texting, I'm just on Instagram." Kayla lies.

Carolyn snatches the phone quickly. After reading two text messages she's seen enough.

"You trifling, little bitch!" Carolyn yells.

She reaches over and slaps Kayla in the back of her head and then parks the car in the middle of a bridge. Carolyn hastily unbuckles her seat belt and jumps out of the car. Then she stalks towards the bridge's rail.

Kayla jumps out to chase her down. "You bitch, what are you doing with my phone!" Kayla screams.

"Fuck you Kayla," Carolyn screams over her shoulder, "don't talk to me. And we ain't sisters anymore!"

"That's my phone!" Kayla yells running full speed behind her sister. Carolyn throws Kayla's phone as far as she can into the murky waters below.

Kayla screams out as she falls in the middle of the street throwing a real tantrum.

"I'm sure my husband's money paid for that fancy ass phone," Carolyn says walking past her crying sister, "so that made it my phone bitch. Text my husband now, you *trick*. I guess you gone have to send his ass a smoke signal or something. Come get your trifling ass in this car so we can go."

(20 minutes later)

As the two sisters arrive at their parents' house Kayla is sleeping, and Carolyn is still just angry as she was when they left her house.

"Wake up Kayla," Carolyn says, "now look I'm not gonna tell, mom and dad anything yet... But if you don't do exactly what I say, or if I catch you so much as sending Ralph a friend request on Facebook I'm gonna mess you up big time little girl. You got me acting all ghetto, this not me. Damn! I need to see my man; I can't wait till Friday."

Ch. 11

"School Days"

Calvin

T he Waldorf High School Academy at 10242 Sw. 72nd St in Miami only services 360 students per semester. The tuition isn't cheap, but it's definitely worth every dime. The curriculum, the staff, and the facilities are some of the best in the world. WHS Academy is ranked number one in the state among other private schools, and number four in the entire nation.

(Lucas)

Private school are a lot like public schools now, the only difference is public school is free. My school has bullies, cliques, nerds, gay people, hipsters, weirdoes, and even wanna be thugs.

I say wanna be because none of these kids could ever legitimately claim to be real thugs; because, to even go here their parents have to be exceptionally wealthy and each student has to pass an extensive background check. There's no way you're a legit thug from age 15 to 18 with a squeaky clean record.

We only have about 23 black people in our school total. Now that includes 12 students, and 11 staff members from the lunch crew, the janitors, on up to administration.

Five out of those 12 black students are here solely on athletic scholarships. They're all from some of the less desirable neighborhoods in the city, but even they had to pass a background check. Since they're here they obviously passed with flying colors.

These five students Rocko, Brian, Jason, Ashley, and Calvin are easily the coolest kids at the WHS Academy. They walk different, they talk different, they dress way different... they're just so raw and real. You can look at them at times and read the struggle and pain in their eyes... Damn it I want to know that pain, I wanna know what it's like to struggle and then triumphantly survive just like them.

The 5 of them are in a clique everybody calls the YBC, the Yung Ballers Crew. All 5 of them are exceptional athletes in their own right and will go on to have glorious college careers, and one of them the coolest in the clique Calvin Ridgefield is going to the NBA in two years. Yeah, it's rumored he's going to enter the NBA draft right out of high school. The kid is 17 years old, 6 foot 7 inches tall, seemingly gaining weight every day, and he handles a basketball like a point guard.

I used to hate sports, but number 8 on the WHS Academy basketball team has turned me into a fan for life. I mean Calvin is like LeBron James before he became LeBron, "the best basketball player in the universe."

Not to mention the kid is gorgeous, no homo. He has the entire school on lock. He can date any girl he wants, including some teachers. He's dark skinned, with a nice low haircut that usually has some cool design cut in it; his eyes are dark brown and so full of life. His smile could turn Kool-Aid into Cîroc, cheese toast into a New York style pizza, and a fan into a fag instantly. I'm just saying. His teeth are so perfect and white, and his little hood accent gives me chills. It's like he has his own language and his very own street dialect.

I know my dad James Radicon is a borderline racist prick, but I'm not. I love black people. I think I belong with them. I mean why not; white people don't accept me anyway. Needless to say, I wanna be a part of the YBC extremely bad.

It was a long shot because I don't have an athletic bone in my skinny white body. But it was worth a shot just to be cool with Cal, that's what the cool kids call him.

About two weeks ago I got my chance to be cool with the YBC. They were all sitting at a lunch table near me discussing rap music, I love rap by the way. Cal and Ashley were arguing with Jason, Rocko, and Brian about the Canadian rapper Drake, and the down South American rapper Big Krit. Ash and Cal said Drake was the best, and Jason, Rocko, and Brian claimed Krit was the new king. I couldn't help myself, I turned around and told them all that Krit was okay, but he needed to put in a lot more work, and prove a lot more before he could even enter a conversation about being the best.

Cal and Ashley invited me, a rich uncool white kid to sit with them at their table, and I've been "bangin' "with them ever since. Apparently bangin' means hanging out, not actually shooting guns or gang banging so don't worry.

But I've been hanging out with the YBC, inside and outside of school ever since that day. Cal and I text all the time, he even gave me a nickname, he calls me Luke Skywalker. Apparently that's a guy from the movie Star Wars.

The craziest part is as cool as he is from far away; he's just as cool when you become his friend. Damn, Cal Ridgefield, the top high school basketball recruit in the nation and I, are actually friends.

Lucas is standing in the hall at school by his locker waiting for school to start.

"What's up Luke?" Ashley says coming down the hallway alone.

Ashley dresses better than anybody in the YBC; she's definitely a true tomboy.

Lucas thinks she's a lesbian, but she's such a pretty girl he's really not sure.

"Nothing," Lucas replies in his cool voice, "where's everybody at?" "Oh, the guys are in the gym," she says, "come on let's go see what they're up to."

As Lucas and Ashley walk in the gym they find Rocko, Brian, Jason, and Cal all shooting some hoops. Lucas is hoping they'll all finally notice how he's changed his swag up lately to look more like he fits in with the clique.

Calvin looks back at Luke and Ashley.

"What up Ash," Cal says, "throwing her the ball."

"Chillin'." she replies dribbling the ball towards Rocko, Brian and Jason.

Cal continues walking towards Lucas. "Come holler at me for a second Skywalker." Cal throws his long black arm around Lucas' shoulders as he walks him outside the gym.

As they walk Lucas' heart is pounding right out of his chest. He's sweating more right now than he ever has in 16 years of life. His insecurity level just shot through the roof, well beyond its all-time high. This is the longest walk of Lucas' life. He doesn't want to have this talk with Calvin, but he knew it was possible because he definitely doesn't really belong in the YBC. Lucas knows he doesn't deserve to hang out with the school superstars; they've been more than nice to him long enough. But nobody wants to continue to drag along a little rich white dork forever. The other guys must have told Cal to get rid of him he thinks, because Cal is way too nice a guy to have ever done this on his own.

Once they reach the back of the school outside of the gym, Cal turns Lucas around so he can look at him.

"Look Luke," Calvin says, "I like you bro, I really do. But you don't have to lie to kick it."

"What are you talking about Calvin?" Lucas asks.

"You're changing bro; you're not the same S k y w a l k e r   a n y m o r e ." Calvin looks him up and down.

"Changing," Lucas says, "hell no I'm still me Calvin."

"Seriously Luke," Calvin questions him, "look at your new haircut bro... your new Jordan shoes, your gold chains, you don't even tuck your little Polo shirts in anymore. This is cool... But it ain't you Luke."

Lucas looks down at how he's dressed and he instantly feels foolish for trying so hard to fit in with Calvin's crew.

"Besides," Calvin says, "you and I know the real truth about you anyway." Lucas blushes.

"And what is that Calvin?" Luke asks trying not to stare at Calvin's full lips.

"Come on Luke," Cal prods, "I see you; I'm not like everybody else. I'm like you... And I can see through you Mr. Skywalker, to the real you."

"What do you mean the real me?" Lucas asks.

"Luke," Calvin smiles, "it's in the way you walk, the way you talk, it's beautiful to me bro, and so easy to see... So just be who you really are. Shit, I wish I could... but my name and my career won't allow it right now fam." Calvin winks at Luke, slaps him on the butt, and then runs off to catch back up with his crew.

(Lucas)

I'm frozen solid. I literally can't move. So now I know that Calvin is... Gay? Or at least he's sure I am. But I know I'm not. I mean I've been through some strange things in my life, and sometimes I have these disgustingly wonderful thoughts, but I know I can't be... Gay. Hell no. But he thinks I'm beautiful? And he smacked me on my ass. I don't know if I should feel disrespected or flattered by that entire exchange Cal and I just had.

Lucas' phone vibrates in his book bag, violently snatching him away from his own confused thoughts. He pulls his phone out of the small compartment in the front of his bag. It's a text. It's from Cal, it says, "I hope I wasn't too weird out there bro. Don't over think anything we said, just take it slow and find you. I'm not going anywhere. I think me and you can be friends for a very long time Skywalker."

Lucas smiles as he walks towards his new fire red BMW coupe. He decides to skip school for the day to go catch a few movies and think things through. Besides he has four AP classes with Cal, and if he sees him again today it'll be way too awkward.

Ch. 12

"Justin Tolls"

(Carolyn)

I needed that time with my mom and dad. Especially my mom I really opened up to her about everything, and she helped me put it all into perfect perspective. I know what I need to do now, and that's play my loyal position until I can be what I want to be to the man I love.

I'm still angry with my little sister Kayla, and I know I will be for a very long time. None of it even seems real to me. In my mind Kayla is still that little yellow girl with the pigtails, running around singing Hannah Montana songs, clutching a raggedy old hand me down Barbie doll. When did I blink and miss this transformation of my baby sister turning into this money hungry, sex crazed, trifling slut?

(Kayla Williams)

Kayla

Standing there in her bedroom mirror Kayla Marie Williams believes she is the baddest bitch on the planet. She actually has that title written in and on everything important that she owns.

As she admires her hazel eyes and distinct dimples she can't help but be intoxicated by her own beauty. No one loves her smile more than she does. She had over 1,500 selfies in her phone smiling into the camera all alone; as if every picture was the very first time she ever smiled.

She's wasn't sad about her sister throwing her phone over the bridge into that lake for long, because she knew she could make one of the stupid boys at her school who have a crush on her buy her a new one. A twelfth grader at her school named Landon Carter used his mother's credit card to order her new iPhone last night. It will arrive in three days.

Kayla runs her thin yellow fingers through her long dark brown weave. It's accented with bright blonde streaks throughout it. Staring in the mirror at her body she understands exactly why everybody is so obsessed with her.

They should be obsessed with me, and they should thank me for blessing them with the opportunity to look at me. I give people their only legit reason to live. My school and this city would cease to exist without me. I wonder what my baby Ralph is doing. Ooh he just makes me feel sooo Mmmhm.

I still remember when we first kissed. It was the night of my sister's wedding reception here at my parents' house. I was only 14, but he already had his eyes on me. Everybody in the house was drunk except for me of course. I went into the kitchen to get my dad another beer and Ralph was in there all alone. He was just standing there staring at me with his eyes all low.

It was so sexy. And I hate my sister Carolyn so of course I flirted with him. I walked past him twisting my hips harder than usual.

When I got to the refrigerator I opened it, grabbed a beer, and then turned to smile at him. I knew he was checking out my ass. Hell I was bigger than Carolyn back then. I was walking back out of the kitchen when he said, "hey." I melted on the spot. I finally found my voice and I replied, "Huh..." Oh I was sooo cute. He said, "Is that beer for you or for me?" I blushed and told him it was for my daddy, but I would come back and give him one if he really wanted one. I knew he was fully capable of getting the beer himself but the smell of him intoxicated me. He smelled like a man, I guess. But he had that scruffy little beard, a cute little pot belly, and huge shoulders. I had to have him.

I took my dad the beer and then I came back in the kitchen and got Ralph one. When I handed him the beer, he grabbed my arm, I felt a connection. It was instant and electric; I felt it in my heart. Then he kissed me.

It doesn't matter what my sister Carolyn says or does; Ralph Olivier will always belong to me, the baddest bitch on the planet.

(Carolyn)

As Carolyn pulls up to the winery, she can feel an air of relaxation falling all over her body. Working here for Carolyn gives her the feeling most people take vacations from their job to feel.

It's almost like being back in High School, trying to look cute every day because you know at some point during the day you're gonna run into that person you're crushin' on.

She parks her car in her designated company parking

spot, finishes her coffee from McDonald's, grabs her briefcase, and hops out of her car. As she heads towards the building she presses the lock button on her keychain to secure her car. It honks twice.

Carolyn reaches for the front door, but before she can grab the handle, Daniel one of her coworkers pulls the door open from the inside. As she walks in Mariah Carey's music is playing on the speakers and a large banner is hanging from the lobby ceiling. It reads, "Congrats Carolyn!!!"

Everybody is standing around clapping for her. Standing right there in the middle of them all is the blonde billionaire James Radicon.

Carolyn finishes hugging everybody and shaking hands on her way towards her handsome boss man.

"Thank you James." she opens her arms to hug him.

"You're welcome Mrs. Olivier." he replies stepping back from her to dodge her public hug and instead shake her hand.

"How embarrassing." she whispers to him.

"You'll be fine darling," he says, "meet me up in my office in 5. For now, go check out your new office, I think you're gonna like it."

"Okay people," James yells to his staff, "show's over for now, enjoy your cake and champagne and get back to work ASAP."

He let's go of her hand and turns to leave. Carolyn stands there unsure what to do next. She reaches up to check her hair nervously and then follows Radicon to the elevator, so that she can get up to the third floor and check out her new office.

As the elevator door closes Carolyn notices she and James are alone. "That was very disrespectful James." she tells him.

"Oh shut up bitch." he turns around to pin her against the back wall of the elevator kissing her passionately.

As he plunges his large tongue in her mouth and caresses her soft pretty face her brain begins to explode with ecstasy.

As he squeezes her behind through her tight blue sundress; her hormones are raging and ready to erupt with volcanic intensity.

As he bites the left side of her neck he uses his right hand to lift her right leg. "James..." she moans.

"What baby?" he growls. "We're in the only elevator in your entire building someone's gonna need to use it."

"Oh, right." he lets her leg down carefully. He turns around and presses the green button to go to the third floor. As the elevator begins to ascend he forces her back against the wall and sticks his big sweet tongue in her mouth again.

"I wanna love you," he moans squeezing her ample breast, "out loud, in public, for the whole world to see... without a worry in the world."

He kisses her once more before the elevator opens. Carolyn is lost in a daze; she doesn't even know who she is at this point. As she follows him off the elevator, her lips are numb, her tongue is anxious, and her mouth tastes like his.

"So Mrs. Olivier," he says in a professional tone as they exit the heavily tinted elevator, "go see your new office, and then come see me when you are finished."

He clears his throat and then walks away headed towards his own office.

"Yes sir." she says.

As Carolyn walks in her new office, the huge corner office overlooking the vineyard she gasps. She's trying not to faint at the sight of all the yellow and white roses set in beautiful crystal vases all around the room. On her beautiful wooden desk is a metal nameplate that reads, "Mrs. Olivier."

The company laptop from her old office has been set up on the desk just the way it was in her old office. Her radio is in the back window, her trash can is by her desk, and her Miami Heat poster is hanging on the back wall.

James definitely did everything he could to make her new office feel as homey and familiar as her old one.

Carolyn sits her briefcase down on her desk; then she walks back out of her new office closing the door behind her.

As she heads down the hallway towards James' office she sees Justin Tolls heading in her direction. She quickly doubles back and walks back in her office to hide.

"I see all, I hear all, and I know all. I may let things go for a time... But I never forget a thing." James' very precise words he said to her on that plane are ringing in Carolyn's ears loud and clear.

There's a knock at her door.

"It's Justin Tolls, Mrs. Olivier..." he says.

She doesn't respond.

"I just saw you walk in here Mrs. Olivier," he says, "I just wanted to congratulate you on your new promotion... I mean I thought we were friends."

Carolyn opens the door quickly. She peeps her head out of the door past Justin, to look down towards James' office. She doesn't see him. She quickly snatches Justin in her office.

"Are you okay Mrs. Olivier," Justin asks, "You look like you just saw a ghost."

"A ghost would be easier to deal with," she admits, "and a lot less frightening."

"Look Justin," she continues, "you are a great kid and I..."

"Kid," he interjects, "I own my own everything. I am just as grown as you and everybody else here. I'm a man Mrs. Olivier, let's get that straight."

"You're right. I apologize, Justin," she says, "You are a

man and a very, very handsome man at that. There are things... Freaky, erotic things that I would undoubtedly do to your body that would make you know you're a man... And in another lifetime maybe we could explore that fact, but..."

"But what," he interjects again, "say no more Mrs. Olivier I'm yours."

Looking down she notices the nice sized bulge growing in the front of his pants. Her mouth begins to water.

"You see Justin," she pauses, "we... You and I can't do this or anything here... because I uh... I'm married. Right, I'm married so I can't cheat on my husband at work you know..."

"Girl meet me at McDonald's," he grabs his ever growing penis, "or we can do it right here. If you don't tell I won't tell. That's on my life. This can be our little secret."

Carolyn wipes the excess moisture from around her anxious mouth. "Boy you are gorgeous," she says, "I'm not denying that. But I'm in love and I'm loyal, so no... No this can't happen. So please just forget I exist if you can." She pushes him back towards her door.

"Na I'll never forget you exist Mrs. Olivier," he says, "but I see I'm gonna have to come a little harder if I wanna get you." "Perfect, yes sure whatever," she mumbles walking out of her office, "do whatever you have to, but please don't come back to my office again. You're going to get me in trouble."

"Sure thing Mrs. Olivier," Justin smiles, "we're a lot closer than you think. And I know more than you think I do. I'll see you soon beautiful."

Carolyn turns away from him headed to James' office. Justin is left standing by her door, watching her perfect ass as it sways and jiggles through the back of her sheer sundress.

Carolyn walks in James' office.

"Do you knock?" he asks. "I'm sorry Mr. Radicon," she says, "but I..."

"Don't be sorry correct your mistake." he tells her pointing towards his door. Carolyn follows his finger and looks back at the door.

"Seriously," she laughs, "you want me to go out and knock, just to walk right back in?"

"Precisely," he replies, "you go out and knock, and I may or may not permit you to come back in depending on how I feel."

"Fucking ridiculous..." Carolyn mumbles walking out of his office.

She knocks twice. Radicon says nothing.

She knocks again, there's still no reply from the inside.

As she lifts her hand to knock yet again he yells, "Who is it?"

"Mrs. Olivier." she replies dryly.

"Come in." he says.

"Now what were you saying before," he asks, "and make it quick I'm hungry I didn't eat breakfast this morning. I had to take my daughter Katherine to school."

"Um," Carolyn starts, "James isn't your daughter..."

"Fifteen," he interjects, "yea but she's still my   little princess. I've decided to start spending a lot more time with her."

"James baby," she says, "I don't think that's healthy..."

"Not healthy," James interjects again, "of course it's healthy. Katherine is my only daughter, and after her hospital stay she needs me more than ever now."

"Okay James." Carolyn says.

"So," he says, "do you like your new office?"

"I love it," she replies, "thank you again."

"No worries," he replies, "you look like something's on your mind though. Come sit down and tell me about it."

"There is a lot on my mind James," she admits, "but the

possibility of being homeless with my kids is at the forefront of it all I guess."

"Homeless," he says, "why what happened? Don't I pay you well?"

"Well, yes sir you do," she admits, "but Ralph, my husband pays all the bills. I always give him the money to pay the rent. But... he has a... problem. And as a result of that problem our rent and bills are three months behind."

"Why didn't you just ask me for the money," he asks, "I don't mind helping you and Ruford out?"

"Ralph, my husband's name is Ralph," she corrects him with a smile, "And I didn't want to ask you love, you already do so much for everybody here."

"You're different Carolyn." he tells her.

"Am I," she asks, "I wasn't aware."

"Don't be silly," he tells her, "Tell me how much. I'll write a check right now. You know what never mind." he pulls out his checkbook from a drawer on his desk.

As he writes she waits quietly, she has simply forgotten every word she's ever known. So this is what love is supposed to feel like, she smiles pleasantly.

"Here you are Mrs. Olivier." he hands her a sizable check that could pay her rent for the next year and then some.

"Oh, also," he continues as he reaches deep into his right pants pocket, "take this and run to Starbucks for me. Get us both some coffee and something to eat."

"Something to eat like what James?" she stands to take the cash from him.

"I trust you." he says as his office phone rings.

"Hello." he answers.

"Just a minute," he says into the phone before covering it with his large right hand, "Carolyn I have to take this... Run along to Starbucks, I'll be here waiting when you return."

She obeys.

(30minutes later)

Carolyn returns to the winery with James' food. As she rides the elevator to the third floor she checks to make sure she has everything she paid for. She does. She also has his change from the crisp hundred dollar bill he gave her to pay for the food.

The elevator opens and Carolyn exits quicker than she should have dropping one of the coffees she's carrying spilling some of it on her dress.

Luckily she didn't burn herself with it, but she'll have to eat her food without anything to drink since the other coffee is for Radicon.

As she rounds the corner to his office she hopes the stain on the front of her dress doesn't look too terribly tacky. Her plan is to leave the food with James and then quickly go back and clean up the mess she made in the hall near the elevator.

There are a hundred different scenarios Carolyn could have thought up as far as what she might find when she returned to Radicon's office with his breakfast, but nothing more tragic than this.

On his door James left a note on a sticky tab that reads, "Emergency at home had to go check on my daughter. Be back shortly."

"Grrrr," Carolyn growls to herself, "Radicon is losing his mind. First he said he took his daughter to school this morning, now he thinks she has an emergency at home. None of that is true, but he's not my husband or my man, rightfully... so it's not my damn business."

After cleaning up her mess near the elevator, Carolyn returns to her office. Her door is no longer closed or locked.

She immediately panics because other than her, only one person has access to a key to her office and he's supposedly gone home for a family emergency.

As she pushes her door open more she sees what appears to be a red silk tie, three nice sized lit red candles, and a red piece of paper on the edge of her desk. She walks towards her desk unsure what to think.

The red paper she thought she saw is an envelope. It reads, "Carolyn." What beautiful handwriting she thinks to herself.

Carolyn sets the food down on her desk and carefully opens the beautiful envelope. Inside she finds a small white note folded in half.

She takes a deep breath before opening it. As she opens the note she swears she can smell the scent of him. The letter is written in red pen.

"Don't turn around," it reads, "put the blindfold on now and wait for me."

The letter is signed Master Radicon. Her heart stops, but she obeys. As she ties the expensive silk tie around her face securely, the lights go off, and she hears her door close and lock.

She stands there waiting completely blind and oblivious to everything around her. She can hear herself breathing, and so can he. Her heart is pounding in her own ears now. He's standing right behind her. He kneels down close to her and lifts her left leg up back towards him to remove the heel from her left foot.

Then he places that foot back down on her soft carpet. Next he lifts her right foot up behind her and removes her right heel.

His anticipation for the moment he will enter her body is unmatched by anything he has ever desired before in his life.

As he stands back up he runs his loving hands up the sides of the curvaceous masterpiece that her body has become, since he first saw her.

He reaches down to grab the very bottom of her dress. Then he pulls it up, until he pulls it up completely over her curly brown head.

He smiles as he realizes she's not wearing any panties at all. Leaning forward he kisses her neck softly three times.

He takes the delicious smelling food from her desktop and sits it on the floor carefully. Then he moves the three beautiful red candles to the back edge of her desk.

Next he lifts Carolyn up in his arms and lies her face down on her huge office desk.

She moans happily and anxiously. He unfastens her white Victoria's Secret bra, and prompts her to lift her upper body up for just a moment so he can remove the enticing piece of lingerie completely.

She sighs as she lays back down flat. Tat, tat, tat... She flinches and grabs hold of the edge of her desk as the warm liquid drips slowly on her back from one of the redolent candles.

She squirms sensually as he drips the crimson toned wax up and down her beautiful caramel back. He moves her hair out of the way of her neck, before giving it the same ecstasy evoking treatment.

As the warm candle wax splatters all over her neck and shoulders Carolyn involuntarily arches her back in, as her toes and her head lift upward towards her ceiling.

He makes his way down to her legs. As he drips the wax along her firm but soft left leg; he uses his free hand to caress her round supple behind.

He sits the first candle down on the floor near the almost cold food and coffee, before reaching over Carolyn's body to retrieve the second candle.

Now for her right leg... As the wax pours over her right thigh down to her calf, she begins to spread her legs apart. As the pinkness of her forbidden center becomes finally visible to him he bites his bottom lip, as he grabs himself. His erection is definite now.

He quickly sits the second candle down on the floor, and starts to remove his shirt. Carolyn listens closely as he hastily unbuttons the first button on his dress shirt.

She sits up and turns in the direction where she believes he is standing. She tightens her blindfold first and then scoots towards the edge of her desk with her legs and arms spread wide open for him.

He steps into her arms. She reaches up and starts unbuttoning his shirt for him. After she has finished with the bottom button, she reaches up high and pushes the shirt off over his broad shoulders down to the floor.

Then she grabs his chest. She's shocked for a moment because the hair on his chest is gone, and he doesn't feel as big as he usually does.

She quickly reaches down to grab his penis. Oh yeah that's him, she smiles to herself.

She unfastens his belt, unbuttons his pants, and then pulls his zipper down. Next she reaches around inside of his pants to squeeze his behind, before pushing his pants off him down to the floor.

Carolyn leans forward and kisses his rock hard abs several times. She notices not only has he shaved his chest but James must be working out quite fiercely now, because his stomach is even more ripped up than it was before. His beautiful six pack feels to her greedy hands, lips, and tongue like a full eight or ten pack now.

Enough of this she thinks to herself, this is his fantasy not hers. She's lucky to even still be desired by him so heavily.

She turns around and crawls teasingly along the desk before lying back down on her stomach with her legs spread just as she was positioned before.

He steps out of his shoes, pants, and boxers. In nothing but his socks he leans down over her lower body with his head near her crimson candle wax stained upper thighs. He can't be hesitant anymore; his heart is racing so fast; he needs her now.

He begins to hastily kiss and grope her perfect ass. Then he leans in close between her firm inner thighs and spreads her wider with his hands and his head. He dives in, sucking, licking, and eating her into a new realm of erotic explosions.

She tastes like crushed apples and she's wetter already than he anticipated she would be. Up on her knees now she pushes her round butt deeper into his face. He continues to explore her completely with his tongue without even a thought of fatigue.

Carolyn smiles as she puts her face down on her cold desk. This new youthful vigor that James has is more than exciting for her.

She wonders if it's her new hairdo or maybe the new dress she wore to work today. Hell it doesn't matter this man... this earthly god obviously can't get enough of her, and that's good enough for her.

The sound of his guttural moans between the powerful, unforgettable strokes of his massive tongue are like soothing, angelic, music to her ears.

As he eats her body he begins to lose himself in what seems to be an erotic lucid daydream. He's no longer himself he's a powerful handsome sex gladiator with a gold tipped penis, and Carolyn is a gorgeous wench given to him to do whatever he wants with her.

He bites the inside corner of her right buttocks before wiping his wet mouth on his forearm.

He kneels down to his pants and retrieves an extra-large magnum condom. He opens it quickly tossing the wrapper in the trash can by her desk.

Carolyn heard him opening the condom. She knows James hasn't used a condom to have sex with her in a long time, but she's so wet she doesn't care enough to question him about it now.

He picks her up by her hips and places her on the edge of her desk. She stretches out to push herself back on him. She can feel his glorious condom covered penis throbbing as it sits triumphantly atop her perfect butt.

He smacks her butt with himself several times teasing not only her, but himself as well. He puts himself right there, waiting for her to beg for it.

She pushes herself back towards him even more now. He pulls away and smacks her ass with himself yet again.

"Please baby..." she begs. He smiles.

He reaches forward and grabs a hand full of her beautiful curls. Then as he enters her body, he simultaneously pushes her face down flat on its right side on the desk.

"Yes baby." she moans as he strokes deep inside her slowly.

"Harder, baby harder..." she demands seconds later. Without hesitation he begins to pound Carolyn from behind mercilessly.

He's trying his hardest not to look at her hypnotically jiggling behind. He knows staring at it for too long will end this sensual session sooner than later. He feels it coming near. He stops, he pulls back. She waits for him.

Her hormones are raging like a pack of hungry starved lions, being teased cruelly by a fat scrumptious roast being dangled over their heads by a string.

He marches towards the front of her. He grabs her beautiful face and plunges himself in her greedy wet mouth.

She chokes instantly, he doesn't care. She tries to grab it and take control. He quickly slaps her weak hand away and pushes the back of her head up and down on him.

He's had enough. He pushes her head back playfully. Then he turns her around towards him.

Reaching behind her head he tightens her blindfold for her. As she waits for him, she explores his impressive stomach and thighs with her soft hands and long fingernails.

He picks her up, and slowly enters her body as she wraps her long legs around him.

Then he walks comfortably to the nearest wall and begins rising up and down on the tips of his toes with each hard pump.

As they grunt in unison, they both pray his erection never ends. The sweat from his face is dripping down on her tense body and face. She welcomes, licking a few drops as they land near open her mouth. His sweat feels so cool to her sensitive skin. Her gorgeous moans are becoming more frequent.

A couple of more pumps and he'll be done for sure, he can't hold on any longer.

He squeezes her ass as hard as he can as he rises all the way up to the very tips of his toes this time. He's deep inside her stomach now.

"Ahhh!" she screams out. He moans and grunts joyfully as he comes back down off his toes. As he finishes inside of her, his entire body is shaking uncontrollably.

As she holds on to him tightly, he walks her carefully back to her desk, never coming out of her tight, wet, body.

"Damn Mrs. Olivier..." he speaks for the first time since they began.

"What the hell!" she snatches the sweaty blindfold off. Looking in his young blue eyes she becomes overpowered by panic and frustration.

"What?" he asks.

"Justin Tolls what the hell did I tell you?" she fumes.

"I don't remember," he smiles that stunning smile, "but it's gonna be real hard for you to get rid of me now Mrs. Olivier."

"Damn it," she says, "so now what? What is this? What is this supposed to turn into?"

"Look I'm not stupid," he says still tucked deep inside her pulsating body, "neither is anyone else who works here. We all know you belong to the boss. I'm not gonna get in the way of that, but the man is married Mrs. Olivier, and so are you. So what the hell why not just keep this thing going? Let's just have fun."

"Just have fun..." she questions.

"Hell yes," he replies confidently, "Tell me you didn't just enjoy this. Tell me this wasn't some of the best sex you've ever had."

She hesitates, lost deep in her own thoughts.

"But the note," she says, "Why would you write Master Radicon on it?"

He smiles. After finally pulling out of her, he sits down on the floor to begin putting his clothes back on.

She watches him, waiting for him to speak.

He says nothing.

"Answer my question," she demands, "why did you sign the letter Master Radicon?"

He stands up almost fully clothed again, walking towards her he begins to button his shirt up. He bends down trying to taste her pouty lips once more. She dodges him, catching his handsome face in her hands in the process.

Turning back to face him, she stares deep into his curiously familiar blue eyes. "Answer my question Justin Tolls." She pleads with him.

"No." he replies with a mischievous grin. He tries to kiss her again. This time she doesn't resist she falls back on her desk melting away into his young powerful arms.

Ch. 13

"Ralph Olivier"

When less attractive, unintelligent, middle to lower class men luck up and marry a dynamo like Carolyn Olivier there are always going to be problems. The woman is an unreal powerhouse on every front.

Sure she's head over heels for her boss now, and doing very well with and for his company, but she would have become great even if she never met James Radicon.

She graduated from the University of Miami at the age of 21, after attending the school for just three and a half years, on a full academic scholarship. She didn't just graduate, she finished Summa Cum Laude. The woman graduated with perfect honors, her academic career at the U was amazingly flawless in every aspect. Her G.P.A. never once fell below her perfect 4.0 from orientation to graduation.

While enrolled at the U, she also pledged Alpha Kappa Alpha Sorority Incorporated, maintained a position in the student government association, she was a student ambassador, and also one of the most beautiful women on the campus throughout her tenure there.

With all that said it becomes apparent that Ralph Olivier's marriage to Carolyn Williams was pure dumb luck. The man knew he didn't deserve Carolyn, nor could he hide her from the world forever. In the back of his mind Ralph was always waiting on Carolyn to meet some gorgeous, smart, wealthy guy who could... and eventually would take her away from him. It only seemed right.

Every year she remains married to Ralph is a dead year, another year she didn't break away and through... To become who she was born to be, a beautiful, more than influential, dynamic juggernaut in the world of business. In time James Radicon will undoubtedly help her become just that.

(Ralph)
Carolyn is... Well she's great okay? Damn it she's perfect. I could never give her the kind of life she really deserves. I mean look at me. I'm not a smart man, I've never been much to look at, and I'm not the best father or provider... And hell I'm not even faithful to her.

Everything the world is seeing now in my Carolyn, I saw in her when she was still a teenager. And her little genius brain was like putty in my black hands. I was all she knew... her first everything. So of course she believed and did everything I said. I was her boyfriend and her father.

You see, about five years ago Carolyn didn't even believe she was pretty or smart. And honestly I tried to keep it that way, for as long as I damn could. The more she realized her own potential, the harder it was gonna be for my black ass to keep her. I stole money from her purse, I've beat her... lied to her.

I think I've been trying to sabotage myself all along. I cheated... Lord knows I've cheated on Carolyn a thousand times and it's sad because I know I'm the only man she has ever slept with. Carolyn would never cheat on me, I'm the best and only lover she has ever had.

And her sister Kayla, well she is now what Carolyn was 5 years ago emotionally. She thinks I'm the best thing on the planet, and she would die for my old fat ass in a second. It's sick; but I think I been training Kayla to replace her big sister Carolyn just in case she ever does leave me. But she won't, Carolyn can't live without me, and no other man wants her anyway.

Worst of all I tried to sabotage Carolyn's career. We shouldn't be struggling at all. Hell, right after she graduated from the University people started calling the house offering her all these big time jobs. I would always lie and tell them she wasn't interested. I didn't mind her working in that grape garden at that old booze factory. But now she's working inside, in an office. And she's walking, talking, and even dressing different. And the clothes and heels she's wearing are not the cheap kind she used to wear. Her hair and makeup are different. And then she just took an all-expenses paid business trip all the way to California last week. If I didn't know better, I'd think some kind of fancy man was...

Carolyn's work cell phone vibrates. Ralph looks over at her, she's still sound asleep in their bed. He looks at his raggedy old fake fossil watch. 6:15 a.m. Who could be calling her this early he thinks.

He quietly walks over to her brand new yellow and white striped MK tote purse, sitting in the tattered old gray rocking chair near the bathroom.

Ralph reaches down towards the bag. Carolyn rolls over in bed; he jumps back from the bag in a panic.

She's still sleeping. He reaches down to open the purse, the phone is still vibrating.

The purse is full of all kinds of assorted things. Ralph finds two roses one white and one yellow, a red envelope addressed to Carolyn, a gorgeous red silk tie, a pair of Carolyn's lace panties, and an empty extra-large magnum condom wrapper.

Ralph picks up the condom wrapper and stares at it with his head titled to the left side. Then he looks over at his beautiful sleeping wife with malicious intent.

He sits the wrapper to the side in the raggedy old chair, and picks up the red envelope. He opens it; inside he finds a folded note. As he reads it his temperature begins to rise.

"Don't turn around," he whispers to himself, "a blindfold... Master Radicon? Radicon... Wait, that's the rich white fuck that owns that whole damn place." Ralph drops the note.

His hand begins to shake as he picks up the red silk tie. The knot that Carolyn tied in it to blindfold herself is still in it.

Ralph covers his mouth with his right hand. As he holds the sweat and maybe even semen stained tie in his right hand, it begins to shake again with absolute rage.

He throws the expensive tie down on the floor in a fit. Her cell phone begins to vibrate again. Ralph grabs it as it stops vibrating.

"Three missed calls," Ralph whispers, "and a text all from Mr. fucking Radicon." Ralph opens the text, it reads, "Good morning love, I couldn't sleep because I couldn't stop thinking about you. You really are one of a kind, and I don't give you enough credit. I'm sorry you're going through a rough patch right now, but I do hope that check will cover all of your bills and keep you from losing your home. See you at the Office. Master Radicon."

Ralph holds the phone in one hand, as he searches her bag with the other hand. There's the check. He picks it up. His eyes begin to water as he reads the large amount.

He's upset, but Ralph is no fool. He puts everything he found back in her purse just the way it was originally. He closes it back, and then exits the room.

In the kitchen he finds one can of Bud Light beer on the top shelf of the refrigerator. After opening it he takes a big gulp of it, as he opens the front door and walks out to the front porch. It's still dark outside, and their street is completely deserted.

(Ralph)

What the hell has Carolyn been doing to that man to get a check like that? I'm a fool. I'm a fat old fool. I should have known. No woman is just silently happy like that, at least not in a situation like ours. He's screwing my wife... And he's paying her for it. My wife Carolyn is this man's whore. Damn. I'm mad as hell, but I ain't stupid. I can't get my job back. We need that money real bad. I'm not gonna even bring it up. I'll let her do what she has to, to take care of me and the kids. In fact, I'm not gonna even try to get another job. Since she wants to be his whore, I'm gonna let her do it. But in return I'm not gonna work period.

Ralph takes a few more sips of his beer before throwing the almost empty can out on his unkempt front lawn.

Back inside he takes his shirt off in the front room and throws it on the sofa. Then he takes his jeans off and leaves them right there on the floor.

In nothing but his holy socks and underwear he walks back into his bedroom. With specific intent he climbs in the squeaky old bed on top of his sleeping wife.

"Ralph," Carolyn moans, "What are you doing babe, I'm trying to sleep?"

"I missed you baby." he says, roughly pulling her underwear down to her ankles.

"Not right now Ralph..." she pleads.

"Yeah," he replies, right now."

He turns her smaller body around in front of his. She obediently positions herself on her knees as usual. He enters her body. She barely feels a thing. He pumps five times, and then falls flat on top of her.

Carolyn quickly rolls him off of herself. "Ralph did you just..."

"Just go pee it out," he smiles that annoying toothy smile, "you'll be fine. It ain't like we ain't married baby."

Carolyn jumps out of bed with her panties still around her ankles. She pulls them up just high enough to run adequately.

Inside the bathroom she hastily squats on the toilet and tries hard to push Ralph's contaminated semen out of her body.

(Carolyn)

Forcing yourself to pee is one of the most difficult things any woman could ever do. I really hope my body just rejects Ralph's semen all together. I think I feel it now... sliding back out of me. Yes, some of it is definitely coming out now, but deep down any woman who has ever done this before knows there is no way she's ever going to actually get it all out. Oh my God! This is so damn frustrating. He doesn't care; Ralph does not care about anything... And he definitely doesn't give a damn about me or my body. He knows another kid is the last thing we need right now... And the last thing I want. Lord forgive me; I love my children to death, but if I could give them back to you now and start over fresh, I would... gladly. And James, what would James think if he found out I was pregnant? Mental note... Buy a Plan B pill today!

Ch. 14

"She's My Wife"

Carolyn taps away carelessly on her laptop trying to remain focused on the goals she's set for herself today, but she can't stop thinking about him.

(Carolyn)

His eyes are so deep they penetrate me with ease, his body is more than a blessing it's becoming almost a necessity, and his hands know me all too well. What is this feeling? It's not love of course, it's way too soon for that. No, it's more like a burning curiosity... There's like this primal instinct inside of me that's willing me to continue to explore this relationship... Or whatever it is. If James ever knew, or thought that I was... Even thinking about messing around with another man he would...

There's a knock at the door.

"Come in." Carolyn says.

The door opens, and in walks a tall handsome dark skinned gentleman, wearing a classy black suit, and a nice pink tie.

"Are you Mrs. Carolyn Olivier?" he asks.

"Who wants to know?" she removes her reading glasses to take a better look at her more than attractive visitor.

"I'm sorry," he heads back towards the door, "it's my fault, I must have the wrong office number, my apologies." He turns to leave.

Carolyn stands. "Wait a minute," she says, "I'm Carolyn, but who are you?"

From behind his back the tall man pulls out a bouquet of pink roses, a pink heart shaped box, and a bottle of Radicon's finest red wine. He walks towards her with obvious elegance. He then politely hands the pink box and the beautiful fresh flowers to her. Then he sits the bottle of wine down, and a crystal glass. Next he takes one step back and closes his lively brown eyes.

"You are sooo beautiful to me..." he pleasantly begins to sing the 70's song made popular by the English rock and blues singer Joe Cocker.

Carolyn is blown away by his beautiful voice and perfect tone. She calmly sits back down in her chair as an array of warm emotions wash all over her body.

"You are so beautiful," he continues to croon to her, "To me... Can't you see...? You're everything I hoped for... You're everything I need... Carolyn... You are sooooo... damn beautiful, to me..."

"Wow..." Carolyn smiles at him.

"Sir," she continues, "whoever you are... your voice, is absolutely gorgeous."

"Well thank you Mrs. Olivier," he smiles modestly, "but that's song is not from me, it's from your boyfriend, Justin Tolls."

"Boyfriend..." she wrinkles her brow.

"Yes ma'am," the man replies, "You have a wonderful rest of your day Ms. Carolyn, and enjoy your candy and wine."

"I will, thank you very much." she replies as he exists her office.

Carolyn opens the box of chocolates and finds a small white piece of paper inside. She unfolds the note to find beautiful cursive writing in pink ink. The note reads, *"Don't ever allow fear or judgment to discount or destroy the moments that force you to know that you're truly alive... I can only live for... and through you. Please never change."*

The beautiful note is signed again, *"Master Radicon."*

She quickly opens the bottle and pours herself a glass of wine. She takes a sip and then closes her dreamy hazel eyes as the sweet liquid tickles her palate. She smiles.

"Carolyn..." James bursts into her office unannounced.

"James," she quickly looks down at the items splayed across her desk, "Don't you knock."

"I'm sorry," he glances at her wine, and new pink treasures, "I see I interrupted something. You want me to just come back..."

"Yes please, that would be perfect." she tries to mask her nerves and steady her heartbeat. She takes another big sip of wine.

"Fine," he walks closer to her desk, "I understand completely."

Carolyn balls up the small note in her left hand and places it in her lap below her desk.

"Tell me Carolyn," he says, "did I miss s o m e t h i n g ? Isn't your birthday in April?"

With her balled up left hand Carolyn eases the left side of her skirt up her nervous caramel thigh, and stuffs the dangerous note in the side of her full panties.

"Yes sir my birthday is in April." she replies so happy that she decided not to wear a thong today. She takes another sip; her glass is now empty. She picks up the bottle.

"Here, allow me..." he takes the bottle in his own hands.

"Wow," he eyes the bottle, "this is a bottle of my *Passion Absolute* 1985, I'm impressed. This is what $2,500 a bottle now?" James pours her a full glass of the sweet wine.

"Thank you." Carolyn sips more of the strong beverage.

"So tell me Carolyn, since it's not your birthday... What is all of this?" he asks taking a chocolate from the beautiful pink box and popping it in his curious mouth.

"I uh," she hesitates, "you know me... My husband, Ralph just wanted to surprise me today... Isn't it sweet?"

"Lovely." Radicon replies void of emotion through a

strange half smile. "And roses too I see." he continues. Carolyn takes another sip.

"Right," she says, "was there something you actually needed Mr. Radicon, or have you grown bored of running your billion-dollar company?"

He takes another chocolate, and pops it in his mouth.

"Yes, how are you doing with finalizing everything on the Los Angeles front?" he asks.

"Everything is done," she replies happily, "the only thing left to be done at Nielsen and Brown, is to change the sign out front to Radicon."

"Wonderful." he says through another half-smile taking yet another piece of candy. Carolyn turns the expensive glass up as she finishes her second glass.

"Right... wonderful," Carolyn watches her boss curiously, "are you hungry sir? Because if you want I can run to McDonald's..."

Radicon laughs boldly. "No ma'am Carolyn I am not hungry," he says, "but if I were you would not be running to McDonald's, the border, Burger King, or anywhere else that advertises a dollar menu. No, see I'm not your husband Rupert, I'm your boss."

Carolyn squints, her eyes at him as the left side of her lips curls upward a bit.

"You see," Radicon continues taking her bouquet of roses in his right hand, "I would never send you a dozen roses, and never just one color. Simple men, do simple things Carolyn. The trick is, to not be simple yourself. Well, I have more work to do my love, I'm sure I'll see you around."

He takes one more piece of candy and waltzes out of Carolyn's office. He's fully aware of how angry his jealous display of arrogance must have made her. She's more thankful for the wine now than before, she knows she's gonna need it to make it through this day. She pours herself another full glass. This ***Passion Absolute 1985*** is the very best thing she has ever tasted in her twenty-three years.

(Jessica Radicon)

The temperature in the room is far below what any normal person would find comfortable. The room itself is generic and not the least bit comforting. The air is thick with several indefinable odors.

The door opens, a nurse walks in. "Mrs. Radicon..." the nurse says.

"Yes." Jessica replies. "How are you doing today?" the nurse asks writing something on a clipboard, never actually looking up to at least pretend she cares what Jessica's response will be.

"I'm not doing well," Jessica says, "as I'm sure you're aware, or maybe you're not, but ever since my daughter's stay here, I'm no longer fond of hospitals in the least bit."

"Right," the nurse says still writing, "I'm very sorry to hear that. Well the doctor will be in to see you very shortly... I just need to ask you a few questions for my paperwork please."

"No." Jessica replies turning towards the window in the back of the uncomfortable room.

"No?" the nurse asks.

"Hell no," Jessica tells her, "you are the third nurse to come in here since the first nurse told me an hour ago, that the doctor would be in shortly to speak to me. I am not going to answer all of those same damn questions a fourth time. The answer is no. Go tell Dr. Cole, Mrs. Radicon said to get his ass in here with my results right now, or my husband and I will no longer be funding his weak little annual charity golf tournament."

The flustered nurse exits the room quickly.

(Back at the winery)

Carolyn finished her bottle of wine and half of her box of chocolate an hour ago. She doesn't think she's quite drunk yet, but she's definitely feeling the wine now. She's on her way to James' office.

Using the master key James gave her to gain access to his office anytime he's away from the office Carolyn makes her way inside. He called her from his cell phone and asked her to go in his office to get the manila folder that contains some paperwork she needs to set up the new bank account for the Los Angeles winery.

As she walks in she pauses; as she thinks she hears a noise inside the large empty office, a rat maybe, or a raccoon. God she hopes not; she's never been good with animals especially small furry animals with beady eyes. She shakes her head as she enters the office, she's sure it was nothing. She heads toward the filing cabinet behind his desk.

"Third drawer from the top," she tells herself, "should be the very first folder... Where the hell is it?"

Carolyn hears the sound again. She's definite this time that she heard something, some kind of animal, something bigger than a raccoon in James' office closet.

She has no intention on finding out what it is. The problem is she's really tipsy, and she has to pass by the closet door to get back out of the office.

The closet door opens a bit.

"Oh God." she whispers taking a shaky step from behind the desk.

The door opens wider. It's completely dark inside the closet. She knows it's impossible, but she swears she can feel something inside the closet staring at her with vicious, deadly intent.

She doesn't want to be standing here in fear like this when James returns to his office. He'll definitely make her feel like an incapable, black, idiot, and he won't be happy that the company's very sensitive banking file is missing from his filing cabinet.

Okay it's now or never, she thinks to herself. She takes another step; the door opens a little more. She runs.

Whap! Carolyn is quickly snatched into the closet by two large gloved hands.

She tries to scream, but with one hand on her mouth and one hand on her neck it's physically impossible.

She knows she's going to die. She just hopes whoever this creep is kills her before he rapes her.

"Did you eat all of the candy baby girl..." the familiar voice whispers.

He releases her mouth. "Justin?" she whispers back.

"The one and only." he replies.

She can't see his face in the dark closet, but she's sure he's smiling.

"Justin Tolls, what the hell are you doing in Mr. Radicon's closet?" she asks.

"I could ask you the same thing Mrs. Olivier." he replies. You snatched me in here!" she whispers loudly.

"No, I mean, why are you in his office while he's not?" Justin asks.

"That's none of your damn business," she fumes, "but if you must know, James... I mean Mr. Radicon called my cell phone and told me to come in here and grab a very important file. Now if you don't mind..."

Justin covers her mouth again with his gloved right hand, pressing her softness back against his rock hard form. He can tell she's drunk, and this fact alone is turning him on immensely. She feels him, all of him pressed against her. She knows how wrong this is and how dangerous this could be if James were to catch the two of them together like this is his office closet.

Carolyn is almost certain James would kill them both. Afterwards he would quickly and masterfully dispose of their bodies just like he did Patrick Brown's old bloody body in California after she killed him.

Somehow all of these dangers, threats, and possibilities swirling around in her mind just seem to be turning her on even more as she grinds her round ass back against him. Alcohol is the devil she thinks to herself. She smiles calmly to herself, ready to be taken complete advantage of by her young lover.

Justin can barely contain himself. His mind is gone, his strict instructions are forgotten, and his body belongs to her. He kisses her neck with an open mouth. The warmth of his mouth on her now tilted neck sends instant chills up and down her anxious spine.

"Justin..." she whispers.

"Yeah baby..." he replies between kisses.

"I... Need you..." she admits.

"No worries... You got me baby girl..." he assures her.

He forces her head to the side as he kisses her hard in the mouth. His greedy curious tongue is sending her mouth and her entire body into a state of pure sexual euphoria.

Holding her face with his left hand as he kisses her, then he reaches around with his right hand to caress her glorious thighs. Instinctively he begins to pump her round behind back against himself. His erection is undeniable now.

He turns her around so that he can stare into her eyes as he kisses her. In the darkness the only thing they can see is each other's eyes. He grips her firm ass, as he drives his tongue deeper in her insatiable mouth. She pulls back breaking away from his kiss.

"What's wrong Carolyn?" he asks. She hesitates looking up at him, while wiping the moisture from around her mouth.

She drops down to her knees. She hastily unbuckles his belt and undoes his pants completely. She takes him in her hands, stroking him with awesome precision. Then she engulfs him whole. He puts both of his gloved hands comfortably on top of his head to relax.

Carolyn loves making him happy now. But is he taking James' place? As she continues to throat him she ponders her life and her situation.

This is a child he's not even twenty-one years old yet. There's no possible way he can understand and be able to do the things Mr. Radicon can do for her mentally, emotionally, and especially financially. And as far as her career goes, without Radicon she would be back to square one.

She goes down deep now, as deep as she can. Her eyes begin to water as the wetness spills out from the sides of her more than full mouth. She chokes. He snatches her up. He plunges his tongue deep in her mouth again.

He turns her around, and bends her over in front of him. Justin snatches her short skirt up. Then he pulls her panties down to her knees. Her note from the chocolate box falls carelessly on the closet floor.

With her hands on her knees she waits for him. She hears him rip open a condom. She turns around and snatches it from him. She carefully places the exclusive cherry flavored magnum condom in her mouth, with her tongue in its center.

Back down on her knees she skillfully covers his penis completely with the condom, using only her mouth to do so.

Then she stands back up and takes her anxious position back in front of him.

He steadies himself. He still can't believe this is happening. Blindfolds and masks are one thing, but to be pulling this off all alone is utterly amazing to the nineteen-year-old.

He slides in slow reveling in the moment. He hesitates thinking he hears something. She pushes back on him forcing him deep inside of her. She gasps; he reaches forward to cover her mouth with his gloved hand.

The office door opens and the lights outside the closet come on. Both of their hearts stop cold in their throats.

Carolyn stands straight up against his body with him still deep inside of her. All the pleasure is gone, she can't feel a thing. She no longer feels drunk in the moment, her focus is vital to her survival now.

"Yes Mr. Olivier," James says, "what exactly is it that I can help you with sir?"

"We have a problem **Dradicon**..." Ralph tells him.

"It's my husband..." Carolyn whispers to Justin. "Oh shit." he replies sweating profusely now.

"We have a problem?" James asks shutting his closet door as he walks by en route to his desk.

"Yeah Ralph," tells him, "You and me, we got a huge problem."

"And what might that be?" James asks obviously intrigued by the conversation.

Ralph looks behind him, before closing the office door. "You're fucking my wife Dradicon!" he steps closer to his desk.

"My name is Radicon, with an R," James corrects him; "now that's the second time you've made that mistake. Do not make it a habit Rupert."

"And my name is..." Ralph starts to speak.

"Man nobody gives a damn what your name is!" Radicon assures him adamantly.

"How about now..." Ralph slams his gun down on James' desk.

Justin bends Carolyn back over and begins to stroke. He figures if he's gonna die he might as well go out with a bang. He's never going to let Ralph or anyone harm James. He'll die himself first.

James doesn't flinch at the sight of the deadly weapon.

"You do realize," James starts, "that when people like

me are killed, very bad things happen to those who   kill them right?"

"Man do I look like I give a damn about what would happen after I kill yo rich white ass," Ralph says, "you already got the whole world... Damn you gotta screw my

wife too?"

"Sir," James says, "I do work very closely with your wife; she is my assistant. But I can assure you we are not in any way involved in..."

"Look man," Ralph picks up his gun and aims it at James; "don't blow smoke up my ass. Now I read all your little text messages in my wife's business cell phone. I know you're fucking her. I may not be a very smart man, but you ain't just gone piss on me and try to tell me its rain."

"Um," James hesitates, "first off I don't want to pee on you or blow anything up your ass Mr. Olivier, and I have no clue what texts you're referring to, but I..."

Ralph cocks the gun. Justin stops in mid stroke inside the closet at the sound of the gun being readied to fire.

James puts his hands up.

"You know what Ralph," he says, "you're right... You are absolutely right on all accounts. I will speak to your wife today and I will tell her we can no longer..."

"So you are admitting to me, Carolyn Olivier's husband that you have been having sex with her?" Ralph asks leaning closer to James with his gun only inches away from the nervous sweat on the tip of his nose.

"Yes sir," James admits, "I had sex with your wife... and I apologize. I will speak to her on the matter today. Now please put the gun down."

"No you're going to fire her today," Ralph tells him, "and then you're going to give me five million dollars to keep quiet."

"Keep quiet," James repeats, "about what?"

Ralph smiles his hideous smile as he pulls out an electronic recorder from his sneaky back pocket.

"Mr. Radicon, he says, "do you have any idea what happens to married men like you when they get caught up in work place affairs, without prenuptial agreements?"

"Well now," James laughs lightly as his face reddens, "you're much smarter than you give yourself credit for there Mr. Olivier."

"Fuck all that Dradicon," he says, "do we have a deal or don't we?"

"I'll tell you what," James pulls out his checkbook, "how about I write you a check right now for double what you're asking and you leave the recorder here with me?"

"Hell no," Ralph hands James an old business card with his free hand, "this is my cell number. You call me and then I'll text you the account numbers to deposit the money in. I want one million in each account."

"Fine..." James says as Ralph conceals his weapon before exiting his office.

James immediately picks up the phone and dials her extension. Carolyn's phone rings five times before the voicemail answers.

"You know who this is," he says, "I'll be waiting for you in the very back corner of the wine cellar downstairs. Hurry up."

Then James rushes out of his office locking his door behind him.

Justin starts stroking harder now. She can feel all of him. As Carolyn leans forward reaching towards her toes she feels something on the floor near her feet.

Carolyn bites her lip as she tries hard to concentrate on grabbing the item on the floor. It's a manila folder. The tape across the bottom of the folder is bright red.

Carolyn can see it clearly. It's the sensitive bank file she came in the office looking for in the first place. She now knows why Justin was in James' office. He's trying to steal money from the company. It's definitely wrong, but as he continues to please her as only a real man could she's finding it hard to be mad at him. Besides she's more than sure Justin was going to steal Radicon's money just to spend it on her anyway.

Carolyn reaches down all the way to the floor and grabs the file. Justin pushes the closet door open, and bends Carolyn over Radicon's desk. Carolyn strategically tosses the top secret file underneath James' desk without Justin noticing. He closes the closet door behind him and then begins to pound her from the back with magnificent force.

(In the wine cellar)

Beneath the Radicon winery building is a large cellar used to house more than twenty percent of the world's supply of Radicon produced wine. The cellar itself is state of the art. It looks simple enough, but each barrel is actually opened, filled, dated, and set in place by a machine.

There is one main hall down the middle of the cellar. All around the middle of the huge room are rows and rows of delicious, expensive, aging Radicon wine.

James has been down here for at least thirty minutes waiting for her. He's pacing back and forth frantically, hiding in the very back corner of his enormous wine cellar. His entire face and neck are red. His thoughts, steps, and hand gestures are all quite irrational at this point. He looks down at his expensive new diamond encrusted Rolex watch. "Damn it," he says, "where the hell is she?"

"I'm right here, calm down." the familiar voice says in the darkness.

"Damn it…" he says again walking past her.

"What's wrong James?" she pretends to be clueless.

"I should have known better than to ever…" James starts.

"Ever what…" Carolyn interjects.

"Trust you… or someone, like you." he tells her. "Now what the hell does that mean?" Carolyn asks.

"Exactly what it sounds like…" James says.

"So you don't trust me James?" Carolyn asks. "Please," he says, "call me Mr. Radicon."

Carolyn looks down at the concrete floor shaking her head with a distant smirk on her face.

"After everything we've been through," she says, "you seriously still don't trust me James?"

"How can I?" he asks.

"Really," she says, "how can you trust *me*?" She takes a couple steps closer to him. He backs away from her with both of his arms up to shield himself from her. "Seriously James," she says, "all of this though…"

"You don't understand," he backs further away from her, "you don't have a clue what you've done to me."

"*Me*," she says, "James what the hell have I ever done to you? Damn near everything I ever do is *for* you… but never *to* you."

"Carolyn…" he stares down at the cold floor with no emotion.

"Yes James…" she replies knowing full well what he's about to say. "I'm going to have to let…" he starts.

"Let me go…" Carolyn sheds a few real tears.

"Is that what you were going to say James," she asks, "Because that's who you are to me… You're James. You can never just be my boss or Mr. Radicon again. Don't you understand that? We're in way too deep..."

"Obviously not." he interjects.

"And what the hell is that supposed to mean James?" she asks with a hand on her left hip.

"You know what I'm talking about Carolyn, so don't play cute with me!" he demands.

"So just because my husband threatened to..." Carolyn's words get caught in her throat. "Damn it..." she whispers aloud.

James walks towards her. "I knew it." he says.

"Knew what James?" she asks unable to look him in his eyes now.

"You and your husband," he says, "you're working together."

"No!" she screams.

James slaps her hard across the face. "I was going to try to give you the benefit of the doubt..." he says.

"I'm not working with him James." she cries. "Stop lying!" he yells.

"I'm not lying to you baby..." Carolyn pleads with him. "I am not your baby," he assures her, "I never was."

Her tears are falling more heavily now. "James..." she pleads.

"Tell me," he bends down to be at eye level with her, "if you're not working with Ralph... How did you know what I was talking about without me telling you?"

"I... I can't tell you." she stutters backing away from him slowly.

"No, you better tell me right now you little black bastard." he screams in her face.

"I was there..." she admits. "I was there," James repeats, "I was there, what the hell does that mean?"

"In your office James, when my husband came in…" she says.

"No you weren't…" he says. "Yes I was," she tells him, "in the closet." "Why the hell were you in my closet Carolyn?" he asks stepping back close to her.

"I went in your office to get that banking file you asked me to get," she says, "and when I saw you and Ralph walking in I hid in your closet."

James considers the likelihood of this being true. "And you heard everything he and I talked about?" James asks. "Yeah…" she replies. "Every single word?" he asks.

"Yes James." she tells him.

"Prove it." he says.

"What…" Carolyn replies. "If you were in my closet when **Rupert** and I walked in, prove it." he tells her wanting so badly to believe her.

"How?" she asks.

"What did he bring with him," James asks, "other than that hideous denim outfit he wore and a terrible body odor? He brought two things with him, what were they?"

"A gun," Carolyn says, "a gun, and a recording device. You offered him double the five million dollars he asked for to leave the recorder with you, but he refused. I am not perfect James Radicon, and I'm nowhere near it. But I would never… I will never do anything to purposely hurt you or this company. You have both changed my meaningless life for the better. I am not working with Ralph to extort you; I swear to God."

James looks deep in Carolyn's eyes and believes every word she just said, mainly because he wants to believe her. She notices the look in his soft blue eyes, but she's not quite sure what it means exactly.

"James..." she says. "What Carolyn..." he replies turning away from her. She doesn't know if she should touch him or not. "Do you... Trust me?" she asks him. He doesn't respond to her.

"James, do you trust me..." Carolyn repeats. "More than I trust myself," he admits, "damn it Carolyn. Your husband is going to single handedly ruin everything we've built together."

"No he won't." Carolyn wipes a few tears away.

"Are you serious," James says, "You don't know my wife. Jessica isn't very big, but she can be as mean as a rabid pit bull from hell when she's pushed. The woman has loved me since the very first time she saw me..."

"Join the club..." Carolyn mumbles. "What did you say, I couldn't hear you?" he asks.

"Nothing," she replies, "Finish what you were saying."

James takes a deep calculated breath. "I'm saying," he starts again, "if my wife gets word about us, she's going to divorce me and take half of everything. I will no longer be able to run both wineries. And I've already invested over three hundred million dollars in the reformation of the Los Angeles property."

"Everything is going to be okay James." Carolyn tells him rubbing his lower back just the way he likes.

"How can you say that Carolyn?" he asks.

"Because it's true," she says, "no matter what happens you're going to be okay. And I'm not going anywhere."

James looks down into her loving hazel eyes.

"So if Jessica divorces me," James says, "takes half of my money, the house, all the cars, and ultimately guts both wineries financially, you're still gonna be right here..."

"I wouldn't even flinch." Carolyn says with no hesitation.

"Now see, you never even blinked when you lied to me that time." he acknowledges with a genuine smile.

"It's not a lie James," she tells him, "I don't love your money. I love you… and *exactly* who you are… I always will."

"Come here." he picks her up in his strong arms.

Carolyn can't even breathe as she's been pressed tightly against his large chest, but she doesn't care. As she hangs there in the balance… in his arms, she knows full well being his everything takes precedence over all else.

He kisses her finally, more genuine now and more passionate than ever.

"I believe you," he whispers, "I believe you because I want to. I trust you Carolyn… with my life."

James sits her atop a nearby barrel of wine. Carolyn smiles at him, as she's overjoyed she took the time to go to the bathroom, to wash Justin's scent off of her body before coming down to the cellar to meet Radicon.

"What are you smiling at?" he asks.

"Nothing," she replies pulling him close in between her gaping caramel legs, "just shut the hell up and kiss me." He obeys.

"You are going to leave your husband immediately." James says between kisses.

"What…" Carolyn breaks away from his soft sweet lips.

"I said you're going to leave Rupert." he repeats.

Carolyn leans back from him, to look intently in his eyes.

"And are you going to leave Jessica?" she asks.

"Hell no." he replies taking a step back to look at her now.

"Exactly," she says, "hell no, I didn't think so. So if you're not leaving your wife I'm damn sure not leaving my husband."

"You belong to me," he barks, "You do what I say!"

"Yeah, while I'm with you," she tells him, "but whenever I go home James... my job is to successfully satisfy another man's every desire."

"You better watch your mouth little girl." he threatens.

"It's true James," she says with a teasing grin, "when I leave you... I belong to him. Because you... don't want me enough to keep me full time. You just like me enough to rent me from time to time. But Ralph Olivier has the owner's manual.

Whap! James slaps her hard across the face. She grabs her mouth in reflex and then smiles.

"Poor baby," she says, "not man enough to marry his beautiful black whore. Scared of what his colleagues and the outside world might say if he had a lowly black wife."

"I don't have to marry you," he turns to leave the cellar, "you already belong to me, and only me."

"Hmm, that's what you think." she jumps down off the wine barrel.

Radicon spins around on his furious heels and rushes back towards her. He picks her up high in the air and then quickly slams her back down on the wine barrel. His face and neck are bright red again.

"Do not play with me Carolyn!" he demands.

"Then stop playing with me James," she says, "I can't be your secret slut forever; I'm too good for that James."

He let's go of her and backs away. She hops down from the barrel again. She licks a sweet drop of blood from the left side of her pouty bottom lip. She smiles again.

"You see James," she walks towards him, "Other men do find me attractive too."

"They all want to do what you do to me… and maybe even a little more." she continues.

Every seductive step she takes towards him is more powerful than the last. "The difference between you and them James baby," she says, "Is they don't mind taking it a step further."

Carolyn steps behind the quiet thoughtful Radicon. She reaches up and begins to run her tiny fingertips up and down his powerful red neck. The hairs on his strong neck respond to her delicate touch immediately. She giggles.

"What you gonna do James," she finally allows the alcohol in her system to take complete control of her mouth, "What you gonna do, if some handsome, strong, smooth, young guy comes along and steals my heart away from you? Then what…"

"Carolyn, shut the fuck up!" he yells turning around to grab her again.

This time James lifts her up by her neck and carries her back to the same wine barrel once more. Carolyn believes he's going to kill her right now. What a beautiful death; to be murdered via a crime of passion, at the hands of someone you would die for anyway. She knows full well her way of thinking when it comes to him is not healthy to say the very least. It never has been.

Holding her in place atop the barrel with his left hand gripping her small throat, he uses his right hand to remove her panties. Once he takes them off completely he tosses them away behind some more dusty old barrels.

Carolyn smiles, even though she can't breathe at all.

The pain and anger in his eyes from her words is the

satisfaction and the reaction she was searching for. James unfastens his clothes. Within seconds he's inside her.

"You are my bitch," James growls between strokes, "I don't give a damn about your husband."

"Neither do, I." Carolyn moans.

"Never say his name in my presence again," James demands, "he will only be referred to as Rupert."

"Yes sir daddy!" she screams.

"Daddy, oh daddy I love you!" she continues to scream out loudly.

"More than him..." James asks pumping harder and harder inside of her warm wet body.

"I never loved him," she moans, "I have only been in love once in my life."

"Who do you love?" he growls in her ear.

"Mr. James... Radicon!" she screams out arching her back to thrust her body towards him more.

Deeper... and deeper he continues to pleasure her; while mentally marking his territory on her precious vagina.

James picks her up. He quickly turns her around and prompts her to lean forward and grab the sides of the wine barrel. James smacks her round behind over and over again as it jiggles and begins to redden. Stepping forward James grabs hold of Carolyn's neck as he enters her body from behind.

Carolyn is damn near delirious now. She believes these two men; James and Justin are turning her into a nymphomaniac. Sex is all she ever thinks about now. And they're both so spontaneous she literally never knows when, where, or if she's going to get screwed at all.

She can't breathe or see now. She is so drunk. Her mind is playing tricks on her now. She can't focus. She has no clue, which man is behind her diving deep into her very stomach.

She panics, she tries to regain her composure, but he's way too deep now. He obviously hit something that sent her mind spiraling near temporary retardation.

"Say my name!" he growls smacking her ass again with his free hand and choking her even harder with his right hand. Carolyn doesn't respond.

"Say my name!" he demands again. "Okay I will…" she mumbles as saliva drips from the corners of her excessively wet mouth.

"Now damn it!" he bellows with finality. "I love you Justin!" she screams out.

James' face angrily contorts instantly. He pauses briefly, then he punches Carolyn hard in the back of her head. Everything goes black.

Ch. 15

"Burn in Hell"

Its late morning, and she still can't quite wake up. Her headache is throbbing intensely. Her body is sore, and her legs feel like rubber. She wants to open her eyes, but she's more than sure the light around her will be way too bright for her to stand right now. So she continues to just lie there silently, never moving a muscle.

She tries to pray several times, but God's not listening and she can't find the words anyway. She truly believes she's on her own now and that God stopped loving her and protecting her long ago. Probably around the time James Radicon became her god.

This isn't healthy she knows that. She never wanted to build up, or put stock in a relationship that she can't take to God. She's in the middle of a once secret, lust-filled, affair that has already caused unfixable damage in her life, and the lives' of others. But, she did in fact allow it all to take form in the name of love, so for that fact alone she has no regrets and would do it all again in a heartbeat if he asked her to.

Carolyn finally opens her eyes. Too much pain, the light is way too bright, she closes them again instantly. She waits. Then she opens her eyes again.

(Carolyn)

What the hell? Where am I? Did I get drunk last night? I must have gotten really, really wasted last night. My head is killing me, my body hurts like I fell down a flight of stairs or something, and I don't have a clue where I am. This room looks like it belongs to a ... teenager. And why are there so many flowers in here? Am I sick, wait... am I dying? What the hell is going on? I can't remember anything that happened last night or yesterday period. Wait... Justin, Justin was in Radicon's office... hiding in his closet. He was stealing the bank file I was in there looking for. It's under James' desk now, that's where I hid it. Oh my God... Justin and I, we had sex in James' office. What the hell was I thinking? And Ralph, my husband Ralph was there. Damn it; that's right Ralph, is trying to extort James' and the company for five million dollars. He put a gun to James' head and everything. I'm gonna kill his fat ass. Why the hell did I ever marry that man? Wait... so how did I get out of that closet?

A door opens. "Rise and shine baby girl," James says through a strange smile, "daddy is here." He sits down a tray of food near the foot of the bed. Then he walks over to Carolyn and bends down to kiss her on her confused forehead.

"Good morning baby." he says.

James pulls the covers down off of her. He's wearing nice dark Polo jeans, and a bright red shirt that reads, "Katherine's Dad." Carolyn knows his relationship with his daughter is a very sensitive subject so she decides not to say anything about the shirt.

James carefully puts the tray over her lap. Carolyn sits up a bit to survey the tray of treats. There's a bowl of

Apple Jacks cereal, a glass plate with scrambled eggs, bacon, grits, and toast. And a tall glass of orange juice.

"Eat up baby," James says through another creepy smile, "we have a lot to do today." As he heads for the door, Carolyn notices something different about the way he's walking. Just before walking out of the room he turns back to look at her. "Can I get you anything else Katie?" he asks with open eyes.

Carolyn chokes on her cereal. James rushes to her side.

"Are you okay?" he asks kneeling way down to rub her back.

"What did you call me," Carolyn asks, "just now when you were walking out what did you say?"

James smiles as he stands back up. "I said can I get you anything else Carolyn..." he tells her.

"No James you didn't," she says, "You called me Katie, as in Katherine your Fifteen-year-old daughter. I'm not her James and I think it's time you realize..."

"Don't be stupid Carolyn," he interjects angrily, "I called you *your* name. Your name is... Carolyn Olivier and that's what I called you." He quickly exits the room.

As he leaves Carolyn shakes her head. She's worried about James' emotional state, but way too hungry to stop eating. As she continues to eat she smells something foul. She leans over to look on the side of the bed where she finds a small trashcan full of her old dried up vomit. Now she knows she was drunk yesterday.

(Kayla Williams)

As she rides along in his car, she feels like she won again. She's not sure what the game is, but she knows she must be winning. As he nears the school he takes a wrong turn.

"Ralph you idiot," she yells, "don't pull up in front of the school you know better than that."

"I'm sorry baby." he says in a weak tone.

He turns the car around quickly and continues driving around the school.

"Right there..." she says pointing near a trailer on the backside of her school's building.

He parks exactly where she tells him to. She arrogantly checks her phone for any new text messages or social media notifications from her adoring fans. Then she slides her new phone that, that idiot senior bought her in her pocket. At this point she doesn't even remember the kid's name. She's trying to think of what letter it starts with as she stares at Ralph though an adorable evil grin. She reaches over and begins to kiss him with an open mouth as she rubs his fat belly. She breaks away from his embrace suddenly and opens the passenger side door.

"Ralph," she looks back at him before getting out, "you need to find a job. I told you before we got serious that I needed to be kept... and you're not keeping me anymore."

"Baby I got you," he says through a confident ugly smile, "I told you I'm about to be... No we about to be millionaires."

"You promise baby?" she asks. "I swear to you." he tells her. Then Kayla scoots back over, and then leans over in Ralph's lap to kiss him one more time before hopping out of his car.

(The University of Miami Hospital)
(Jessica Radicon)

All these rooms look and feel the same. Every nurse here talks and acts the exact same way as the others. Is this what life has become? A vacuum filled with superficial colorless inhuman robots? These people don't seem human

166

at all. It is our ability to choose and be different that makes us special... set a part as a species. But everywhere I look everybody is a slave to somebody else.

I wanted more for my children. I pray my son Lucas decides to embrace his uniqueness. I hope he has the strength to be bold, and stand out above the influence. I'm his mother I'm not blind. I knew when he was born he was different. And as he got older his father James and I both could see it. We pretended we didn't know, but we knew. Then of course we tried to hide it and subliminally change him and his way of thinking. But my son is who he is, and when I leave this hospital I'm going to go give him a big hug and a kiss. I'm going to let him know who he is, is good enough for me. He's a good, smart, handsome young man and I am more than proud of him.

His lifestyle hit his father James the hardest though I'm sure. When I was pregnant with Lucas, James used to always brag about how it was going to be raising up the heir to his own throne. He and Lucas were going to play catch, go fishing, boating, hunting, and work on cars. Most of all he used to visualize Lucas' high school graduation, and the very first time he would walk him into the winery as his top manager, and his ultimate protégé.

He always said Lucas would be better than him, I think he already is. My marriage is falling apart. I'm white... damn it I'm white and my husband is a gorgeous, rich, smart, successful business owner. I should never have to feel this way. We never have sex. He barely even looks at me anymore. I often smell her perfume on his clothing, but I never say a word, because I owe him everything. Right... I mean before him I was nothing and I had nothing. Now through him I own the world, or at   least *it feels like it. I was destined to marry some factory worker, or some abusive, ignorant, redneck… but James Raymond Radicon swept me off my feet and landed me in a dream world fit only for a queen… his queen.*

The door opens. "Baby, what's going on?" James asks approaching Jessica's bed. He quickly throws his jacket on the chair next to her hospital bed. "I don't know hunny." she replies. James kneels down to kiss her pale, thin, pink lips.

"Jessica you're crying baby," he acknowledges, "you must know something. What have they said?" "They haven't said anything yet," she says, "but the fact that I'm still here is telling me more than I want to know."

James kneels down close again one by one he begins to softly kiss each one of her tears away. From the bottom of her chin, back up to her lips, and up to her gorgeous aging eyes her tears are guiding his careful lips like a translucent treasure trail.

"James…" she whispers in his ear.

"Yeah babe…" he replies.

"We used to be so damn good together, didn't we?" she asks.

"Hell yes Jessie," he says moving back to look in her eyes, "we still are baby."

The uneasy stillness in her wise gray eyes tells him just how wrong he is.

"What is that look, Jessica," he asks, "what's   wrong? What did I do?"

"Oh James baby," she cries, "my beautiful, beautiful James. I knew, I always knew there was no way in hell I was going to be that girl forever."

"What girl Jess, what the hell are you talking about baby?" he asks.

"That young girl that stole your heart away all those years ago," she tells him, "back when you vowed that if there was only going to be one lifelong faithful man on God's Earth… it would be you."

"I meant every word Jessica." he swears.

"Yes," she replies, "it was in your eyes. I knew you meant every word back then. But that was before the two kids, cellulite, menopause, and the fifty strands of gray in my withering old head."

"Baby," he leans in closer, "don't say that. And don't use words like withering, it makes you sound…"

"Old," she interjects calmly, "I am James, and so are you.

"We are both getting older, but *you* are a different beast. You, you transcend time, age, and even love. You possess the type of genetic makeup that will allow you to be to any and everybody whatever you want to be to them at any given moment. So in the end… I lose."

"Jess… What the hell are you talking about?" he asks stepping away from her.

She's trying to stop crying, but she can't. Sometimes when your heart has been truly broken, it just feels good to cry your eyes out until you have no tears left to give. That hurt… that undeniable gut wrenching pain defines us as people and it forces our hand to know full well that we are alive. We try to take and accept the good embedded in the bad, but that pain is definite and deafening… who among us can find the good in that?

"Jess," James says, "get out of your head and talk to me. What's going on, what are you losing baby girl?" James begins to cry himself.

"You," she says, "I lost you the moment you saw her. I don't know who she is, and it doesn't matter, but all I do know is that I've become a lonely, foolish, old housewife who toils each loveless day away just like the one before. You don't love me anymore James." Jessica's red face is covered in useless tears. She cries out with deep pain.

James rushes to her.

"Baby what's wrong... What hurts?" he asks. She shakes her strawberry blond and gray streaked head. "Baby," James says, "Jess, baby I can't help you if I don't know what hurts."

"My heart," she says, "you broke my heart James Radicon... And you can't save me. I won't divorce you or take you to court. I don't want your money. All I ask is that you give me a nice burial. Bury me next to..."

"Shut up Jessica," he explodes wiping his salty tears away, "You are not dead, and you are not dying."

"James," she says with knowing eyes, "you still haven't dealt with..."

"Jessica," James grabs his jacket off the nearby chair, "I asked you to **shut the hell up**! No one is dying, and no one is going to die."

"People die James..." she cries.

"No they don't, not on my watch, and you are not going to die anytime soon." he tells her.

Jessica smiles a defeated smile.

"You can't save me James," she tells him honestly through her sad smile, "you can't save me or Katherine. Go to that woman. Go, go now. Run back to that woman you love. She is the only one who can save you and bring you to the truth."

James doesn't respond. He puts his hat on, pulls the brim down tight, and walks out of his wife's hospital room never knowing if he'll ever see her beautiful, pale, tear stained face again.

(Hours later)

Marvin Gaye is blasting on the radio. All the sheets are on the floor along with the pillows and their clothes. The bed is rocking steadily. This room hasn't seen this much action since the last time she snuck over here. If only the walls in the Olivier's bedroom could talk. The whole world would only pretend to cover their ears. The deceit, lust, and infidelity that live and breathe in this room have taken on a demonic life of their own. A love affair this wrong can only end in hell fire and brimstone.

Kayla's legs are high in the air. Her knees are pinned down by her ears. Ralph is on top of her, inside of her pumping as hard as his inconvenient belly will allow him to.

"Did you make sure my kids were asleep?" Ralph moans.

"Yes baby, yes baby yes!" she screams.

"I love you Kayla." he moans.

"Who's the baddest bitch on the planet..." she asks.

"You are..." he moans.

"Say my name," she begs, "Say it baby please... Tell me. Who is the baddest bitch on the planet?"

"You are," he moans trying to concentrate on not finishing, "Kayla... Kayla Williams. You are the baddest bitch on the planet."

"Who's the prettiest?" she screams.

"Kayla..." he moans.

"Who got the fattest ass?"

"Kayla..." he moans again.

"Who's the hottest bitch baby?" she asks.

"Kayla..." he moans yet again.

"Who has the best pussy..." she screams.

"Hot..." he moans.

"What?" Kayla frowns at him.

"Hot…" he repeats.

"No Ralph you idiot," she yells, "We already did the hottest bitch. I said…"

"No," he interjects between his weak strokes, "it's really hot in here. You don't feel that? And I can hear the kids crying in the front. Something is wrong… I think the house…"

"Oh shut up," Kayla demands spreading her legs even more, "you better not cum before me, or you ain't gettin' none for a whole month."

"I'm telling you baby," he moans, "Something ain't right. I think I smell smoke. What if Carolyn came home? Just let me go check."

He tries to pull out. She quickly pulls him back down.

"So what you just gone run to her," Kayla screams,

"hell no, you belong to me keep hittin' this good shit." Ralph continues to stroke obediently.

The smoke in the room is way too thick to ignore now.

"What the hell…" Kayla says.

"What," Ralph says between pumps, "I didn't cum bae…"

"Not that you fool," she yells trying not cough, "look by the door. It's a whole bunch of smoke."

Wham!!! Something heavy slams against the bedroom door. They both jump. The crying in the front room is much louder now.

"Get off me fool!" Kayla screams.

"Go see what the hell is going on out there." she tells him.

Ralph falls clumsily to the floor in a coughing fit. He hastily pulls on his raggedy old sweat pants, still coughing heavily.

"I have asthma…" he tells her.

"I don't give a damn," Kayla yells, "go see who just hit the door like that!"

He obeys.

After finally reaching the door Ralph tries to open it, but it's stuck.

"It won't open!" he yells.

"I think the house is on fire," he continues, "and we're stuck baby!"

Wham!!! Something else heavy falls in the front room. The crying stops immediately. Kayla stands up on the bed completely naked.

Ralph races back to the bed for some running room. Then he rushes back at the door full speed. **Bam!!!** His shoulder feels like its crushed now, and the door is still stuck. He tries again with his other shoulder. **Bam!!!** Same result. Kayla is coughing nonstop now due to the heavy smoke.

"Baby get me the fuck out of here I'm scared!" Kayla screams.

Ralph is in position to try to break the door down once more. This time he races full speed at the door head first.

Crash!!! His head and upper body break through the door this time, but Ralph is knocked out cold. The smoke is upon Kayla now like a dark heavy blanket. Her coughs are constant and painful.

Through the door Kayla can now see the huge flames engulfing the front of the house. They seem to be growing by the second. "Ralph!!!" she screams. He doesn't respond.

"God, please save me!" she screams. The flames begin to engulf Ralph's bloody head and body. Kayla is screaming and crying in full force now.

"Ralph," she exclaims, "Ralph wake up baby you're burning."

The smoke is even worse now, and the flames are only getting bigger. Kayla can't think straight. But she knows if she stands here on this bed she is going to die just like Ralph and the babies.

She jumps down off the bed still completely naked. She can't see a damn thing now. She tries to open the bedroom window first. She soon notices its nailed shut from the outside.

She tries to feel her way to the bedroom door. The fire is blocking her path out of the room. She steps back and then dashes forward through the door way. She immediately trips over Ralph's dead, burning, body and some other unseen object. Then she falls face first into the scorching flames.

Ahhh!!! Kayla screams out, but no sound ever leaves her deceitful teenage throat. She pulls herself up covered in flames from head to toe now. She races to the front door screaming aloud now. She opens the door and falls out on the front porch. With one last valiant effort Kayla crawls out on the front lawn and begins to roll around.

"Lay still." a voice says from nearby. Kayla's body is completely numb now; as a traumatized neighbor puts the remaining flames on her nude body out with his garden hose. Everything goes completely black.

James' blood is ice cold now. Suddenly everything that felt so right, just took an unbelievably bad turn. James turns around and looks solemnly at the backseat of his black SUV parked just down the street from the house. He shakes his head and begins to say a silent prayer.

There's nothing left that he can possibly do to change what he's already done; using one of his gloved hands to sit one of the large empty cans of kerosene on the floor of the passenger side of his SUV, James quickly drives off.

Ch. 16

"Atlanta"

An hour later James swerves into the driveway of his mansion. He cuts the car off as he tries to c a l m his nerves. He's no longer just an accomplice to the murder Carolyn committed in Los Angeles. He's now a killer himself. He killed a grown man, and a teenage girl. He steps out of his SUV both of his feet feel numb as they touch the ground. Everything around him looks... Well normal. He smiles. Nothing has changed. He killed people and his world has not ended. Everything is going to be fine.

James sticks his key in his front door's keyhole, but before he can turn it, the door opens from the inside.

"Carolyn," he says, "What are you doing out of bed baby?" She doesn't respond.

James reads her face.

"My wife," he whispers, "she came back? Is she here now?"

"No James," Carolyn says, "Don't worry your precious Jessica didn't come home while you were gone. Although, I did enjoy that *fucking shrine* you have dedicated to her in your bedroom."

Wham!!! James slaps her hard to the floor.

"Damn it," he kneels down to pick her back up, "I'm sorry baby. You just catch me off guard with your..."

"With my what James," she asks, "with my **words**? Because that's what they are James, just words. You may be able to spend countless hours with me, and fuck me on a daily basis, and never even begin to feel **anything** real for me. But I'm not you; I am a female. We're built differently."

"How so…" James asks.

"How so…" Carolyn repeats.

"You know what James," she stands back up to her feet, "I am not going to do this with you." James grabs her hand.

"Do what?" he asks. She snatches away from him.

"This," she says, "all this stupid shit. James… Damn it… I love you. And don't worry I realize exactly how stupid that really is. My mama… She didn't tell me not to continue talking to you, but she did warn me that you… Or me… wanting you could very well be a dead end."

"Baby loving me is never a dead end for you…" James tells her with open arms.

"I'm not stupid James!" she yells. "I know you're not stupid baby," he tells her, "you're special that's why I…"

Carolyn laughs a very painful laugh aloud. She shakes her head at him.

"Boy you can't even say it," she tells him, "love… Love James. It's simple, its only four letters. You can't say it to me now, and you never will, because it's a lie. You do not love me and you never will."

She steps back from him. He never takes his watery eyes off of her.

"You see James," she seductively lifts up his XXL t-shirt that's she's wearing, "you love this ass. You love my vagina. You love how seductive and submissive I can be…

You love the way I suck you, massage you, and bite you... You love the idea of me. But baby... You do not love me."

James drops his head.

"I'm sorry." he mumbles.

"What? I can't hear you." Carolyn leans in.

"I said I'm sorry." he repeats a bit louder this time.

"For what James," she asks, "sorry for not loving me? Don't be sorry baby... No, I'll be fine I have a husband, my own husband, that..."

James feels his heart start to race.

"Carolyn about Ralph..." he starts.

"No," she interjects, "let me finish. Ralph, my husband isn't perfect. He may not look as good as you, be as rich, or as smart as you... But he can take me to the movies or out to eat on his arm and feel proud. He can stand there and know that I... his wife am a gorgeous black woman. I'm black James, my pigment ain't going anywhere. I'm black now, and I'ma be black again tomorrow. Come into the present you redneck! Its 2015 nobody cares about color anymore. There are interracial couples everywhere; they look good together and they make beautiful babies. But you don't have to worry about all that. You already have the precious wife that you always dreamed of... your perfect Jessica. Me, I'm just a toy you play with to keep life going... Just to make sure your blood's still flowing. Go to her James, go to your precious Jessica she's the only one that can save you."

James smiles at the familiar idea. "Did I say something funny Mr. Radicon?" she asks.

"Yeah," he laughs lightly, "you said that... Jessica is the only person who can save me."

"Yeah so..." Carolyn replies.

"It's funny because, she said the same thing about you." he tells her.

Carolyn tries to remain composed even though she suddenly feels awkward and foolish. She leans to the right balancing most of her weight on her almost steady right leg.

"Why... Why would your wife say that?" Carolyn asks. James laughs again.

"It's the funniest thing," he says, "She said that because, she knows with every fiber of her being just like I do that... I love you Carolyn Olivier."

Her heart stops. Her mouth is completely dry now. She can't move. She will never in a million years get that moment back. James Radicon just said that he loves her, Carolyn Olivier for the very first time ever and she can't utter a word. He's standing there silently waiting. She knows she has to say something, anything.

"Police..." she says.

"What where?" James ducks quickly near the front door.

"No not now," she says, "while you were gone two detectives came by looking for you."

"What did they want?" he asks standing back to his numb feet.

"They were from L.A. James," she says, "we're under investigation for Patrick Brown's murder."

"Atlanta." he says.

"What..." she replies?

"We're going to Atlanta for two days. We need time to figure things out." James explains.

"What about my kids and my husband James," she asks, "What am I supposed to tell them?"

"Damn it Carolyn we're flying to Atlanta tonight!" he barks with finality.

"Yes sir." she submits.

James pulls his cell phone out of his pocket and scrolls through it looking for a specific number.

"Hello yes, this is the Miami International Airport right," he asks, "I do apologize, but your accent made it hard for me to understand you sir. I understand. Yes, well in any event... I need two round trip tickets to Atlanta, Georgia." He pauses. "Within the next hour," James says, "okay great." James laughs. "No, that won't be necessary this is James Radicon and I could care less what the tickets cost. Book em'... Awesome! Thank you Fidel, my... *Girlfriend*, my *black* girlfriend and I... will be there shortly."

Carolyn smiles at the thought of being James' actual girlfriend.

"Oh James..." Carolyn says.

"What," he replies, "What did I do wrong now?"

"Nothing baby," she says, "it's just I don't have any clothes for this trip. I'm gonna have to go home first."

"Nonsense," he says with an arrogant, handsome, grin on his face, "you'll buy whatever you need or want in Atlanta. That what this is for." He hands her a card.

"James," she gasps, "this card has my name on it."

"Yeah, I know baby." he heads up the stairs.

"But James," she yells up the stairs, "this is a *black card*..."

He smiles down at her from over the stair rail.

"The woman in my life should never have limits to anything she does," he says, "especially spending my money."

He spins around and disappears into his bedroom.

(The Miami International Airport)

A million different scenarios are running through James Radicon's mind as he races to the Miami International Airport. He's a murderer. He's a criminal and not just in California anymore. He just pulled a home invasion and grand arson in Miami. In L.A. he was guilty of grand theft auto, reckless endangerment, and he was accomplice to murder among other assorted crimes. The charges just keep piling up. If he gets caught, he knows not even his massive bank accounts can save him.

But somehow as he looks over at the angel sleeping next to him in the passenger side of 2015 Mercedes Benz coupe he knows everything is gonna be okay. And even if he does get caught he believes the time he's had with Carolyn Olivier is worth any punishment a judge might slap him with. James like Carolyn always believed a love like this only exists in fairytales. And it's still not perfect, nor will it ever be. But he said it... out loud. He can't believe he actually confessed his true feelings for Carolyn to her.

(James)

Telling Carolyn, I love her was something I never planned to do. Because now I can be held accountable for everything I do, because mutual feelings have been established. I wasn't going to say it... Damn it. She forced my hand, she was pushing me to Jess, and Jess was pushing me to her... But in the end and from the moment our eyes met it has been and will always be Carolyn. She is my true heart. But I can't let her weaken me. I can't allow her to build up too much confidence. She's too powerful already. The woman is unreal. She's an absolute monster in the business world. I don't even wanna know how many other companies are trying   to steal my talented little protégé from me. And she's never been quite just a protégé to me has she? I don't mean the sex; I mean she listens to me. She listens to everything I say and teach her in respect to business. Carolyn soaks it all up like an unquenchable sponge; she's doesn't just mimic me and the things I teach her. She goes back and studies what I show her, she researches, analyzes, breaks it all down, and then brings my teachings and philosophies back to me much more improved than they ever were before. Got damn it! The woman is an angel... an absolute Godsend to me. But now you see it's a whole different ball game. With love in the mix everything changes. She's going to expect more from me, she's definitely going to hold me to a much higher standard now, as she should. But it won't end well for her or her heart. The last thing I want to do by any means, is hurt Carolyn, but what choice do I have? I am almost forty years old. My personality for all practical purposes was set at the age of nine. I have not changed my thinking much since then. I have grown and just become more and more like my father the great Raymond Radicon. God how I idolized that man. And when he died I... Damn it! My father was a pioneer in sustaining one's wealth; not only for his own lifetime but for the next generation to come as well. He always said, "Image is everything and perception sadly will always be reality. When you're rich what people think you are from the outside is what you are. He told me what you do doesn't matter; the only thing that does matters is what people think you do. You'll never be able to change that. So keep a clean nose. Have a beautiful, presentable, respectable wife, and always keep her happy."

He loved Jessica, he said I chose well. I can't disappoint him now. Damn it, I'm crying again. I don't want to ever lull Carolyn into a false sense of security because I know and she knows she will never be my actual wife. She'll never bear the name Radicon. Jessica is my wife and she always will be.

(Lucas Radicon)

The Regal Cinemas South Beach Stadium 18 Movie Theater at 1120 Lincoln Road in Miami is filled to capacity this afternoon. Everybody is here to see the new "Teenage Mutant Ninja Turtles" movie. Lucas would have preferred to watch the comedy "Let's Be Cops," but sitting there in the top row next to that empty seat he knows he made the right choice. He's not as nervous as he thought he would be, but he's extremely nervous just the same. He's wiped the sweat from his forehead, checked his breath, and secretly smelled his armpits a thousand times since entering the lobby of the theater tonight. He wanted to stop at the concessions counter on the way in, but he was too afraid to say anything. He didn't want to say the wrong thing or seem awkward, so he just remained silent. He sees him coming back. As he takes one step at a time up the mighty steps of this glorious theater; Lucas is locked in on not only Calvin, but the beautiful purple aura that surrounds him. Lucas believes this man child is a god in the flesh. Lucas realizes he has to stop staring now, because even though it is rather dark in the theater; Calvin is almost close enough to be able to tell that Lucas is staring at him.

"Okay," Calvin says with a comforting grin, "Sour Patch kids, popcorn, nachos and cheese, **and** an extra-large blueberry icee." Lucas laughs.

"Shut up Calvin." he says.

"What," Calvin smiles.

"They don't sell extra-large icee's." Lucas says.

"They do now," Calvin says, "I made em' create one especially for you. Look at the cup." Lucas studies his cup.

"This is a popcorn container Calvin." Lucas says.

"Exactly Skywalker," Calvin says, "and I guarantee you, that big ass cup is way bigger than any icee cup ever was." They both laugh.

"Hey, be quiet back there!" a guy two rows in front of them says.

"Hey, you better shut the hell up before I make you!" Calvin barks back to the man.

The man turns back around towards Calvin.

Calvin stands up. The man looks up at Calvin's gargantuan size, and immediately turns back around quietly.

"Faggots." the man mumbles.

"What you say, you fat mother fucker!" Calvin jumps back up; Lucas pulls him back.

"Calvin sit down; the movie is starting. Forget him." Lucas pleads.

Calvin looks down into Lucas' soothing eyes. He hesitates. Then finally he obediently sits back down.

(The Hartsfield-Jackson Atlanta Airport)

As the almost happy couple exits the Atlanta airport hand in hand, they are pleased to walk out and find the temperature much better than they expected.

"Let's find a cab." James surveys the area.

"Lead the way…" she sighs happily. He smiles down at her.

"Where do you want to go first baby," he asks, "are you hungry or do you wanna shop first?"

Carolyn looks down at her outfit, and then back at James.

"Shopping." they both say in unison. James laughs.

"I don't know Carolyn I kinda like the way you look now." he says in jest.

"Yeah right," she replies, "I am not walking around Atlanta wearing your wife's "Say No to Obama" sweat suit."

They both burst into loud jubilant laughter as they continue down the sidewalk in front of the airport in search of a taxi. People around them are genuinely intrigued and impressed by their adorable exchange. Some of them are even a little jealous of how happy they seem to be.

"Do you know how stupid I look right now?" Carolyn says still laughing joyfully.

"Yes," James says, "I know exactly how stupid you look right now." They laugh again as James signals a cab driver to pull over.

They get in. "Take us to the **W**, please ma'am." James tells the driver.

"A female cabbie huh…" James leans forward.

"Yes Sir Mr. Radicon," the driver says, "been driving twenty years now."

James looks at Carolyn. She shrugs her shoulders.

"That's impressive," Radicon replies, "But how do you know…"

"Your name," she interjects, "everyone knows your name James. Most people are just afraid of ya."

"What," James laughs, "That's not true…" He looks at Carolyn again.

She drops her gorgeous hazel eyes.

"Baby…" James looks intently at Carolyn.

"Is that true?" he asks

"Well, hell yeah it's true," the cabbie interjects, "she ain't gonna say it, bless her heart she's probably scared of you too."

"I'm having a conversation with my girlfriend thank you," James tells her, "Baby... Are people scared of me?"

Carolyn still can't look James in his eyes.

"It ain't all bad," the cabbie says, "it's kinda like a gift and a curse I guess you could say. People fear you Radicon, but they fear you because they respect who you are. Well, at least who they think you are."

"And what the hell does that mean?" he asks.

"Well," the driver replies, "let's just say from your television, radio, and magazine interviews you just don't seem like somebody who should be messed with. See Radicon, you're like the Grinch, except you're rich, and much, much prettier." Carolyn laughs briefly. And then she quickly focuses her attention outside of her window. James stares at her anxiously.

"Carolyn," he says, "Say something, damn it!"

"My phone has been dead for like two days now." Carolyn says with a pleasant smirk on her face.

"You can charge it when we get to the hotel," he tells her, "but wait, why are you smiling. Don't you want your phone to be functioning?"

"Oh yeah," Carolyn says, "Of course I want my phone to function. Who doesn't? It's just..."

"Just what baby?" James asks.

"The W..." the Cabbie announces as she pulls up to the front door.

"Fine," James climbs out of the car, "wait here. We'll be right back down."

James and Carolyn check in the hotel and carry their bags up to their room. Carolyn plugs her phone up before she and James exit the room and head back down to the cab.

"You know what's crazy about the cell phone situation James?" Carolyn asks.

"What babe?" he replies.

"Well," she says," my phone has been dead plenty of times before… but this time was different."

"What do you mean Carolyn?" James asks.

"Well," she starts, "I've been with you or at least at your house for the better part of the past forty-eight hours and my dead phone never even crossed my mind until now."

"Yeah so…" James replies.

"Don't you see baby," she grabs his big warm hand, "When I'm with you… in your presence, nothing else in the world matters outside of us."

James kisses her full lips with his eyes focused on hers.

"So I'm all you need huh?" he asks with his forehead lightly pressed against hers.

"Yes Sir Mr. Radicon," she says, "I could totally exist in a world that only revolved around you and making you as happy as your pretty ass makes me." She giggles.

"I'm not pretty little girl, I'm handsome…" he joins in her laughter.

"Now that is just cute as hell ain't it Mr. Radicon?" the cab driver watches them nosily in her rear view mirror. They ignore her.

"You ready to shop until you can't feel your feet love?" he asks her with a genuine smile.

"I can't feel my feet now," she laughs, "you got me floating on cloud 9 constantly James Radicon. Tell me this is really real. Tell me this not some magnificent dream that one of my kids or Ralph's fat ass is going to rudely wake me out of."

James kisses her. Then he holds her faces gazing into the hazel clearness of her two gorgeous eyes.

"Everything you feel, hear, and see right now is very real," he assures her pouty face, "but I will warn you Carolyn... it's only going to get more unbelievable."

"Well of course it is," the cabbie interjects again, "you're richer than God and well, she's your whore. It's your civic duty to spoil her life away..."

"Lady, shut the hell up," James fumes pounding both of his clenched fists down hard on the seat, "are we at Saks yet?"

"Told you," the driver mumbles, "mean as a rattle snake."

"What was that cabbie?" he barks.

"I said yes sir; we're pulling up at Saks now." the driver tells him.

James pays the woman and conveniently forgets to tip her. She looks down at how much cash James handed her.

"I told you, mean as the Grinch." the cab driver says through her window as she drives off.

"That wasn't nice James." Carolyn says.

"What..." he replies.

"You should have tipped her." Carolyn says.

"Well she should learn to shut the hell up." he tells her.

"I guess..." Carolyn sighs as they walk along the sidewalk towards a few stores. James takes her left hand in his right hand and intertwines his fingers with hers. Her heart is really racing now.

(Carolyn)
Does he know people can see us? Well of course he does its broad daylight outside. Wow. I could live every

second of the rest of my life walking with this man, in this moment, just like this. My feet, my hands, and my heart would never get tired. Hint, hint Lord... Make this man, my man... My forever!

"James..." she says.

"Yes Carolyn." he replies.

"Should we go get something to eat first?" she asks.

"I'm fine for now darling," he says, "besides I have plans to eat you all night..."

"Oh..." she smiles.

He smiles down at her.

She blushes and looks in the opposite direction.

"Are you always gonna be this perfect?" Carolyn asks James.

"Uh," he says, "for as long as I wake up every morning with only you on my mind and go to sleep every night praying I dream about you."

Carolyn blushes again.

"You coulda just said forever..." she teases.

"*You coulda just said forever,*" he mocks playfully, "that's not my style. I don't ever wanna give you the watered down version of anything Carolyn... especially not my love."

(Back in Miami)

(Justin Tolls)

The Miami sunshine is beaming in through the front windshield of Justin Tolls' newest addition to his fleet of luxury cars. When he left his second home this morning he had a lot on his mind. His mission, his career, and his inevitable future were all forcing him to look at himself under a very fine microscope. He'd give every dime in his offshore bank accounts to just have an easier route to becoming a loved, valued, accepted part of his biological family. He's naturally a sweet person who would never purposely harm or sabotage anyone's life or career, but his grandfather does not take no for an answer.

He's fully aware that without his wealthy old grandfather he would have nothing. And if he falls from the old man's grace that's exactly what Mr. Tolls is going to have, absolutely nothing. It's crossed his mind several times to just go to his father one on one and tell him the truth. But he knows better. There's way too much doubt in his mind to take a huge chance like that, instantly risking losing everything he's worked so hard for. Plus, he owes his grandfather; the old man spent some major cash bailing him out of jail three years ago. He kept him from going to prison for a very long time. In total the old man spent about twenty grand to buy Justin out of his lengthy prison sentence and basically clear his record completely. Not easy to do for a half black kid in South Miami who committed a string of high profile robberies. Justin is dressed comfortably today as he rides along the back roads of South Beach. He's a huge fan of Michael Jordan apparel. He owns hundreds of pairs of Jordan shoes. He has on black and blue Space Jam retro 11 Jordan shoes, matching socks, black Jordan basketball shorts, a blue Jordan shirt, and a matching hat. On his wrist he has a large rose gold and diamond Rolex custom watch.

As he nears his destination he's fully aware that the news he has to deliver is not going to make for a good visit. His grandfather is likely going to punish him. He wonders more and more if maybe his conscious is causing him to purposely fail the majority of the mission's his grandfather has given him lately.

He parks his car in the driveway. He hesitates. Then he repositions his rear view mirror so that he can look   at himself. He stares into his own faded blue eyes, wondering deeply what life would have been like if his father's side of the family had wanted him all those years ago. Obviously things would have been much different. Justin's mother Katrice knew exactly who his father was, but she absolutely refused to tell him. Justin found out the truth on his own.

He opens his car door and steps out onto the pavement. He closes the door and makes his way to the strange front door of the mansion. It's made mostly of stained glass. Since the first time Justin saw the strange door almost three years ago, he has never really understood it. It appears to him; that a group of evil spirits are circling over the unsuspecting heads of Mary and the baby Jesus just waiting to swoop down and devour them.

The door opens to reveal a gorgeous black woman in her seventies. She dressed in fine black linen pants and a matching shirt. Her sandals are open at the top as they reveal her well-kept feet.

"Ms. Dee…" Justin gushes as he reaches out to hug her.

"Hello Justin baby." She hugs the handsome young man tightly.

"How you feeling today?" he asks her.

"I'm doing good love, how are you?" she replies.

"I don't know yet," he whispers, "what kind of mood is he in today?"

Ms. Dee hesitates as she looks over her shoulder towards the winding staircase.

"I think he's okay," she says, "been kinda quiet all day. He's been waiting to hear from you…"

"I know Ms. Dee, but I…" he starts.

"It's, okay baby," she interjects, "you never have to explain yourself to me. Explain to your grandfather he'll understand. You'll be fine I'm sure…"

"Well at least one of us is." Justin replies bleakly.

"You'll be fine love," Ms. Dee tells him, "he's upstairs in bed. Go see him."

Justin takes each one of the pristine white step very slowly as he tries to figure out exactly what he's going to tell the old millionaire.

As he finally reaches the top of the stairs he notices the door to the master bedroom is already open. He walks in slowly.

"Justin…" the old man says.

"Yes grandpa…" he replies. "Do you have the Radicon bank file?"

"No sir Master I don't." Justin says dropping his head somberly.

(Saks 5th, Atlanta)

After taking Carolyn on a luxurious two-hour shopping spree, James is starving. "I don't understand." Carolyn says as James open the back door of the Louis Vuitton store for her. "Oh," he says, "leaving out of the back door has nothing to do with you love. We spent a considerable amount of cash just now; and as a courtesy to us the store manager is allowing us to leave through the back just in case someone was in there watching us with ill intentions."

"That's not what I was talking about James," she says, "but now that you mention it I did find our exit strange."

"I'm sorry baby, what is it that you don't understand?" he asks.

"Well," she starts, "you gave me a black card…"

"I did," he replies, "You still have it right?"

"Of course." she replies as they walk around the back of some more stores. "Good." James says.

"But what's the point of having it baby," she asks, "everything we bought today you paid for it. I never had to swipe my card once."

James laughs as he holds her hand tightly.

"Your black card is for you to spoil yourself when I am not around love," he says, "but when I'm with you I'm going to do all the spoiling myself."

"I love you James," she says, "So when are the stores supposed to deliver the rest of the items I picked out to the hotel?"

"Probably in the morning love," he says, "it's almost closing time now."

A stranger bumps into James abruptly.

"Watch where you're walking asshole..." James barks at the much younger man.

"Sure thing pops." the young hooded black man says.

He's with two other hooded men, one white and one black.

"Damn, your girl has a fat ass." the guy says looking at Carolyn as she and James start to walk away.

James let's go of Carolyn's hand and spins around with vicious intent. He quickly hands her all the bags.

"James, don't," she says, "There are three of them. Can we please just go to the hotel?"

He can't hear a word she's saying.

"What the fuck did you just say punk?" James asks the man, who doesn't appear to be backing down from the much larger James at all.

"I said your girl has a fat ass." he repeats.

As James walks closer to the man, his two friends step up by his side.

"Dude," the white guy says, "this is James Radicon."

"James who…" the second black hooded man asks.

"The wine dude…" the white guy says.

The first guy looks back at his white friend with a crooked smile.

"Billionaire James Radicon…" he asks.

"Hell yeah, bro!" the hooded white man exclaims.

"James let's go baby…" Carolyn pleads pulling him by his left arm.

"Carolyn," he says, "I will never tolerate anyone disrespecting you. These punks couldn't take me if there were five of them."

"It's, okay baby," she says, "it was a compliment. He said I have a nice body."

"Na," the first hooded man says, "I was saying you a fine ass bitch and I wanna fuck you."

At this she steps back calmly shaking her head.

James hastily snatches his polo shirt off. Once he gets the shirt over his head he finds three guns pointing at him.

"You fucking cowards…" James says.

"Shut up gramps," the first gunman says, "let me get it."

"Get what?" James asks.

"Don't be smart, fuck face," the man says, "everything, let me get everything you got!"

One of the hooded men walks towards Carolyn.

James turns around.

"If you touch her…" James says.

The second one cocks his gun and puts it to James' head.

"If you move," he says, "I'll blow you pretty white head off."

While James is held at gun point the white robber snatches his wallet out of his back pocket and puts it in his own pocket.

"Come here bro." the first robber tells his white friend.

"What we got here," the white man asks, "oh some Louis Vuitton gear. I can get off all this tonight."

"Shut up man!" the first gunman barks at him.

"What Doug..." the white robber says.

"Nigga you just said my name," the first gunman says after slapping his friend hard in the face.

"Man," the first robber says, "both of ya'll take her bags and her purse and go wait for me at the spot."

The other two gunmen obey as they quickly run off with Carolyn's purse, as well as her new clothes and shoes.

The lone gunman points his gun at James, and then reaches behind Carolyn and squeezes her behind.

"Nice..." he smiles at James.

He searches her and only finds her black card. Then he spends a little extra time rudely checking her empty back pockets.

"That's enough man!" James yells walking towards the man calmly with both hands high in the air.

The gunman begins to back away from Carolyn.

"You got everything we had," James continues, "unless you plan on killing us can you please just run along behind your little friends. Have a little heart man..."

"This ain't **The Little House on the Prairie, Gomer Pyle**..." the robber says.

"It's two different shows." James says.

"What you say *white boy*?" the robber asks stepping closer.

"Its two totally different television shows," James explains, "The character Gomer Pyle, was played by an actor named Jim Nabors, he became famous on the "**Andy Griffith show**," not "**The Little House on the Prairie**," that was Michael Landon who played..."

"Shut up *cracker*," the robber says with his finger still on the trigger, "damn lady you sure know how to pick em'. This crazy white dude is trying to debate about old ass T.V. shows while he's gettin' his ass robbed..."

BAM!!! James catches the robber off guard and punches him hard in the face.

The robber falls back on his behind and quickly pulls the trigger in a panic.

Carolyn swears when the shot was fired she saw sparks and fiery lightning fly from the barrel of the robber's gun as her entire life flashed before her eyes.

James and Carolyn both fall hard to the ground.

The robber jumps up and runs out into the street. After forcing a couple of motorists to stop as he weaved through the oncoming traffic the criminal disappeared in the distance.

James and Carolyn are both still lying on the ground completely still.

(Lucas Radicon)

The radio is loud enough to hear, but nowhere near as loud as it usually is in Lucas' fire red BMW coupe; and for once he's riding on the passenger side of his car. If his dad knew Lucas let anybody else drive his new car, he would kill him mercilessly. Well, probably not, but he would at least ground him for a week.

But Calvin isn't just anybody, he's special.

Back to the music. Lucas' speakers are always blaring some new song as loud as they possibly can. And why not, music is the soundtrack of our lives and car speakers serve as teenager's most useful device to ruin their hearing at an early age. Lucas reaches forward to turn the volume down a bit more.

The music is low now, but they both can still hear it faintly as they ride along and it doesn't matter that the music is uncharacteristically low because they're both lost in their own deep thoughts anyway.

Ah, deep teenage thoughts like; what socks am I gonna wear to match my shoes tomorrow, or I wonder if Nicki Minaj has to get her butt implant redone once a year. As the beautiful red coupe turns into Calvin's hood, and I do mean *hood*, Lucas' face changes a bit.

His smile has faded and his forehead and armpits are increasingly moist. He stares out of the passenger window as if he's a tourist riding through a jungle, gazing fearfully out of a safari jeep at dangerous, rare, wild animals. Everything Luke thinks he sees appears so alien to him. The obvious poverty is mind numbing.

Luke looks over at Calvin, Cal smiles down at his frightened friend.

"You good in the hood white boy," Calvin assures him, "you with the king."

"Don't, call me white boy, you fake ass LeBron," Lucas teases, "and what do you mean you're the king?"

"Fake LeBron," Cal smiles, "boy you better get a copy of my issue of Sports Illustrated ASAP Skywalker... They said I'm gonna be better than dude. Don't get it twisted, that's my idol... but I could take Bron one on one any day."

"I bet you'd like that." Luke mumbles.

"What you say Skywalker..." Cal asks.

"I said what makes you the king?" Luke lies.

"I'm the ruler of my kingdom," Cal says, "Look around you Skywalker. Ain't nothing out here. I came from *nothing* and I ain't sposed to *never* be *nothing*. But I am... I'm next up. I'm Calvin Ridgefield. I'm the only hope these people got Luke. Once I become a huge star I can come back and help… and change things around here you know? But if I fail…"

"You won't fail." Luke tells him.

Calvin pulls up in front of his apartment building.

"I hope not." Cal replies solemnly, putting the car in park.

"How can you," Lucas says, "no other high school player, or college player for that matter is gonna be recruited harder than you next year. You're guaranteed to be an instant star bro."

"Bro…" Calvin turns to look at Lucas.

"Yeah," Luke says battling hard not to blush noticeably, "we're bros right?"

"Yeah Skywalker, we're bros."

Calvin extends his left hand to Luke. They do their secret hand shake, and just as their hands lock in the final sequence of the handshake, Cal pulls Lucas to him. He hugs him tightly.

"Man, honestly I don't know what this is," Calvin holds Lucas close, "I'm confused about a lot of things… but, you Skywalker you're not one of those things. You are the best and truest friend I've ever had. You're pretty cool for a white boy."

Lucas pushes himself away from Calvin as they both laugh.

"I'm cool period." Luke tells him.

They spend the next three hours parked right there, lost in conversation, deep thought, and most notably each other.

(Atlanta)

As Carolyn lays there in the warm uncomfortable liquid, she can't hear or see a thing.

(Carolyn)

Am I dead or alive? I can't see anything. It's so dark, what the hell is this? Wait... is this Hell? I can't move, if nothing else I must be paralyzed, I can't feel anything except the wetness beneath my head. I must be in a coma. Damn it! I'm obviously dead or at least extremely fucked up... and the only thing I can think about is the fact that some other woman is going to take my James away from me. My eyes are closed. Wait, I think I can... The sky, it's so clear. Only a few stars are visible. I can feel my legs, and now my arms... wait I'm shaking. Why the hell am I shaking?

"Baby, wake up are you okay?" a distant voice says.

"Carolyn..." the voice says. She's fighting her way back to consciousness.

She can see a face, a beautiful face, and two panicking blue eyes...

"James..." she whispers.

"Yeah baby," he replies still calmly shaking her body.

James takes a quick second to retrieve his polo shirt from the ground near them and put it on.

"Here," he says, "can you sit up." James kneels down closer to help her up into an upright position supporting her back and her head.

As Carolyn sits up, she feels more and more coherent. She looks around to try to figure out how she got on the ground. James' left hand is covered in blood.

"Come on Carolyn," James picks her up, "we gotta get you to a hospital before..."

"James," she gasps as she lay weakly in his arms, "that blood on your hand... whose blood is it?"

He doesn't respond.

"Daddy's got you." James says calmly.

"Don't you worry about a thing baby girl," he continues, "I'm gonna save you and everything is gonna be alright."

As Carolyn looks up into his eyes, James' appears to be in tears as he carries her wounded body along the dark street.

"James," she says, "Why am I bleeding? Did that asshole really shoot me?"

James looks down at her.

"No," James says, "he missed you, but when we fell back you bumped your head on the brick wall behind us. You were out cold for like ten minutes. I thought you were... I thought I had lost you."

"Awe baby..." Carolyn says with a faint smile on her face.

"I don't ever wanna lose you Carolyn Olivier... not ever." James bends down and kisses her on her warm forehead.

"I'd rather have bad times with you," he sings, *"then good times with someone else, I'd rather be beside you in a storm, then safe and warm all by myself. I'd rather have hard times together than to, have it easy apart... I'd rather have the one who holds my heart..."*

"That was beautiful James," Carolyn cries, "God, I love Luther Vandross..."

"God, *I love you* Carolyn Olivier **Radicon**." He assures her.

"I love you too Mr. Radicon." Carolyn cries.

"I'm serious Carolyn Jane," he says, "a tragic situation with you is much better to me now, than being happy with any other woman... including my wife."

James walks her in the front door of some kind of clinic with Carolyn cradled tightly in his huge arms.

"Awe James…" Carolyn moans.

"Sir…" a security guard near the front desk says.

James ignores him and continues to walk.

"Sir…" the man says again.

James sits Carolyn comfortably in a wheelchair sitting idly against the wall. Then he begins to push her further inside in the wheel chair.

The security guard draws his weapon with his right hand and approaches James with his walkie-talkie in his other hand calling for back up.

James continues on to a counter with two nurses standing watching the security guard curiously.

The guard grabs James' shoulder.

James turns to look at him with a blank stare on his face. The guard places his walkie-talkie back in its holder, and aims his gun at James' head. James smiles down the barrel of the deadly black weapon.

"Go ahead sir;" James tells him, "I've already been shot at once tonight. Let's just make that the common theme of the evening."

"Shut the hell up man," the guard says, "you just waltzed in here without even checking in with me at the front. And this is not a hospital so I don't know what's wrong with this one, but you both need to leave now!"

James calmly steps in front of Carolyn… and even closer to the end of the powerful gun.

"*This one*," James says, "is my wife. And she sustained a serious head injury about thirty minutes ago after we got robbed at gunpoint and then shot at. Where were you and your mighty gun when me and my wife were being assaulted and harassed in that alley?"

"That's not my job." the tall black guard says.

"I'm sure," James replies, "you're better suited drawing your weapon on innocent non-threatening, non-armed people in need of medical attention."

"This is not a hospital!" the guard contends again.

"Damn it," James fumes, "I wouldn't give a fuck if this was Chuck E. Cheese, I see a bunch of nurses in here doing absolutely nothing, just like you. Somebody is going to check on my wife, and tell me she's okay!"

"It's okay Ronnie," the older black nurse walks from behind the counter, "put your gun away love. It's no problem I can check the young lady out for her husband."

James continues to stare at the guard.

The nurse puts her old wrinkled yellow hand atop the gun and calmly forces it down to the guard's side.

"Go back to your post Ronald;" she tells him, "I can't wait till I see your mama at Wal-Mart again, so I can tell her…"

"No ma'am Ms. Talbert that won't be necessary." the guard walks away back towards his post.

"Hello," the nurse takes James' hand in hers, "my name is Ms. Talbert, call me Coleen. Now what's wrong with this beautiful young lady?"

"Well she…" James starts.

"I can talk James," Carolyn interjects calmly, "we got robbed. James hit one of the robbers and he panicked and shot at us, I fell back and hit my head pretty bad."

"I see." the old freckled faced nurse says as she checks the wound on the back of Carolyn's head.

"Honestly," the nurse pulls a small bandage out of one of the pockets of her dark blue scrubs, "it's not that bad. The gunshot itself probably just scared you and amplified the severity of the situation."

"So I'm okay?" Carolyn asks.

"You'll be fine love," the nurse assures her, "now just let me check your vitals for you."

James walks over to sit down in the waiting area to calm his nerves.

"My wife..." he whispers to himself agitatedly, *"James, what the hell are you doing to this woman? She will never... ever be your fucking wife! Stop saying that stupid shit!"*

"Well your blood pressure and everything else seem to be normal." the nurse says.

"You know," she continues, "that's quite some husband you have there. It's obvious he doesn't love you... he's *in love with you honey,* there is a huge difference. It's in his eyes. And girl he is gorgeous too."

"Well, thank you Ms. Coleen." Carolyn says as they both share a light laugh.

"But he's not my husband..." Carolyn admits.

"Oh he will be... he will be." The nurse whispers as James walks back up to them.

"She's all patched up Mr. James." Coleen smiles at him.

"Thank you," James looks down at Carolyn, "now let's get out of here I'm starving."

"Okay," Carolyn replies, "but I don't know how we're gonna eat. They took my card, and your whole wallet baby."

Coleen reaches down in her pockets once more.

"Here..." she hands James all the money she has on her.

It's less than five bucks, but it sure beats nothing.

They both thank the old lady and exit the building hand in hand.

As they stand on the curb of the busy Atlanta street they both eagerly check their pockets to see what they have left.

Carolyn has nothing, all James has is the money Coleen just gave him, his dead cell phone, both his and Carolyn's I.D.'s, and their folded up plane tickets back to Miami in his front left pocket.

James looks down into Carolyn's face.

She doesn't even look worried. The calm stillness of her eyes brings him into a beautiful comfort zone of his own.

"What was that look about, Mr. Radicon?" she asks.

"You don't even seem worried..." he says with an almost comfortable smile on his handsome face.

"About what," she asks, "James this is only one-night baby. You are a billionaire. Tomorrow morning someone is going to deliver exclusive Louis Vuitton apparel to our presidential hotel suite, tomorrow night we fly back home to Miami. Every single thing those assholes stole can be replaced. Oh, you might want to have that black card cancelled ASAP though."

They both laugh as they continue to walk down the street.

The easiness of their interaction is refreshing to them both. They have always felt forced and very calculated in conversations with their respective spouses, but with each other every action and reaction between them is so beautiful and purely natural.

"So, I get all that I'm rich and this is only one-night stuff," James says, "but you still should be a little more shaken up babe. We just got robbed at gunpoint; you hit your head and passed out in a dark alley..."

"James," she says with a smile, "I'm not saying I grew up in the hood, but I've been through a lot in my life and I have been robbed before. And only having five dollars to eat with... been there plenty times before too. I think it made me stronger."

"I bet." he replies quietly.

"I mean of course I'm never gonna let myself live like that again," she tells him, "but it's a humbling experience and I think... no, I believe for some reason God wants us to feel this right now."

James looks at her. "I didn't know you were religious." he raises his left brow.

"I'm not," she says, "I'm... well I used to be very spiritual. There is a major difference in being religious and being spiritual James..."

"I'll let you teach me about that one day before I die," he says blankly, "but right now I'm starving. What are we gonna do with this $4.57?"

"Look there's a McDonald's up there on the corner." Carolyn points towards it.

The closer they get to the restaurant James can't help, but stare up at the glorious golden arches. He never thought old Ronald McDonald and his dollar menu would ever look so good to him.

They walk inside. James quickly hands Carolyn the $4.57.

She looks up at him, as he looks away from her. She's tired and not in the mood to question him. Her hair is a mess and her makeup is less than perfect to say the least, but at this point she's so hungry she doesn't even care. She steadies herself and then walks towards the front counter. James follows behind her at a considerable distance with both of his sweating hands dug down deep in his pockets.

Carolyn is third in line.

For years Carolyn had gotten used to feeling the way she looks right now. Being married to that insecure scumbag Ralph Olivier for four years, would destroy any woman's confidence and self-worth.

Ralph made her feel dumb, when she's more than ingenious. He made her feel fat, when her body has obviously been crafted by God's angels. He made her feel absolutely alone in this world, without even breaking a sweat. But James, Mr. Radicon need but touch her face or taste her lips and instantly she becomes alive again.

She becomes more than just a female; she becomes a sexy, vibrant, intelligent, relevant, super woman. In his arms she can do anything, with him her potential knows no rational boundaries. James Radicon created Carolyn's ability to love, and he alone possesses the capacity to sustain its prowess until the end of all time.

Carolyn smiles to herself, as her joyful cheeks begin to flush. She's next in line. She turns around to look at James.

"Come here James." she says.

He obeys hesitantly with his head down and his hands still dug deep in his shameful pockets.

"Pick your head up..." Carolyn whispers to him.

"You are James Radicon," she reminds him, "tomorrow night you can fly back and buy this entire restaurant if you wanted to. It's okay... We're okay, and this too shall pass baby..."

"May I help the next customer please?" a tall, red-headed, pimply faced, teen says, donning a black McDonald's managerial shirt. He sounds as if he's irritated, so of course Carolyn takes her time to respond.

She looks up at James.

"What do you want baby?" she asks.

"Oh, let's see," James rubs his stubble laden chin, "I'll have the Filet Mignon, medium well please."

"Ma'am," the tall boy says, "Do you wanna eat, or don't ya'?"

Carolyn ignores him.

"James," she looks up at him, "do you want a cheese burger or a hamburger?" James finds himself impressed with her ease, and her command of the situation.

"Cheese is fine." he replies gazing down into those two precious hazel orbs.

"Ma'am can you…" the red-headed kid starts.

"I'm ready," Carolyn interjects, "I'll have the two cheeseburger meal medium size please."

"$4.89." he replies.

Carolyn hands him the $4.57. The young irritated manager counts the money, and then he looks down at her.

"You're short…" he says.

"And, you have acne." she replies.

"No lady," he says, "I mean you don't have enough money for what you ordered."

"I know what you meant kid, but it's only 32 cents, damn give me a break here." she leans on the counter with both hands.

An older white man nearby hears their conversation.

"I can't give you a break ma'am," the red headed manager says, "I have food costs that need to be covered and…"

"Thirty-two cents kid," Carolyn says, "really though?"

"I'm sorry." the pimply face kid says attempting to hand Carolyn her money back with a hideous sneer on his red face.

"Look sir," she says, "I know you don't know me, and you probably don't care… but I just got robbed and this is all the money I have in Atlanta."

The manager's face never changes.

"You're right," he tells her, "I don't care. Who's next in line this lady can't afford cheeseburgers..."

Wham!!!

"Here's fifty cents," an old man slams two quarters down on the front counter, "now give the lady her fuckin' food! And hurry up with my damn coffee, it don't take twenty minutes to make no damn decaf coffee!"

The pimply faced manager immediately finishes ringing up Carolyn's order, and opens his register. He throws the money in the register, and then grabs the change.

"Here's your change sir." the kid says to the old man.

"Keep it," the old man says, "you might need it for cab fare *asshole*."

The teen frowns, and then walks off in pursuit of the old man's coffee.

Carolyn smiles at the charismatic, bald headed, white gentleman.

"Thank you sir." she says with a stunning smile.

"Don't mention it," the old man tells her, "the kid's an asshole. I told his mother somebody is gonna kick his ass real good one day."

Carolyn steps closer to the elderly man. "So, you know that asshole?" she asks.

"Here's your coffee," the redhead returns to the front counter, "now please go wait in the car grandpa; I get off in five minutes."

"Boy," the old man tells him, "I'm leaving in exactly six minutes. If you ain't in my car, you're calling a cab." Then he snatches his coffee from the kid.

The old man looks at Carolyn.

"You can't pick your offspring, or the offspring they create." he tells her.

"That's true." Carolyn says absolutely enchanted by the old man's animated spirit.

"It was nice to meet you miss…" he says.

"Carolyn." she tells him.

"Carolyn, that's a lovely name." he tells her as he shakes her caramel hand.

Then he walks towards James. He shakes James' hand as well.

"Mr. Radicon," he says, "I've been drinking you for over fifteen years now. Best brand of wine on the planet. My idiot grandson there doesn't realize when he's in the presence of American royalty."

"Thank you sir…" James replies with a genuine smile. The old man looks back at Carolyn as she gets their food.

"And that one," the old man says, "She's a keeper. Now, I come from a different day and age than you kids, but one thing I know is love has absolutely no color at all. Have a goodnight son."

The old man exits, as Carolyn approaches James with their food.

"What were you and the man talking about babe?" she asks.

"Well," James says, "he said you're a keeper, and that love… has no color."

"Smart man," she replies with a sexy grin, "let's go, that gorgeous hotel shower is calling my name."

As they finish their food a few blocks away from McDonald's Carolyn and James stumble onto a homeless woman and her two small children. The unfortunate threesome is sleeping on a bus stop bench on the side of the street.

"James," Carolyn whispers, "look, that could be me and my two sons. I don't know what I would do if I ended up homeless and couldn't provide for and protect my kids."

James hears Carolyn speaking about her kids but he decides not to prolong that part of the conversation.

"We have to help them." Carolyn says.

James looks in the McDonald's bag and decides it would be disrespectful to offer the woman and her children the few crumbs left from what he and Carolyn just ate. He tosses the bag in a nearby trashcan.

Carolyn is staring up at James as they get nearer, and nearer to the lady and her kids. James looks down in Carolyn's desperate eyes and then decides at this very moment that whatever she wants, or asks for… is his duty to fulfill.

He looks down at his hand and pulls off his expensive diamond encrusted, gold wedding ring.

Then James approaches the woman.

He places the ring in her hand.

She smiles.

"In the morning," James says, "Take this ring to any jewelry store in the city and tell them you got it from James Radicon. They will gladly buy it from you. The amount they will give you will be enough to get you and your sons off the street and on your feet for quite a while."

"Thank you Mr. Radicon," the woman cries, "may God bless you eternally sir."

"Amen," he replies, "and here take one of my business cards just in case the jeweler wants to speak directly to me."

The woman smiles at him.

"Thank you again Mr. Radicon." she cries.

James walks back to Carolyn and takes her by the hand as they head on towards the hotel.

"James was that your wedding ring," she asks, "you can't be serious. I asked you to help the woman not give her your ring…"

"Carolyn," James interjects, "my marriage ended the day I laid eyes on you. I'll be fine, and I'm sure the ring you'll pick out for me, for **our wedding** will be even more beautiful than that one was. You make me feel, think, and say things before I have time to dissect it all."

"Thanks I guess," she says, "and **our** wedding, that sounds nice."

Carolyn squeezes James' hand tightly in hers.

(An hour later)

The hotel door opens. James waits until it slides fully open and then carries Carolyn's inside. Once he makes it up to their room, he walks her sleeping body inside their warm, luxurious, presidential suite.

He carries her directly to the enormous bed and gently lays her down in the middle of it.

Next James heads to the bathroom. Inside he turns the shower on, adjusting the dial so that the water pressure and temperature will be just right.

He reaches up above the bathroom door and grabs four towels, two large towels and two smaller face towels.

He sets them all on the bathroom sink. He opens up one of the large bars of Dial soap that he requested be placed in the bathroom of his suite prior to his arrival. Then he grabs the clear shower cap from the back corner of the sink and heads back out into the bedroom area of the suite.

First James walks over and sits the shower cap down on the table near the bed. Then he takes his size thirteen shoes off and sits them on the side of the bed. Then he takes a seat in a nearby chair. He takes each of his socks off his sore feet. Next he removes his Polo shirt again for the second time tonight. He takes his expensive watch off and sits it on the table next to the bed.

Next he stands up and unbuckles his belt as he looks lovingly at his sleeping lady, resting angelically in the center of their bed. He sits back down to take his pants off completely. Walking towards the bed he drops his boxers. The steam from the bathroom is making its way into the room now.

James carefully removes both of Carolyn's pure white slip on Louis Vuitton sandals. Then he rolls her over on her back and gently pulls her shirt off over her head. He grabs the shower cap off the nearby table and sits it on the bed next to her. With his hand he calmly wraps Carolyn's hair around her head to the best of his ability.

Once he has it just right he holds her hair in place as he places the shower cap over her head. Then he pulls her pretty pink Louis Vuitton leisure pants down off of her.

Reaching behind her James unfastens her expensive white bra, and then removes it. Then he pulls her matching white panties down off of her body as well. Next he picks a nude Carolyn up in his strong arms and walks her into the bathroom.

"James..." she yawns.

"Yeah baby..." he replies.

"Where are we going?" she asks with her eyes just barely open.

"We walked a long way to get back here to the hotel," he says, "We both need a good bath."

"No baby, I know," she says, "but I'm too tired to shower tonight and my feet hurt so badly, I just can't. Not tonight..."

He smiles down at her with those big, deep, blue eyes.

"You can," he tells her, "and you shall."

Holding her mostly with his right arm he moves the shower curtain to the side with his almost free left hand. Then he steps into the bathtub with Carolyn nestled in his perfect loving arms.

"Baby…" she moans.

"It's okay love" he tells her as he holds her body slightly beneath the stream of the wonderful warm water.

"Whenever you can't do for yourself," he kisses her warm face, "I will always be there to do for you…"

He steps closer to the water with her still cradled in his arms. As the water begins to cover her and mind numbingly soothing her sore tired body, Carolyn closes her eyes and opens her mouth. James kisses her open mouth deeply.

She moans softly.

(Carolyn)

Lord God… Who is this angel you have blessed me with? No woman deserves a man this special, a man this potentially perfect and complete. His skin feels like the soft, warm, flesh of a baby, but his arms and his stomach are as solid as stone, and his eyes… God every time I look in his eyes, they take me straight to heaven. I love James Radicon Lord and I always will.

James kisses her again.

"Can you stand up for me baby?" he asks.

"Mmmm…" she moans.

James lets her down so she can stand on her own. Facing the tantalizing warm stream of water with her back to him, Carolyn reaches up to fix her shower cap.

James steps out of the shower. Carolyn is now left alone, lost in her affair with the steamy water. Every bead that touches her body is sending her senses and her mind into a deeper realm of ecstasy.

James steps back in the shower with a towel and a bar of soap in hand. He reaches around Carolyn's body and wets the Dial soap as it sits in the center of the small white bathing towel. Once the towel is wet enough James begins to lather it fully. Then he sits the yellow bar of soap in the soap holder on the side of the tub in the wall.

He starts with her neck and begins to massage her back and her entire body with the soapy towel, paying special attention to her most sensitive parts.

Carolyn turns towards him as he continues to massage her body with the soapy towel. Her entire body is covered in the strong white suds now. She takes the towel away from James and rinses it out and then she takes the soap herself and lathers it again.

Looking intently in her enchanting hazel eyes James awaits her next move. Carolyn reaches up high and begins to massage his rock hard body deeply with the soapy towel.

His shoulders, neck, chest, stomach, and back are now covered in suds.

She turns him around switching positions with him, so that his back is in the water stream, and his body is shielding her from the water completely.

Carolyn kneels down and begins to wash his lower body. First she does his feet, then his ankles and legs.

Next she begins to wash his thighs and his growing passion sword. As she strokes him he steps back closer to the water. His eyes are closed tightly as she pleasures him with the towel and her soft hands.

He moans deeply several times. This moment and this feeling is so intense neither one of them can even speak. Their eyes are doing all the talking for them. Carolyn continues to stroke him masterfully.

He can't take it anymore. He picks her up in his arms and allows the warm stream of water to wash all the soap off of the both of them. Next he steps out of the shower with her in his arm just like she was originally and carries her back to the bed.

James throws Carolyn's wet body on the bed like a wild animal, then pounces on her like she's his helpless prey.

As he climbs on top of her, he bends down close to kiss her perfect lips. Her phone rings loudly.

The ringtone is **Boyz 2 Men's** old hit song, "Mama".

"Baby..." she moans between his tasty kisses.

"Whoever that is can just wait..." he growls.

"No baby," she says, "that's my mama, she's gotta be worried about me." Carolyn quickly slides from under him and rushes to her phone.

James rolls over on his back growling in agony. His entire body is tense with lust; as he wants to do things to Carolyn right now that's he's never done before.

Carolyn's phone stops ringing.

Looking at it she sees missed calls from several strange numbers. Also she has twenty-three unread text messages from her mother. She opens the text messages one by one and begins to read.

As her eyes taste the pain in each word of every text her entire body turns ice cold. Her hands are shaking. Her face is all, but numb to the real tears streaming down it.

She closes her eyes tightly; she can't breathe at all. She finally opens her eyes again and the messages... every one of them are still right there in her evil phone. She tries to pray. Nothing, she can't find any words.

No meaningful words exist in her prayer vocabulary. Nothing matters every single damn thing is meaningless now. We work so hard and at least try to live right, but in the end we all die... and all the things we've built or broken become meaningless. But she has to pray. She tries again...

"Lord my God..." she whispers aloud.

James' heart stops as he hears her cry out to the Lord. He rolls over and sees Carolyn's devastated face.

Oh my God, she loved him. James thinks to himself.

He tries hard to speak... but no sound is available in his throat. He knows that Carolyn now knows what he did. She doesn't know he is actually responsible, but she has definitely been given the news. He knows one day he is going to tell her... but that day is not tonight.

Carolyn taps the name Mama on her phone's screen.

She stands up and then she falls back down in the chair as her legs give way to pain and fatigue. Her mind is cracking. Her phone is pressed way too hard against her ear, but she can't feel a thing as it continues to ring.

No answer.

Carolyn drops her phone in her lap and lets her tear stained face fall helplessly into her unstable hands.

"*Mama... Mama you know I love you...*" her phone's ringtone startles her. She answers the call.

"Mama..." she cries.

She stands up and rushes to the bathroom. Once inside she closes the door behind her.

"Mama, what happened." she cries.

James quietly creeps to the bathroom door to try to hear what Carolyn is saying on the phone to her mother.

"But how did the house catch on fire in the first place Mama?" she asks.

"What do you mean a *freak accident*," she cries out, "we have lived… in that house for over *four years mama*! That house is new… it ain't a mansion by any damn stretch, but it was not prone to *spontaneously fucking combust!* Something had to happen mama something is wrong."

Carolyn begins to cry harder now.

James can't stop shaking. It's hard for him to hear Carolyn's every word because his heart is pounding extremely loud in both of his deceitful ears.

"This was no accident Mama," Carolyn says, "This was murder. But why would somebody kill my babies…" Carolyn falls down to her knees on the bathroom floor, crying harder now than she ever has in twenty-four years of life.

"What do you mean they couldn't find their bodies mama," Carolyn asks, "They didn't find Jr., or Karan? That's just stupid they couldn't possibly be alive. Where would they go… where would they be now?"

Carolyn listens closely.

"No, Mama," she cries, "my babies are dead… Mama, I'm so sorry, and I just want my babies back. *I'm sorry God*, I am not a good woman, and I'm an unfaithful wife… I'm an *adulterous slut!* I am *more* than lost Lord… But, I am… *I was* a damn good mother! I tried to be…"

James suddenly feels sick. He rushes to the trash can near the front door. Before he can make it he trips over one of his own large shoes. James makes it the rest of the way to the trash can on his hands and knees, and vomits several times. Then he rushes back to the bathroom door.

"Where is Kayla now?" James hears Carolyn asks her mother.

"How bad does she look Mama?" she continues.

"No Mama..." Carolyn screams out.

"Damn it," James whispers to himself, "the girl on the front lawn never died. She could have seen my truck. Now I have to find her and kill her too."

The bathroom door opens. Carolyn falls into James' arms and continues to cry her life away.

"James..." she cries.

"It's okay baby." he tells her holding her close to him.

"It's not okay James," she cries, "*my house burned down. My husband is dead, my children are... missing probably dead too, and my little sister is in a hospital bed right now barely breathing. Her entire body was burned in the fire. My family is dead James... and I have nowhere to go.*"

Her cries are squeezing and painfully piercing his very heart and soul. James picks Carolyn up in his arms rocking her back and forth like a little baby.

"You have me." he says.

Ch. 17

"The Big C"

S taring out of the window in the distance Jessica Radicon tries to clear her discontented mind. She knows she's sick, she just doesn't know how sick. But to be lying here all alone is the worst part. She could handle dying, but she doesn't want to die alone; in a dim, smelly, hospital room. With no husband, friends, nor kids there to comfort her in her time of ultimate need.

(Jessica)

A fool... I Jessica Radicon am a damn fool. I pray no other woman ever knows my exact pain. I'm sure every woman has known at least once in her life what it feels like to be the absolute sole object of a man's affection. Even if that man is not the man she wants or ever wanted. It's a good feeling to be needed and wanted. Men are creatures of habit they tend to transform more and more over the years. As they get older they begin to question themselves and wonder if they still have what it takes to do the things they once did as much younger men.

James Radicon, the billionaire, my husband is no different. He is still every bit as gorgeous as he ever was, but my telling him that constantly would have never been enough. He's a lover, a true romantic. He's had my heart forever; so he no longer feels the need to sustain me and my feelings for him. But this new woman, he's still building an emotional and physical resume' with her. I'm sure he's going out of his way to wow and woo her with expensive trips and nice pretty things. Why is it even possible that materialistic things... can make us love people?

Right now James is locked in on his new woman wholeheartedly as she is still just falling in love with him. He's still very careful with her at this point... He's gentle, nurturing, and thoughtful. He's belligerent, but charming in the same breath. He's her father, her brother, and her man. Lord knows I remember those days. She's very happy right now I'm sure, but I hope she knows those happy days do in time expire.

The hospital door opens. In walks a moderately attractive tall white man, with brown curly hair. He's adorned in a white doctor's jacket, so it's obvious this man is not just another annoying and clueless nurse.

"Who are you?" Jessica asks.

"I'm Dr. Franco, Mrs. Radicon," he walks closer to her, "I'm your doctor."

"No Dr. Steven Cole is my doctor." she replies.

"Not anymore," he tells her, "but I do have your lab results for you Mrs. Radicon."

She pretends not to hear his last statement.

"What do you mean not anymore," she asks, "Of course he is. Where is he, where is Dr. Cole?"

"You have both Ovarian and Breast Cancer Mrs. Radicon." he tells her.

Bang!!!

Dr. Franco's words ring out and instantly penetrate Jessica's heart, shattering her entire being.

His lips just continue to move on and on, as his plain face and head move from side to side, and then up and down at times.

He's still talking alright, but Jessica can't hear a single word he's saying. The queen of the Radicon Empire is more than devastated.

Her only comforting thought is that James no longer needs her. He will be just fine after she passes away.

"How long..." she interjects while the doctor is still aimlessly talking.

"I'm sorry, what?" he asks.

"How long do I have Dr. Franco, before I'm going to die?" she asks.

He looks down at his clipboard as if he doesn't know off the top of his head.

Before this asshole ever entered her room, Jessica knows he had the number tattooed on his brain. It's right there screaming at the forefront of his mind. He knows exactly how long his calculated assessment has told him she's going to live.

"Two maybe three weeks..." he says.

BANG!!!

Another shot to the head. At least now she can be with all of her loved ones that she lost just this year.

Dr. Franco pats her on her left foot and then he leaves the room, taking with him all sound, meaning, and light. Most of all, the prick is leaving with any hope Jessica had of surviving her painful illnesses.

Oh how she wishes she could turn back the despicable hands of time. Jessica calmly folds her arms across her sore chest and closes her eyes as the tears begin to force themselves out through the sides of them.

(Justin Tolls)

As Justin Tolls waits in the parking lot of the Starbucks on Biscayne Boulevard in his expensive car; he has no clue what today's meeting could possibly be about, but he skipped work to be here. Not that his boss would notice that he's not there, hell Mr. Radicon hasn't been back at the office in over a week now. Even if his billionaire boss was at the winery, Justin still wouldn't have missed this secret meeting for anything. After all these years he's wondering why she just now decided to contact him to speak to him privately.

A 2015 yellow Mercedes Benz pulls up and parks two spaces down from Justin. She pulls her Chanel shades down low on her elegant face and looks down towards his car.

Justin immediately turns his car off and prepares to step out of it. He hesitates as he sees her opening her door instead.

She gets out of her gorgeous vehicle and walks along the sidewalk towards his. She motions for him to let down his passenger window.

He does.

"How are you baby?" she asks with a faint smile.

"I'm okay Ms. Dee." he replies returning her smile.

"I'm gonna run inside and get a latte. Do you want anything?" she asks.

"No ma'am, I'm fine," he tells her, "but I do have to get back to work…"

"Boy," she says, "you have more money in your trust fund than that little office job could pay you in three lifetimes. You'll be fine. I'll only be a second."

With that said she heads off inside the restaurant. Justin watches the older woman as she walks inside.

He shakes his head. Ms. Dee ain't lost a step. She's just as fine as she wants to be.

Justin smiles, and then shakes his head again.

She emerges back outside moments later with her latte in hand. She opens his passenger door and sits down in his car closing the door behind her.

"Dang that was fast." Justin says.

Ms. Dee smiles at his surprise.

"Cause and effect son." she says.

"Cause and effect," he repeats, "What you mean by that Ms. Dee..."

"Well," she says sipping her latte carefully, "I gave the young lady a $100 tip and in return I got some speedy customer service."

Justin shakes his head again as they both share a comfortable laugh.

"Drive." she says.

"Drive where?" Justin asks.

"Doesn't matter," Ms. Dee replies, "just crank up and drive."

He obeys.

"So to what do I owe the pleasure of this meeting today, Ms. Dee?" Justin asks.

She doesn't respond.

"And I've always been curious," Justin says, "What's really up between you and my Grandfather?"

Ms. Dee continues to sip her latte.

"What the Master and I do is our business." Ms. Dee finally responds agitatedly.

"No," Justin says, "I respect that Ms. Dee. But he treats you very well... what exactly is it that you do?"

"I do it all," she claims raising her voice, "he treats me the way I deserve to be treated! I'm owed a lot! Know that! The life that I live is exactly as it should be! But I didn't ask you to meet me here to talk about me."

Justin nervously clears his throat.

"Okay," he says, "and, I'm sorry Ms. Dee I just…"

"Don't be sorry," she says, "Just don't ever let that happen again son."

"Yes ma'am," he says, "So what did you want to talk about?"

"You…" she tells him.

"What about me?" Justin asks.

"First of all," she says, "take on your father's name Justin. It's a very powerful name. It holds a lot of weight and it belongs to you just as much as it does to him."

"But Ms. Dee," Justin interjects, "My father doesn't even…"

"Relationship or not," she cuts him off smoothly, "his blood flows through your veins. Never be forced to hide or shy away from who you are… especially not because of the color of your skin. Your bloodline is a very proud one Justin Tolls. You deserve to enjoy it just like the rest of them have."

"Wow," he replies, "I never even thought about…"

"Think more," she tells him, "Most importantly Justin, I want you to remember… Your grandfather has made some huge mistakes in his life. Some you know about, most of them you will never know about. I do not want you to allow him to use you anymore. Your money is your money he can't ever take it back from you."

"I just want him to respect me," Justin says, "and I want my father to pay for not being in my life as a kid."

"Your grandfather's respect," Ms. Dee says, "is not worth ruining your life or anybody else's. I love Master very much, but he can be a very evil and sick man."

"I don't..." Justin starts.

"Enough," she interjects, "I don't want to hear anything else. I have said what I felt the need to say. This conversation and this meeting never happened. Are we clear son?"

"We're clear." he replies solemnly.

"Fine," she says, "Now take me back to my car, and do not forget what I said today Justin. I only want what's best for you and this family... I always have."

Ch. 18

"The Cover-up"

As James drives away from the Miami International Airport with Carolyn lying across the backseat of his SUV, he's already formulating a plan to cover his ass. He was more nervous before, back in Atlanta he considered doing some really drastic things. He doesn't want to lose Carolyn, so he thought about killing her in her precious sleep and then killing himself so that he could die right beside her.

(James)
I was actually going to kill myself and Carolyn. I prayed about that idea and eventually decided against it. She was just lying there asleep in that huge hotel bed. She was breathing like a sweet angel and just barely moving. I could have easily smothered her or choked her to death and ultimately put her out of our misery. We're killers both of us have actually killed people. Part of me believes that maybe she wouldn't mind dying by my hands; it would mesh our souls together for all of eternity. No this shit is crazy! I know what I need to do. I have to tell Carolyn the truth and deal with the outcome. She'll understand... one day.

Her husband threatened me with a gun. He held my company, my career, and my marriage hostage with a fucking recording. He deserved to die as horribly as he did. He's not a good man, I can tell because of how unhappy Carolyn used to be... before me that is. It's time.

James turns around to look towards the backseat of his SUV. Carolyn is sound asleep.

"Baby..." he says.

She moves, but doesn't wake up.

"Carolyn baby," he says, "wake up we need to talk."

She slowly gets up and then sits upright in the backseat, rubbing both of her tired eyes.

"Where are we?" she asks looking out of the window.

"Headed to your mother's house," he tells her, "that's where you wanted me to take you right?"

"The hospital," Carolyn says, "Just drop me off at the hospital. I need to be with my sister now."

"Okay." he says.

"James..." Carolyn starts.

"Yeah." he replies.

"What's on your mind," she asks, "something is not right with you, I can tell."

James looks in his rearview mirror to find Carolyn's tired red eyes staring directly at him.

James hesitates.

"Speak baby," she says, "what's wrong now? It can't be any worse than everything else that's already going on."

"Carolyn I just don't want you to..." he stops in the middle of his sentence.

"Don't want me to what James," she asks, "you don't want me to cry anymore? I cried all night and all morning... I am all cried out. And if you think what you have to say now is going to make me cry again, then that means you're leaving me... again."

Carolyn's eyes begin to well up with new painful tears.

"No baby…" James says.

"What the hell did I ever do to you *James Justin Radicon*," she asks, "I've lost everything because of the incessant sins I've committed with you and for you. But it's still not enough for you to love me back is it? No, I know it's not… Because nothing I will ever do, will make me good enough to become your wife."

"I killed your husband." James says.

Carolyn continues to stare at James in his rearview mirror as her animated sobbing stops almost instantaneously.

The look in her eyes turns James' stomach upside down and his body feels completely numb.

Pure hatred has never had a face until now.

"Say that again." she says void of emotion.

"I killed your husband," he tells her, "I was there I started the fire baby… I'm very sorry."

She doesn't respond.

"Baby…" James says.

"Pull the car over." Carolyn says calmly.

"What, I'm not pulling the car over." he tells her.

"James," Carolyn says unable to look at him anymore, *"pull the fucking car over now!"*

"You are nowhere near the hospital or your house baby…" he reminds her.

"According to my mother I no longer have a house James," she says with a deadly smirk on her face. "I don't have anything, because you thought it was a good idea to take everything away from me… and still not give me you! All I wanted was you!"

"You got me baby…" he says.

"I don't want you anymore James," she says, "You're a very evil and sick man. Pull the car over and let me out now!"

James continues to drive.

Carolyn slides over behind the driver's seat and then quickly lunges forward covering his eyes as he drives.

He's blind.

James can't see a thing as he tries to keep his composure. In a panic he swerves left and then right; James screams out in real fear.

The truck spins around to the left as they are vaulted off to the side of the road in a high-speed, reckless, fashion.

Carolyn is calm, completely ready to die. James has his foot down hard on the breaks, but the truck won't stop, it continues its deadly spin.

The car spins three more times and then comes to a halt, just a few feet away from a huge tree.

Carolyn lets go of James' eyes, unlocks the back door herself, and jumps out of the truck.

She closes the back door, snatches open the driver door, and reaches up slapping James hard in the face.

"You weak bastard!" she cries.

"You weak inconsiderate bastard," she slaps him harder this time, "you don't want me, that's a given. I'm just a toy you use to distract yourself from your real life, and the people you really love…"

"No baby, that is not…" he starts.

"Do not cut me off again," she screams, "you don't love me enough to confess it to anybody other than me, that's how I know it's a lie James!"

"Baby," he interjects again, "I told everybody in Atlanta you were my wife."

Carolyn reaches up and slaps James again even harder this time.

"Damn it!" he yells in obvious pain.

"And now I know why," she screams, "James... you're only willing to love and marry me because you single handedly stole my family away from me. You sick bastard!"

"That's not true Carolyn," he claims, "I've said openly that you, not Jessica are my wife baby..."

"Telling those people in Atlanta that lie don't mean shit to me," she yells painfully, "Tell Jessica I'm your wife; tell your son Lucas I'm your wife. Tell somebody who actually matters to you!"

"Fine, I will!" he claims as he steps down out of the truck.

He tries to hug her. Carolyn step back from him with her tiny arms extended to block him from getting close to her.

"No it is not fine," she screams, "you killed my husband. Ralph wasn't perfect but at least he wasn't ashamed to say he loved me. You disfigured my eighteen-year-old baby sister! She is going to feel like an ugly ass monster for the rest of her fucking life James! And my kids..."

"Now Carolyn," James steps towards her, "In all fairness I never knew you had kids. You never talked about them. But I can promise you everything is not quite as bad as you think it is right now."

"It doesn't matter James," she screams, "it will never matter again! My kids are dead and gone! What the hell, what if my mom and dad had been there? You would have burned them alive to right? The whole world; can rot and fucking pass away, as long as Mr. Radicon is happy right!"

"Baby... the kids..." he tries to put his arms around her.

"It's over James," she tells him, "I never wanna see your evil face again as long as I live. If you come anywhere near me, I will not hesitate to tell the police everything!"

With that said Carolyn turns around and begins walking back up towards the street. "Carolyn," James yells out, "I'm... I'm sorry baby. I did every single thing I did for us baby!"

Almost to the street now, she turns around to look at him.

"There is no us," she yells, "there never was! Everything was always for and about you!"

Carolyn in her tight denim shorts easily flags down a truck driver who immediately slows his truck down and stops just up the road from her.

Carolyn runs to the truck and then jumps in. James watches from the brush as the truck drives away with Carolyn inside.

(At the Hospital)

On the elevator Carolyn can envision her entire life before her eyes. The good times, the bad, the successes, and the monumental mistakes she has made as a mother, a wife, and a person in general.

As she approaches her sister's room she finds her mother and father standing out in the hallway crying.

Watching them stand there in so much pain forces Carolyn's tears to begin falling again.

"Mama, Daddy..." Carolyn cries.

"Oh baby..." her mother says as both of her parents wrap their arms around her and each other.

"Daddy," Carolyn cries, "Daddy what am I going to do?"

Carolyn's father Marcus Williams kisses his wife on the forehead and asks her to go wait in the hospital room with Kayla while he speaks to Carolyn privately.

She obeys.

"Carolyn," he holds her close to his heart, "this is an awful, terrible tragedy... but this is not going to break us."

"My babies are dead Daddy," she cries, "both of my babies burned to death in my house... And I wasn't there to save them."

"No baby this is not your fault," he tells her, "if you had been home, you would have been hurt too; or maybe even killed."

Carolyn breaks away from her father's embrace to look deeply in his eyes.

"No daddy," she says, "if I was there, the devil never would have turned my house into a hell on earth. If I was at home like I was supposed to be, the fire would have never even existed. It *is* my fault Daddy."

"Baby, I don't know what you're saying, but Daddy is gonna help you through this." Mr. Williams pulls his baby girl back into his protective arms again.

"Now I don't want you to worry about this right now," he continues, "but at some point you're going to have to speak to the police. They just want to ensure that this was a freak accident and no foul play was involved. They also have concerns about the fact that Karan and little Ralph's bodies were never found."

Carolyn doesn't respond. "You
hear me baby..." he says.

"I just want to see my little sister," she says breaking away from his grasp again.

Carolyn Olivier walks into her sister's hospital room. Her mother hugs her as she exits the room back into the hallway to be with her father.

"Comfort her baby..." her mother whispers before closing the door behind her.

The cold room is deathly quiet as Carolyn has lost her ability to hear. She stands there frozen near the door as she has also lost her ability to walk.

She would speak, but her mouth refuses to open. Even from this distance Carolyn can clearly see the damage that James has done to her once stunningly beautiful baby sister Kayla.

Carolyn knows she will never forgive James for this. She plans on taking time tonight to pray hard to the Lord and ask him what she should do in respect to her evil, murderous, ex-lover. He is responsible for the death of her husband, her children, and the permanent disfigurement of her teenage sister.

(Carolyn)
Well I have to say something. Her skin looks like burned meat from what I can see. Most of it is covered in bloody bandages and gauze. But it's definitely worse than I ever imagined it would be. That's it one foot after the other. Come on Carolyn you can do it. I'm almost there; Aw damn it, I'm crying again. Damn it! If she sees me crying she's gonna cry too. Suck it up Carolyn, come on now.

Carolyn reaches up and dries her face the best she can. In her right hand Kayla is clutching a hand mirror that she's holding down by her side. As Carolyn gets closer, she can see Kayla's face fully now, it's not covered much at all. Her sister's face looks like it's been held down on a scorching hot grill for hours, as every inch of her youthful beauty melted away into the grill's pit.

Kayla looks weakly up at her beautiful older sister. She smiles a dark heart chilling smile.

Carolyn forces a smile in return. Kayla brings her mirror to her face.

As she looks the monstrous young girl in the face, Kayla wonders who she is.

"This can't be possible..." she mumbles.

"What Kayla?" Carolyn asks.

"I," Kayla mumbles on, "I'm a... I look like a monster."

Carolyn strategically covers her mouth and calmly shakes her head.

"No you're not Kayla," Carolyn tells her baby sister, "you are not a monster and you do not look like one. How bad did they say your..."?

"Second degree burns," Kayla mumbles, "over eighty percent of my body. I'm fucked."

"Don't say that Kayla, you'll be fine." Carolyn tries to console her dispirited baby sister.

"Tell me I'm pretty sissy..." Kayla prods with the little strength she has.

"What?" Carolyn asks.

"Well you're obviously in the lying mood right *mother fucker*," Kayla asks, "So damn it tell me I'm pretty and you better fuckin' mean it!"

"You're... pretty." Carolyn says.

CRASH!!! Kayla quickly slams her hand mirror down on the ground crushing it into pieces hurting her arm in the process.

"You know," Carolyn says, "you can't keep breaking mirrors. It's bad..."

"*Luck*," Kayla interjects obnoxiously with much less power than she'd like, "Sissy please; luck, a miracle, and God all rolled up into one ain't gone fix my damn face. Nope, it's over with."

"Kayla..." her big sister starts.

"It's okay," Kayla blurts out awkwardly, "And you... big sister, you should be happy."

"Happy about what Kayla..." Carolyn asks, covering her mouth as she begins to cry again; fearing what her damaged baby sister will say next.

"Look at me," Kayla laughs, "you're the pretty sister now. So, now Ralph will leave me for you."

With her left hand still over her mouth, Carolyn covers her heart with her right hand, as her eyes double in size.

"What the hell is that look for?" The severely burned teenager asks.

"Kayla, Ralph is..." Carolyn starts.

"Your husband," Kayla tries to snap with her weak voice showing no regard for her severely damaged body, "Yeah I know Carolyn. But he spends every second thinking about me... my breasts, my ass... If you and I were the same age, your husband would be mine. I love him Carolyn. He is *my* man."

Carolyn grips her heart even more as her tears continue to fall. She begins to shake her head calmly, as she rocks from side to side.

"What," Kayla groans, "It's true Carolyn. Ralph is..."

"Kayla Ralph is dead." Carolyn tells her.

"You're such a liar," Kayla mumbles, "he can't be dead; he came to see me last night. I know he... unless I was dreaming. No... I couldn't have been drea..."

Kayla begins to tear up. "You're lying sissy," Kayla cries, "please tell me you're lying to me..."

"Ralph died in the fire Kayla." Carolyn explains through her tears.

"No," Kayla screams, "what about Junior and Karan..."

Carolyn gently lies down on her sister's bandaged stomach. Carolyn's deep groans answer her sister's question.

Kayla rubs her sister's curly brown head as they both cry for very different reasons indeed.

(Police Station)

After crying with her baby sister for what seemed like an eternity, Carolyn asked her father to drive her to the police station.

"Now baby," Carolyn's father Marcus says as he drives along the road, "you don't have to answer any questions that you don't want to. You are not on trial today and you're not even a suspect. You can leave whenever you want to."

"Come with me daddy." she cries.

"Oh, of course princess." he replies as he protectively takes her hand in his and kisses it.

"Daddy..." she says somberly.

"Yeah baby." he replies.

"Why can't I find a man like you," she asks, "mommy found you, so there has to be someone like you for me."

Marcus furrows his brows tightly.

"Baby don't talk like that," he says, "You just lost your husband..."

Carolyn laughs as she continues to cry.

"It's very disrespectful to Ralph hunny." Marcus explains to his daughter in the midst of her conflicting emotions.

"*Dis... respectful*," Carolyn says, "I am far from alone in *that* category father."

"What do you mean baby girl?" Marcus asks her.

"Ralph," Carolyn starts, "was never half the man you are daddy." she smiles a strange smile as she wipes a few tears away.

Marcus parks his new white Cadillac near the rear of the police station. After removing his seat belt, he reaches over and wipes some of Carolyn's new tears away from her precious reddened face with his warm hand.

"Did you love him Carolyn Jane?" her father asks.

She doesn't respond. Carolyn's father unfastens her seatbelt for her.

"You don't have to answer that love." he tells her before exiting the car.

Fifty-three-year-old Marcus Williams has seen many things over the years, but can't quite grasp what's at the root of his family's present plight. But he can definitely sense that something is being kept secret from him.

He has a million questions and thoughts swirling around in his mind as he walks around to the passenger side of his car to let his daughter out.

He opens the door and helps her out on to the sidewalk. Marcus closes the door.

As they walk he tries hard to find the words to say to find out the secrets that are being withheld from him.

As they reach the front door to the station, Marcus steps in front of Carolyn and opens the door for her.

Once inside they make their way to the front desk.

"May I help you?" a short pudgy white woman asks with no detectable emotion.

"Ah yes," Marcus says, "My daughter and I are here to see Detective Larky."

"And your names are?" she asks.

"My name is Marcus Williams," he tells her, "and this is my daughter Carolyn…"

"Williams, my name is Carolyn Williams." Carolyn interjects.

"Fine," the pudgy lady replies, "Go have a seat somewhere and I'll let him know you're here."

"Somewhere," Marcus says, "What do you mean go have a seat somewhere?"

"Just go sit down sir." the homely woman stresses again.

"This is a damn shame..." Marcus says as they walk away in search of a place to sit.

On the far wall they spy an almost empty wooden bench.

At the end of the bench sits a scantily dressed woman adorned with handcuffs and hideous makeup.

Marcus and Carolyn both take a seat at the opposite end of the bench from the now smiling woman.

"Well hello there daddy..." she breathes towards them.

The loud foul stench of liquor and God knows what else on her breath is all but nauseating to Marcus and his recently widowed daughter.

Carolyn covers her mouth and nose, as her father covers his stomach.

"How are you?" Marcus waves back politely. Then he turns his back to the lady and faces Carolyn.

"So what was that?" he asks.

"Oh daddy she's obviously a working girl." Carolyn tells him.

"A working girl..." he repeats.

"A whore daddy, you know like a prostitute..." Carolyn explains.

"Oh, not her," Marcus says, "I'm talking about what you said to the clerk up front."

"What did I say?" Carolyn asks.

"Well baby," he says, "you told her your last name was Williams, instead of Olivier."

"So what." she says.

"Your husband and children, who all bear that name just died in a fire," Marcus says, "how can you in good conscious just lie your married name down so quickly? That won't go over well with this detective at all."

"Don't worry about it daddy." she says.

"You can be my daddy too..." the whore at the end of the bench says.

They both ignore her comment.

"What am I missing baby," Marcus asks Carolyn, "What is it that you're not telling me hunny."

"It doesn't matter daddy," she tells him, "It's the past... it's not going to change anything in the present or future."

"Baby..." he says.

"No daddy," she interjects, "some things are just much better left unsaid. What's done in the dark can stay there if people leave it there. And that's what I fully intend to do."

An officer approaches the whore at the end of the bench and motions for her to stand up.

She obeys.

Then she looks down at Marcus and winks at him with her long dark tongue protruding disgustingly far outside of her crusty, dry, lipstick crumb covered mouth.

"Bye daddy," she says, "sure hope I see you around sometime..."

Marcus waves politely, and then turns his back to her once again.

"Carolyn, now baby you are not being up front with me about everything." Marcus tells her.

"Where the hell is this detective," Carolyn says, "we've been here over twenty minutes."

"To hell with the detective," her father says forcefully, "you tell me what's going on *right damn now Carolyn* Jane!"

"Fine," she says, "Ralph was having…"

"An affair…" Marcus interjects.

"I'm sorry so baby," he continues as he tries to hug her, "but if you…"

"I wasn't finished daddy." she tells him pulling away from his attempted hug.

"I'm sorry baby keep going." he tells her.

Carolyn exhales deeply, as she carefully decides how to deliver her next delicate proclamation.

She looks in her father's waiting eyes and forgets what she was going to say.

A tall, bald headed, white man, with blue eyes wearing a suit approaches them.

"Mrs. Olivier I presume…" he says.

Carolyn nods.

"I am very sorry about your loss," he says as he shakes her tiny caramel hand, "If you can just come with me, I just need to ask you a few simple questions."

"Detective Larkin is it…" Marcus asks.

"Yes sir," he replies, "and you are?"

"I'm Carolyn's father," Marcus shakes the detective's hand, "we are in the middle of a very important conversation so…"

"It can wait daddy." Carolyn stands up from the bench.

"Sit your ass down now!" Marcus tells her.

"I am not a child." she says.

"Now!" he says with finality.

She obeys.

"After we are done talking I will bring her to your office myself," Marcus says, "I saw the office over   there to the left from which you came. Just give us five minutes please."

"Yes sir that's fine." Detective Larkin walks back to his office.

"Finish what you were…" Marcus starts.

"Ralph was having sex with Kayla dad." Carolyn interjects.

Marcus' eyes triple in size as he scoots much closer to his daughter.

"Kayla who?" he asks.

"Kayla Williams," Carolyn says as new tears begin to trickle down her tired face, "my little whore of a sister was sleeping with my husband behind my back and has been for years. She caused him to lose his job, she was taking money out of our home… she ruined my family daddy."

"Oh my Lord…" Marcus hugs his daughter tightly.

"I knew it," he continues, "they found Kayla butt naked burning to death on the front lawn."

"Junior and Karan; are dead daddy," Carolyn cries, "They're both dead because of Kayla."

"Did Kayla start the fire baby?" Marcus asks.

"Not in a literal sense," Carolyn wipes more tears away, "but she is the reason the house was burned down."

"Did you do it baby?" Marcus whispers to his daughter.

"No daddy," she stresses her words, "I would never hurt my babies."

"Who started the fire Carolyn Jane?" Marcus inquires.
Still crying, she stares into her daddy's eyes. His name is on the tip of her tongue. She can hear it being whispered inside her head over and over, "James, James Radicon."

"Who started the fire Carolyn Jane?" Marcus asks again.

"Stop calling me Carolyn Jane," she tells him through red blurry eyes, "the fire is Kayla's fault dad. She may not have physically started the actual fire, but she started the chain of events that led to it. It's her fault they're dead; and it's her fault the rest of her face is lying somewhere on my charred front lawn! I hate her daddy!"

"Don't say that baby." he tells her.

"Fuck that dad," she cries, "it's true she's a little evil, conniving whore, and I hate her!"

"Carolyn, listen," he says, "family is all we got in this world. If you can't trust family who can you trust?"

"Love." she replies.

"This is not all your sister's fault baby." he says.

"I agree," Carolyn says, "it's Ralph's fault too."

"And your sister she's just different Carolyn." Marcus says.

"Tell me about it..." Carolyn scoffs.

"No, baby," Marcus says, "I mean Kayla didn't get a lot of attention as a child, not as much as you did when you were growing up."

"So what..." Carolyn says.

"She is your sister," Marcus tells her, "and she loves you very much."

"No she does not," Carolyn replies, "that is a lie daddy. Damn it! People just go through life believing and saying the same stupid shit until they die. Well, I'm not one of those people dad. Right is right and wrong is wrong. Kayla is not a baby she knew exactly what she was doing. If she wanted... or needed attention she should have come to you, like I did when I was her age."

With that said Carolyn storms away from her father across the hall into the detective's office.

Ch. 19

"Lakeside"

(Carolyn)

*T*he investigation of my husband's death and the mysterious case of my children's missing bodies is ongoing, but with so many burdens to bear now, I don't know which one to succumb to first. I hate giving up on anything, but I'm definitely smart enough to know when too much, is just too damn much. With nowhere else to go I was forced to move back in with my parents. Damn it! I said no matter what I would never, ever move back in with my parents. I can't get comfortable at night, no matter what I damn do. Rather than sleep in my bed in

*my old room, all alone I decided to sleep in the den on
the sofa.*

A few days have passed and Carolyn still hasn't been
able to create anything close to a comfort zone at her
parent's home. Her days are filled with the planning of
the triple funeral and listening painfully to her father's
plans for her future going forward.

Carolyn loves her parents dearly, but living with them
is something she could never survive long term.

She went to visit Kayla in the hospital yesterday. The
doctor said her skin is healing fast, but it looked noticeably
worse to Carolyn. The only positive is that destroying
Kayla's face has seemed to give new life to her soul.

Her entire outlook on life has begun to change
drastically. She's nowhere near depressed like everyone
expected her to be. She sits up most days talking about
how she wants to start mentoring young girls about
molestation, rape, and the dangers of teen sex.

She seems adamant about teaching young girls and
teens to be strong enough to speak up when something is
happening to them that shouldn't be.

Carolyn still hasn't forgiven her baby sister for sleeping
with her husband and lying to her for years, but she does
believe that there is hope of them being friends again one
day.

As Carolyn lies alone on her mother's couch tonight the
rain is falling fiercely outside. The thunder is obnoxiously
loud and the lightning strikes are blindingly bright.
Tossing and turning for hours is the worst recipe for a
good night's sleep.

(Carolyn)
*How do you survive trapped in a life without a man
that has become your whole world? Never possible, I'm*

no fool. If his heart ever stops beating, mine will stop immediately with his. We are bonded together, connected forever.

Carolyn continues to check her phone and every social network site she's a member of to see if Radicon has tried to reach her. But there's nothing. Carolyn finally accepts the fact that the only man she has ever been in love with has moved on. He's gone forever.

And deep down in her soul, she knows she's the one who pushed him away. She left him stranded on the side of the road and drove off into the sunset in a random transfer truck.

She rode for thirty minutes next to a smelly old black guy in soiled overalls, bashing James' name for something he did out of pure love for her.

She's sure he never meant to hurt Ralph Jr., Karan, or Kayla; they were just there with Ralph. He probably didn't know.

Unable to lie down any longer Carolyn sits up on the sofa. With her head in her hands she tries to clear her mind of all the dangerous thoughts that are clouding it. She would like to think she would never really take her own life, but a life without James Radicon is no life at all.

She stands up on shaky legs. Her equilibrium has long escaped her and her ability to focus no longer exists. When she returns to work at the winery, she's sure James will fire her. Life goes downhill from there.

If you choose to take the time to invest yourself wholly into an unsavory relationship, be ready to whether the storms it will undoubtedly create.

From where she's standing, Carolyn can see clearly out of the window next to the front door. The rain is still falling steadily. The pattern in which the drops are hitting the window is almost soothing to her.

She begins to walk towards the window slowly, she can't help it. She feels drawn towards it and the methodic sound of the now lightly crashing rain.

With both hands on the window, she softly presses her ear to the glass and listens calmly to the outside world. She can feel a pulse in the window, its James. She can feel his heart beat in every fiber of her parents' house.

With her face forward now pressed gently against the cool rain covered window Carolyn can see something outside the house.

It's a truck, a black truck. *It appears to be James' SUV.*

Her heart stops instantly, but she can still feel his beating deep inside her chest. She walks a few steps to her left to the front door.

She opens it slowly. As Carolyn walks out of the front door, she's unsure why James' truck is parked in front of her parents' house.

The closer she gets to the car she can see him sitting in the front seat.

Her heart stops again as she takes yet another step forward. He's crying. James' face is down in his hands and he's crying openly like a vulnerable child. Carolyn's heart breaks instantly, as she has never seen this man be so transparent and real.

She stands there in the rain watching him cry through his window. Her hair and makeup don't matter right now; to him they never really did.

A love like theirs' transcends and penetrates all levels and forms of worldly relationship stereotypes and statistics.

Their love is one that is real and raw… and most importantly undeniably everlasting. She believes deep down in her soul only death could truly separate the two of them.

James looks up with wide eyes laced with panic. He immediately aims a gun at her.

She jumps back in real fear. James quickly lowers the gun.

At the genuine pain on his face Carolyn begins to cry herself. He opens the door.

"Baby, I don't care how much time I get in prison," he cries, "I'll do every day. I deserve it. I never meant to hurt anybody but your husband Carolyn. I am… eternally sorry for causing you pain, that was never my objective. And I'm sorry about your sister Kayla as well. But I do not apologize about what happened to Ralph. He put his hands on you and I will not tolerate that. I couldn't focus baby… so many things were going through my mind. Jessica is sick; I think my son Lucas might be gay, and my Katie… If I was to ever lose my daughter I don't know what I would do Carolyn. Baby, I am so, so sorry for hurting you… I didn't know you actually loved your husband."

Carolyn jumps into James' lap and kisses him deeply.

"I love *you*." she admits.

"And you're not going anywhere, James Justin Radicon," she cries in between kisses, "I didn't tell the police a damn thing."

James pulls her in his truck completely and closes the door behind her to shield her from the rain.

"Are you serious?" he asks.

"It never even really crossed my mind." Carolyn lies.

"Well it did," she admits, "but if I had told the   police what you did, I know I would have regretted it for the rest of my life."

James turns Carolyn around in his lap to face him.

"Look at me Carolyn," he stresses to her, "I never want you to leave me again, okay? No more serious fights, no more break ups... this is it."

"Okay Mr. Radicon..." she says with a rejuvenated smile.

Their tears begin to intertwine as James presses his warm face against Carolyn's. Kiss after kiss James regrets more and more every second he's spent away from this woman from the moment he met her.

The rain has stopped; and the sun is trying to peek through the clouds.

James looks deep in Carolyn's eyes for a long silent moment. Then he kisses her hard on the mouth and then softly again.

"Damn I missed your lips..." he growls happily.

"And you know what else?" he continues.

"What?" she asks.

Carolyn closes her beautiful, tear stained, hazel eyes as she takes in this moment with all of her senses.

"I have a confession." James says.

"Confess baby..." she says with an adorable closed eyed smile.

"When I'm with you," he says, "things change all around me. But most importantly I change, you make me better in every way; and my wife of almost seventeen years never crosses my mind. Carolyn Jane Olivier there is no comparison between the two."

"Between me and Jessica..." Carolyn asks.

"I never in my life loved my wife the way I am so completely, unconditionally, drowning in love with you hunny..." he vows.

Carolyn opens her eyes as they light up instantly.

"Oh James..." she moans.

"Come with me now baby…" he says.

"Where James?" she asks.

James reaches in the passenger seat and hands her an envelope with familiar red handwriting on it.

"Open it…" he says with an anxious grin.

She obeys.

"This is an invitation to Master's house to go swimming," she says, "but, he doesn't have a pool does he?"

"No, he has a lake Carolyn." James tells her.

"That's great," she replies, "but I'm not going to swim in it."

"Why not baby?" he asks.

"Black people don't swim in strange lakes James." she tells him.

"It's not strange," James says, "the lake is secluded and manmade baby so there's almost nothing in the lake that he didn't have put in it himself."

"Almost doesn't count James," she says, "that means that there could almost be a big ugly alligator in that lake just waiting to eat me."

"Nobody's gonna eat you but me…" he growls with his lips against her blushing cheek.

"Please…" he continues.

His electricity is calmly, triumphantly penetrating her mind, body, and soul.

"Fine James," she says, "but first explain to me what your fascination and your connections are with the Master and his house."

"I told you," he says, "when my parents past away my father left me a note, asking me to contact the Master. I know the Master is a little strange, and mysterious, but he is the only connection to my father that I have left on this earth Carolyn."

"I understand," she tells him, "just let me go change and get some extra clothes. I'll be right back."

As she rushes back into the house James shakes his head with a distant smile covering his face.

He pulls his rear view mirror down to look at himself. He dries his reddened face and uses his chap-stick to moisten his almost dry lips.

His phone rings.

"Hello," he answers, *"Yes Dr. Franco this is Mr. Radicon. Damn it... Are you sure? Well what else can be done sir? Nothing... How long does she have now Doc? I understand Dr. Franco, yes I understand, but right now I have to be here. I messed up really bad and I have to fix it before it's too late. I'm sorry you feel that way sir. Doc if she's going to die either way then why... Well, tell Jessica I am very sorry, but I... Sir, I contribute millions of dollars to that hospital, if you don't... fine!"*

James hangs up his phone riddled with anger, regret, and frustration. Seconds later Carolyn runs back outside with one of the Louis Vuitton duffel bags he bought her in Atlanta and a much smaller Michael Kors make up bag. She gets in and he tosses her bag in the backseat for her. Carolyn opens her makeup bag as he cranks up.

As they drive off Carolyn pulls down the overhead mirror and begins reapplying her makeup.

James shakes his head because he wants so badly to tell her she should never wear makeup again. She doesn't need it. But, he's already told her this before and he knows full well *that* statement will spark an even bigger conversation that he's not emotionally ready for in this moment. So instead he just drives and keeps his precious endearing thoughts to himself for now.

After putting the pretty finishing touches on her face Carolyn turns the volume up on the radio. Luther Vandross' old hit song, "If This World Were Mine," is on. Carolyn sits way back in her seat and takes James' hand in hers.

"James..." she turns the radio down a bit.

"Yes love." he replies.

"Your radio is always on the old school or slows jams station." she says, smiling to herself.

"Yeah most times." he says.

"Why though," she asks, "How did you start listening to so much black music; growing up in an affluent white household?"

"Ms. Debra." he replies with a real smile.

"Ms. Who..." Carolyn asks.

"Ms. Debra Bennifield," James says, "she's dead now. She was my father's old secretary. But she was really more like an all-around assistant to him, like you are to me."

"And Ms. Bennifield was white right?" Carolyn asks.

"Just as white as you are." he replies smiling at her playfully.

"Wait, so let me get this straight," Carolyn says, "Your father and his black assistant were fucking too, just like us?"

"Hell no," James snatches his hand away from hers to turn the music back up; "My father loved my mother dearly. He was loyal to her until the day they died."

Carolyn can sense the tension in his voice. She turns the music back down a little, and covers the top of his pale right hand with hers.

"Calm down baby," Carolyn says, "Ms. Debra... So that's where your love for soulful music came from huh?"

"Yes ma'am," he replies, "now I do love old school music baby, but I also gotta have my country too; Alan Jackson, Toby Keith, Rascal Flatts…"

"Every long lost dream…" Carolyn begins to sing the popular country song by Rascal Flatts. *"Led me to where you are…"* James joins in singing with her in joy and surprise. *"Others who broke my heart,"* they continue to sing together, *"They were like Northern stars… Pointing me on my way… Into your loving, arms… This much I know is true… That God blessed the broken road… That led me straight to you…"*

"Wow," James smiles from ear to ear, "Are you serious right now?"

"Now that was cute." Carolyn says laughing giddily.

"Why *the hell*… Do you know the lyrics to *"Broken Road,"* Carolyn Olivier?" James asks staring at her in pure awe.

"There are still things that you don't know about me Mr. Radicon." she tells him as she brings his large hand to her mouth and kisses it gently.

(Carolyn)

"So when are you moving in?" James asks Carolyn.

"Moving in what?" she asks as her necks snaps to the right.

"You're moving into my house." James tells her."

"No I'm not." she replies.

"Of course you are," he says, "where else are you gonna go? You can't just stay at your parents' house forever."

"So you really expect me to live at your house with you and your wife?" she asks.

"I bought that mansion," he tells her, *"my* blood, sweat, and tears… *nobody else."*

Carolyn leans way back in her seat and stares straight ahead holding James' hand tightly inside of hers. He presses the button on his steering wheel and turns the radio volume up to its original volume, as Keith Sweat sings his old hit song, "*Twisted*."

(The lake)

As they pull up the hill into Master's driveway at his mansion, Carolyn dives into the backseat and begins searching her bag frantically.

"Damn it." she says.

"What's wrong now?" he asks.

"I didn't bring a swim suit," she tells him, "damn it, that was the main reason I went back inside my parent's house."

"It's ok you won't need one." he replies.

"What do you mean I won't need a swimsuit James?" Carolyn asks.

"You ask way too many questions little girl." he tells her.

"Little girl," Carolyn repeats, "Um, James we are going swimming, so I do need to know what I'll be swimming in. That's kind of important."

"No worries," James says, "everything will be fine. I just want you to relax and tend to *my desires*. We've both been through so much lately we just need to take a step back and realize our positions."

Carolyn remains silent with her arms crossed in the backseat.

James looks up into his rearview mirror.

"What the hell is wrong with you?" he asks her.

"You," she replies, "You're right on one account. We have *both* been through a lot lately. So, what the hell do you mean you want me to *relax and tend to your desires?*"

James smiles at her.

"Carolyn," he says, "I am your man. You are my woman... all I mean is that I want you to be my everything... and I want to be everything to you."

"You are everything to me James," her brows wrinkle gently, "but this has to become more of a two-way street between us..."

"So you no longer want to be my fantasy," he says, "that's fine Carolyn I..."

"I never said that James," she interjects, "those words never once came out of my mouth. I only mean that I want more."

"More what?" he asks.

"More everything..." she replies.

James laughs.

"Oh, I see," he says, "no worries Carolyn Jane I'll be rich forever."

"And what is that supposed to mean?" she asks with her left hand on her hip in the backseat.

"It means," James stares down at his expensive gold Rolex watch, "you don't have to worry, because I have more than enough money to keep your fine ass in *Gucci and gold*, and *Prada and pearls*..."

Carolyn's right hand quickly finds its way to her right hip, as her brows wrinkle even tighter.

"Really," she says with a venomous glare on her face, "And what about Dolce and diamonds James..."

"Oh of course," he says, "diamonds are a girl's best..."

"*Oh shut the hell up James Radicon,*" she interjects, "I am not a gold digger, never have been, never will be. I am not with you because of money..."

"Is that right..." he scoffs.

"I was married to Ralph," she reminds him, "if money was my motive I would have left his broke ass a long time ago."

James continues to stare at his flawless watch in curious silence.

"Where the hell did this conversation even come from?" she asks.

"You said you wanted more," he says with a smile, "I'm just letting you know you can have it…"

"I didn't mean material shit James," she yells, "You've already bought me enough clothing to last me a couple of lifetimes. If I sold all the jewelry you've given me, I could retire now and probably buy a small country and live well until I die."

James reaches deep in his left pant pocket.

"Are you listening to me Radicon…?" Carolyn asks.

"Here," he reaches his hand over the seat behind him, "Your new black card came in the mail yesterday."

"Damn it James!" she screams knocking the card out of his hands.

"Is that really what you think of me?" she asks.

"It's not your fault love, it's just the nature of the beast." he explains.

"The nature of what beast Radicon?" she fumes.

Unable to look in her eyes James continues to fidget with his watch.

"Carolyn," he says, "I've been rich all my life. And I've been around a lot of rich people. I know when a young black chick gets the opportunity to date an older wealthy white man *love* is usually not a part of the true agenda."

"Well James," she says, "***I'm not a usual bitch.*** I'm a respectful, loyal, young black woman who happens to love you very much… although you make it hard as hell at times. And stop mentioning color, there are no colors. My love is blind."

"I believe you baby," he tells her, "I'm just being a little insecure I suppose."

Carolyn's poisonous scowl melts away from her face as she leans forward behind James' seat and throws her arms around his broad shoulders.

"How is that possible," she asks with a calming smile, "What on this earth could possibly make a man as gorgeous as you even consider doubting himself?"

"Dating a woman as perfect as you Carolyn Jane." he admits.

"Awe baby," she gushes, "That was sweet, but stop calling me Carolyn Jane, *my dad* calls me that."

"I am your daddy..." he tells her with a flirtatious smile.

"I'm serious James," she whines, "stop it."

"Yes ma'am," he replies playfully, "so can we go swimming now?"

"I have nothing to swim in James." she reminds him.

"Neither do I." he opens the front door of his expensive SUV.

With the front door still open James takes his shirt off exposing his gorgeous upper body to the thirsty rays of the bright Miami sun.

Then he takes off his shoes and socks and throws them in the front seat.

"Let's go baby..." he heads off towards the back of the enormous house. Carolyn hastily jumps out of the car to try and catch up to him.

Once out of the car she attempts to pull her extremely short shorts down to cover the exposed part of her behind.

"James wait up..." she calls out to him.

By the time she turns the corner, he's already way behind the house headed down to the lake.

As she follows behind him Carolyn looks ahead to the decent sized body of water that lies in front of them.

The water is calm and inviting. Around the lake lie several small boats, a raft, and a cute white canoe. The canoe bears the word, "Master" on the side of it.

They're about five hundred feet away from the lake now. Carolyn's still not sure what's she's going to swim in, but doesn't have the nerve to ask James again right now.

James turns around quickly and grabs Carolyn by her shoulders. Her heart sinks to her stomach and stops instantly. He's looking deep into her eyes piercing her with the pure blueness of his.

"We said a lot of stuff back there..." he says.

"Yeah..." she replies.

"Forget it," he smiles, "forget all of it. You belong to me. I want you to always be my fantasy."

"Okay..." she replies meekly.

"A woman should be her man's own personal porn star." he tells her.

James bends his head down just low enough to fill her warm, wet mouth with his strong tongue as his passionate lips graciously massage hers.

He pulls away from her, and starts back walking towards the lake. She follows him.

At the edge of the lake James dips his left foot into the water to test it.

"Perfect..." he says.

He looks around the lake momentarily as if something is missing.

James shakes his head and then smiles.

"This is really nice." Carolyn rubs James' back.

"What is?" he asks.

"Master letting us swim in his lake…" she says.

"Oh yeah, he's a good man." James removes his cargo shorts.

In nothing but a pair of boxer briefs James steps back closer to the lake.

He looks back at Carolyn with that infectious smile on his face.

Carolyn has no clue what that smile means, but she returns it anyway. James snatches off his boxers, bearing his tanned behind for the world to see and then dives into the beautiful water head first.

With folded arms Carolyn watches him as he slices through the water like a human fish. After swimming under water to about the middle of the lake James breaks the surface.

"Whoo hoo!!!" he yells.

Carolyn jumps as the loud echo of his voice startles her.

"Get in little girl!" he yells.

"The water is perfect…" he continues.

"James you're in that lake completely naked…" she says.

"So what," he laughs, "You will be too in a minute."

"Um no I won't." she tells him with a defiant smile as she calmly walks further away from the waters.

"Little girl you are really blowing my high." he says playfully before disappearing beneath the beautiful waters again.

Seconds later he emerges from below again this time near the edge of the lake.

Looking at him and the gorgeous view that is surrounding him, Carolyn feels completely overwhelmed by the plethora of personified beauty that is before her at this very moment. Her heart is pounding fiercely and she feels a little lightheaded.

"Jump in baby." James snatches her mind away from her wondrous daydream.

"I can't James." she takes a few more steps back.

"Ok that's fine." he tells her.

James climbs back out of the water and walks up the bank towards her.

Carolyn pleasurably takes in every one of his perfect steps as he draws closer to her.

Standing there completely nude dripping lake water, James Radicon's body has never looked so magnificently perfect as it does right now. Carolyn can't help but stare at the glorious size of him.

Her eyes greedily take in every inch of his chiseled body until they finally reach his smiling eyes.

Carolyn bites her bottom lip then she swallows hard to rid her extremely wet mouth of some of the excess moisture inside of it.

"You're not gonna swim with me baby?" he asks.

Carolyn playfully shakes her head no.

"Come on **Carolyn Jane**..." he pleads with her.

"No **James Justin**." she says with a playful grin.

"Fine..." James walks towards her, "You don't have to swim if you don't want to."

Standing face to face with her, James slowly runs his fingers through her recently straightened hair. Smiling down at her with bright wise eyes James tries to imagine what she's thinking right now.

He kisses her gently on her full pink lips. As he kisses her he pulls the straps of her thin shirt over her shoulders and lets it fall off of her.

Next James unbuttons her shorts and pulls them down. Carolyn steps out of her shorts that have fallen down around her ankles. She also finishes removing her shirt.

Standing there in nothing but her panties Carolyn stares up into James eyes wondering what's next. He bends down and pulls her panties down low, Carolyn steps out of them one foot at a time.

After he stands back up James picks Carolyn up in his strong arms and she wraps her legs around him.

"Now what..." she breathes deeply on his neck.

"I'm gonna throw you in the water..." he whispers.

"I can't hear you baby." she tells him.

James starts walking towards the water.

"James..." Carolyn says.

He smiles at her.

"James no baby," she screams, "I don't want to go under... James my hair!"

James starts to run towards the water.

"Baby noooo!" she yells out.

"Oh shut up Carolyn Jane..." he replies with a mischievous smile.

Closer to the lake now, James starts to pick up speed with Carolyn nestled tightly in his powerful arms.

From the edge of the lake James leaps off one foot as far out into the water as he possibly can.

Splash... A warm rush takes over Carolyn as their bodies' crash into the beautiful water.

As they sink deeper into the lake Carolyn can see bubbles all around her floating back up to the surface. Careful not to open her mouth, Carolyn soon realizes she can't breathe.

James can feel the panic in her progressively tense body. He kicks his feet out towards the bottom of the lake to speed up their ascent back to the surface.

Once they break through the lakes surface Carolyn starts coughing. After she regains her composure she pushes away from James.

"Are you okay babe..." James asks swimming towards Carolyn.

"Fuck you James!" she yells pushing him away again.

"Awe baby," he forces his arms around her,
"I'm sorry..."

He kisses her on her forehead.

Carolyn pushes him away yet again.

"That was the worst thing you have ever done to me." she wipes some of the runny makeup from around her eyes.

"I'm sorry Carolyn..." he says.

"No you're not James," she whines, "that was really mean and I don't appreciate it at all!"

"Awe, come here baby..." James wraps his arms around her again.

Looking at him, her anger begins to melt away down into the lake waters.

Suddenly James picks her up in his arms and throws her towards the shallower area of the lake, a few feet away from him.

"Ahhh!" she screams as she breaks the surface again.

James is laughing heartily.

"James my makeup," she cries, "Look at my face... I hate your stupid ass!"

"No you don't," he tells her, "have some fun little girl. And who wears makeup to swim anyway?"

"Look at my face James," she cries, "I'm not perfect like the white women you're used to. I saw pictures in your house of Jessica when she was my age. She was fucking perfect James. I have a lot of flaws, but my makeup makes me feel good enough... not quite good enough *for you*, but good enough to look at myself in the mirror and not be too terribly insecure."

"Are you serious right now," James asks, "are we really having this conversation in the middle of this beautiful lake?"

Carolyn turns away from him as she begins to cry.

James' heart breaks at the sight of her new tears.

He swims towards her quickly.

"Baby no," he says, "don't cry. You are a very intelligent, talented, diligent woman... but you gotta be one of the *blindest* bastards I've ever seen in my life..."

Carolyn holds back a smile and a laugh.

"What are you talking about James Radicon?" she asks.

"Less than perfect," he says, "no you are more than perfect to and *for me*. Do you know what I see when I look at you?" "No."

she replies.

"Well I'm gonna tell you," he pulls her into his strong arms, "when I look at you Carolyn Jane Olivier... right now, no lipstick, no makeup, hair every damn wear... I see a creature so stunningly beautiful, that if God himself gave me the power to create my own angel... she could have never turned out as perfect as you are baby. Yes, you do have flaws. So does Jessica, so do I, but it's our flaws that make us all unique baby."

"Whatever James..." she says.

"I am so serious," he pulls her even closer to him, "baby you don't even need all that makeup, you don't need anything, but you to keep me satisfied for a lifetime."

"Stop lying to me James Radicon…" Carolyn cries.

James holds her face steady in his hands, right there in the middle of the lake and looks desperately deep into her hazel eyes.

"Right now," he says, "butt naked, with no makeup on, in the middle of this lake you are more beautiful to me than ever before."

Her eyes tell him she believes him with every thread of her being. Carolyn jumps in his arms. The primal fire between them is raging ferociously.

Carolyn hastily wraps her legs around James' hard body. He steadies his feet in the bottom of the shallow part of the lake, then uses his hand to guide himself inside of Carolyn.

She gasps. He kisses her open mouth as he begins to grind in and out of her precious body. Every kiss James blesses her greedy mouth with is just as powerful and real as the one before it.

Carolyn screams out in pure ecstasy. She continues to scream and moan with her lips pressed gently against his handsome face. Sex with James gets her so high she never wants to come down. They both pray the undeniable power of the love they share never dies.

"I love you," James moans, "I love you more than anything in this whole damn world."

He begins to fuck her harder, and harder, he can't help himself.

Her screams are deafening now; her nails are dug painfully deep into his powerful back. His precious pain feels so good to Carolyn's anxious hungry body. She can feel him all the way in her tiny stomach again. Carolyn begins to bounce up and down on him, as she feels the need to take control now.

She closes her eyes and bites down hard on her bottom lip as she strains to take all of him. James is gripping her ass harder than ever before. He wants her to have no doubt that her mind, body, and soul all belong to him... but especially her body.

Carolyn begins to bite James' neck as she rides him. He's deeper now, but she wouldn't dare ask him to stop. A strange feeling suddenly rushes through Carolyn's body. She opens her eyes.

Behind James on the far side of the lake she sees three men watching them. Master draped in a black bath robe, is standing in between the other two men who are both wearing black masks.

The other two men are both completely nude. Carolyn covers her mouth with bulging eyes, as James continues to penetrate her wet body.

Master and his two servants are obviously aroused by the show she and James are putting on, as all three of them now have obvious erections.

Carolyn licks her lips, and starts back biting James' neck as she watches the three men pleasure themselves as they watch her. Carolyn can't help but to feel like a gorgeous sex goddess who has the power to drive any man wild.

She realizes now that being watched is something she's always wanted to do. James pulls out, and then turns Carolyn's body around so that he can hold her up and enter her body from behind.

While fucking her from behind James slowly turns around in a half circle so that her body is facing the Master and his men at the edge of the lake.

James begins pulling Carolyn's small body back towards him as hard as he can. He can't stop looking down at her round, plump ass, as it bounces off his rock hard six pack abs.

Harder, harder, harder still James is trying to make Carolyn scream out even louder than she already is.

"Oh baby," she cries out, "are they gonna join or just watch us..."

"Do you want them to join?" James asks with two more powerful strokes.

"Only if you want them to," she moans, "my body belongs to you baby..."

"James..." the master calls out.

James looks towards the old man.

"I'll be right back baby," he says, "wait here; I need to get something out of the car."

He pulls out and then turns her around to kiss her hard on the mouth. As James swims back to the grassy edge of the lake, Carolyn stands there awkwardly waiting for her next command.

At the edge of the lake, James engages in a private conversation with the Master.

Carolyn's body is on fire now, with both hands beneath the water Carolyn continues to pleasure herself. She watches as James begins to climb out of the lake. She licks her full lips as his naked form emerges fully from the water.

James picks up his shorts off the ground and puts them on. As he begins to walk back up the hill to the house, Carolyn stares through anxious and curious eyes at   the three men that remain. The one to the right has a body that is even better than James'.

Master lifts his left arm and points towards Carolyn. The two naked men immediately dive in the lake and begin swimming towards her.

The first man to reach her picks her up in the air; with her legs wrapped around his head he begins to suck her body.

James can hear Carolyn moaning as he turns the corner at the top of the hill. He shakes his head.

He storms towards his SUV with evil thoughts flooding his confused mind.

After opening the door, he jumps in the front seat and slams the door behind him. He can still hear Carolyn's obvious pleasure in the distance.

He sticks a finger deep in each of his ears trying to drown out the sound, but no luck.

Carolyn's joyous screams are only growing louder.

James quickly takes his cell phone out of his   pocket. After scrolling through his contacts he clicks on her name.

The phone rings.

It continues to ring as he waits patiently.

He hears her voice.

"Hello… Katie," James says into the phone, "What you doing baby? Are you okay? Daddy misses you. Yes, I'll be home tonight. The father-daughter dance is in two days; I wouldn't miss it for the world. Okay baby, I'll see you soon. I love you Katherine Grace."

He presses end on his phone's screen, and then places the phone back in his pocket.

James opens the door of the SUV and rushes to the back corner of the house. He gently peaks his head around the corner to see what's going on now.

Carolyn is out of the lake bending over holding on to an old tree, as the three men have their way with her gorgeous caramel body.

James turns away and makes his way back to the front of the house. He looks towards the front door and pauses for a second.

He wants to go inside, but at the same time he fears the Master and what he was told he's capable of.

His father told him in the detailed letter he left behind when he died ten years ago, to obey the Master no matter what, and never cross him, because he would surely die.

James absolutely worshiped the ground his father walked on so disobeying the Master is an idea Radicon's mind only flirts with, but never seriously considers.

He walks to the front door. The beautiful art that is the stained glass in the front door catches James' eye once again. James opens the door quietly. He slowly walks in closing the door behind him gently.

James has always felt a strange sense of familiarity inside the Master's house. The very first time he was invited inside it felt like and even smelled like his childhood home.

The Master was apparently very close to James' father Raymond, so the young billionaire wonders why his father never introduced them while he was still alive.

Maybe they had grown apart, he thinks, or maybe his father had a few secrets he didn't want to be exposed by James having a relationship with the Master himself.

James has often wondered if his mother and father ever engaged in the Master's sexual exploits. He realizes now that it's very possible they did because the Master has a very convincing personality to put it mildly.

Radicon almost feels at times like he's been brainwashed by the Master; he feels powerless around him. Whatever the man says James will see to it that his request is done as quickly as possible.

This for James is not familiar territory at all; he has been the biggest boss in his own life for the past twenty plus years.

To come into this man's world and become one of his lap dogs is very unnerving for James Radicon the self-made billionaire, but he would never disobey this man whom his father instructed him to respect.

James makes his way to the back window and stares out of it, down towards the lake. The master is joyfully having his way with the woman James loves. He turns away again, this time in pursuit of the kitchen.

As he walks into the kitchen area he heads straight towards the refrigerator. He opens it. He grabs a bottle of water and then closes it back.

After exiting the kitchen James makes his way to the mysterious stairs that lead up to the upper deck of the Master's mansion.

James takes each step one at a time all the while trying to look up ahead to see what is awaiting him at the end of his ascent of the gorgeous black marble staircase. The Master's stairs are just as beautiful as the rest of his home. The black topped gold railing on the sides of the stairs look fit only for a king. This enormous house is an American castle and the Master is the king of its domain. At the top of the steps James can't decide if he should go left or right. He looks down at the tattoo on his left wrist and decides to check out the left side first.

As he walks he's careful not to make any noise even though he's more than sure there's nobody else in the house. He passes a couple of large rooms that are both empty for the most part.

He passes yet another room on his left side, but this time he pauses just after this room. Out of the corner of his eye he saw movement in the third room.

James walks backwards towards the room. He slowly pushes the door open a little more. Sitting in front of a mirror he sees a woman.

She hasn't noticed him standing there yet. A small digital radio beside her is playing one of James' favorite songs of all time, *"Fire and Desire"* by Rick James and Teena Marie.

As James watches her from behind, the woman sitting there in the mirror brushing her hair, feels so familiar to him. She begins to sing along beautifully with the radio. Her voice brings back so many wonderful childhood memories for James.

He closes his eyes and listens to the woman flawlessly hit every note along with the legendary singers on her radio. James walks closer to her.

James doesn't want to startle her so he subtly clears his throat. She turns around quickly.

James looks deep into her eyes as both of their hearts begin to melt instantly. The woman smiles at him as she starts to cry. She stands up.

"Ms. Debra," James says, "what are you doing here?"

She steps forward to hug him tightly.

"Oh James," she cries, "I am so sorry about your mother... and your father."

"Thank you Ms. Debra," he replies as she steps back to look at him, "but weren't you on the plane with them? We thought you died in the crash too."

"It's so good to see you son," she tells him wiping a few tears away, "and you look... exactly like your father did at your age."

"I know Ms. Debra, but how are you alive?" he asks.

She smiles.

"Your mother," she says, "loved you so much James."

"I know that Ms. Debra," he replies, "but why are you dodging my question?"

"How are Jessica and the kids James?" Debra asks.

"They're fine but..." James starts.

"That's good to hear." Debra interjects.

"Damn it Ms. Debra, what are you hiding?" he asks trying not to raise his voice.

"James," she says, "I'm a grown woman, I don't have to *hide* anything."

"Why aren't you dead Ms. Debra?" he asks agitatedly.

"Wasn't my time." she replies dryly.

"Is that some kind of joke Ms. Debra?" he asks.

"No James, calm down baby," she says, "Look I didn't die in the plane crash because... there wasn't one."

James' eyes triple in size instantly. "What the hell do you mean there was no crash Debra?"

She shakes her head.

"No, I didn't mean to say there was no crash," she tells him, "of course there was a crash I just wasn't in it."

"Obviously," James says, "and my question to you is why the hell not?"

"I wasn't on the plane James." she says.

"Then why weren't you at my parents' funeral?" he asks.

The front door opens downstairs.

They both panic.

"Quick," Debra says, "go down the hallway to the bathroom near the stairs. Do not let the Master know you ever saw me."

James obeys.

He looks out of the room first to see if anybody is coming up the stairs.

He sees nothing. He hastily creeps down the hallway to the bathroom. Once inside he closes the door behind him.

In front of the large picturesque bathroom mirror James doesn't recognize his own reflection. He feels dizzy and nauseous.

So many things he has believed for over ten years may very well be a lie. The only person who can tell him what he needs to know is at the other end of the hall seemingly scared for her life.

"James…" a female voice calls from downstairs. James quickly washes his reddened face in the sink and then dries it on a towel hanging up near him.

He opens the door to the bathroom and heads towards the stairs.

"There you are." Carolyn says.

James begins to quickly descend the stairs.

"Well you're just all smiles aren't you." he says.

"I had fun baby," she says, "it would have been more fun if you were there with me though."

She wraps her tired arms around his strong form, and lays her messy head on his strong chest.

The door opens. Master walks in with his two lackeys following closely behind him both wrapped in black towels.

"What are you two doing inside my house?" the old man asks looking James square in the eye.

James can't find any words to say.

Carolyn looks up at James curiously. Then she turns towards the Master.

"We just came inside a second ago Master," she tells him, "We were just admiring your lovely home again. We didn't mean to upset you."

"Yes sir," James says, "well we really have to get back now… I don't want Carolyn to have to walk into her parents' house too late."

James takes Carolyn by the hand and leads her out of the front door.

As they exit, Master looks up at the top of the stairs where two sad brown eyes are staring back at him.

Ch. 20

"Father daughter dance"

(The Radicon home)

T he room is filled with steam and the large bed is drenched with their sweat. Lust fires are burning their long awaited desires into every inch of his usually lonely bedroom. In his mind this has to be a dream. It's all wrong, very wrong, but it feels so right. He has never felt alive until this very moment.

(Lucas)

Oh God, to be held ... finally. To be touched, consensually for the first time in my whole life. This is what life is all about. Through this boy, my man, I know who I am. I know what I am. I don't want to hide anything; I want the world to know that I am happy with who God has allowed me to be. No more dating close female friends just to fit in, and keep the whispers to a minimum. Calvin Ridgefield is making me a man; he's making me free.

"Skywalker..." Cal whispers.
"Yeah..." Lucas moans.
"I can't... I can't do this. It's not me." Cal claims as he continues to pleasure the heir to the Radicon fortune.
Lucas looks at him and smiles.

"Oh shut up Calvin," Lucas replies happily, "this... is exactly who you are, it's who *we* are."

"Lucas!" James yells from downstairs.

"Oh shit..." Lucas whispers.

Cal stares into his boyfriend's eyes unsure what to do next. Cal begins to pull his pants and boxer shorts up.

"The window..." Lucas whispers.

"Hurry up, just put your shirt and shoes back on, and climb out of my window." Luke continues.

"What," Cal says, "I'm black Skywalker, I ain't jumpin' out no damn window..."

"It's either that or you can introduce yourself to my dad." Luke tells him.

Cal jumps out of the bed and quickly puts his shirt on. Next he grabs his shoes.

Luke runs into his bathroom.

Cal watches as Lucas' naked body disappears into the bathroom. After putting both shoes on, Cal opens the window.

"Lucas," James yells again much closer this time, "I know you hear me son!"

Cal pushes the window up more. He climbs out onto the roof.

Luke rushes back near his bed with a can of Febreze. He sprays it generously all around his room.

Cal begins to push the window down from the outside.

"Wait Cal..." Luke whispers.

James knocks on his door.

"Luke!" his father yells.

"Just a minute dad." he replies.

Luke grabs his car keys off the floor and then rushes to the window.

Cal kneels down so that he and Luke will be almost eye to eye.

Luke hands him the keys.

James knocks on the door harder this time.

"Damn it Lucas open this door! What the hell are you doing boy?" James asks.

"Take my car," Luke tells him, "scale the roof all the way to the left over there and then climb down the ladder."

"Okay baby." Cal replies.

Luke stands up on his tiptoes and kisses Cal twice.

"Come back and pick me up around two." Luke tells him.

Then he closes his window from the inside.

On the floor near his bed he finds a pair of Calvin's XXL basketball shorts. He quickly puts them on.

"Damn it Lucas…" James says as the door opens finally.

James pushes his son out of the way and rushes into his room. James searches every possible hiding spot to try to figure out what took his confused son so long to come to the door.

"Dad…" Luke says.

James walks into Luke's bathroom.

"Dad…" Luke repeats.

"What Lucas?" James barks.

"What are you looking for?" the sweaty teen asks.

James turns to face his son. Looking at his flustered face, James is all but sure the boy just had sex.

"Nice shorts son," James analyzes the boy even closer, "a little big for you though, don't you think?"

Luke looks down at the huge shorts that reach all the way down near his ankles.

"Oh, um these," Luke mumbles, "they are just…"

"Save it Luke, I don't wanna know," James interjects, "Where is your sister?" Luke's face wrinkles quickly as his head leans to the side involuntarily.

"Dad," Luke starts, "Katherine is…"

"You know what never mind," James smiles, "I'll find her myself. The father-daughter dance is tomorrow night. I want to practice dancing with her for an hour or so, so we'll be ready for tomorrow."

James approaches his son.

"Clean your room son." he says.

"Yes sir…" Luke sits down on his bed with his face still distorted.

James heads for the door to exit his son's smelly room. On the floor near the door James grabs an empty condom wrapper off of the floor.

He turns to look at Luke with the condom held up near his own head.

"What's done in the dark son," James shakes his blonde head, "will always come to the light."

"Yeah, well let's hope not for either one of us dad," Luke snaps, "how is your black assistant by the way? Have you given her any *special assignments* lately?"

James drops his head.

Then he looks back up at his son.

"Luke," James hesitates, "I love your mother very…"

"Yeah whatever dad," Luke barks, "mom is dying and you really just don't give a fuck! You're too busy giving your favorite employee special *perks*."

James drops the condom wrapper back on the floor and exits his son's room closing the door behind him.

(The hospital)

James walks into the University of Miami hospital with one goal on his mind and he will not be denied. He hops on the elevator.

As he arrives at Jessica's room he finds another woman lying in her bed.

"Who the hell are you?" James asks.

"Gertrude Petty," the lady responds, "are you my doctor?"

James storms out of the room.

He quickly approaches the first nurse he sees.

"Where the hell is my wife?" he asks her.

"Who is your wife sir?" she asks.

"You know exactly who the hell I am," he tells her, "cut the shit."

"Okay calm down sir," the nurse says, "what is your wife's last name?"

"I'm James Radicon," he yells, "My wife is a Radicon! She's the richest patient in this fucking hospital now where is she?"

"Radicon…" a strong voice startles James from behind him. He spins around quickly to find a young male doctor.

"Who the hell are you?" James asks.

The doctor approaches James quickly and shakes his hand.

"Dr. Franco," the man replies, "we spoke on the phone a couple of days ago."

James let's go of the man's hand.

"You called me an insensitive prick…" James recollects.

The doctor smiles nervously.

"Yeah I uh…" the doctor stutters.

"Whatever man, where the hell is my wife?" James asks with authority.

"Follow me." Dr. Franco tells him.

James follows the man all the way back onto the elevator. After riding up two more floors both men exit the elevator and begin walking down a new hall.

Lying there just outside of an actual hospital room in a hospital bed is Jessica Radicon. James approaches her quickly. He gently grabs her frail, cold, pale white hand.

James kneels down to kiss her dry cracked lips.

She doesn't move. James can't tell if she's dead or just sleeping. But he would never dare asks. He doesn't believe in death. Not anymore.

He lost his mother and his father ten years ago on the same day. He refuses to ever lose anybody else again.

He would rather die first. Her lips are so dry they look as if they could bleed at any given second.

"Why the hell isn't she in a room?" James fumes.

"They're cleaning it Mr. Radicon." Dr. Franco tells him.

James can no longer be strong.

His frustration finally gives way to desperation. With his shaky left hand, he pulls a cherry chap stick out of his pocket. He pulls the top off, and then twists the bottom of it to expose the bright red tip of the lip balm.

He carefully applies it to his wife thin pink lips. The tears that are flooding his deep blue eyes are making it very difficult to adequately apply the balm to Jessica's peeling lips.

Jessica opens her steel gray eyes just barely.

She smiles at the sight of her handsome husband and then closes her eyes back as she no longer has the strength to keep them open.

Jessica knows full well she is living in her last hours. Her mind, body, and spirit are so tired of fighting to stay on this pain-filled earth.

She gave up long ago, when it became evident that she had lost the rights to her biggest reason to live.

She lost her husband to another woman. A younger, prettier, much more vibrant woman than her, she's sure.

"Jessica..." James whispers through his warm tears.

"Hey you..." she mumbles trying hard not to cough.

"I love you Jess..." he cries.

"I know you do tiger..." Jessica replies.

James can't help but smile at the sound of his wife's high school nickname for him. His favorite cereal has always been Frosted Flakes. When they were teens, Jessica used to tell him he was gonna turn into Tony the Tiger one day.

"How are you?" she asks him.

"Me," he smiles through his tears still holding her hand tightly in his, "how are you Jessica?"

"Well you're here," she mumbles, "so this goes down as a good day in my book."

She smiles a weak smile. As James looks down into her fading eyes, he can clearly see her life has long left her body. She's almost ready to go.

"How is she?" Jessica coughs painfully several times.

"Who..." James replies caressing her frail shoulders.

"Don't play anymore games with me James," she cries, "I'm not..."

"Please calm down Jess," James interjects, "I don't need you getting yourself all worked up over nothing."

"What do you mean nothing James Radicon...?" Jessica asks.

"You are my wife Jess," he tells her, "that's what matters. Everything and everybody outside of us are irrelevant."

Jessica smiles as her eyes close and then open again.

"That is what you men do isn't it," she asks, "You down play your emotions for one woman when you're with another. Don't do that James. I'm a big girl now. I'm actually happy for you... for **both** of you. You really like her from what I've heard in the media. I hope she's a good woman, and I hope she can replace me when I'm..."

"Shut the hell up Jess," James cries, "nobody can replace you. You hear me? Nobody, don't you ever let me hear you say that again."

Jessica laughs weakly.

"What's so funny?" James asks.

"James you are *so* disrespectful." She shakes her tired head.

"What the hell are you talking about Jessica?" he inquires.

"You could have at least buried me before you stopped wearing my ring." James quickly hides his hands in his pockets.

"The room is ready now Mr. Radicon, I am so sorry about this." Dr. Franco says from behind him.

"We don't need the room doctor." James tells him.

"Excuse me..." Dr. Franco frowns.

James sees Jessica's eyes open again.

He bends down to kiss his wife on her fragile lips.

"What are you saying Mr. Radicon?" Dr. Franco asks.

"I'm taking my wife home," James never takes his eyes off of Jessica, "and I'll be taking one of your best nurses with me. I'll pay her whatever the going rate is for in home caretaking."

"No, James I don't think you understand..." Dr. Franco tells him.

"No sir," James replies, "obviously you don't understand. This is my wife. You have given her only a few days to live. You have more than expressed the fact that you cannot save her. So if she's going to go to sleep... eternally, she can do it at home with her family."

(Carolyn's parents' house)

"Carolyn Jane where are you going with all your stuff?" her father asks.

"To James' house daddy," she replies, "he needs me."

Marcus Williams is shaking his head, as his wife walks in the room.

"What are you doing baby?" her mother asks.

"Mom," Carolyn sighs, "*I... am* going to James' house. He needs me right now."

"What the hell is she talking about Marilyn?" Marcus asks his wife.

"Calm down Marcus," his wife placates him, "Carolyn has been through a lot this past week."

"So have we." he replies sitting down abruptly.

"We have darling," Marilyn agrees, "but we have never experienced what she just did. Not in her position."

Carolyn exhales abruptly. "Can we please stop talking about this already damn?" Carolyn asks her parents.

"It happened," she continues, "you both have told me it's not my fault and I couldn't change what happened even if I was there. Fine! Well, I need to move on with my life; I cannot do that reliving this every single day!"

"Moving in with another man ain't gonna stop the pain either Carolyn Jane," Marcus tells her, "**Who the hell is a James anyway**? Does he have a job?"

Carolyn laughs.

"James Radicon baby..." Marilyn tells her curious husband.

"Radicon," Marcus stands up, "*the* James Radicon... your boss, the billionaire?"

"*Mama*..." Carolyn cries.

"Baby it's better that he knows the truth," Marilyn reaches for her daughter's hand, "we can't keep secrets from your father it's not right."

"Well you've both been doing a damn fine job keeping it a secret so far!" Marcus yells.

"Marcus I wanted to tell you baby," Marilyn insists, "but Carolyn asked me not to."

"And why the hell not?" he stands to his strong feet looking directly at his daughter.

"Because dad," Carolyn cries, "look at how you're acting now."

"And just how long has this little fiasco been going on," Marcus asks, "You know he's married right?"

"We know dad." Carolyn replies with an agitated sigh.

"And did you know that his wife Jessica is in the hospital dying from Cancer?" he asks.

Carolyn looks at her mother with wide eyes.

"How do you know that, Marcus?" Marilyn asks her husband.

"It's all over the damn news," he screams, "if that poor woman found out that you were... you and her husband, are..."

"Enough dad," Carolyn interjects, "It's not like that with me and James." she claims.

Marcus takes a seat at the opposite end of the sofa that Carolyn is seated on and looks directly at her.

"Then please by all means Carolyn Jane, tell me what it's like." he says.

"Don't call me Carolyn Jane anymore dad," she tells him, "James calls me that."

"Well I'm sure he does," Marcus scoffs, "he is old enough to be your father."

"James is only thirty-seven dad," Carolyn explains, "and he looks like he's thirty. Only black people have kids at thirteen."

Marcus stands up, and then looks at his wife with his quivering mouth gaping open.

"What did you just say?" he asks his daughter.

"I said black people are the ones who have babies as young teens not white people," Carolyn tells her father, "unless they're from the backwoods or something."

"Kids of every ethnic backgrounds make mistakes little girl," Marcus chastises her, "And don't think just because you're shining this rich white man's golden sword, that you're better than anybody else!"

"Marcus..." Marilyn gasps.

"Damn it Marilyn," he screams, "this is wrong. If we don't tell our child what's right who the hell will... definitely not her pimp **Mr. Radicon**!"

Carolyn storms out of the den towards the bathroom.

"Damn it Marcus!" Marilyn exclaims.

"What?" he asks.

"What are you doing right now," she grabs his face in her hands, "she is our daughter not some whore on the street!"

"Well damn it, right now I can't tell the difference." he pulls away.

"Really dad..." Carolyn cries.

Marcus turns around quickly to find his daughter standing there in the doorway staring a teary eyed hole through him.

"Baby..." he says walking towards her.

"Save it dad," she interjects, "you know this isn't easy for me, none of this! I didn't just wake up one day and decide to fall in love with that man. But I am in love with him daddy, and he is a good man."

"He's married Carolyn Jane!" Marcus reiterates.

"Yeah dad, we've been over that already," Carolyn replies, "but so what, we love each other **to death**. I'm not going to live without him dad!"

"Like hell," Marcus replies, "I am forbidding you to see that man, and that's final!"

Carolyn laughs obnoxiously.

She steps closer to her angry confused father.

"Dad I'm not a kid anymore," she tells him, "and maybe if you hadn't kept me sheltered so long, just maybe I would have had the sense to not marry Ralph in the first place."

"Damn it Carolyn," Marcus yells, "now we both know Ralph wasn't perfect, but can we at least put the man in the ground before you move in with another man?"

"No dad we can't." she tells him.

"And why the hell not..." Marcus asks.

"Because I'm not mom and James isn't you, dad." she tells him.

"What the hell is that supposed to mean Carolyn?" he asks looking back at his wife.

"I want love too dad," she cries out, "I want real love that I can feel on a regular basis. I want tangible love dad. With James I can see, hear, taste, and feel his love all around me. Everybody is not lucky enough to just land in the middle of a perfect Marcus and Marilyn style relationship."

"Carolyn," Marcus hesitates, "your mother and I aren't perfect..."

"Oh I know." she replies snidely.

"Carolyn Jane..." her mother stands up.

Marcus looks at his wife.

"What the hell is she talking about Marilyn?" Marcus asks.

"Nothing hunny." she lies.

"Fuck that mom," Carolyn yells, "Mom told me that your marriage isn't as perfect as you make it seem. She said that you have both dealt with lies, regrets, and infidelity."

Marilyn covers her mouth, closes her eyes, and drops her head.

"Lies and regrets maybe," Marcus admits, "but there was no infidelity... *ever*."

Marcus turns to look at his wife again.

"Marilyn what is she talking about infidelity," he laughs uncomfortably, "She's lying to me right?"

Marilyn doesn't respond.

"Now Marilyn, baby," Marcus steps towards her, "Tell me, she's lying. Baby, just tell me..."

"Oh save it dad," Carolyn interjects with an evil smile, "you cheated on mom and she obviously caught you. Since we're talking about me, let's put all of our business out there. Right..."

"Carolyn Jane, please..." her mother cries.

"No mama," she replies, "he's in here condemning my relationship and he walks around like he's God or at least the perfect husband, and he is neither!"

"Who the hell are you talking to little girl?" Marcus asks his daughter.

"Tell him mom," Carolyn prods, "tell dad how you told me that you both had to go to the clinic three years ago, because he gave you some disgusting STD..."

Marilyn's face is covered in warm tears now.

Marcus turns to look at her.

"You told me we had to take those pills because of something you contracted from a urinary tract infection." Marcus says to his wife.

She continues to cry.

Carolyn takes a seat on the couch slowly realizing what she just accidentally did.

"So you lied to me?" he asks.

"And you... *you* cheated on me? **Damn.**" he continues.

Marilyn continues to cry, no longer able to even look in her husband's eyes.

"How could you Marilyn," he asks, "twenty-five years of marriage, and I never once stepped out on you."

Carolyn covers her mouth.

"**Now** I understand," he turns to look at his daughter, "your mother was able to give you sound advice about being that man's whore... because she's been that same whore before herself."

Marcus walks past Carolyn and grabs his car keys. Then he walks out of the front door slamming it shut behind him.

"Marcus!" Marilyn screams as she races to the door.

She watches through the front window as her angry husband speeds off down the street in his Cadillac.

"I'm so sorry mom," Carolyn cries, "I thought you were saying dad was the one who cheated..."

Marilyn falls to her knees right in front of the door screaming out in real pain.

(Father -Daughter dance)

As James pulls up to the Miami Dade Civic Arts Center he is genuinely excited for this night to finally be here.

He finds a decent spot to park near the front of the building.

"Are you ready Katherine?" he asks.

"Yeah dad, I'm ready." she replies with a sweet smile.

He jumps out and makes his way around to the passenger side door. He opens the door to let his daughter out.

James watches proudly as his almost pretty, soon to be sixteen-year-old daughter steps out of his Mercedes Benz coupe.

He closes her door and presses the button on his keychain to lock the car. Hand in hand James and Katherine walk towards the building.

From the outside he can already hear the sweet music wafting through the air. **Luther Vandross'** hit song, **"Dance with my Father,"** is just coming on as they hit the dance floor together.

James holds his daughter close to him, as they sway back and forth. His eyes are closed for the most part, but every time he opens them he notices that all eyes are on him.

The other father and daughter couples all seem to be shocked that he's there. They're all watching him and Katherine, some are even pointing at them.

"Daddy, why are they staring at us like that?" James hears Katherine asks.

"They're not staring at us baby." he whispers.

"Yes they are daddy, I see them." Katherine replies.

"Nope," James says, "they're all staring at you not me baby girl."

"Me," she says, "but why would they be staring at me daddy?"

"Because you are the prettiest daughter here," he tells her, "and I'm the luckiest dad here, because you belong to me."

"Thanks dad." she says with a toothy smile.

James always loved his daughter's less than perfect smile.

Everybody in the room is whispering vigorously now and they're still pointing and staring at James. Even the couples near them are whispering to each other.

James honestly doesn't care he wouldn't have missed this moment in his daughter's life for anything in the world.

"Whoo, let's hear it for James Radicon, and his beautiful daughter Katherine!" A man shouts from near the refreshment table.

Now everybody in the room is clapping and cheering for them. A few people are even clearly crying.

"You're a good man Radicon." one of the fathers says as he passes by.

"Wow, that is so sweet..." his daughter cries.

"Best couple here by far." a black guy says standing nearby dancing with his biracial daughter.

"Daddy, why are those girls crying?" James hears Katherine ask.

"What girls?" James asks.

"Over there by the table, right here next to us, every girl here seems to be crying." Katherine says.

"Nothing matters tonight," James says, "you planned a long time for this night Katherine. It's all yours hunny."

"I love you daddy." James hears her say clearly.

"I love you too... Katherine." the tears stream down his proud regretful face.

"Daddy..." James hears her whisper.

"Yeah baby." he replies.

"I just wanted to feel this moment," she says, "and now that I have I want to go home and rest."

"Can I go home now?" she asks.

"Yeah baby," he replies, "you can go home."

Ch. 21

"Finally Home"

"James!" Carolyn yells from the kitchen.

Radicon smiles at the pleasant sound of her voice in his house, as he walks down his stairs.

"James!" she yells again.

"I'm here Carolyn." James walks into the kitchen.

Carolyn lifts her left brow as he approaches her with obvious pride in his step. He kisses her twice on the side of her lovely face.

"James I don't know what the hell I'm doing." Carolyn whines through the confused scowl on her face gripping a large white egg in each of her hands.

"I don't know what the hell you're doing either baby." James says with a joyful laugh.

"Poached eggs," Carolyn says, "I can boil an egg, I can scramble an egg, I can even make deviled eggs, but I don't have a clue how to poach an egg."

"Who wants a poached egg?" James asks.

"Your wife…" Carolyn replies.

James burst into laughter again.

"What's funny James," she asks, "I've been in here for twenty minutes trying to get my mother on the phone to ask her what a poached egg is."

"Did you ask Jessica what a poached egg is?" he asks trying to control his laughter.

"No," Carolyn replies, "I didn't want her to think I'm stupid."

"You should have asked her?" James continues to laugh.

"Why James," Carolyn asks, "and what's so funny?"

"A poached egg," he smiles genuinely, "Jessica doesn't know what the hell a poached egg is either probably."

"Then why would she expect me to know what it i s ?" Carolyn asks.

"She doesn't expect you to know," he tells her, "she's messing with you because she knows you're the one."

"The one what," Carolyn asks, "No hell I am not the one. This is not funny and I'm gonna curse her pale ass out as soon as I get back upstairs."

Carolyn attempts to walk past James.

He grabs her before she can get far.

"I mean she knows you're the *other* woman, Carolyn." he tells her.

Carolyn's eyes instantly bulge.

"No she doesn't," she whispers, "You said you were gonna tell her I was just hired help James."

"And I did baby," he replies, "but she's known me for over twenty years Carolyn. Jessica is very sick, but she's far from dumb."

"And what does that mean?" she asks.

"She can feel it." he replies.

"She can feel what James?" Carolyn asks.

"Jessica is almost forty, love," he tells her, "I'm quite sure her women's intuition is strong enough that she can easily detect how I feel about you. There's probably a certain look in my eye or a variation in the tone of my voice when I talk about you."

"What?" Carolyn laughs.

"I'm serious." James tells her.

"No you're not serious," she replies, "that's the stupidest thing I've ever heard."

"Nope," James contends, "I read about it somewhere. Women, especially women over the age of thirty-five can pick up on a man's affection for another woman based on their tone of voice, facial expressions, and or body language. She knows Carolyn. I'm telling you she knows."

Carolyn listens closely to James, as if he's some hot young college professor giving her the key notes to pass his extremely difficult exam.

"So again Mr. Radicon," Carolyn wets her full lips, "what do I do now? I can't live here in your wife's home knowing she wants me dead."

"Don't be silly baby," James smiles comfortingly, "she doesn't hate you, and this is not her house. I bought this house and everything in it, the only person who can evict your ass is me."

Carolyn exhales deeply.

"I don't like this James," she pouts, "this is very uncomfortable for me."

"My wife of seventeen years is going to die at any second Carolyn," James says, "please forgive me if I'm not as sympathetic to your plight as you would like me to be."

"I'm not a victim James..." she says.

"I'm glad you realize that." he interjects.

James walks away from her towards the refrigerator. He grabs a large carton of orange juice out. He opens it and begins drinking directly out of the carton.

After he's had enough he wipes his mouth off with the back of his wrist, he burps loudly, and then he closes the carton back, as he replaces the juice to its original spot inside the fridge.

"Now," he looks back at Carolyn, "scramble two eggs for my wife; take them to her with a piece of bacon, and a lightly toasted piece of bread."

"Um yes sir..." Carolyn replies.

"Good girl." James says as he walks past her.

Carolyn makes her way to the pantry to find what she needs to carry out Radicon's request.

"Oh..." he walks back in the kitchen.

Carolyn jumps as his sudden return startles her.

"Damn it James!" she exclaims.

"What, why are you so jumpy?" he laughs.

"I thought Jessica had snuck in here to kill me," Carolyn explains, "I just knew it was time. I thought she was about to stab me in the back with a huge knife."

James laughs again.

"Baby calm down," he rubs her back, "no worries Jessica is definitely not the murdering type."

"Why did you come back in here James," she asks, "you already made your demands. I'm going to cook this food and then go serve your wife in bed like I'm some old *house nigger*."

"Good girl," James smiles, "Wait... why did I come back in here?"

"You're getting old Mr. Radicon." Carolyn grins.

"Shut up," he returns her grin, "oh I remember now I'm going to the drugstore to pick up some medicine for my wife. I'll be back shortly, don't forget to take her a glass of orange juice with her food as well."

"James, get the hell out of here please." Carolyn tells him.

"Yes ma'am Mrs. Radicon." James bows out of his kitchen backwards.

Carolyn smirks.

"Don't call me that James that is not my name… yet." she whispers the last word only loud enough to hear it herself.

After walking up the steps to the second floor of the Radicon home, Carolyn stands there at the top of the stairs staring down at the tray of food she has prepared for the enemy.

(Carolyn)

Come on now Carolyn, you can do it just a few more steps. Damn it. My legs aren't working. Okay, I'm ready. I can do this. Nothing Jessica can say or do will alter my emotional balance. If this is war, I will win. Every great general knows the key to winning a war is defense and an innovative explosive attack. I used to be so effectively intelligent before I fell for James. Why can't I be brilliant and smitten at the same time?

Looking at her I can't tell if she's sleeping or not. That boring ass, monotone, White Christian music she's playing makes me feel like I'm dying too.

Carolyn sits the tray of food down on the bed near Jessica. Jessica opens her fading gray eyes. She looks up at Carolyn with a deadly scowl just barely masked by a fake smile.

"This is for me?" she asks.

"Well if it were for me Mrs. Radicon, I would have just eaten it downstairs." Carolyn tells her.

"It was just a question," Jessica replies, "no need to get snippy."

"I wasn't getting…" Carolyn starts.

"I'm sure," Jessica interjects, "so what is this?" Jessica asks looking down at the tray Carolyn has brought to her.

"Have you lost your eyesight as well Mrs. Radicon," Carolyn tries not to raise her voice, "no, so I'm sure you can see exactly what *this is*."

"I asked for a poached egg!" Jessica exclaims with the little strength she has.

"Your husband told me to bring you this." Carolyn replies.

"Where is he anyway?" Jessica asks.

"He ran to the drugstore to refill a couple of your prescriptions." Carolyn tells her.

"So, he left me here alone with you?" Jessica asks.

Jess continues to talk, but Carolyn can't hear a word she's saying, as she begins to fall deeply into her own thoughts again.

(Carolyn)

The acute minimal lethal dose of arsenic in adults is estimated to be 70 to 200 milligrams. That's all it would take is the right amount of Arsenic in Mrs. Radicon's scrambled eggs, to put her out of her misery much sooner than expected. I'm losing my mind in this house, and at this point I can't remember if I poisoned her food or not. Guess I'll have to wait till she eats it to find out. I wonder if I killed her what James would do. He killed my husband, so why shouldn't I have the right to kill his wife? It's only fair right?

Carolyn sits near the edge of Jessica's enormous bed. Jessica begins to pray over her food looking in Carolyn's unclear eyes the entire time.

Carolyn plays it cool, she knows if she makes a false move Jessica is going to suspect that she did something to her food.

Jessica takes a bite of the bacon, and then scoops up some eggs in her spoon. She swallows them both. Carolyn watches her closely waiting for her body to react to the Arsenic. She realizes that if there is poison in the food it will take more than just a couple bites for the Arsenic to kill Jessica.

"You know," Jessica says, "I realize you're probably one of James' whores but you're okay with me. I'm trying hard not to like you, but part of me just wants to save you."

"Save me," Carolyn says with an obnoxious burst of laughter, "save me from what?"

"My husband..." Jessica replies.

"I don't have a clue what you're talking about Mrs. Radicon."

"Girl, I am not stupid," Jessica says, "I have known my husband a long time. I know when there's a new young fish on the line... and *you're it*."

Carolyn stands up, and puts a defiant hand on each hip.

"First off my name is not *girl*," Carolyn tells Jessica, "Respect me, and I will try to respect you. Second I am not some *new young fish on a line*... *do not* refer to me as such."

Carolyn turns to leave.

"Wait, don't leave," Jessica pleads, "I'm not the enemy. I want you to take care of him for me, I don't have long to live. My James is not well mentally, I'm sure you've noticed his focus on our daughter Katherine as of late. It's really not..."

"Look lady," Carolyn interjects, "you may not be the enemy, but we're damn sure not friends. I don't get into things that are not my business. Enjoy your food, Mrs. Radicon."

Carolyn turns to leave again.

"Nice shade of lipstick by the way." Jessica takes another bite of the crispy bacon.

Carolyn stops cold in her tracks. She turns to look back at Jessica with her brows furrowed gently.

"Yeah," Jess continues, "It's been really hard washing that same cheap color out of the necks of all my husband's shirts."

Carolyn doesn't react, she steadies herself and then exits the room headed back down stairs.

Ch. 22

"Back to Work"

(The Radicon Winery)

As she rides down the street towards the winery in her new red Mercedes, Carolyn has Trey Songz's new album playing loudly through her speakers. She's always been a huge fan of the super R&B crooner also known as *Trigga*, but this morning she can't hear a word he's singing. She really can't control what she thinks at all anymore. The possibilities and the unknowns are destroying or at least changing who and what she is.

Someone is blowing their horn. Carolyn looks to her left to find a young white man waving at her. She smiles at him nervously. The light up ahead turns red, so she's now forced to stop next to him for at least a minute or two.

As both of their cars come to a complete stop Carolyn politely lets her window down.

"Hey that's a really nice car…" the man says.

"Thank you," Carolyn replies, "it's new."

"Yeah I know," he replies, "I work at the Mercedes dealership."

"Oh…" Carolyn responds.

"Yeah, I uh, I sold that car to James Radicon just two days ago." the man tells her as if she didn't know who bought the car.

"Is that so." she replies.

"Yep," he says, "he said it was for his wife. *Are you* James Radicon's new wife?"

Carolyn hesitates, hoping the light will turn green, but it doesn't.

"Well are you," the man asks, "because if you are... he is a very lucky man."

Carolyn smiles and blushes wildly.

The light turns green.

"Have a great day Mrs. Radicon..." he says as he drives off.

Carolyn pulls off slowly from the light. She feels almost fearful as she nears her turn to enter the parking lot of the Radicon Winery.

After she pulls into her special parking spot she turns her radio off, puts the car in park, and then cuts the ignition off. She pulls her rear view mirror down to look at herself. She still looks the same, but the way she feels is so foreign to her.

As Carolyn Olivier walks in through the front doors of the winery it feels different to her as well. She no longer feels like James' assistant, she feels like his partner. She feels like this is her winery and it is for all practical purposes.

Carolyn heads towards the elevator.

"Good morning Mrs. Olivier," one of the young interns speaks to her, "I'm sorry to hear about your loss."

"My loss..." Carolyn replies wrinkling her brows just a bit.

"Yes ma'am," the young white girl says, "your husband and your kids, the fire..."

"Oh right," Carolyn smiles, "Yes, thank you. I'll be fine."

"I'm sure," the intern says a little alarmed by Carolyn's nonchalant attitude, "well in any event I forwarded the location and details of the funeral this weekend to the entire staff. I hope that's okay."

"Yes that's fine love," Carolyn replies, "and what was your name?"

"Melody Diggins," she replies, "I've been your assistant for a month now."

"Right, Melody I'm sorry," Carolyn tells her, "hey do you know if the boss is in his office?"

"Well Mr. Radicon has been in his office all morning," Melody tells her, "but you're my boss Mrs. Olivier."

"Right Melody," Carolyn steps into the opening elevator, "well I'll see you in a bit I'm sure."

As she rides up the elevator Carolyn can't believe she let her recent tragedy escape her mind like that. She can't let that happen again. If she makes that mistake while talking to the wrong person she could cause a huge problem for herself and James in respect to the police.

The Miami P.D. is looking for a reason to classify the fire as murder instead of an accident.

As she steps off the elevator she looks down to check her outfit, it's perfect of course. With her office keys in one hand and her Michael Kors clutch bag in the other hand Carolyn makes her way down the crowded hallway.

Instead of taking a right to go towards her own office, she heads straight towards James' office. She calmly runs her fingers through her freshly curled sandy brown hair before approaching his door.

She lifts her hand to knock but decides not to. Through James' office window Carolyn can see her boss talking to a young female. Carolyn can feel her temperature rising wildly.

The young light skinned lady is leaning over whispering to James as he sits behind his desk.

Carolyn can't watch anymore; she bursts into the office.

"Carolyn..." James stands up quickly.

"No need to stand now Mr. Radicon," she says, "Sit on back down love, I just came in here to tell you I ran into the salesman that sold you my new *2015 Mercedes*."

"Oh." James says.

"Yeah," Carolyn continues, "he said you bought the car for your wife."

"Carolyn..." James holds a shaky hand up towards her.

"It's such a cute gift love," she interjects, "but since I'm in here, I was just wondering... since you and this bitch are the only two mother fuckers in here, why would she feel the need to whisper in your ear?"

"Excuse me," the lady says, "did you just call me a bitch?"

"I sure did bitch," Carolyn replies, "now, how many more bitches would you like to be? You can be a stupid bitch, a ratchet bitch, a..."

"Mr. Radicon..." the light skinned lady says.

"Carolyn," James warns, "be professional..."

"Fine," Carolyn opens the door with a smile, "I'll just see you at home tonight baby. Bye, bye now."

Carolyn waves to the young lady before closing the door behind her and walking away.

As Carolyn walks towards her office she can feel her weak façade crumbling piece by piece, as reality is brutally shattering all the lies she created for herself about James Radicon.

After unlocking her door Carolyn walks in her office and throws everything down on the floor near the door. The pain in her heart is strong and definite as the tears quickly storm her beautiful face. The questions in her mind are screaming so loud she's praying to be rendered deaf immediately.

(Carolyn)

I knew it. Jessica Radicon told me this was going to happen. She's not dead yet, James and I aren't married yet, and he's already trying to replace me... and with a light skinned bitch. She's a redbone, but damn it she's still black! I thought he wasn't attracted to black women...

Her office door swings open violently. Carolyn looks back with both eyes wide open. He walks in and slams the door behind him.

Carolyn gasps painfully as he stalks towards her with an intent scowl on his face.

"James I..." she starts.

"Oh shut up." he tells her as he grabs her by the neck and pushes her towards the nearest wall.

"Don't move bitch..." he growls.

James makes his way back to the door and locks it.

Carolyn can't breathe and she doesn't dare move. She fully regrets the way she disrespected James in his office in front of the pretty young lady.

James grabs her hard by her neck and lifts her up on the wall. Carolyn instinctively wraps her legs around him.

She still can't breathe. She's more than frightened by the look in his eyes.

"You will respect me..." he demands.

"Yes sir." she mumbles.

"Shut up," he growls, "you will never disrespect me again!"

"Yes sir James..." she cries.

James slowly lets her slide down the wall closer to his face. He looks deep in her eyes still clutching her neck tightly in his large hands.

James leans in and kisses her harshly on her lips.

"Don't you ever be jealous," he tells her, "I belong to *you* and you only."

He kisses her again.

"Let me down..." she mumbles close to his lips.

"What?' James asks.

"Please..." she asks.

James lets her down. Carolyn immediately drops all the way down to her knees, and quickly unfastens James' belt. After ripping his pants open she takes him in her hands gently.

James watches her from up above with both of his hands on the wall in front of him. Carolyn carefully tastes the head of him, working her longish tongue around it in a perfect circular motion.

He's all most ready now. She lifts him up and lays him on her forehead as she licks his scrotum gently.

Now that he's as hard as he's ever been before she engulfs him quickly. James reaches down and pushes her head back against the wall. She doesn't resist.

James begins to slide in and out of Carolyn's hungry mouth deeper each time. Every time she gags he gently slaps her with his left hand. The more she chokes the harder he slaps her.

Whap!

Carolyn smiles as the last slap was considerably harder than the rest knocking a considerable amount of saliva from her wet mouth. James has absolutely no idea how much he's turning her on right now.

Carolyn grabs hold of his thighs as she leans forward to take on more of him with her throat and mouth.

Her lips are dripping with spit. James grabs her chin in one hand and the back of her head in the other. Then he begins stroking quickly in her mouth.

He pulls back.

"More baby…" she moans.

James grabs her head again and positions it perfectly. Then he slides in even deeper this time.

She gags.

He slaps her again.

Carolyn pulls away from him. She stands up and unfastens her pants and then lets them fall to the floor.

"Perfect…" James growls as he snatches her panties down to her ankles.

Carolyn kicks her pants and panties off in the distance. Then she jumps on James wrapping her legs around him.

James doesn't hesitate; he forces himself inside her extremely wet center.

"James…" she gasps.

"Shut up!" he growls.

"I'm so sorry baby…" she cries as she takes him on.

James doesn't respond. He pins her hard to the wall and begins to pump as deep into her wet, warm body as he possibly can.

James' phone rings in his pocket. He stops in mid-stroke to grab it.

"Really…" Carolyn complains.

He looks down at the flashing screen of his expensive rare smart phone.

"It's the front desk," he says, "Hello. Yes, Nancy I'm still here. No, no I'm not in my office… Damn it Nancy I'm here in my building, my exact whereabouts at all times is not your business! Now what is it you need? Reverend Green? Oh from the airport, yes send him to my office. I'll take care of him."

James hangs up his phone and lets Carolyn down off the wall.

"You are not leaving me like this…" Carolyn quickly puts a defiant hand on each of her firm hips.

"I'll see you at home." James says.

Then he leans in to kiss her as he fixes his clothes.

"James…" Carolyn whines.

He doesn't respond.

After he has repaired his exquisite outfit to the best of his ability he kisses her once more then leaves Carolyn's office without another word.

Carolyn locks her door and plops down on the floor with her back to it.

As James turns the corner to his office he finds the ruggedly handsome black man dressed in a decent suit and a beautiful tie.

"Mr. Radicon," the man speaks, "I told you I would come."

"Mr. Green," James smiles and shakes the older man's hand firmly, "you did say you would come and I told you I would be here. So you're a reverend?"

"I am." Reverend Green replies.

"That's beautiful," James flashes another genuine smile, "well come on let's go in my office and talk."

As they walk in James flips his light switch up and then turns on his automatic cappuccino maker.

"Have a seat Reverend." James says.

Reverend Green sits down in one of the chairs in front of James' desk as James takes his place behind it.

"This is a really nice office Mr. Radicon." Reverend Green says.

"Thank you Reverend," James replies, "so why didn't you tell me you were a preacher?"

"You didn't ask." the old man replies with a light laugh.

"No I didn't." James replies joining in with Mr. Green's laughter.

"Tell me James," Reverend Green says, "how did everything go in Atlanta?"

"How did you know what was going to happen?" James asks.

The reverend flashes a wise grin.

"I didn't know what would happen, James," he tells him, "I was warning you against what could have happened."

"Well you were right on the money," James tells him, "my girlfriend and I got robbed at gunpoint, and we almost got killed."

"You were covered by the blood of Jesus James, so don't worry about it," Green assures him, "now about that job…"

(Two days later)
Carolyn
So the funeral of my family went like this… every single black mother fucker in attendance silently blamed me for my husband's and my children's deaths. I was not happy by any means, and yes James has shown me a life anybody would probably kill for, but for anybody to think I physically had anything to do with my house being destroyed and my children burning to death inside of it is just absolutely ludicrous. Even in the midst of their ignorance the service was still beautiful overall. I know how cliché that sounds, but I really did do my very b e s t

in arranging everything and for it to have been the only funeral I've planned to date, I think I did exceptionally well. Certain parts were harder to sit through than others; and watching my babies' symbolic caskets lowered into the ground was unforgettably traumatic. But the sickest part is... in my mind laying my children to rest made room for and gave birth to my potential future with James Radicon. Yes, I do feel like scum, and I deserve the despicable accolade of the worst mother on the planet award, but at least I'm honest. James Radicon and the life I could have with him was, and is more important to me than my kids were. Most women would claim they don't understand that, but then most of those women are not involved in successful relationships either. I know so many old friends who destroyed potentially good relationships because of nonsense. Some of them then focused all of their lonely, bitter, anger on their kids. I'm no psychic by any means, but I'm willing to bet anything that those bitter and lonely women who are becoming overbearing mothers, who can't help but take out all of their frustrations on their kids are not going to raise anything close to future productive citizens. Bitter hatred and malice are contagious and hereditary. But I digress. Some children from my mother's church said poems and sung songs inside the church long before the procession ever headed to the old graveyard. Their little voices were more powerful than they know, even though the concept of death is too much for them to fully comprehend at this point in their carefree young lives. I'm sure I looked beautiful in my new black dress, but I felt anything but. I spoke to everyone I made eye contact with, whether they ever stood a chance of speaking back to me or not. They blame me, they all blame me and it was not my fucking fault! James did it, he did it for me in a sense, but I definitely didn't... and never would have told him to commit such a heinous crime. Did they want to see me cry? I did cry, I cried a lot actually. Do not get me wrong, I do miss my kids, but just probably not as much as some people would think I should, but I miss them nonetheless. The strangest thing is the fact that they never found my children's bodies. We know they were in the house so even though their bodies' were never found the conclusion wasn't hard to make. Inside Ralph's closed black casket he wore a nice black suit. Inside the two smaller caskets I laid two tiny suits that matched Ralph's perfectly to symbolize my babies' bodies. I bought the suits a couple of months ago actually. I didn't have a reason to buy them; I think I must have bought the suits because of the deep guilty feeling that was living at the pit of my stomach. The feeling isn't gone now, but it's definitely different. Well damn it, with nothing else to lose but James, I have no reason to ever focus on anything outside of him again.

(At the Mansion)

Dressed in all black Carolyn walks in through the front door of the Radicon mansion. She didn't have to ring the doorbell this time because James gave her a key last night. Carolyn Olivier has **her own personal key** to Billionaire James Radicon's mansion.

None of these things even seemed to be possibilities when she was first hired at the winery after graduating from the University of Miami. Carolyn can't help but just stand in the doorway of the mansion, staring straight ahead at the beautiful, lonely stairs.

She walks towards them. Every step she takes she can feel her body becoming weaker, and weaker.

She planned to go upstairs and shower but she doesn't have the strength to right now. The familiar warm wetness on her beautiful face lets her know her powerful performance she gave at the funeral is over now, and reality is starting to set in.

(Carolyn)

My God is anything real anymore? Does anything matter beyond my insane love for one man? I keep pretending and trying to be strong, but I just buried my husband... and both of my children surrounded by familiar strangers. I put two tiny caskets in the ground today... forever. Saying bye to Karan, and Ralph Jr. was the hardest thing I've ever had to do. Lord, what do I do when I'm so tired of crying? I don't know who to turn to... you never talk back to me, ever. I can't turn to James this time, because he's the one who killed my kids. My parents don't understand period, so I can't go to them...

"Carolyn," James says from up above, "Awe baby... Damn it I'm so sorry."

James rushes down the stairs to her. He picks her up and hugs her tightly.

"When does all the pain just fade away?" Carolyn cries.

"I don't know baby," he replies honestly, "but I swear on my life whatever you want or need on this earth I'll give it to you. You are my... *everything*, I waited way too long to admit that to myself."

"You don't owe me anything James..." she cries.

"I owe you my life little girl," he tells her, "My entire existence only matters because of you and what you mean to me."

"James it hurts *so* bad..." she cries deep in his arms.

"I know baby," he says, "and I'm so sorry. I will spend eternity making this up to you… and even then I still won't be perfect, but I'm yours."

"All mine…" she asks.

"All yours." he replies.

Ch. 23

"Fix my child"

I t's late in the evening and the weather outside is fair. The sky is as clear as it has ever been over Miami. There's a cool breeze whistling through the sweet south Florida air. The dark trees are swaying rhythmically   in submission to the light breeze.

The inside of the Radicon mansion is more quiet than usual. Country music is playing softly through the speakers in the kitchen. The sink is cluttered with slightly dirty dishes. The trashcan near the kitchen door is almost full with empty fast food containers and bags. Most of the lights in the kitchen are off except for the small one just above the oven.

Upstairs almost all the bedroom doors are closed. Only one man is in the hallway. The king of the Radicon castle is listening closely outside of his young prince Luke's bedroom door. James' eyes are closed, his face is red, and a lone tear is sliding down his cheek.

"Baby..." Luke moans.

"Yeah bae..." Cal replies.

"I love you." Luke admits.

"I love you too Skywalker." Cal moans.

"Don't stop bae..." Luke tells him.

"I'm not." Cal groans.

"Don't stop bae..." Luke moans again.

"I'm not ..." Cal whispers.

Luke's bedroom door bursts open.

The frightened teen turns around to find his confused father standing there frozen in his bedroom doorway.

"Dad..." Luke says.

"You are *not* my son anymore." James says with real disgust written all over his face.

Radicon storms out of his son's room slamming his door closed behind him.

Every heartbreaking step James takes down the hallway hurts more than the one before. James is more confused now than he's ever been before. He doesn't know if he should go to his sick wife's room and tell her that he now knows something they had feared for years is actually true. He has now seen his young son engaged in a sexual act with another man.

James knows this information wouldn't do anything to help his wife's emotional state. Jessica has been more than depressed lately.

James wisely takes a left down his long hallway towards his largest guest room. This is the room he moved Carolyn into a week ago.

"Damn it!" James storms into the guest bedroom waking Carolyn up.

"What baby..." Carolyn tries to steady her heart rate.

"I just caught..." he starts.

"What baby," Carolyn pleads, "you just caught what?"

"Damn it!" James yells as he falls back hard on her bed simultaneously slamming his fists down by his sides.

Carolyn climbs on top of James. He covers his face with both of his hands. Carolyn grabs both of his hands and places them on the bed behind his head. James tries to free his arms but he can't. Carolyn applies a little more pressure to keep both of his arms pinned down.

"What's wrong James?" Carolyn asks.

"Damn it!" James growls as his face turns yet another shade redder.

"James Justin Radicon, what the hell is wrong with you," Carolyn asks, "tell me now!"

"It's Luke..." he says.

"Your son Luke?" she asks.

"Of course my son Luke," he barks, "what the hell other Luke would I give a shit about Carolyn!"

"Whoa, whoa, whoa," she says, "No sir, you are not going to use whatever this is as another springboard to go off on, and ultimately mistreat me."

"What?" James wrinkles his brow.

"Those days are long behind us," she tells him, "I am no longer your emotional punching bag. I am submissive to a fault, but you will not fault me, or punish me for shit that has nothing to do with me."

"Carolyn," James says, "what the hell are you talking about?"

"I'm just saying..." She replies climbing off of him.

"Luke is gay." James says aloud for the first time in his life.

"Yeah I know." she replies.

"What do you mean you know?" James asks.

"It's kinda obvious James," she tells him, "was it supposed to be a mystery or something? Because I knew the first time I saw him."

James has no clue, what to say next as he stares back at Carolyn. He slowly rolls out of the bed in the opposite direction of where she's laying. As his feet hit the floor again he has no clue what to do.

James walks towards the window at the back of the guest room. Carolyn watches him very carefully searching her mind desperately trying to find the right thing to say. But deep down she knows there is no right thing to say or do in a situation like this. You just let people deal with what they're going through; and be there for them if they need or want you to be.

"You know," James stares out of the large window into the darkening distance, "I think you're right. I think on some level we have always known that he *was*... he *is* gay. There is no surprise, but I think I fooled myself into believing that it was just a phase. But now that it's here... now that everything is definitely out in the open I don't know if I can..." James drops his head in real defeat.

Carolyn jumps off the bed and walks up behind him. She wraps her arms around him from behind and carefully kisses his strong back.

"It's okay," Carolyn says, "it's nothing you did wrong baby, and you cannot change the way he feels. He's just wired differently; and being *that way* is the only thing that will allow him some form of happiness. He has to be true to himself James."

"I know," he replies, "but it's embarrassing because he's my oldest, and my only male heir to my empire."

"Right," Carolyn says, "so now you have to be in total control of this situation from here on out. You have to stay on top of damage control."

"What do you mean by that Carolyn?" he asks.

"Luke is gay," she says, "so what. He's your son... *and* you love him no matter what..."

"He's no son of mine," James starts, "when he decided, he..."

312

"He is your son," Carolyn interjects, "and yes you do still love him. You just need to work overtime now training him in the ways of your company."

"He can't take over for me." James tells her.

"He can and he will," Carolyn tells him, "Luke is more brilliant than you James. I've done my research on the boy, and he has a tremendous upside. I for one am kind of excited to see what new heights he could take your company to, once you relinquish the reigns to him."

"Never gonna happen," James says, "but what did you mean by damage control..."

"Oh," Carolyn says, "I just mean that you and I have dealt with some sharks in this business. We both know if they think they feel a weakness in someone they go in for the kill."

"Your point..." James says.

"My point is," Carolyn says, "build Lucas up. Do not allow him to feel less about himself, than what you feel about yourself. If you do he will be a sitting duck. And once you are no longer capable of holding his hand, someone could swoop in and destroy everything we've built."

(Lucas)

Sitting on the edge of his bed next to his boyfriend Cal, Luke is absolutely speechless.

"Now what..." Cal says.

"I don't know Calvin." Lucas replies.

"I... I mean," Cal stutters, "is your dad gonna like..."

"Is he gonna what Cal?" Lucas asks with his forehead wrinkled tightly.

"Don't play with me Skywalker," Cal says, "your father knows who the fuck I am. If he leaks this to the media my career is over."

"So your plan is for me to forever be a secret right?" Lucas asks.

"This ain't the time for all that bullshit Skywalker!" Cal barks.

"Oh this is the perfect time nigga…" Lucas says.

"This shit is getting old Skywalker." Cal tells him.

"What are you talking about Cal?" Luke asks.

"If your dad tells the media I'm gay…" Cal stops in the middle of his statement.

"Baby, my father…" Lucas starts.

"I'm not ya baby Skywalker." Cal tells him.

"What the hell Cal…" Lucas says.

"Fuck it I'm gone." Cal grabs his clothing and storms out of Lucas' room.

Luke falls back on his bed, even more confused than he was before.

(Mount Zion Miami Missionary Baptist church)

Early Sunday morning Carolyn is lying alone in the guest bedroom. She slept well for once, but she's being awakened now by the smell of food. Someone is down stairs cooking breakfast and it smells perfectly delicious.

Carolyn rolls over on her back smiling with her eyes closed. The food smells wonderful in the distance but she owes her current smile to none other than James Radicon. He snuck in her room late last night and made sweet love to her for what felt like a private eternity. After he came, she climbed on top of his face and grinded rhythmically on his mouth for the better part of thirty minutes.

Then she scooted down to sit on his rock hard abs and eventually laid down flat on him face to face blessing his lips with her own.

The door to the guest room opens slowly. James walks in with a tray of food just like he did the time she woke up in his house mysteriously. To this day Carolyn is not sure how she ended up at James' house that day.

"Good morning beautiful…" he says.

"Hey baby." she replies with a smile.

"Here," he places the tray on her lap, "eat up. I want to take you to church with me in an hour."

"Church…" Carolyn says.

"Yeah Carolyn," he replies with an uneasy grin, "Are we that bad that we can't even set foot in churches anymore?"

Carolyn laughs.

"Oh, you and I are terrible James," she admits, "but I think we are still not beyond forgiveness. I was just caught off guard by the thought of us attending church… together."

"Well just eat your food," he tells her, "I bought you a nice outfit yesterday. You wear a seven in heels right?"

"I do," she smiles, "James…"

"Yeah baby?" he replies.

"Why do you know all of my sizes?" she asks.

"You're a part of me," he smiles proudly, "It's my job to know everything about you. I'll go get your dress and your heels, go ahead and eat love."

"Perfect." she replies.

An hour later as they fly down the street headed towards the church Carolyn is lost in the mirror checking every single detail of her gorgeous face. No matter how pretty she knows she is somehow she still feels like she could be prettier around James.

"You look fine Carolyn." he tells her glancing over at her briefly while turning into the church parking lot.

"Thank you James," she says, "What made you want to come to church today anyway?"

"Reverend Green invited me," he responds, "He's the guest preacher here today."

Carolyn looks up from the mirror at the church. Then she looks at James with an amused smirk.

"What..." he notices the way she's looking at him.

"You do know you will be the only white man in this church don't you?" she asks.

"So what," he replies, "God doesn't see color, he sees hearts and souls."

"Amen baby." Carolyn replies as he finally finds a decent parking spot. James cuts the car off and then hops out to walk around and open Carolyn's door for her.

"Thank you." Carolyn takes his hand and steps out of yet another one of James' beautiful sports cars.

Inside the Mount Zion Miami Missionary Baptist church, the décor is absolutely breathtaking. The walls are lightly sprinkled with exquisite religious art. The blood red carpets that span from wall to wall seem regal and inviting. The air is sweet and soothing to the mind. The music playing from all of the large surround sound speakers just outside of the sanctuary is soul touching.

"I'd rather have Jesus than silver and gold..." Carolyn sings along gracefully as she and James make their way into the sanctuary.

"Good morning." a short, old, chubby black woman greets them with a comforting smile as she hands them both a program.

As they walked down the aisle in search of somewhere to sit all eyes are on them. Well most eyes are on James, but as the congregation stare at James they can't help but see the beautiful Carolyn as well.

Near the middle of the sanctuary Carolyn spots some empty space on a pew. She squeezes James' hand gently to get his attention. He looks down at her. She points towards the empty space on the pew just a few rows ahead of where they are now.

They politely slide past several members of the church and then take seats on the comfortable pew.

"Well Amen." another older black woman says from behind them. She leans forward and hugs them both from behind.

"Welcome to Mount Zion my young brother and sister." she says.

"Thank you." Carolyn and James reply.

Two ladies on the row in front of them turn around simultaneously and smile at James.

"Well amen." they both say.

Carolyn shakes her head with an uneasy smile plastered on her face.

(Carolyn)
God I hate some black women. They're so transparent. They all look at James and see everything he's not. He's not looking for some cheap thrill. He's not going to have sex with one of them and then just magically fall in love with them and whisk them off into his glamorous life... Wait; is that what he did with me? Am I one of these women?

Carolyn looks over at James. He feels her eyes on him. He smiles down at her, before directing his attention back to the pulpit as three young kids are just finishing up telling the church what they learned in Sunday school this morning.

From the rear of the pulpit an old black man is approaching the podium.

"There's Green sitting on stage." James whispers to Carolyn.

She doesn't respond, as she's still very much lost in her own disturbing thoughts.

"Thank you to all of our kids who blessed us this morning with their growing young knowledge of the word," the man says, "to all of our visitors, welcome to Mount Zion Missionary. My name is Pastor Calhoun. I won't take up much of your time this morning; we have a very special guest today. Reverend Bernard Green is a very wise and passionate man of God. He has journeyed near and far and he has been through so many things good and bad, but he is here now with a powerful testimony, and words from the Lord. Without further delay I would like to welcome my brother in Christ to the podium, Reverend Bernard Green."

Pastor Calhoun turns to look at the reverend as he approaches him. The entire church stands to their feet and clap loudly for Reverend Green. The two men in the pulpit shake hands and then hug.

"Good morning church," Reverend Green speaks into the microphone, "First of all I would like to thank you Pastor Calhoun for inviting me to have this time with your congregation this morning. Church let's give your pastor a hand, he has really grown into a powerful soldier for God."

The congregation stands to clap and applaud again.

"Okay," Reverend Green smiles, "please be seated church. Today is a special morning Mount Zion. I am… born again."

Reverend Green smiles out at the congregation as they clap and holler hallelujah in response to his words.

A teenage boy approaches the podium with a tall glass of water covered by a white napkin. He gently sits the glass at the edge of the podium.

Reverend Green thanks the boy.

"Yes," he continues, "church I am born *yet*... again. You see, at times... we become complacent in our faith. We begin to believe that... everything we have, we deserve. We may even begin to feel like because we go to church, and tithe, and participate in communion that God himself owes us wonderful things in our lives. I know how easy it is to adopt and accept this mind frame church... because I have been there."

Reverend Green takes a sip of water from the glass nearby on the edge of the podium.

"For those of you who don't know me," he begins again, "I am Reverend Bernard Lee Green. This was once my church many, many years ago." He turns to smile at Pastor Calhoun.

"To those of you who have been here for over seven years," Green says, "those of you who do know me, I want to say I have missed you all very much. I had to leave you before because I was overtaken by addiction. *Crack cocaine* took over my life. Church, there are so many forms of addiction. The most popular addiction most people suffer from today is themselves. So many of us are addicted to keeping up these façades to impress people, who really don't even care about us at all."

The church claps for Reverend Green again.

"But my addiction was cocaine," he continues, "I have been through so many ups and downs over the years, but I'm here now, and I'm doing so well. I have a new job, a home, a car... and a new beginning all because the Lord blessed me to meet a very special young man by the name of James Radicon. James, if you're here today please stand up."

James stands. The entire congregation stands with him as they applaud him graciously.

"Ladies and gentlemen," Reverend Green holds back tears, "this very successful and wholesome man put me in a house, bought me a car, and gave me a job at his local winery. He has changed my life forever, and mended my broken mental state. Thank you Mr. Radicon, I am eternally grateful for you. You may all be seated."

James nods to the reverend in kind acknowledgement.

"James," Carolyn whispers, "What the hell, you bought him a house and a car? And when did you hire him?"

"Carolyn," he whispers harshly in her ear, "My money is *my money*. *Never* question me. Besides I couldn't spend all my money in three lifetimes. Its time I start giving back and changing lives."

"I'm not here to talk about me today," Reverend Green says, "but I want to show you what kind of man Mr. Radicon really is. When I invited him to come here today, his only request was that I not tell you all what he has done for me. I apologize, James but you are a godsend for me and I have to spread the word about the blessings I have received."

Reverend Green takes another sip of his water, and then he gently sits it back down.

"Today church I want to talk about helping," he says, "stepping in to help, or correct sin, when you have the power and influence to do so. It is our duty people of God… to help each other when we see fault in what one another are doing. When I'm messing up, let me know. And trust and believe I will always do the same for you…"

After the service is over James and Carolyn remain seated until the majority of the congregation has already left the sanctuary.

Reverend Green finishes talking to Pastor Calhoun and then he makes his way down to James and Carolyn.

"Thank you for coming James," Reverend Green shakes his hand firmly, "and you must be Ms. Carolyn... you are even prettier up close and personal."

She blushes as she shakes the reverend's hand.

"Thank you," she gushes, "that was an amazing sermon by the way."

"I appreciate that," he replies with a smile, "but where is everybody else James? I told you to bring your entire family..."

"I did." James assures him smiling down at his gorgeous girlfriend. Reverend Green smiles at the obvious real love he's witnessing between the two of them.

"You know," he recollects, "it really felt good to be back in the pulpit."

"You could get another church Reverend Green," James says, "I could..."

"James," Reverend Green interjects, "you have done more than enough for me. It felt good to preach again, but I understand that, that part of my life is over now. I fell way to hard that last time, and I caused a lot of good people to stumble. I would never take that risk again."

"I understand," James replies, "but if you ever..."

"I won't." Reverend Green cuts James off with a smile.

"I promised Pastor Calhoun I would take him to lunch after service; the two of you are welcome to join us."

"Thanks Reverend," James replies, "but I need to get back home, next time though we'll be there."

"Okay James," Reverend Green grins, "I'm gonna hold you to that. Thanks again for everything, and may God always show you favor my son."

The two men shake hands again and hug. Carolyn hugs Reverend Green, then she and James both leave the church filled with the spirit, at least for the moment.

(Hours later)

Carolyn is in her personal bathroom at the mansion that's connected to the guest bedroom that has become her room. She's curling her long brown hair. Her body is covered in chill bumps as she only has on a sports bra and some extremely short shorts.

"Carolyn," James bursts in the room, " I need your help."

"Sure baby," she replies, "What do you need?"

"Here," he hands her a small roll of cash, "I want you to fix my child."

Carolyn looks down at the cash and then back at James.

"You want me to what?" she asks him.

"I want you to fix Lucas." James tells her.

"Okay," she replies sitting the cash down on the bathroom counter with a nervous smile on her face, "James, what the hell, are you talking about? How do you expect me to fix Lucas?"

"What do you think Carolyn," he asks, "you're not *that* stupid."

"You want me to counsel him?" she asks.

"No." James replies.

"Well then what the fuck are you talking about James," she yells, "because I am not going to…"

"You," James quickly interjects, "will do as you're told!"

"I can't with you," she screams, "This is a nightmare! Every single time I feel like we're making progress you hit me with some off the wall crazy shit like this!"

"Carolyn I really don't care how you feel about what I'm asking you to do," he admits, "I just gave you more money than you make in a month. Now go fix my son. This is nothing new; men of affluence have done this for hundreds of years."

"Newsflash James," she looks at him with pure poison in her eyes, "Slavery is over. You do not actually own me, you never will. I am not some little black wench locked away in a slave hut waiting to be used to break in your little *faggot* son..."

WHAP!!!

"**You stupid black bitch**..." James slaps Carolyn down to the floor.

"I'm sorry James..." she says from the floor wiping the new blood from her bottom lip.

"No baby I'm sorry." James picks her up from the floor. He grabs the towel at the edge of her sink and wets it with cold water and gently wipes her lip with it.

"I don't understand you James," she cries, "you want me and then you don't. I'm your wife and then I'm just a pawn you use whenever you can."

James grabs her softly by her shoulders and looks deep in her hazel eyes.

"You are the love of my life," he says, "and you're gorgeous. If anybody can fix my son it's you."

"What do you want me to do James?" she asks.

"Fix him..." James says.

"Say it James," Carolyn demands, "stop beating around the damn bush! What are you saying, what are you telling me to do?"

"I am telling you to go in my son's room and have sex with him," James says, "do that, and the money's yours."

"Why would I need your money when I have you," she asks, "that's just stupid?"

"Girl," he growls, "go fix my son."

"Fine." she replies walking out of her bathroom cutting the light off on her way out. James stands there frozen as she walks out of her room down the hallway towards Lucas' room.

James cuts her bathroom light back on and stares into his aging blue eyes.

"This is for the best..." he whispers to himself.

"As a father," he continues, "I can't just sit back and allow my son's confusion to ruin him. He's not gay, he can't be... *gay*, because I'm his father and I'm all man. Carolyn would die for me, she is the woman of my dreams, but I have to remain careful and precise. If I show her too much affection she will gain more power than I have over her. She always obeys me... but this time I think part of me didn't want her to."

James shakes his head and then finally cuts the bathroom light off. Sitting alone on the edge of Carolyn's bed James searches his soul for all the answers he realizes he may very well never know.

Unable to fight his screaming curiosity anymore he rises from her bed and exits her room en route to Lucas' room. James sees Katherine walking down the hall towards him.

"Kate baby," he says, "do daddy a favor and go down stairs and watch T.V. for a little while."

James looks nervously towards Luke's door and then back down the hallway for Katherine but somehow she's already gone.

James closes his eyes and then shakes his head violently. He looks again and Kate is still not there.

James then turns his attention back to his son's door. With his ear to the door James can't hear anything inside. He tries the knob, it's not locked. He closes his blue eyes and turns the knob slowly, careful not to make any noise. Once the knob will no longer turn James waits, then he slowly pushes the door open. He continues to push very gently.

It's wide enough now for him to peek inside, but he's afraid of what he may find. He realizes now that he will not come out of this situation happy either way.

He opens his eyes and looks inside. There they are; and they don't see him. Carolyn is lying atop Lucas' body in nothing, but her bright yellow panties. Lucas' arms are flat on the bed. Carolyn is kissing his neck and running her skilled fingers through his hair. Now she's touching all over his body. Then she picks her head up and looks in his eyes. She's grinding on top of him the entire time. She kisses him deeply on the lips.

James pushes the door open completely and rushes to the bed.

"James..." Carolyn gasps.

"Dad..." Luke's heart attempts to jump out of his chest.

James quickly picks Carolyn up off of his son and kisses her hard on the mouth in front of Lucas for the very first time.

Then without a word he carries her in his arms out of Luke's room all the way back down the hallway to her own room. Once inside he lays her down and makes sweet love to her.

Ch. 24

"The Proposal"

S itting in her office behind her new red cedar desk Carolyn Olivier is hard at work on a list of things her boss asked her to do today. Although most people would find this list impossible to complete in one day's work, Carolyn's professional skill set and drive are of such that her boss trusts her to handle everything he throws at her on any given day. She doesn't mind, she gets a thrill out of blowing his socks off with more than just her sexual prowess.

The look in his eyes when she breaks another company sales record or lands a new contract that never seemed obtainable before is priceless to her. That moment or two of gratification is all the satisfaction she needs to wake up every morning and take on whatever he throws at her each day.

With a moment to reflect Carolyn notices she hasn't seen Justin Tolls in a while. She wonders if James found out about them and fired the kid, or worse killed him. Carolyn feels terrible now. She pulls out her cell phone and texts Justin.

No response. Carolyn jumps up from her desk in a panic. She rushes to the back of her office and closes all of her blinds. Then she rushes back to her desk and closes her laptop after shutting it down properly first.

"James, please tell me you didn't kill that boy..." she whispers to herself.

Carolyn jumps up. She rushes to her door and quickly turns her office lights off. After opening her door, she hears her phone's text tone going off behind her desk.

She closes her door back and rushes to her phone.

It's Justin. His text says, "Hey, I'm fine. How are you?"

Carolyn plops down in her chair and exhales loudly.

"Wow..." she says.

Justin goes on to tell her he's been working down in the cellar lately. James assigned him to cellar duty last week. James gave him a week to inventory all the wine in the cellar.

He's almost sure this task was given to him as a punishment. He and Carolyn both realize James did this more than likely so that the two of them couldn't see each other during the day.

Carolyn tells Justin to finish his assignment and to just text her later. He agrees to do just that.

Carolyn opens her laptop so that she can get back to work herself. After signing in with her password she starts back typing up the invitations to the annual tasting the winery holds every October.

Carolyn hasn't seen James all day. She decides he must be at home tending to his wife. She can't be angry at that; hell Jessica is his wife. She built her entire life around James Radicon and she deserves to have his company during her final days.

And even though Carolyn is intelligent enough to understand the situation as a whole that will never stop her heart from being extremely jealous of it. The winery doesn't feel right to her; knowing he's not around the corner in his office calling the shots.

She misses the days when they used to both do random things just to find themselves on each other's hallway, just so they could sneak a peek of one another. God they were like giddy high school kids with crushes on each other. But now that Carolyn has moved into the Radicon mansion she's afraid the spark between them is gone. That's the last thing she wants of course. Hell James is all she has now.

Her parents are in the middle of a nasty divorce because of her big mouth. Her husband and kids are dead because of her choices, and what's left of her sister is hardly capable of being her support system.

Carolyn tries hard to do all the extra things around the house to make James' life as comfortable as possible. She does everything he wants and needs, but at the same time she doesn't want to live forever chasing something that she may never actually obtain. Carolyn often wonders with all the beautiful things James Radicon tells her, how much of what he says is actually authentic.

He's never dated a black woman until now, so she realizes he may just still be attracted to the mystique of her. She's like an exotic toy to him. But when he speaks of marriage, are those words just bait to string her along until he meets a better option than she could ever be?

If they ever did get married the pictures of the two of them together on nationwide magazines would definitely turn some heads, and maybe even some stomachs. But Carolyn doesn't care, it's a new day and people are always going to be people. Hell, people talked about Jesus and He was perfect. The only thing Carolyn Olivier cares about is being happy and making her man happy.

If she loses him now, she has no clue what her next move will be. She grabs her cell phone to text him, but then quickly drops it back in her purse. He's obviously busy. Otherwise he would have at least called to check on her. Unless, unless he just really doesn't care anymore.

Carolyn closes her laptop again, this time she bypasses the safe shutdown method and just closes it as is. She finds it unnerving that one man could have the power to make her feel amazing, and amazingly insecure all at the same time.

The sadness that has become common place to her is taking over her mind again. She grabs her phone from her purse and decides to text Justin again. He replies asking her to meet him at Starbucks for lunch.

She agrees.

Carolyn grabs her purse and leaves her office locking the door behind her.

(Starbucks)

When Carolyn arrives at Starbucks Justin is already parked near the front door. She parks near him and then gets out and walks towards his expensive car.

As she approaches him he lets down his driver's side window.

"I'm curious..." she says.

"Oh yeah," Justin replies, "Curious about what love?"

"Well," she hesitates, "just how the hell does a struggling college student afford a car like this?"

Justin smiles at her.

"Who said I was struggling?" he asks.

Carolyn steps back as Justin opens his door. After getting out he leans in and kisses her on the lips. Carolyn pushes away from him.

"Justin, damn it," she wipes her mouth, "we can't do this anymore. I live with James now."

"So fucking what Carolyn," he replies, "Now the old bastard has some extra built in pussy at his gaudy little mansion! That doesn't change anything between you and me."

He leans in and tries to kiss her again.

Carolyn pushes away from him once more.

"You're so stupid," he tells her, "it's all a game Carolyn! You can't win, and you won't win because you're not supposed to! But as soon as the contracts on the Cali winery are done Radicon is gonna lose big too, so you won't be alone in that respect."

Justin laughs obnoxiously at the obvious confusion on Carolyn's face.

"What is that look for," he asks, "God it's priceless."

"What game are you talking about Justin," she asks, "and the final Cali contract was done over a week ago."

"Now that I didn't know," he says with an evil smirk on his face, "thanks for the info."

Justin pulls out his cell phone and makes a call.

Carolyn stands there watching him as he holds his phone to his ear.

"Hey Grandpa," he says, "Yeah, *wake and bake*. Yeah it's in, go ahead and pull the plug on the big bad wolf. Okay, see you tonight. I love you Grand…pa."

Justin looks at his phone as he begins to blush.

"Um, he probably just didn't hear me." Justin lies to himself.

"Who the hell was that, and what are you up to Justin Tolls?" Carolyn steps close to him with a hand on each of her hips.

"Look Carolyn," Justin says, "you will never truly belong with him, we will both probably die, as black shadows, in Radicon's perfect white world."

"What do you mean, we?" Carolyn asks.

"What?" Justin says.

"You said we," Carolyn contends, "you said we as in *you and me* will both die as black shadows in James' perfect white world... That's what you just said Justin Tolls! And now I'm asking you what did that mean? Who is Radicon to you?"

Justin smiles a strange but intriguing smile.

"I," he hesitates, "*am Radicon.*"

"What the hell does that mean," Carolyn asks, "*I am Radicon*... No the *hell*, you're not, so what the *hell* are you talking about? And what is that tattoo on your left wrist... I swear I've seen it somewhere before?"

He smiles again.

"You don't get it," he shakes his head stepping back inside his car, "goodbye Mrs. Olivier, I gotta get back to work."

Justin drives off.

(Back at the office)

With no time to waste Carolyn rushes into her office back on the winery's property. After logging in on her company laptop, she quickly pulls up Justin Tolls' employee file. She searches everything she possibly can about the college standout turned Radicon protégé.

"He's up to something," Carolyn whispers to herself, "but what... There has to be some kind of clue in his file. And what if he was right? What if James is just using me as a stepping stone to some other woman? The woman, that was in his office. Damn it!"

RING, RING, RING!!!!!

"What the hell!" Carolyn yells.

Her door opens.

"Come on Ms. Olivier," her assistant Melody yells, "there's a fire in the building we have to evacuate immediately."

Carolyn grabs her purse and bolts for the door. Behind Melody Carolyn runs full speed to the door that leads to the stairs. As she bounds down the stairs two at a time Carolyn's heart is beating faster than it ever has before. She doesn't smell any smoke but she's sure the fire must be bad because she didn't see anybody left in the building on her way to the stairs.

"Hurry up Ms. Radicon," Melody prods, "we're almost there."

"I'm coming," Carolyn yells back as they reach the exit door, "wait... what, did you just call me Melody?"

Melody ignores Carolyn's question as she pushes the back door open and holds it open for her. Carolyn is staring at Melody in complete confusion as she stands there in the doorway.

Carolyn finally turns to look out of the door.

A sudden chill comes over her entire body. Every member of the staff at the Radicon winery is dressed in all white, and they are lined up on either side of the door creating a more than perfect aisle between them.

They're all staring at her. Carolyn begins to walk down the aisle between them all, still completely clueless as to what is going on.

On her left side up ahead she sees Justin Tolls lined up with his fellow employees as well. Carolyn looks back to find Melody still standing in the doorway watching her every step.

Melody turns to signal someone behind her. Almost instantly Luther Vandross' hit song, *"If This World Were*

Mine", begins to play loudly through the speakers at the back of the building.

As Carolyn nears the middle of the manmade aisle, all the employees begin to shift as they turn the aisle into an imperfect circle surrounding her.

"What the hell is this?" Carolyn asks to anybody who might respond to her. No one does.

In the distance some kind of loud noise can be heard high in the air. Everybody surrounding Carolyn stares way up into the sky towards the ruckus that seems to be getting closer, and closer.

It's a helicopter, and dangling by some kind of rope ladder hanging from the helicopter is a man in a white suit. Carolyn covers her face as her chills return once more.

The helicopter flies the man in close and then allows him to let go of the rope ladder near the ground at the center of the circle.

As he hits the ground with a large bouquet of beautiful, vibrant, assorted flowers James walks towards Carolyn with the most handsome smile she has ever seen tattooed on his perfect face.

She can barely feel the warm tears rolling down her blushing cheeks, as her entire body has gone numb.

James hands her the bouquet. Then he turns briefly to focus on the employees that are surrounding them.

"Thank you all for being here, to share the special moment in our lives." he smiles.

Then he looks back at the wet, reddened face of Carolyn Olivier.

"Carolyn..." he smiles down at her perfect damp face.

"Yes James." she replies wiping her face gently.

"I don't know everything," he says, "and I never claimed that I did. I have made some huge mistakes in my past, and I can't promise that I won't make more in the future. I don't know if what I'm doing is right or wrong, but the one thing I do know is that I am so in love with you. The love I have for you isn't matched by anything I have ever felt in my entire lifetime. There is not now, nor will there ever be *a me,* without you. I would gladly die painfully a thousand times just to live one second in your precious and perfect presence. You will always have my heart, mind, body, and my very soul..."

James drops down on one knee.

"Carolyn Olivier," he says, "will you please... make me the happiest and most blessed man on the planet... and be my wife?"

"You already have a wife James Radicon," she replies with joyful tears and a permanent smile, "but I would love to."

"Is that a yes?" he asks.

"Of course it is." she replies.

The circle explodes around them in joyous cheers and laughter, all except one young man who doesn't look to be pleased at all by this new turn of events.

James slides the gorgeous three-million-dollar ring on her finger. Carolyn's eyes bulge right out of their sockets as she views her beautiful ring for the very first time.

James stands to his feet and kisses his new fiancé in front of everybody for the very first time.

"Oh, I almost forgot." Carolyn bends down to reach deep inside her purse. Then she pulls out her own ring and puts it on his finger as well.

"How did you know I was going to do this?" James smiles down at his new ring lost in his own confusion.

"I didn't, I was actually going to propose to you this weekend myself..." Carolyn admits.

"Wow." he smiles taking her deep in his strong arms to kiss her again and again.

(That night)

Carolyn is in her personal bathroom down the hall from James' master bedroom where his ill wife Jessica is resting as usual. Carolyn is putting the finishing touches on her hair and face, as if her modest perfection could be elevated to yet another level. She's smiling as she works her silent magic in her enormous bathroom mirror, but she's not exactly happy. Though she's not happy yet, she's as close as she could probably get at this moment considering everything that's happened as of late.

(Carolyn)

Is this life? Is what I'm doing okay in the eyes of God? Do I care? I want this man so bad it hurts sometimes, actually it hurts more times than not. But, am I really living here... in this house, or is this all a dream? Did the beautiful, stern, filthy rich, genius James Radicon really move my black ass into his mansion? The man proposed to me today; and I know it's real, because he purposely involved so many other people to plan the surprise proposal for me. He proposed in front of virtually everyone who works for him. That moment is, and will forever be unforgettable to me. I cannot get close to enjoying this moment the way I want to though. I'm literally living in this man's house day in, and day out waiting for his wife to die, so that I can replace her. That is wrong, no matter how much I love this man I am not blind at all. How does she feel? I wonder how much Jessica Radicon hates my ass. I would not be as calm as she is if we were to switch positions. And it's not that farfetched to believe that one day I just might be in Jessica's very shoes. Of course I won't grow old before James, and hopefully I won't become deathly sick... but he is very attractive and charming and... well the man is perfect. So, I'd be a complete idiot to believe that no woman has a chance to obtain at least some of his attention and or lust. He's taking me out to eat tonight. He didn't give me any specifics he just told me to dress well and be ready by eight. It's getting close to time and I'm as ready as I can get. You know, I don't miss that evil, cheating son of a bitch Ralph at all... but I am beginning to miss my babies very much so. I think... I keep trying to trick myself into believing I didn't love them like a mother should so that the pain of losing them wouldn't be so unbearable. No time for this now, after my new fiancé and I go enjoy our evening I can come back here and cry my eyes out all night if need be. I have to wear this mask for now, I can't let him see me cry again, I don't want him to feel any guiltier than he already does.

Carolyn cuts her light off in her room, steps out into the hallway, and gently closes the door behind her. Her gorgeous gold dress fits her magnificent body like a silk glove. She looks down at her Chanel watch and panics immediately. Somehow she lost track of time; its five minutes after the hour, and she knows that James is a punctuality freak. As she takes her first step down the hallway her heart stops as she locks eyes with him.

"You're late Mrs. Radicon." He tells her dressed in a custom made suit that would give any version of James Bond a run for his money.

"I'm sorry James I…" she starts as she walks close to him.

336

"I'm only kidding," he smiles as he straightens his tie, "You are my fiancé tonight, not my employee. This is our world... not just mine."

Carolyn blushes as he takes her arm in his and walks her down the stairs to the first floor.

James opens the front door and then politely waits for his fiancé to step outside first. After stepping outside, himself he carefully locks the front door and then they both head to his new blue Ferrari.

James lets Carolyn in on the passenger side first and then makes his way to the driver's side. Once seated and almost comfortable James cranks the car up and prepares to head down his driveway. He puts his sweaty hand on the gearshift and then looks back at the windows of the house.

He knows it's time to reveal the rest of his secrets to the woman he loves. He pulls out his cell phone and sends a quick text message. After placing his phone back in his jeans pocket he closes his eyes and exhales deeply.

Carolyn looks over at him. "Are you okay James?" she asks.

He doesn't reply.

"Look babe," Carolyn puts a comforting hand on his shoulder, "your wife is in there on her death bed, so if you don't feel like taking me out tonight you definitely don't have to."

"Go inside." He mumbles.

"What?" Carolyn frowns.

"Go inside..." He says more clearly this time, but with even less emotion.

"Wait, so you're leaving me here?" she asks.

"Carolyn, just go inside." He pleads.

"Fine!" She huffs.

After grabbing her purse off the floor of the car, Carolyn opens her door and then storms away from the car leaving the passenger door wide open. James shakes his head.

By the time Carolyn reaches the door her flaming anger has flooded into unavoidable emotion. In her mind, now that she's James' woman, he has another woman somewhere taking her place as his fantasy. After unlocking the front door, she steps inside and softly closes the door.

As she begins to walk towards the living room the thoughts of James eventually leaving her for his new woman are screaming rudely inside her head. Carolyn swears she can hear her children. She knows how crazy that is, so she pretends she doesn't hear a thing. Standing in the living room she waits to hear James drive off. Tiny footsteps sound like they're approaching her.

"Mama, mama!" as she turns towards them the familiar screams from the familiar faces evoke immediate tears from Carolyn's gorgeous hazel eyes.

"Oh no," she cries as her kids wrap their warms arms around her legs, "I'm turning into James. I'm finally losing my mind. This is so bad. I can't, I cannot live with these ghosts.

"It's real," a soft voice says from the nearby kitchen, "these are not ghosts Carolyn they're your living breathing children."

Carolyn looks up at her face.

"You," Carolyn cries, "you're the bitch that was in James' office that day whispering in his ear."

"Nice to see you again too Mrs. Olivier..." the attractive light skinned woman replies.

"I wanted to tell you right away." James says from behind.

Carolyn drops down to her knees and kisses both her crying babies as they continue enjoying just being near her.

"Ralph Jr.," Carolyn cries, "watch your baby brother for mommy, I need to go into the next room to have grown up talk."

"What's grown up talk mama," Ralph Jr. cries, "don't leave me again mommy."

Carolyn smiles at his adorable cheeks.

"I am never going to leave you again," she promises, "and grown up talk is something I'm going to make damn sure you and your baby brother Karan can have one day."

She kisses Karan between his two wide teary eyes and then stands back to her feet.

"James," she says still looking down at her babies, "I need to see you right now."

"Babe," James says, "You just got your children back... basically from the dead, don't you want to spend..."

"*James Justin Radicon,*" she barks walking past him, "get your ass over here now!"

Once in the hallway Carolyn makes her way to an empty room with James not far behind her. After she opens the door and walks in James reluctantly follows her inside.

"I did want to tell you but I knew you couldn't think clearly at the time and I couldn't risk..." he claims.

"Risk what James," Carolyn interjects, "you would already have been charged with a triple homicide I know damn well a kidnapping and child neglect charge didn't scare you."

"It sounds dumb now..." he admits.

"You think so." She interjects brashly.

"It sounds dumb now," he repeats, "but I was drunk as hell that day and I couldn't figure out how to... damn it Carolyn can't you just be happy that your kids are alive?"

"Hell no," she exclaims, "I still don't even know   how they *are* alive. Nobody is telling me anything!"

James exhales deeply looking down at the well-polished floor.

"After I finished setting the fire," he explains, "I barricaded your husband in your bedroom. Then I retraced my steps carefully. As I was headed out of the front door I heard your youngest crying. I rushed in their room and grabbed them both and then rushed back out to my truck."

"*Oh my God.*" Carolyn cries.

"I felt terrible," James admits, "Had I known you had kids with him, I probably wouldn't have even killed the poor bastard. Boys need their fathers; Lord knows I wish I had been there for Lucas..."

"No," Carolyn screams, "you will *not* make this about you! My children didn't deserve this!"

"No," James agrees, "They didn't, but I promise you they were never neglected; Sheila took very good care of them."

"I bet she did." Carolyn scoffs as Sheila steps into her room.

"Yes, I did take very good care of your adorable children even though you were very rude to me." She says.

"Well excuse me lady I thought you were screwing my future husband," Carolyn says, "I didn't know at the time you were conspiring with him to kill my husband and hide my kids from me, as I buried them in front of everybody I know."

"I'm sorry." Sheila replies.

"No," Carolyn screams, "sorry doesn't work! It **does not** work; it is not okay! Damn it! I'm going to go back in here to my kids right now, **but this is not over**!"

The End

Passion Everlasting

(Stolen Moments)

De'Lure

(Prologue)

*P*assion *is defined as a strong and barely controllable*

emotion. An example often used is the suffering and death of Jesus on the cross in the bible, commonly referred to as the Passion of the Christ. Good or bad most people are passionate about something; and that passion drives us all to do things that not everybody can do. When you are blessed with a passion for another human being that feeling can be beyond scary. But if you're lucky enough to have the person you're passionate about reciprocate your passion back equally to you... that gives b i r t h to a love most people will only read about throughout the course of their lives. To connect with your true soul mate, you have to be in the right place, at precisely the right time, and be open to receive them. He or she may not look anything like what you think you want, or the person you always dreamed of, but passionate love surpasses all earthly laws of attraction. The trick is once you find that absolute passion, work on it, and give it time to evolve into a passion everlasting.

Chapter 1

Radicon Mansion

Sitting in the chair near the bed that Jessica used to always sit in James is watching his wife as she sleeps. Over the course of the past five days James has spent an extreme amount of time in this chair watching his wife sleep. She doesn't do anything else.

Her nurse bathes her and takes care of all her personal needs and then Jessica just sleeps. James loves Carolyn, but he still misses the woman his wife Jessica once was. Her thin hair is completely lifeless, all of the color has drained from her once near flawless face, and she never utters a single word.

James stands up to walk closer to her. As he stares down at her peaceful face he smiles. Then he leans down and kisses her cold forehead.

Jessica opens her eyes.

"Jess…" James says.

"Hey." she replies with a weak smile.

"How do you feel baby?" he asks.

"Tired," she mumbles, "I am *so* tired James."

"I know love." he responds.

"Just rest Jessica," he continues, "everything is going to be fine…"

"No James," she says, "everything is not going to be fine," she mumbles, "and I don't want it to be… not anymore."

"What are you talking about Jess?" he asks.

Jessica coughs several times.

"You don't love me anymore James," she whines, "I am dying James, and you still spend all your time with her."

"Jessica you don't understand..." he starts.

"Of course I do," she interjects, "I understand perfectly. Honestly I'm not mad anymore. She deserves you, and as soon as she gets older or sick, you will replace her and destroy her heart just like you did mine."

"Don't do this Jessica..." James pleads.

"I am being so serious," she mumbles with her eyes fading in and out by the second, "you know when old dogs... are uprooted from their homes and the families who raise them they often die of home sickness and a broken heart. This cancer is kicking my ass, but you are the reason I'm dying James Radi..."

Jessica falls into a strong coughing spell.

"Baby..." James cries.

Jessica's coughing isn't showing any signs of stopping or slowing.

Her young Caucasian nurse Lisa rushes into the room. She quickly helps Jessica sit up. Jessica leans forward still coughing. There's blood everywhere; and the smell in the room is horrid.

"Mr. Radicon," the nurse yells, "Call a paramedic now! I think it's time..."

"It's time," he repeats, "what the hell does that mean lady? She's sick; she's not having a fucking baby!"

"She's dying Mr. Radicon," the nurse yells, "go call a paramedic now, or have your girlfriend call one! I left my cell downstairs, hurry up!"

"Do not disrespect me!" James demands as his wife continues to choke on her own blood.

He rushes towards the door to go get his cell phone from Carolyn's room. As he runs down the hallway full speed he can still hear Jess fighting to breathe. James barges in Carolyn's room. James' heart stops cold as his eyes triple in size at the unbelievable sight in front of him.

Carolyn is bent over the end of her bed taking back shots from Luke. James looks down at her hand. She's still wearing the engagement ring he just gave her earlier today. Luke looks up at his father, and then right back down at the perfect ass in front of him. His hands are gripping her hips gently as he strokes slowly.

"Carolyn, what the hell are you doing?" James screams.

"I fixed Lucas for you, baby," she moans with a smile, "and he's good baby, he's *sooo* good. This is our third time today..."

Before she can finish her statement James rushes forward and pushes his son hard to the floor.

Luke flies all the way to the far wall and smacks his head on it.

Carolyn quickly crawls towards the head of the bed, and pulls her blanket over her naked body.

Luke looks up at his father with pure fear in his eyes and heart. "I thought this is what you wanted me to do Dad..." he cries in confusion. "I just wanna make you proud," Luke continues, "I don't wanna be a faggot Dad... I don't!"

"You have a boyfriend Luke," James yells, "that ship has already sailed boy!"

"No," Lucas tells him, "Cal left me... for good."

"Lucas," James yells, "Boy, get your little ass the hell out of here before I kill you!"

Luke stands up completely naked and then runs awkwardly past his father out of Carolyn's room down the hall to his own room.

"Don't get quiet now bitch," James says, "so you're fucking my teenage son behind my back!"

Carolyn doesn't respond.

"Speak bitch!" he screams. "I should have your black ass arrested," he continues, "this is rape!"

"James," she cries, "I was only doing what you told me to do. That boy... idolizes you. He just wants to be accepted by you. He loves you James..."

"Shut the hell up you slut!" he screams.

"No," she cries out, "you do not call me that! I don't deserve that! I am what you made me, I did *everything* I could to become your perfect fantasy. And now you're..."

"You know what," James interjects, "get the hell out of my house. I'm going to see about my sick wife..."

"Oh so now that bitch is your wife again huh," Carolyn screams through her burning tears, "Ugh you make me sick James Radicon! You gave me a ring damn it! This ring is mine and it symbolizes our future together..."

"Bitch when I get back you better be out of my house!" he screams.

"No James," Carolyn cries, "I don't have anywhere to go!"

"Screw you," he replies, "And make sure you leave my damn ring as well."

James then snatches off the ring Carolyn gave him and throws it at her with violent force.

"*James*!!!" the nurse screams from down the hall.

James quickly grabs his cell phone from the table near her bed, and rushes back out of her room.

He sprints back down the hall but he no longer hears Jessica coughing.

As he runs in his room the nurse is gently closing Jessica's eyes for her.

James falls to his weak knees in surrender. Jessica Denise Radicon is finally free from her nightmarish last days on this Earth.

Carolyn walks out of the guest bedroom fifteen minutes later with two Louis Vuitton duffel bags filled with her clothes and personal items. Looking down the hallway she sees James lying on the floor, in his doorway. She immediately drops her bags and runs to him.

"James..." she cries painfully as she reaches down for him. Before she touches him she looks up to find Mrs. Radicon's nurse staring a hole through her, standing right beside the huge bed.

Lying there next to her with closed eyes is the obviously deceased Jessica Radicon.

"Oh James," Carolyn says lying down on top of him, "baby I'm sorry."

Carolyn can't hear him crying, but his body's convulsions let her know that's exactly what he's doing.

"It's okay baby," she coddles him, "it's okay James, you can cry forever if you need to. I'm not going anywhere."

"You both killed her..." the nurse snaps approaching them.

"What the hell are you talking about lady?" Carolyn asks from the floor.

"She wasn't happy at all," the nurse tells her, "she would have lived quite a bit longer if the two of you weren't in her face breaking her heart again *every single day!*"

The young red faced white girl walks past them into the hallway.

"I hope you're happy Radicon, you bastard," she yells, "Your wife was a good woman, and you killed her off for this worthless black whore!"

"Bitch," Carolyn barks, "You better get the hell out of here before you need a nurse your damned self!"

The doorbell rings.

"The paramedics are here," the angry nurse tells them, "I had to call them myself from your dead wife's cell phone. I'll let them in on my way out. Go to fucking hell both of you."

"That's fine," James says looking up at the young lady through his teary eyes, "I hope you realize I will not be paying you for the terrible service you gave me and my wife."

"Mr. Radicon," she snaps walking back towards them, "I don't want a dime of your damn money! Keep it, you keep it all! I promise you this though, *all* your millions..."

"*Billions*." he corrects her.

"All your *billions* won't buy your way into Heaven," she tells him, "you will suffer. I promise you, you will suffer you evil *bastard*."

"It's not about money Lisa," James says trying to dry his tired face, "I loved my wife very, very much. I just made the mistake of falling in love with another woman even more. And I tried, but I could no longer sleep at night without this woman in my house. She is a part of me now... a part of me, that could never be replaced."

"Poor Mrs. Radicon," Lisa says looking over at Jessica, "she's right there James. I sure hope she can't hear you."

The doorbell rings again.

"Damn it Lisa," he yells, "go let the paramedics in already and get the hell out of my mansion!"

Chapter 2

"The Service"

The funeral procession for the late Jessica Radicon stretches more than a few miles long. The ride from the church to the graveyard isn't long at all, but all the cars and news trucks are causing everything to take a lot longer than they would have otherwise.

Inside the church there were cameras from different news stations in every corner of the sanctuary. James was too distraught to handle them the way he wanted to. Today is about celebrating Jessica's life so there was no way he was going to cause an ugly regrettable scene inside the church.

As they ride along inside the limo James, Carolyn, and Lucas are all silent. Luke is obviously agitated, but he wouldn't dare voice as much to his father right now.

James looks to be praying with his head down deep in his hands as he mumbles to himself. Carolyn is softly rubbing his back. She's trying to take her mind off the ugly headlines that are going to be all over the news in the morning.

Billionaire widower James Radicon shows up to bury his wife with his black mistress on his arm.

Carolyn doesn't care, but she's unsure how James is going to react to it all.

James opens his eyes and looks at Carolyn.

"What baby?" she asks.

James doesn't respond. He has a glazed over look in his dim blue eyes.

"What's wrong James?" Carolyn asks.

"Where is Katherine," he asks, "she should be here with us..."

"*Oh God Dad*..." Luke explodes.

"Lucas," Carolyn interjects, "don't, not right now."

"Why are you *even here*?" Luke barks at Carolyn.

"Because your father asked me to be here Lucas." she responds.

"Stop saying my name like that!" Lucas demands.

"Like what Carolyn..." wrinkles her brow.

"Like you're white," he spits, "You ain't white... *never will be*."

"Hmm," Carolyn smiles, "That's funny coming from you Lucas, someone who has... or *had* a black boyfriend."

Lucas forgets what he was going to say next and instead turns and looks out of his window.

The limo stops.

"Come on James," Carolyn says taking him by the hand, "it's time to go."

The chauffer opens the door for them, and they all step out.

The walk to the gravesite feels excruciatingly long. The grave is already surrounded by thousands of random people who just wanted to be able to say they were here.

James, Carolyn, and Lucas take their seats in front of the grave.

Reverend Green walks forward with a microphone.

"Instead of me talking everyone's head off again like I did in the church," he says with a comforting smile, "I'm going to hand the microphone over to Mrs. Radicon's brilliant young son Lucas. Lucas wrote an original poem for his mother just last night. His words will be the last words spoken as we lay his mother to rest. Lucas…"

Lucas takes off his jacket and makes his way to the podium next to the reverend. Reverend Green hugs Lucas tightly, then he hands him the microphone before taking several steps behind him to stand at the rear of the podium as Lucas readies himself to deliver his late mother's poem to the world.

As Lucas stares out into the unfamiliar crowd he locks eyes with one familiar pair of sad brown eyes. Calvin is staring back at him, waiting for him to speak just like the other thousands of people on hand.

Suddenly Luke has forgotten every word of the magnificent poem he wrote.

Lucas clears his throat. He tries not to look back in Cal's direction but he can't help it. Their eyes lock again, Cal nods in reassuring approval.

Lucas clears his throat once more.

"Every step I take, every sound I will ever make,
I am sure I will never break because I am
formed in the likeness of you,
The likeness of you,
Mama, you taught me to fly high above
any earthly standards
You taught me manners but more importantly you
taught me what matters
In your eyes I could do no wrong, no wrong
from the womb you blessed me with
a forgiving heart
Because my father was not there,
and at times he is still not there
but in my heart you always are

You placate all my tears and scars
And I don't know how far I will ever go now
That you left me all alone and I'm
not even yet grown
Mama, mama, mama, you're gone
I'm left in a powerfully unpeaceful zone
And unpeaceful is not even a word... this I know
But, you and no one else can tell me how to feel or
what feelings to show
I followed no law or rule when
constructing this poem
I will continue to make you proud as
your love makes me whole
But I will never be the same... Now that my
beautifully blessed mother is forever gone
Amen

Reverend Green walks back up to Lucas and hugs him once more. As Lucas leaves the podium there isn't a dry eye in the audience.

Even Cal is crying now. Lucas takes his seat back next to his father. James wipes his face and then hugs Lucas as hard as his weak body will allow him to.

"That was a beautiful poem Lucas." Carolyn says leaning over closely to him.

James lets go of Lucas as they begin to lower his wife into the ground.

"Carolyn..." he whispers.

"Yes baby." she replies.

"Where is my Katherine," he asks, "she should be here."

"She is here James." Carolyn says as the salty tears flood into the sides of her open mouth.

"Where is she?" he asks, in a childlike tone.

After standing to look around for his red headed teenage daughter, James can't find her anywhere.

"Lucas," James says to his quiet son, "Where is your baby sister?"

Lucas doesn't respond. Instead he just shakes his head at his father and walks away from him in search of Calvin.

"James..." Carolyn pulls him back down to his seat.

"What," he replies, "what's wrong with Lucas?"

"James baby," she says, "all the time you've been spending with Katherine is unhealthy."

James stands up again pulling away from her.

"What the hell do you mean," he barks, "she's my daughter. Of course spending time with her is healthy."

"No James it's not." Carolyn contends trying not to cause a scene.

"And why not," James yells, "Can somebody please tell me why this woman is saying I shouldn't spend time with my own daughter."

"Because she's dead James..." Carolyn cries.

James sits back down next to her.

"What..." he cries.

"Baby," Carolyn cries, "she's been dead for months now. She never left that hospital room alive after she tried to kill herself. The cuts were way too deep James. And... you just... you made yourself believe she survived. You told yourself that you could save her, but by the time you were ready to save her she had already died James."

"When," he cries, "when did she ... when did my baby pass?"

"While we were on that plane to California love," Carolyn tells him, "remember Jessica texted you and told you Kate died in her hospital bed baby."

James falls to his burning knees in the dirt in front of his chair.

*"No, no, no… **god damn it!**"* he cries.

"I'm so sorry baby," Carolyn cries holding onto his strong back, "I tried to let you hold on to her for as long as possible, but it's time to let go now baby."

Carolyn reaches down and helps James back up to his feet.

"Come on," she cries leading him towards the graves, "it's time to say goodbye."

Next to Jessica's grave there's a second plot baring the name Radicon in big bold letters.

"Katherine Grace Radicon…" James reads aloud.

Carolyn can't breathe now, watching James cry this hard is killing her.

"James baby," she says, "it's okay, we're gonna be okay."

His pain is unfixable.

"Baby," Carolyn continues, "I know it won't change the pain you will always feel for your Katherine but my doctor told me I was pregnant last month… If it's a girl, you can name her anything you want to baby."

"Princess," he cries, "I'm going to name her Princess Katherine Radicon."

"Radicon's Princess," Carolyn smiles through her tears, "I love it James, its perfect."

James closes his tired red eyes tightly, he throws his arms around Carolyn, and everything goes black.

Passion Everlasting

(Stolen Moments)

(Coming Soon)

Characters

James Justin Radicon

Carolyn Jane "Williams" Olivier

Lucas Bradley Radicon

Katherine Grace Radicon

Jessica Denise Radicon

Ralph Olivier

Kayla Marie Williams

Justin Raymond Tolls

Master

Calvin Ridgefield

Marcus   Williams

Marilyn Williams

De'Lure

"Passion Absolute"

An original poem by De'Lure

I COULD SNATCH DOWN EVERY
SINGLE STAR FROM THE SKY
THEN PAINT THEM DELICATELY BENEATH YA FEET
JUST SO I COULD WATCH YOU FLY
I SEE STARDUST WHEN YOU TAKE OFF BUT I'M
RIGHT BEHIND YOU
I NEVER MIND TOO
CUZ THE ONLY TIME MY MIND IN TUNE WIT
HEART IS WHEN I FIND YOU
NOW NEVER MIND THE TUNES
I COULD DO ANIMAE OR MUSIC TOO
MY TALENT IS ON A SWIVEL I CAN
CREATE ANYTHING I DREAM TO
BUT MUSIC IS THE SOUNDTRACK OF
OUR LIVES THIS IS TRUE
AND THERE ARE NO LIES BETWEEN OUR
EYES WE HAVE A PASSION ABSOLUTE
IF YOU NEVER HAD A CLUE WHAT LOVE COULD DO
I COULD SHOW YOU PASSION BLUE
AND EVERY OTHER HUE OF TRUE LOVE
THERE'S MORE THAN JUST A FEW
LIKE HEARTBREAK PURPLE
FEELING THIS IS CERTAIN JUST
DON'T GO IN CIRCLES
OR LONG LASTING LAVENDER

THAT'S THE ONE YOU SHOULD MARRY HER
OR BREAK DOWN BROWN WHEN
YOUR HEART POUNDS
AND YOU DECIDE TO DROWN
IN BUCKETS AND OCEANS OF SORROW
SEE ORANGE IS FOR NEW FLAME
NOT THE LIES THAT YOU CLAIM
IF YOU CAN POWER THROUGH
THE PAIN YOU'LL FIND CHANGE
BUT AS FOR MY BOO
EVERY STEP I'LL EVER TAKE IS
WALKIN CLOSER TO YOU
AND WHEN I'M LOOKIN THROUGH YA WINDOWS
AND IM TALKIN BOUT YA EYES
I CAN SEE YA SOUL AND THAT'S
WHERE MY HEART LIES
AND IF I EVER LIE TO YOU THAT
LIE WOULD ENSUE
THAT I COULD TAKE ANY OTHER
WOMAN ON THE PLANET
AND MAKE HER JUST LIKE YOU
BUT SEE THAT WOULD BE A
PAINFUL CYCLE FOR MICHAEL
TO TRY TO PSYCHE HER UP TO
BE AN ANGELIC IDOL TOO
BABE I ONLY GOT EYES FOR YOU
HEAVEN IS MY LIMIT I'M ONLY SKYIN FOR YOU
AND I'MA KEEP FLYING TILL
MY NAME IS THE TRUTH
PAIN PRODUCES PASSION MY BRAIN IS PROOF
EVEN DEEP INSIDE THAT CAGE
ALL I HAD WAS THE TRUTH

De'Lure

NOW I'M FREE AS A BIRD DOIN
WHAT MASTERS DO
I COULD BE SINGLE FOREVER JUST LIKE
BACHELORS DO ... BUT
I'D RATHER HOLD YO HAND FOREVER AND
BREAK OUR HEARTS IN TWO
SO THEY COULD BEAT FOREVER LIKE
HEARTS IN TANDUM DO
PASSION ABSOLUTE

Author Bio:

D e'Lure is a dreamer who writes with his heart and a very realistic imagination. His first passion was acting, but from that love spawned an even deeper passion for the art of writing. The imagery he uses to create stories is packed with all the components' legendary writing careers are made of. Expect great things from Dreamer De'Lure.

If you enjoyed this novel you should check out these other *AMAZING* titles by De'Lure

Onyx Cielo: Book 1 -The Tree of Transformation-
Take My Breath Away: Orlando Nights –RELOADED-
Take My Breath Away 2: When Love Calls
Take My Breath Away 3: Moments
De'Lure Shorts & Poem
De'Lure Shorts & Poems 2
Kissed
Mental Apex
He Without Sin
The Art of Beauty

Email: ceom.love@gmail.com
FB: Published De'Lure